Wells Meets Dele

CRITICAL EXPLORATIONS IN SCIENCE FICTION AND FANTASY
(a series edited by Donald E. Palumbo and C.W. Sullivan III)

1 *Worlds Apart? Dualism and Transgression in Contemporary Female Dystopias* (Dunja M. Mohr, 2005)
2 *Tolkien and Shakespeare: Essays* (ed. Janet Brennan Croft, 2007)
3 *Culture, Identities and Technology in the* Star Wars *Films: Essays* (ed. Carl Silvio, Tony M. Vinci, 2007)
4 *The Influence of* Star Trek *on Television, Film and Culture* (ed. Lincoln Geraghty, 2008)
5 *Hugo Gernsback and the Century of Science Fiction* (Gary Westfahl, 2007)
6 *One Earth, One People: Ursula K. Le Guin, Lloyd Alexander, Madeleine L'Engle and Orson Scott Card* (Marek Oziewicz, 2008)
7 *The Evolution of Tolkien's Mythology* (Elizabeth A. Whittingham, 2008)
8 *H. Beam Piper: A Biography* (John F. Carr, 2008)
9 *Dreams and Nightmares: Science and Technology in Myth and Fiction* (Mordecai Roshwald, 2008)
10 Lilith *in a New Light: Essays* (ed. Lucas H. Harriman, 2008)
11 *Feminist Narrative and the Supernatural: The Function of Fantastic Devices in Seven Recent Novels* (Katherine J. Weese, 2008)
12 *The Science of Fiction and the Fiction of Science: Essays* (Frank McConnell, ed. Gary Westfahl, 2009)
13 *Kim Stanley Robinson Maps the Unimaginable: Essays* (ed. William J. Burling, 2009)
14 *The Inter-Galactic Playground: A Critical Study of Children's and Teens' Science Fiction* (Farah Mendlesohn, 2009)
15 *Science Fiction from Québec: A Postcolonial Study* (Amy J. Ransom, 2009)
16 *Science Fiction and the Two Cultures: Essays* (ed. Gary Westfahl, George Slusser, 2009)
17 *Stephen R. Donaldson and the Modern Epic Vision: A Critical Study of the "Chronicles of Thomas Covenant" Novels* (Christine Barkley, 2009)
18 *Ursula K. Le Guin's Journey to Post-Feminism* (Amy M. Clarke, 2010)
19 *Portals of Power: Magical Agency and Transformation in Literary Fantasy* (Lori M. Campbell, 2010)
20 *The Animal Fable in Science Fiction and Fantasy* (Bruce Shaw, 2010)
21 *Illuminating* Torchwood: *Essays* (ed. Andrew Ireland, 2010)
22 *Comics as a Nexus of Cultures: Essays* (ed. Mark Berninger, Jochen Ecke, Gideon Haberkorn, 2010)
23 *The Anatomy of Utopia: Narration, Estrangement and Ambiguity in More, Wells, Huxley and Clarke* (Károly Pintér, 2010)
24 *The Anticipation Novelists of 1950s French Science Fiction* (Bradford Lyau, 2010)
25 *The* Twilight *Mystique: Essays* (ed. Amy M. Clarke, Marijane Osborn, 2010)
26 *The Mythic Fantasy of Robert Holdstock: Essays* (ed. Donald E. Morse, Kálmán Matolcsy, 2011)
27 *Science Fiction and the Prediction of the Future: Essays* (ed. Gary Westfahl, Wong Kin Yuen, Amy Kit-sze Chan, 2011)
28 *Apocalypse in Australian Fiction and Film* (Roslyn Weaver, 2011)
29 *British Science Fiction Film and Television: Critical Essays* (ed. Tobias Hochscherf, James Leggott, 2011)
30 *Cult Telefantasy Series: A Critical Analysis of* [8 series] (Sue Short, 2011)
31 *The Postnational Fantasy: Essays* (ed. Masood Ashraf Raja, Jason W. Ellis, Swaralipi Nandi, 2011)
32 *Heinlein's Juvenile Novels: A Cultural Dictionary* (C.W. Sullivan III, 2011)

33 *Welsh Mythology and Folklore in Popular Culture: Essays* (ed. Audrey L. Becker, Kristin Noone, 2011)
34 *I See You: The Shifting Paradigms of James Cameron's* Avatar (Ellen Grabiner, 2012)
35 *Of Bread, Blood and* The Hunger Games*: Essays* (ed. Mary F. Pharr, Leisa A. Clark, 2012)
36 *The Sex Is Out of This World: Essays* (ed. Sherry Ginn, Michael G. Cornelius, 2012)
37 *Lois McMaster Bujold: Essays* (ed. Janet Brennan Croft, 2013)
38 *Girls Transforming: Invisibility and Age-Shifting in Children's Fantasy Fiction Since the 1970s* (Sanna Lehtonen, 2013)
39 Doctor Who *in Time and Space: Essays* (ed. Gillian I. Leitch, 2013)
40 *The Worlds of* Farscape*: Essays* (ed. Sherry Ginn, 2013)
41 *Orbiting Ray Bradbury's Mars* (ed. Gloria McMillan, 2013)
42 *The Heritage of Heinlein* (Thomas D. Clareson and Joe Sanders, 2014)
43 *The Past That Might Have Been, the Future That May Come* (Lauren J. Lacey, 2014)
44 *Environments in Science Fiction: Essays* (ed. Susan M. Bernardo, 2014)
45 *Discworld and the Disciplines: Critical Approaches to the Terry Pratchett Works* (ed. Anne Hiebert Alton, William C. Spruiell, 2014)
46 *Nature and the Numinous in Mythopoeic Fantasy Literature* (Christopher Straw Brawley, 2014)
47 *J.R.R. Tolkien, Robert E. Howard and the Birth of Modern Fantasy* (Deke Parsons, 2014)
48 *The Monomyth in American Science Fiction Films* (Donald E. Palumbo, 2014)
49 *The Fantastic in Holocaust Literature and Film* (ed. Judith B. Kerman, John Edgar Browning, 2014)
50 Star Wars *in the Public Square* (Derek R. Sweet, 2016)
51 *An Asimov Companion* (Donald E. Palumbo, 2016)
52 *Michael Moorcock* (Mark Scroggins, 2016)
53 *The Last Midnight: Essays* (ed. Leisa A. Clark, Amanda Firestone, Mary F. Pharr, 2016)
54 *The Science Fiction Mythmakers: ... Wells, Clarke, Dick and Herbert* (Jennifer Simkins, 2016)
55 *Gender and the Quest in British Science Fiction Television* (Tom Powers, 2016)
56 *Saving the World Through Science Fiction: James Gunn* (Michael R. Page, 2017)
57 *Wells Meets Deleuze* (Michael Starr, 2017)

Wells Meets Deleuze
The Scientific Romances Reconsidered

Michael Starr

Critical Explorations in Science Fiction and Fantasy, 57
Series Editors Donald E. Palumbo *and* C.W. Sullivan III

McFarland & Company, Inc., Publishers
Jefferson, North Carolina

ISBN (print) 978-1-4766-6835-2
ISBN (ebook) 978-1-4766-2887-5

Library of Congress cataloguing data are available

British Library cataloguing data are available

© 2017 Michael Starr. All rights reserved

No part of this book may be reproduced or transmitted in any form or by any means, electronic or mechanical, including photocopying or recording, or by any information storage and retrieval system, without permission in writing from the publisher.

Front cover (left to right) Gilles Deleuze and H. G. Wells; background image © 2017 iStock

Printed in the United States of America

*McFarland & Company, Inc., Publishers
Box 611, Jefferson, North Carolina 28640
www.mcfarlandpub.com*

To the Star(r)s

Acknowledgments

I wish to extend my utmost gratitude to those that have, either directly or indirectly, made the completion of this book an actuality. Thank you to friends and colleagues at the University of Northampton, namely Drs. Claire Allen, Richard Chamberlain, David Simmons, Lorna Jowett and Sonya Andermahr, for their input, guidance, and cajoling throughout the entirety of the process. Much appreciation is extended to Sylvia Hardy for her advice and generosity of knowledge pertaining to the project genesis, and to Donald E. Palumbo for the guidance and feedback leading to its publication.

I am indebted to all those in the Whedon Studies Association for their comradeship and infectious enthusiasm, and to the organizers of and contributors to the Philosophy/Science Fiction and Fantasy subject areas of the Popular Culture Association Annual conferences, which are always a source of inspiration and an honor and an education in which to participate.

Much esteem is due to Rosie and Outi Condit-Swayne and family, and Alan Lenton, for simply being their good selves and indulging my (frequently literal) flights of fancy.

Most of all, immutable thanks to the Starr family in its entirety for all the encouragement, support and unequivocal faith in me, in particular my father, who, in reading *The Time Machine* to me when I was young, began my lifelong fervor for all things science-fictional and philosophical.

Table of Contents

Acknowledgments — viii

Preface — 1

Abbreviations — 3

Introduction—Wells, Deleuze and Science Fiction — 4

One—*The Island of Doctor Moreau*: Transhumanism, Spaces and Becoming — 39

Two—*The War of the Worlds*: Martians, Cyborgs and Bodies Without Organs — 72

Three—*The Time Machine*: Time Travel, Crystals and Nomads — 106

Four—H. G. Wells: Conceptual Personae, Minor Writing and Eternal Return — 137

Appendix A: Fictional Portrayals of H. G. Wells — 159

Appendix B: Wells and Deleuze: Chronology of Publications Cited — 165

Chapter Notes — 168

Bibliography — 178

Filmography — 199

Index — 201

Preface

The writings of H. G. Wells have had a profound influence on visions of the human present and its potential futures. Although his oeuvre encompassed many genres, both fiction and non-fiction, it is for his "scientific romances" that he is now best known, and it is works such as *The Time Machine*, *The War of the Worlds* and *The Island of Doctor Moreau* that have bestowed upon him a pivotal significance to the science fiction genre. In keeping with Wells's use of the science-fiction form to explore a plethora of speculative ideas, the philosopher Gilles Deleuze proclaimed that philosophy itself must be a kind of science fiction, in that the latter estranges one from the historical inertia of the "now" and allows a leap into "untimely" futures with singular self-consistency (*Difference* xix–xx). Deleuze himself has become an increasingly powerful force in contemporary cultural theory, offering a challenging new set of conceptual tools to rethink existing texts and critical paradigms, providing unprecedented ways to map the immanence of mind, body and world, and to revaluate literature, film and other fields. Though their respective writings initially appear disparate (at least in terms of the chronology and temporality of their genesis), this study unites Wells and Deleuze, firstly by arguing for the potentiality in Wells's oeuvre for a Deleuzian interpretation (or "deterritorialization"), then demonstrating the power of this theoretical approach by providing a reading of a selection of Wells's scientific romances. Within these specific case studies, various aspects of Wellsian texts are used to exemplify a number of Deleuzian concepts, for example, "Becoming-Animal" in *The Island of Doctor Moreau*, the "Body Without Organs" in *The War of the Worlds* and "Nomadology" in *The Time Machine*. Characteristically, rather than simply applying philosophy to the arts, Deleuzian theory attempts to extract philosophy from them,

Preface

and this approach endeavors to engage positively and constructively with a text, serving to demonstrate "productive use of the literary machine ... that extracts from the text its revolutionary force" (*Anti-Oedipus* 116).

The purpose of a Deleuzian reading is therefore to imbue the subject under investigation with new insights and different readings, thereby liberating philosophical history itself from the hegemony of one limiting perspective, not writing "about" the subject matter (be it art, literature, or cinema), but rather the undertaking of a philosophical "encounter" with it, leading to the formation of new concepts. Via the Deleuzian encounters with Wells that this book imparts, various Wellsian conceits are examined that have subsequently become synonymous with the science fiction genre, such as transhumanism, alien invasion and time travel. In the performance of this process, prior criticisms and assumptions pertaining to Wells are both analogized and advanced upon, resulting in the recasting of Wells as a thinker who demonstrates resonance with Deleuze's theoretical approaches. Ultimately, this serves to demonstrate the "untimely" power of Wells's literature, "acting counter to our time and thereby acting on our time and, let us hope, for the benefit of a time to come" (*Difference* xix).

Abbreviations

H. G. Wells

Moreau   The Island of Doctor Moreau
Time   The Time Machine
War   The War of the Worlds

Gilles Deleuze

Bacon   Francis Bacon: The Logic of Sensation
Cin1   Cinema 1: The Movement Image
Cin2   Cinema 2: The Time-Image
Desert   Desert Islands and Other Texts
Critical   Essays Critical and Clinical
Fou   Foucault
Kafka   Kafka: Towards a Minor Literature
Neg   Negotiations
Proust   Proust and Signs
Spinoza   Spinoza: Practical Philosophy

Gilles Deleuze and Félix Guattari

Anti   Anti-Opedipus: Capitalism & Schizophrenia
Difference   Difference and Repetition
Philosophy   What Is Philosophy?
Thousand   A Thousand Plateaus: Capitalism & Schizophrenia

Terminology

Sf   Science Fiction

Introduction
Wells, Deleuze and Science Fiction

> Our history is just a story in space and time, and to its very last moment it must remain adventure.
> —H. G. Wells *The Work, Wealth and Happiness of Mankind* 895

> There are singular incorporeal constellations which belong to natural and human history and at the same time escape them by a thousand lines of flight.
> —Félix Guattari *Chaosmosis* 27

The purpose of this study is to provide a reading of the scientific romances of H. G. Wells (1866–1946) using the theoretical approach of philosopher Gilles Deleuze (1925–1995). Wells was, for at least two decades at the turn of the twentieth century, one of the most popular British mainstream novelists, his work greatly anticipated and widely and fervently discussed. Working simultaneously as fiction writer, mainstream literary novelist and social philosopher, he published thousands of articles in newspapers and magazines, and over one hundred books. His lifetime ran from one year after the close of the U.S. Civil War to one year after the end of World War II, "[an] astonishing span from cannonballs to atomic bombs" (Wagar *Traversing* 9), and every reverberation of the immense changes taking place in the world about him surfaces in his work. Though rooted in the chief intellectual concerns of his own time (for example, socialism, world government, the role of science, imperialism), Wells's work is simultaneously very much both of its day and timeless. Indeed, "it would be difficult," Wells scholar W. Warren Wagar writes, "to imagine another major literary figure of his generation so intensely conscious of human life on Earth as a process of change over long periods of time, both historical and geo-

Wells, Deleuze and Science Fiction

logical, both past and future" (9). Though a prolific writer in many genres, Wells is of course now best known for his work in the field of what is now termed science fiction (sf):

> Every field of study, like every nation, has its founding fathers and mothers. Figures of legend or of history, they help give the oncoming generations a sense of identity. They instill pride, confidence, and purposefulness.... But who "founded" the study of the future? Herman Kahn? Arthur C. Clarke? Bertrand de Jouvenel? The answer is unsurprising, yet not as obvious as perhaps it should be. The founder of future studies was a man born long before any of these noted seers: the English novelist, popularizer, and journalist par excellence H. G. Wells. No one else begins to rival him [Wagar "Genesis" 25].

Gilles Deleuze was a French philosopher of the late twentieth century who wrote extensively on literature, cinema and art, his most influential books being the two volumes of *Capitalism and Schizophrenia*: *Anti-Oedipus* (1972, translated into English in 1977) and *A Thousand Plateaus* (1980, translated 1987), both co-written with Félix Guattari.[1] These texts have come to be seen as major statements of poststructuralist and postmodern theory, and as such Deleuze has become an increasingly powerful force in cultural theory, offering a challenging new set of conceptual tools to rethink existing texts and critical paradigms, providing unprecedented ways to map the immanence of mind, body and world, and to revaluate literature, film and other fields. Characteristically, rather than simply applying philosophy to the arts, Deleuzian theory attempts to extract philosophy from them. Deleuzian philosophy is based on the idea of rhizomatic thinking, advocating the formation of intricate paths of free flowing associations, as opposed to arboreal, flat trains of thought. Deleuze's modus operandi is based on the revaluation of the role of other thinkers, and the means by which one can use them: new concepts are created out of the works of others, or old ones are recreated, and put to new use.[2] In Deleuze and Guattari's thinking around subjectivity, identity and individuation, they turn away from the possible that on some level has already been conceived (such as any self contained object of scrutiny), towards that which resonates with unexpected potential (Fancy 93); this is therefore not a process of writing "about" a subject matter (be it art, literature, or cinema), but, rather, the undertaking of a philosophical "encounter" that leads to new concepts.

Deleuze's main intellectual trajectory can be observed in his shift-

Introduction

ing relationship to the history of philosophy, and he never lost enthusiasm for writing about other thinkers. Indeed, many of his works name other philosophers as an intrinsic part of the title: Hume, Bergson, Kant, Nietzsche, Leibniz, and Foucault, for example. With regards to the traditional style of the history of philosophy, Deleuze expresses two main problems. The first concerns the politics of the tradition:

> The history of philosophy has always been the agent of power in philosophy, and even in thought. It has played the repressing role: how can you think without having read Plato, Descartes, Kant and Heidegger, and so-and-so's book about them? A formidable school of intimidation which manufactures specialists in thought—but which also makes those who stay outside conform all the more to this specialism which they despise. An image of thought called philosophy has been formed historically and it effectively stops people from thinking [Deleuze and Parnet *Dialogues II* 13].

This hegemony of thought comes under criticism recurrently throughout Deleuze's career, notably in *What Is Philosophy?* (1982, also co-written with Guattari). This criticism also corresponds with a theme general throughout his writings, which is the idea of the immediate politicization of all thought. For Deleuze, philosophy and its history are not separated from the wider world, but intimately tied to it. The second criticism directed at the traditional in the history of philosophy is the construction of specialists and expertise, and this leads directly to the principal element of Deleuze's particular method. In *Negotiations* (1990) he states: "What we should in fact do, is stop allowing philosophers to reflect 'on' things.... The philosopher creates, he doesn't reflect" (122). For Deleuze the history of philosophy embraces a sense of the constructive; each reading of a philosopher, an artist, or writer should be undertaken in order to provide an impetus for creating new concepts that do not already exist. Thus the works that Deleuze studies serve not only as inspiration, but also as a resource, from which concepts can be gathered, along with the force to develop new, non preexisting concepts. The work of Deleuze and Guattari is perhaps best conceived as a "toolbox," a collection of concepts that can be "plugged into" other machines or concepts and made to work. Deleuze implicitly refers to his philosophy in these terms in a conversation with Michel Foucault: "A theory is exactly like a box of tools.... It must be useful. It must function. And not for itself. If no one uses it, beginning with the theoretician himself ... then the theory is worthless or the moment is inappropriate. We don't revise a theory, but construct new ones; we have no choice but to make others" (Foucault "Theatre" 208).

Deleuze published a wide range of texts attacking philosophical essentialism and re-envisioning reality wholly in terms of these "machines," and for Deleuze this machinic "becoming" is something enthusiastically to be celebrated. He commences *Anti-Oedipus* reveling in the machinic cosmos of "desiring production," the strenuously joyful functioning of desire itself:

> It is at work everywhere, functioning smoothly at times, at other times in fits and starts. It breathes, it heats, it eats. It shits and fucks…. Everywhere it is machines—real ones, not figurative ones: machines driving other machines, machines being driven by other machines, with all the necessary couplings and connections. An organ-machine is plugged into an energy-source-machine: the one produces a flow that the other interrupts. The breast is a machine that produces milk, and the mouth a machine coupled to it [1].

In conjunction with philosophy, Deleuze wrote extensively on literature and the arts, and his writings are permeated with literary references. Within his theories he provides original interactions with a variety of literary texts. Aside from dedicating whole works to Proust (*Proust and Signs*, 1964), Leopold von Sacher-Masoch (*Coldness and Cruelty*, 1969), and Kafka (*Kafka: Towards a Minor Literature*, 1975), and a large portion of *The Logic of Sense* (1969)[3] to Lewis Carroll, he also dealt in some detail with a wide range of literary figures such as F. Scott Fitzgerald, Herman Melville, Samuel Beckett, Antonin Artaud, Heinrich von Kleist, and Fyodor Dostoyevsky.

Thus, using the Deleuzian "tool-box," such works can be "deterritorialized"; drawn from *Anti-Oedipus*, this concept equates to the breaking up of order, boundaries and form to produce movement and growth. Although (like most Deleuzian terms) deterritorialization has a purposeful variance in meaning throughout his oeuvre, it can be roughly described as a move away from a rigidly imposed hierarchical, arborescent context, which seeks to categorize things (concepts and objects, for example) into discrete units with singular meanings or identities, towards a rhizomatic zone of multiplicity and fluctuant identity, where meanings and operations flow freely between said things. To deterritorialize is to "turn toward lines of flight so as to dismantle the subject, disorganize the body, or even to destabilize the state" (Olkowski *Deleuze* 34). This is removed from a Derridean deconstruc-

Introduction

tion, as deterritorialization seeks to decenter rather than to deconstruct. Instead, Deleuze proposes a new way of understanding the world; through the concept of deterritorialization, attempts can be made to destabilize the binarisms and hierarchical systems that produce, and are products of, Western society, and thereby produce new readings of culture in its many forms. Hence, to "do" philosophy is "to fabricate concepts in resonance and interference with the arts, past as well as present" (Rajchman 115). Philosophy cannot "do" art (as in being "applied" to art as a theory) any more than art can "do" philosophy, but instead they have a mutual contagion, in which both art and philosophy come alive and discover their resonances with one another.

    This study brings together Wells and Deleuze, seemingly two disparate thinkers, firstly by arguing for the potentiality in Wells's oeuvre for Deleuzian deterritorialization, then demonstrating the power of this theoretical approach by providing a selective reading of Wells's scientific romances. This critical approach to Wells can initially be justified simply because it can be done; by its intrinsic nature Deleuzian theory encourages experimentation and the making of rhizomorphic connections, and Wells's scientific romances, despite being the subject of much critical appraisal, have not as yet been investigated from this perspective: "Make a rhizome. But you don't know what you can make a rhizome with, you don't know which subterranean stem is effectively going to make a rhizome, or enter a becoming, people your desert. So experiment" (Deleuze *Thousand* 277). This statement is central to Deleuze's concept that philosophy only "works" when in a relationship with other disciplines (art, science, or politics, for example, or, in this case, literature). A further case can also be made through the process of explicating existing Wells criticism and evaluating the various arguments for his cultural and theoretical positioning. Despite having been the subject of close critical scrutiny from many perspectives for over a century, Wells's writings have repeatedly resisted easy categorization as to both their historical worth and critical positioning. He occupies a unique space (in contemporary criticism), being acclaimed for his literary and intellectual influence yet often erroneously maligned as a relic of Victorian Empire. Some claim that he "changed the mind of Europe and the world," calling him the "great sage" of his time (Achenbach 112). However, he was writing at a time when literary fashions were changing rapidly and as a result was dismissed by the burgeoning

Wells, Deleuze and Science Fiction

early twentieth-century modernist movement as an outmoded exponent of late Victorian and Edwardian realism, a prosaic, redundant representative of a past age (Hardy "Poststructuralist" 113). Subsequent criticism has attempted to redress this, claiming that far from being at odds with the modernist movement, he was in fact a modernist in his own right, while some more recent criticism has made a case for Wells as an anticipatory postmodernist or poststructuralist. This study is not overly concerned with such specific categorizations, the focus being the interpretation of Wells via Deleuze as opposed to a debate as to whether he in any way anticipated his theoretical approach. However, the very fact that Wells avoids easy categorization is in these terms a strength, as it facilitates his placement as what Deleuze refers to as an "entretien" (a term borrowed from literary theorist Maurice Blanchot) or "in-between" writer; this ultimately facilitates the concluding debate of the study, positioning Wells in relation to what Deleuze calls the "untimely" and "minor" nature of all great literature.

By way of an initial argument, the introduction examines the conjoined subjects; Wells will be looked at in terms of prior critical analysis of the scientific romances, investigating the various positions that he occupies in terms of (and in affiliation to) critical theory. Correspondingly, the Deleuzian philosophical methodology is explicated, and its main themes approached in a broad sense, before specific attitudes to literature and sf are demonstrated. For Deleuze, a philosophical concept never operates in isolation, and in keeping with the rhizomorphic nature of this theory, the philosophical methodology is for the most part explicated in relation to the relevant subject matter as the study progresses, in conjunction with the various literary and ideological themes. Hence, concepts such as the "Virtual," the "Rhizome," "Nomadology" and the "Assemblage" are conjoined with definitions such as science, science fiction, utopia, literature, and the novel. This serves to provide an overview of the key concepts that will be the subject of the subsequent case studies.

While the study as a whole references Wells's entire oeuvre, it is his "scientific romances" that are the explicit focus, and the main body of the study consists of case studies specifically concentrating upon the novels *The Time Machine* (1895), *The Island of Doctor Moreau* (1896) and *The War of the Worlds* (1898). These have arguably been the most critically analyzed of Wells's works, and therefore are the

Introduction

most in need of the new reading that this study provides. They are also the three novels that best exemplify the radical concepts and ideas (such as time travel, transhumanism and alien invasion) from which the entire genre of modern sf has been fashioned. As an element of their deterritorialization Deleuzian theory will demonstrate their significance through the extrapolation of these ideas and their influence upon contemporary sf. There is also the issue of practicality; a balance must be struck between Wells's vast body of work and the overall scope of the study. The literary case studies involve specific chapters in which Deleuzian readings are performed in relation to a variety of issues within the scientific romances, for example, "Nomadology" within *The Time Machine*, "Becoming-Animal" in *The Island of Doctor Moreau*, and the "Body Without Organs" in *The War of the Worlds*. However, due to the rhizomorphic nature of Deleuzian theory, there is inevitably some degree of crossover between these studies. The order of the specific case studies is dependent not upon their chronology of publication, but upon the critical approaches that they encourage; in this way, theories introduced initially will serve to inform later chapters. Similarly, various elements of theory from an assortment of texts will be referenced as is required; this is in keeping with Deleuze's remit (particularly concerning *A Thousand Plateaus*) that, other than the introduction and conclusion, the "plateaus" may be read in any order, emphasizing the rhizomatic nature of the knowledge presented and the infinite number of permutations that are possible for such assemblages. Hence, although the principal Deleuzian texts utilized are both volumes of *Capitalism and Schizophrenia*, other works, such as *Kafka: Towards a Minor Literature, Difference and Repetition* (1968) and *What Is Philosophy?*, will be referred to as required. Also important to note is the inherently political nature of a Deleuzian reading; he believed that there is no separation between the personal and political, the individual and the collective. Hence (while concentrating upon Wells's fiction as opposed to his explicitly political essays) the readings function to draw out the political elements of his oeuvre thus emphasizing the continuing relevance of his political and philosophical ideas that were intrinsic to his fictional works.

Having demonstrated the value of a Deleuzian reading, the study concludes with an argument concerning whether Wells himself can be posited in terms of the Deleuzian "conceptual personae," and ultimately the question of his adherence to the Deleuzian concept of "minor" literature and writing is addressed.

The Scientific Romance: Wells's Legacy

The following sections are concerned with the general issues of Wells, sf, utopia, and their relationships with Deleuzian theory. The various arguments as to the origin of the sf genre, and attempts to strictly define it constitute a study in itself, but suffice to say that more than a century after the publication of such seminal texts as *The Time Machine*, *The Island of Doctor Moreau* and *The War of the Worlds*, Wells (as a major participant in this "evolution") is regarded as the writer most responsible for creating the ideological template and narrative approaches upon which modern sf, both literary and cinematic, is based:

> The plenitude of his conceptions, the visualizing power of his imagination, the sheer grandeur of his mind as it played over things unattempted yet in prose or rhyme constitute Wells' legacy to the new literary form he helped build.... As science fiction developed its distinctive literary character throughout the twentieth century, writers followed the trails Wells had blazed, and their imaginations were tutored by the great sequence of early Wellsian narratives[4] [Crossley 353].

These early writings (usually regarded as those pre–1910) that had such an enormous impact are often referred to as the "scientific romances." The earliest noteworthy use of the term is believed to have been by author and mathematician Charles Howard Hinton, who published a collection of short-stories titled *The Scientific Romances* in 1886, but it is notable that Wells did not of his own accord specifically label any of his fictional works as scientific romances, and it is only subsequently that he has become the author most associated with the term. In an interview with Arthur H. Lawrence published in *The Young Man* in 1897, Wells does state that he is thinking of starting "another scientific romance" (Bergonzi *Early* 140), but this is in reference to Lawrence's own classification; Wells was very much his own man, and did not wish to be assimilated into a group of writers defined by the term (such as Jules Verne, George Griffin and Camille Flammarion) merely for the sake of journalistic convenience. The phrase was retro-

Introduction

spectively attributed to Wells in 1933 when Victor Gollancz issued an omnibus of eight novels under the title of *The Scientific Romances of H. G. Wells*, thus giving the phrase authoritative status.[5] Superseding the term scientific romance, sf itself came into general use in the 1930s, an early appearance being in Hugo Gernsback's editorial introduction to *Science Wonder Stories* (1929), with emphasis upon the necessity of scientific content as opposed to the fictional elements. This notion of sf as a didactic and progressive literature with a solid basis in contemporary scientific knowledge was soon revised as other pulp editors abandoned some of Gernsback's precepts, but the emphasis on science remained. A new manifesto was drawn up by John Campbell in the 1940s, proposing via a "thought-experiment" paradigm that sf should be regarded as a literary medium akin to science itself: "Scientific methodology involves the proposition that a well-constructed theory will not only explain away known phenomena, but will also predict new and still undiscovered phenomena. Science fiction tries to do much the same—and write up, in story form, what the results look like when applied not only to machines, but to human society as well" (Broderick 7–8).

Judith Merril also adopted this definition in the sense of expressing dissatisfaction with the label science fiction, believing that "speculative fiction" was more useful when conducting academic and ideological criticism: "Speculative fiction: stories whose objective is to explore, to discover, to learn, by means of projection, extrapolation, analogue, hypostudy-and-paper-experimentation, something about the nature of the universe, of man, or reality" (quoted in Edwards and Jakubowski 257). Merril states that she uses the term "speculative fiction" specifically to describe the mode which makes use of the traditional "scientific method" (observation, hypothesis, experiment) to examine some postulated approximation of reality. As a result, by introducing a given set of changes (imaginary or inventive) into the common background of "known facts," an environment can be created in which "the responses and perceptions of the characters will reveal something about the inventions, the characters, or both" (Merril 60). In *New Worlds for Old: The Apocalyptic Imagination, Science Fiction and American Literature* (1974), David Ketterer expands on these points at length, dividing sf into three categories (according to the type of extrapolation involved) and concentrating on the third: "Philosophically oriented science fiction, extrapolating on what we know in the context

Wells, Deleuze and Science Fiction

of our vaster ignorance, comes up with a startling rationale, that puts humanity in a radically new perspective" (190). Wells most certainly adheres to this definition.

However, regardless of semantics, it was in his scientific romance novels, in the space of less than a decade, that Wells created a body of work that combined previously disparate elements into the cohesive and modern narrative entity; for example, the utopian speculations of Thomas More, the serious social satire of Jonathan Swift, the cautionary fables of Mary Shelley, and the fantastic voyages of Jules Verne are all present in his novels, yet they are far more than a mere amalgamation of these previous contributions. Mary Shelley, via the medium of *Frankenstein* (1818) and *The Last Man* (1826), presented us with themes of the alien and mad scientist (in the former) and images of the future and the end of civilization (in the latter). Jules Verne added further motifs later in the nineteenth century, namely depictions of space, subterranean and subaquatic travel in *From the Earth to the Moon* (1865), *Journey to the Centre of the Earth* (1864), and *Twenty Thousand Leagues Under the Sea* (1870). Hence by the time *The Time Machine* debuted in 1895, some of the conventions of sf were already in place. Wells was however the decisive shaper of the new form, and *The Time Machine* established the template for his distinctive kind of fiction, with its "critical and educative effects of grand and startling visions" (Crossley 356). To this end renowned sf author Brian Aldiss declares Wells to be "the Prospero of all brave new worlds of the mind ... the Shakespeare of science fiction" (Aldiss *Omnibus* 133). In agreement and extrapolating from the perspective of those Wells has influenced, sf and fantasy scholar Tom Shippey claims:

> The dominant literary mode of the twentieth century has been the fantastic ... when the time comes to look back at the century, it seems very likely that future literary historians will see as its most representative and distinctive works books like.... George Orwell's *Nineteen Eighty-Four*.... Kurt Vonnegut's *Slaughterhouse-Five*.... Ursula Le Guin's *The Left Hand of Darkness* and *The Dispossessed*.... The list could readily be extended, back to the late nineteenth century with H. G. Wells's *The Island of Doctor Moreau* and *The War of the Worlds* [Shippey *Tolkien* vii].

The above quotation encapsulates the fundamental influence that Wells has had upon this broadly termed "literature of the fantastic." Sf theorist Darko Suvin is in agreement, stating that Wells was the first

Introduction

significant writer who started to write sf from within the world of science, and not merely facing it: "He endowed later sf with a basically materialist look back at human life and rebelliousness against its entropic closure. For such reason, all subsequent significant sf can be said to have sprung from Wells's [*The*] *Time Machine*" (Suvin *Metamorphoses* 220–221). Wells scholar Patrick Parrinder concurs:

> Wells is the pivotal figure in the evolution of the scientific romance into modern science fiction. His example has done as much to shape sf as any other single literary influence. This is partly because of his mastery of a range of representative themes (time travel, the alien invasion, biological mutation, the future city, anti-utopia) and partly because his stories embody a new genetic combination, which proved attractive both to "literary" and to scientifically minded readers [Parrinder *Literary* 10–11].

Crossley agrees, but emphasizes that, as far ranging as these themes and concepts are, their specific origins may be lost to the modern reader or cinema-goer, who "may not know who invented them or gave them their first memorable fictional incarnation" (Crossley 356).

Though in agreement as to the vital significance of Wells to the sf genre, these quotes contain various generalizations and assumptions that have both occupied and plagued Wells and sf studies over the last century. Such studies, eager to prove that Wells has more to offer than "just" being the father of sf, are often concerned to espouse the later non-fiction at the expense of his early works, thereby attempting to redress the critical balance towards his entire oeuvre. Indeed, the history of Wells studies demonstrates not only changing responses and perspectives towards Wells and sf in general, but also the evolution of modern critical and theoretical approaches themselves as they are brought to bear upon his works. Initial critique, that is, dating from the early 1900s) lacks any specific theoretical framework. However, Marxism, Russian Formalism and literary deconstruction are gradually introduced as these became significant critical approaches. Early mid-period criticism is also concerned with scientific progress, with both evolutionary theory and psychoanalysis being recurrently employed. Unsurprisingly (considering sf's inherently social commentary) socially and politically based theory is consistently in operation; the source material provides much for the utopian scholar, instigated by a study by Christopher Caudwell (*H. G. Wells: A Study in Utopianism*) in the 1930s, and culminating in works by John Huntington (*The Logic of Fan-*

tasy: H.G Wells and Science Fiction) and Patrick Parrinder and Christopher Rolfe (*H. G. Wells Under Revision among many others*) in the 1990s.

With regards to the scientific romances, opinion is often divided as to the relative merits of the earlier works in comparison to Wells's later, non-fictional texts. For example, Victor Sawdon Pritchett's "The Scientific Romances" (1946) argues that in *The Time Machine*, *The Island of Doctor Moreau*, and *The War of the Worlds*, "the destructive, ruthless" Wells of "fires and fist fights" far outshines the later Wells of "a dream world of plans," although behind both lies "the magic of science" (122–129). This critical train of thought is particularly emphasized by Wells's son Anthony West, in *Aspects of a Life*, published in 1984. West claimed that Wells was by nature a pessimist, and his intelligence and aesthetic sense were hopelessly at odds with the more progressive line he adopted later in his writing career. This study, that Wells willfully abandoned his pessimism lest it impact upon his creativity, had previously been implied by Bernard Bergonzi in his work *The Early H. G. Wells: A Study of the Scientific Romances*, published in 1961. Subsequent to Bergonzi, Wells's novels after 1910 were reclaimed by David Lodge and Parrinder, who disagreed with the view that they were less significant than the earlier works. A similar approach is also pursued by Peter Kemp (*H. G. Wells and the Culminating Ape: Biological Themes and Imaginative Obsession*, 1982) and Huntington, who give primacy to works up to 1900 or 1910. Mark Hillegas begins *The Future as Nightmare* (1967) by announcing Wells to be the father of modern "dystopian thought." To support this, he puts forward the study that twentieth century dystopian thought springs both from the pessimism of the early scientific romances, and rebounds in reaction from the utopianism of the later non-fiction. Within *H.G Wells: Discoverer of the Future* (1980) Roslynn Haynes takes a different stance, treating Wells's entire body of work as a single entity. Huntington's *The Logic of Fantasy: H.G Wells and Science Fiction* (1992) refers to the utopias of modern sf writers that Wells has influenced, seeing his heirs in the visions of Olaf Stapledon and Ursula Le Guin, and he reads Yevgeny Zamyatin's *We* as surpassing Wells in relentless ironies (149).

Notwithstanding the critical arguments attempting to reread Wells's non-fiction, research on the scientific romances has yet to be exhausted, as newer critical theories are brought to bear upon these

Introduction

texts, serving to reinvigorate the analysis of these early works. As a recent example of the renewed critical interest in the scientific romances, the essay collection *H.G Wells's Perennial Time Machine* (Slusser et al. 1995) is concerned with the specific agenda of "approaches from the point of view of the sf tradition on which it [*The Time Machine*] has had such a seminal influence" (Slusser et al. ix). Within this collection, David Leon Higdon's essay "A Revision and a Gloss: Michael Bishop's Postmodern Interrogation of H. G. Wells's *The Time Machine*" is concerned with issues of literary homage, adaptation and pastiche. Wells's novel is discussed in conjunction with Michael Bishop's 1982 novel *No Enemy But Time*, describing the latter as "a Borgesian counterbook to Wells's novel—a counterbook that appropriates, replies, supplements and wraps" (Higdon 177–178). Some texts specifically target and overtly reference Wells's oeuvre as source material, such as Stephen Baxter's *The Time Ships* (1995) or K.W Jeter's *Morlock Night* (1979),[6] while from a postmodern perspective *No Enemy But Time* has a "convoluted relationship with Wells's novel.... It is simultaneously a reply, a parody, a supplement, an interrogation and affirmation, a rebuttal, an homage—paradoxically both an ancestor and a defendant" (184). Although observing that literary references to time travel and time machines are now standard vocabulary for sf, Higdon explicates a number of inescapable intertextual ties to Wells's novels, such as references to "Martian war machines" (Bishop 255). Ultimately, he concludes that in its dismantling of the original work and consequent reconstruction upon radical new lines of thought, Bishop's novel functions as "a problematizing of one of the defining myths of science fiction," concluding that in terms of Wells's oeuvre and influence, "work that endures is always capable of an infinite and plastic ambiguity" (Higdon 184).

Critics such as Larry Caudwell and Wagar have claimed that postmodern traits such as these are in fact evident in the works of Wells themselves. In the essay "Time at the End of Its Tether," Caudwell claims: "Wells's critical affiliation ... is with the postmodern. His radical skepticism about narrative reflects that of his near-contemporary Nietzsche and anticipates stances taken, for example, by writes like Barthes, Derrida and Foucault" (139). Although Caudwell is highly skeptical as to whether Wells would himself embrace the "theoretical lucubrations" (139) of such theorists (particularly taking into account Wells's dismissal of the literary theory of Henry James), he is in no doubt that "his intellectual allegiance is clearly given to the mind that embraces 'hypotheses' together with the narrative subversions they entail.... The fractures and interstitial vacancies towards which postmodernism directs its eye are all familiar in Wells's narrative practice" (139).

John Hammond also emphasizes this point: "Wells sensed that it was not only man who was subject to metamorphosis; it was his institutions, his art, and the novel itself. In parodying the conventions of the realist novel and presenting it within a framework of evolutionary time he was widening its scope in an innovative way and looking ahead to the experimental fictions of the century's final decades" (Hammond *Modern* 206). Wagar concurs with Hammond, though importantly he cites the lack of distinctive boundaries between critical theories as more significant than the problem of placing Wells within them: "Since I have my doubts about the alleged wide disjunction between modernist and postmodernist discourse, I find Hammond's line of argument congenial" (Wagar *Traversing* 309).

Bridging the critical gap between the postmodern and the poststructuralist is Veronica Hollinger's essay "Deconstructing *The Time Machine*" (1987). Adopting a philosophical stance, Hollinger explores aspects of time travel in literature, contending that *The Time Machine* achieves an ironic deconstruction of Victorian scientific positivism. Hollinger states that it is first necessary to "read" time before writing a time-travel story: within the terms of a set of metaphors suggested by Roland Barthes, one can conclude that stories which support the classical Newtonian definition tend to read time as "work" (or "oeuvre"), while stories which explore the Einsteinian paradigm of physical reality tend to read time as "text" (201). Within the classical paradigm, time is linear and homogeneous. Relativity may thus be identified with "free play and différance, the (non) principles of the Derridean poststructure" (201). Further to this, Hollinger claims that in *The Time Machine* Wells anticipates several key Derridean concepts, in particular the idea that metaphysical structures must be undermined from the inside (202). Hollinger's study marks a new direction in Wells criticism at this point, not only in the content of her argument but also the actual philosophical framework in which the arguments are presented.

Other examples of recent criticism have equated Wells's use of language as a refutation of assumptions inherent to structuralist lin-

Introduction

guistics, thus reading him from the position of poststructuralism. In the essay "H. G. Wells the Poststructuralist" (in *H. G. Wells's Fin-de-siècle: Twenty-First Century Reflections* [2007]), Sylvia Hardy disputes previous arguments for Wells's modernist attributes, instead aligning him with the poststructuralist movement. Initially discussing Wells's rejection of the experimental modernist mode of writing (referencing written evidence of his exchanges with Henry James and James Joyce), Hardy cites Wells's staunch belief in the function of the novel as a conveyor of ideas, and for this reason he "dismissed modernist theories of the impersonability of the artist and of literary autonomy" (Hardy "Poststructuralist" 114). More important than this is the "fundamental principle underlying both his style and approach to fiction—his theory of language" (114). It is claimed that as early as 1891, Wells was questioning the notion that language relates unproblematically to pre-existing reality; on the contrary, he believed that "by categorizing and classifying, language *creates* meanings" (114). Influenced in part by William James's view on pragmatism and language, these ideas were developed continuously throughout his writing career. As a consequence, by the 1930s "Wells is outlining a view of language as signifying system which is in many ways as revolutionary and far-reaching as Saussurean claims about the arbitrary nature of the sign" (115).[7] Hardy argues that as a consequence, Wells actually remained ideologically opposed to the linguistic and aesthetic ideas represented primarily by modernism. Where Henry James sought an ideal artistic representation of the real world, Wells considered such an endeavor impossible "because language does not represent pre-existing meanings, but mediates, and to that extent creates, meaning" (115). By subscribing to this linguistic model, Wells's work became increasingly out of step with the prevailing modernist aesthetic of the early twentieth century. Hardy maintains that it was this that led to his work being attacked or ignored by modernist critics: "Wells's rejection of the modernist aesthetic [for example, its emphasis on erudite allusion, syntactic disruption and general linguistic deviation] has resulted in much of his fiction being misunderstood and underrated because it does not measure up to the criteria established by modernism and upheld by its critical counterpart, New Criticism" (113). She concludes her argument by stating: "While the modernist aesthetic ran counter to Wells's practice as a writer in just about every respect, poststructuralist/postmodern literary theory reaches conclusions not far removed from his ideas about texts as "experiments in statement" (125). In response, critic Paul Kincaid acknowledges that Hardy is "not alone in pointing out that Wells's work was out of step with the modernist aesthetic" and that she is "original in her analysis of the linguistic underpinning of this dissonance" (Kincaid "Ignored" n. pag.). He does however remain unconvinced by Hardy's identification of Wells with Saussure, and is "certain that she is taking far too great a step in calling Wells, even tentatively, a poststructuralist." Kincaid does however concede to the value of Hardy's innovative approach, and as Wells still defies easy categorization, "it seems a logical next step to see this as further defining perceptions of his [Wells's] place within twentieth-century literature" (n. pag.). Hardy's poststructuralist approach to Wells is highly significant to this study as a whole, and is discussed at length subsequently. As demonstrated, despite continued debate as to their specific stance and significance within the Wells canon itself, the scientific romances are still open to readings from new and emerging critical theories. Hence, this study represents a re-appropriation (or indeed, deterritorialization) of the scientific romances via the medium of a Deleuzian reading. It is in the context of this gradual emergence of postmodernist and poststructuralist approaches to Wells that this study is positioned, with the conclusion in particular building specifically upon Hardy's poststructuralist positioning of Wells.

Science Fiction and the Virtual

As we have seen, Wells's fiction instigated, and led to the mass popularization of a variety of sf tropes, concepts and ideas; in *The Time Machine*, *The Island of Doctor Moreau* and *The War of the Worlds* respectively we observe the genesis of time travel, genetic engineering and alien invasion. How are these ideas manifested in Wells's texts, and how are they subsequently extrapolated to give birth to an entire genre? To provide an answer to these questions (and in so doing, moving beyond already explored "traditional" taxonomies), we can turn to the theories of Deleuze. It is this "rebellion against enclosure," to paraphrase Suvin (*Metamorphoses* 221), and the idea of *The Time Machine* (along with Wells's other novels) as genesis for an entire ideological

Introduction

movement (or Deleuzian "image of thought," as shall subsequently be explored), that is to be investigated.

In their essay "The Philosophical Appeal of Science Fiction" (*Philosophy through Science Fiction*, 2009) Ryan Nichols et al. claim that sf and philosophy share a fundamental goal: "the discovery of what is essential and valuable in reality" (434). However, through the medium of Deleuze, it is not in fact "reality" that is the vital factor here, but "the virtual." The virtual and the actual are important concepts for Deleuze, who proposes to replace the true/false or real/unreal opposition by the actual/virtual distinction. According to Deleuze virtual and actual are both real, but not everything that is virtually contained (immanent) in this world is or becomes actual. The difference between virtual and actual is an important philosophical claim; simply put, the virtual (imaginations, dreams, memories, pure qualities) is real insofar as it has an effect on us, hence the virtual "insists" on the actual. For example, Deleuze claims that there is a dimension of the body that is virtual in addition to the physical dimension of the body, where potential reconfigurations of the senses are realized. This "virtual" body need not remain virtual, however. Deleuze and Guattari's purpose is to draw these virtual dimensions into reality, to experiment and create rather than simply theorize. The same applies here in terms of literature. While Deleuze's virtual ideas superficially resemble Plato's forms and Immanuel Kant's ideas of pure reason, they are not originals or models, nor do they transcend possible experience; instead they are the conditions of actual experience, the internal difference in itself: "The concept they [the conditions] form is identical to its object" (Deleuze *Desert* 36). A Deleuzian idea or concept (of difference) is not an ephemeral abstraction of an experienced thing, it is a real system of differential relations that creates actual spaces, times, and sensations. This concept of the virtual holds a central position in Deleuzian philosophy: "[it] is probably the most pivotal ... concept in Deleuze and Guattari's philosophical vocabulary" (Massumi *Users* 34). Indeed, Daniel W. Smith writes that "Deleuze's entire philosophy is concerned with the description of this virtual domain" ("Pure Immanence" 172). It is this actual/virtual relationship in Wells's works that this study ultimately explores.

In recent years Deleuze has become a rich source of analysis for sf, particularly with specific reference to his film theories, and hence the emphasis has often been upon sf cinema. To cite but a few examples of studies: David Martin-Jones's *Deleuze, Cinema and National Identity* (2006) features chapters concerning the time image in relation to *Terminator 3* (2003) and *Eternal Sunshine of the Spotless Mind* (2004). Anna Powell's *Deleuze and Horror Film* (2006), despite the title is very sf orientated, subjecting *Event Horizon* (1997), *Alien Resurrection* (1997), *Hardware* (1990) and *The Fly* (1986) to Deleuzian readings. Powell's *Deleuze: Altered States and Film* (2007) also dedicates a chapter to *2001: A Space Odyssey* (1968) and *Solaris* (1972). In *Mille/Punks/Cyber/Plateaus: Science Fiction and Deleuzo-Guattarian Becomings*, Charles J Stivale uses an "admittedly abstract delineation of the concept of becoming" (Stivale *Mille* 67) to examine the Cyberpunk genre, concentrating upon the concept of cyberspace,[8] stating that he "wish[es] to utilize this genre as a narrative vehicle for introducing some terminological distinctions available, but often hard to activate, in *A Thousand Plateaus*" (67). In this process, he draws from a number of cyberpunk narratives, both literary and cinematic.[9] Damian Sutton and David Martin-Jones's *Deleuze Reframed* (2008) takes in many examples of sf literature, film and video games,[10] using them as illustrations for various aspects of Deleuzian theory.

The application of Deleuzian philosophy to the sf genre is unsurprising; indeed, as Deleuze himself proclaimed in his introduction to *Difference and Repetition*, philosophy itself must be a kind of science fiction, in that the strange rhetoric and "monster" slang of sf estrange one from the historical inertia of the "now," and allow a leap into "untimely" futures with their own singular self-consistency (*Difference* xix–xx). Sf also allows a rigorous yet "hallucinogenic" relationship with a scientific discourse Deleuze and Guattari value without attempting to assimilate: "Philosophy can speak of science only by allusion, and science can speak of philosophy only as of a cloud" (*Philosophy* 161). In *A Thousand Plateaus*, Deleuze suggests that sf's plots of "becoming," becoming-woman, animal, even alien or machine,[11] are "antimemories" that reassess traditional hierarchies, challenging any presumption of human superiority or singularity (*Thousand* 324). This, according to Deleuze, is the fluid "ecstasy" of the world, and sf, being a speculative literature of ideas, is ideally placed to apprehend and interpret such concepts. Consequently it is to these marginal and hybrid genres, such as sf and its multitude of off-shoots (for example, sf horror and cyber-

Introduction

punk, and as this study argues, the scientific romance), that one turns to in order to find fitting cultural illustrations of the changes and transformations that are taking place in our post-human present. As a result, they arguably end up being a more accurate and honest depiction of contemporary culture than other, more self-consciously "representational" genres:

> By dipping into SF, they [Deleuze and Guattari] can extrapolate the conceptual imagination into a world transformed by science and technology. How do we conceive of being when the distinction between organic and machinic dissolves? When reality is folded into virtuality, the body morphs, and computer networks suck knowledge into a digital monad? How do we think if thinking is chaotic at its core? [Davis n. pag.].

These questions neatly summarize the methodology of the various studies exemplified above, although as demonstrated, all are primarily concerned with modern sf, the emphasis being upon contemporary film or literature. However, with Deleuzian theory a concept can be retrofitted to understand the conceptual power in the work of an artist or author in a new way. Similarly, this new creative form might better illustrate, and give new dimension to, a concept already developed. Hence this study demonstrates that it is not merely present day sf that benefits from a Deleuzian reading, but also the works of Wells that have served as its inspiration.

Deterritorializing Utopia

Fredric Jameson describes the perspective offered by sf as "a structurally unique method of apprehending the present as history" (Jameson "Progress" 153). This conception of science fiction as a characterization of utopian imagination stems from Darko Suvin's own understanding of utopia as "the socio-political subgenre of science fiction" (Suvin *Metamorphoses* 45). The term utopia itself was popularized by Thomas More's work *Utopia*,[12] published in 1516. Prior to this, utopian themed literature had principally been Edenic or messianic, with Plato's *The Republic* (360 BC approx), and Cicero's *De Republica* (53 BC approx) being notable attempts to elevate utopian concepts from the realms of mere fantasy to a level of social critique. More utilized his concepts of utopia in a practical way, his purpose being the comparison of his ideal state with what he saw as the moral decadence and disunity of contemporary Christian Europe; the tolerance and prosperity of his imaginary utopia was the very antithesis of the society in which he lived. More's contribution to utopian literature is far reaching, as not only did he coin the term that is in common usage to this day, but he demonstrated how a literary mode could be utilized as a form of criticism of society. Once More had set the precedent for utopian literature as a sociological tool, as well as a literary one, *Utopia* was followed by Philip Sidney's *The Countess of Pembroke's Arcadia* (1590) and Philip Stubbes's *The Anatomie of Abuses* (1583), both variants of More's approach, being satires on imaginary countries. The utopias of the seventeenth century include Joseph Hall's *The Discovery of a New World* (1605), Francis Bacon's *New Atlantis* (1626), Francis Godwin's *The Man in the Moone* (1638), Gabriel Platte's *Macaria* (1641), Samuel Gott's *Nova Solyma* (1648), James Harrington's *Oceana* (1656) and Henry Neville's *The Isle of Pines* (1668). The basic characteristics of these works largely follow the model laid down by More, being essentially Christian, hierarchical and authoritarian. Jonathan Swift's *Gulliver's Travels* (1726) is the best known example of eighteenth-century utopian literature. This can be read as an attack upon the utopian ideal itself, being equally critical of concepts of radical liberalism and authoritarianism.

In the nineteenth century the genre proceeded to evolve; due to technological and scientific advancement it became possible to imagine a society wherein, as Asimov put it, "scientific and technological advance might impose a utopia from without" (Asimov *Gold* 101). These speculative technological and economic utopias include Wells's *A Modern Utopia* (1905) and Edward Bellamy's *Looking Backward* (1888) and *Equality* (1897). It is arguable that at such a point in history, it became feasible for utopian literature to take on another form, that of the imaginary dystopia.[13] Dystopia is in direct contrast to utopia as it is intended that the society described be viewed as considerably worse than the current state of affairs. In this manner, both forms fulfill a co-dependent yet separate definable function; utopias provide us with an ideal state of affairs, thus presenting us with the issue of how such a state of affairs may be reached. Dystopias threaten us with undesirable circumstances that society may already be some way towards: they function as a warning that must be heeded. In the late twentieth and

Introduction

early twenty-first centuries, this form has become far more popular than the utopian novel or film. Arguably this is due to contemporary social criticism being intrinsically easier through the medium of the dystopian novel than the traditionally static utopia.

Wells was a practitioner of both forms of critique, his writings embracing both utopic and dystopic forms; *A Modern Utopia* and *Men like Gods* (1923) are good examples of the former in their praise of rationality in science and politics, and *The Sleeper Awakes* (1910) of the dystopia. However, in keeping with the amalgamated nature of the two concepts, he also combined the two, often shifting emphasis from one to the other for added impact. For example, the future world depicted in *The Time Machine* initially appears to the narrator to be a utopian paradise, before the full extent of its dystopian nature is revealed. In non-fictional works, such as *The Discovery of the Future* and *Anticipations* (both 1902) he sets a specific agenda for social change, describing what he believed to be an achievable utopia for future human society, built around the concept of a peaceful and empathetic world state.

Deleuze and Guattari's concept of utopia is intrinsically linked to the vocation of philosophy, transformed into an immanent concept that expresses philosophy's political nature. Deleuze's trajectory of utopia moves from the concepts of time and the distinction between the virtual and actual presented in *Difference and Repetition*, through the very different views of history presented in the two volumes of *Capitalism and Schizophrenia*, and it is in *What Is Philosophy?* where he discusses utopia most explicitly. Deleuze explicitly uses ideas from Samuel Butler's *Erewhon* (1872) at various points in the development of his philosophy of difference. In *Difference and Repetition*, Deleuze refers to what he calls "Ideas" as "erewhons." "Ideas are not concepts," he explains, but rather "a form of eternally positive differential multiplicity, distinguished from the identity of concepts" (*Difference* 288). "Erewhon" refers to the "nomadic distributions" that pertain to simulacra; "Erewhon," in this reading, is "not only a disguised no-where but a rearranged now-here" (333). In this manner, Deleuze and Guattari suggest that utopia stands for absolute deterritorialization, "but always at the critical point at which it is connected with the present relative milieu" (*Philosophy* 99). In *Difference and Repetition* they state:

philosophy is neither a philosophy of history, nor a philosophy of the eternal, but untimely, always and only untimely—that is to say, acting counter to our time and thereby acting on our time and, let us hope, for the benefit of a time to come. Following Samuel Butler, we discover *Erewhon*, signifying at once the originary "nowhere" and the displaced, disguised, modified and always re-created "here-and-now." We believe in a world in which individuations are impersonal, and singularities are pre-individual: the splendor of the pronoun "one"—whence the science-fiction aspect, which necessarily derives from this *Erewhon* [*Difference* xix].

As a result, rather than designating a static representation of the ideal place (or "topos"), utopia then becomes the power of the "ideal" itself, which can bifurcate time and create possible worlds, an ideal form of repetition, rather than the repetition of an ideal form (Lambert "Uses" 148).

Evolution, the Rhizome and the Nomad

It goes without saying that the Darwinian theory of evolution, as a major concern at the turn of the nineteenth century, is an intrinsic element within Wells's works, and has hence been a rich source for literary criticism. The vast school of criticism that these themes have spawned will not be investigated in detail here, but a brief overview of a number of notable studies and their various perspectives on the evolutionary issue is provided. Wells himself writes extensively upon the subject in *The Science of Life* (1930) (one chapter being titled "The Incontrovertible Fact of Evolution"), while fictional texts such as *The Time Machine*, *The War of the Worlds* and *The Island of Doctor Moreau* have been described and discussed in terms of their "biological vision" (Hammond *Time* 137) by later critics. One obvious example is *The War of the Worlds*; the conflict between mankind and the Martian invaders is portrayed as a Darwinian struggle for the survival of the fittest. The alien invaders, whose longer period of successful evolution (the novel depicts Mars as being a far older planet than the Earth) has led to them developing a superior intelligence, are able to create weapons far in advance of humans on the planet Earth (Williamson "Evolution" 189). In *The Early Fiction of H. G. Wells: Fantasies of Science* (2009), *Steven McLean* investigates the scientific romances in relation to contemporary scientific theory: specifically *The Time Machine* and *The Island of*

Introduction

Doctor Moreau in the context of debates on evolution, retrogression and degeneration. McLean claims that in *The War of the Worlds* "Wells utilizes his fourth scientific romance as a means to participate in the debate between Huxley and Spencer over the application of evolutionary theory to human society" (McLean *Early* 112). Sylvia A. Pamboukian's "What the Traveler Saw: Evolution, Romance and Time Travel" (2009) argues that the narrative devices through which Wells presented his ideas added extra gravitas to the Darwinian themes. The mechanical nature of his time machine supports the evolutionary content of the text by allowing readers to visualize continual geological and biological change over a vast timeframe. Since the time machine is a new sort of transportation technology, "Wells (unlike his contemporaries such as [Richard] Jefferies, [W.H.] Hudson and [William] Morris) is able to represent the continual state of flux inherent in evolution through repeated journeys in time" (Pamboukian 18). This also serves to undermine the assumption that evolution is inherently progressive; *The Time Machine's* "terminal beach," in which the time traveler journeys quite literally to the end of the world, is a depiction of regression rather than a progression to "superior" evolutionary forms: "For the first time [in fiction] the evolution of Man was revealed not merely as a biological and social process, but also as an astrobiological development, played out against a backdrop of dying planets and dying Sun" (Brake 277). "People unfamiliar with such speculations as those of the younger Darwin, forget that the planets must ultimately fall back one by one into the parent body," reflects the time traveler himself (Wells *Time* 52), echoing sentiments within the article "Zoological Retrogression" that Wells wrote previously in 1891: "There is no ... guarantee in scientific knowledge of man's permanence or permanent ascendancy.... Nature is, in unsuspecting obscurity, equipping now some humble creature with a wider possibility of appetite, endurance, or destruction, to rise in the fullness of time and sweep homo away into the darkness from which his universe arose" ("Zoological" 246–253).

Even if the scientific romances did not involve the literal depiction of vast stretches of time, evolutionary issues are still a vital element, as present in *The War of the Worlds*, *The Island of Doctor Moreau* and "The Stolen Bacillus" (1894), for example. *In H. G. Wells: Traversing Time* (2005), Wagar discusses Wells's fascination with time, which led to his more obvious books about the subject, such as *The Time*

Wells, Deleuze and Science Fiction

Machine, but also his historical texts. Wagar claims that the depiction of the passage of time was vitally important to Wells, not just with regard to the evolution of life, but also the evolution of society. This can clearly be observed in works such as *The Time Machine*, in which the evolution of Eloi and Morlock can be traced back to the social class structure of Wells's England, but is also present in the manner in which Wells approached writing about the world in general. Wagar poetically surmises that Wells was "like the ambiguous hero of his first novel, an intrepid time traveler, a man whose mind traversed time from its beginnings in the inferno of Earth's creation to the broad spectrum of futures imaginably awaiting our species and our globe" (Wagar *Traversing* 2).

Evolutionary theory also plays a significant role in Deleuzian theory, and functions as a compelling illustration of the rhizomatic thinking that he advocates. Deleuze describes the standard epistemology of Western thought as functioning on the principle of an arboreal structure in which a trunk grows vertically and produces branches which subdivide into smaller and lesser categories, hence an insistence upon linear, hierarchic and totalizing principles. To challenge this, the image of the rhizome is utilized, in which the stem of a plant sends out interconnecting roots and shoots as it spreads underground, to describe the way in which ideas should be conceived as multiple, interconnected and self-replicating. In this manner, rhizomatic thinking advocates the formation of intricate paths of free-flowing associations, as opposed to arboreal, flat trains of thought. This prevents a narrativization of (for example) history and culture, instead presenting them as a map or wide array of attractions and influences with no specific origin or genesis, for a rhizome has no beginning or end: "it is always in the middle, between things, interbeing, *intermezzo*" (Thousand 27). Hence, life itself for Deleuze is an "open, creative whole of proliferating connections" of which the human subject is only the "effect of one particular series of experiential connections" (Colebrook 5).

In the essay within *A Thousand Plateaus* "Becoming-Intense, Becoming-Animal, Becoming-Imperceptible," Deleuze and Guattari illustrate a rhizomatic reassessment of evolution. Natural history and evolution are traditionally realized through "a chain of beings perpetually imitating one another, progressively and regressively, and tending toward the divine higher term" (259). This structured form of beings, one evolving to the next, points to a trajectory whose objective lies in

Introduction

progression and finally in perfection: "Ideas do not die. Not that they survive simply as archaisms. At a given moment they may reach a scientific stage, and then lose that status or emigrate to other sciences. Their application and status, even their form and content, may change; yet they retain something essential throughout the process, across the displacement, in the distribution of a new domain" (259). Here, Deleuze and Guattari compare the history of ideas with that of evolution. Over time even the idea of evolution itself evolves, migrating not only to other sciences, but also into literature and popular culture. It is therefore the linear passage and progression through time of such ideas that they hope to shatter, as the history of ideas should never be continuous; within such a linear chain only imitation remains possible, but within a rhizome the possibilities for different associations and ideas become endless. This proposed destabilization of the arboreal structure, on which so many Western epistemological models are founded, is furthered with the notion of "becoming," via which Deleuze seeks to bring into conjunction artistic, philosophic and scientific machines; this is discussed in the next section of this introduction.

Deleuze's opposition to a linear evolutionary descent of ideas would initially appear to confuse and contradict the positioning of Wells as the "father of modern sf," as the (subsequent) tropes he inspired are typically seen as direct descendants of his literature, in the form of an arboreal evolution of ideas. Indeed, in *The Early Fiction of H. G. Wells: Fantasies of Science*, Stephen McLean warns that the focus on Wells as a "father" of science fiction risks "encourage[ing] the popular conception that the significance of his scientific romances lies not so much in their engagement with scientific debates" than in "the contribution of a number of literary tropes toward the creation of the modern genre of science fiction" (McLean 2). However, as this study argues, Wells's position is rhizomatic not arboreal; he occupies the position of the "virtual," or to connect with another Deleuzian term, possibly that of the "nomadic" writer. The Deleuzian nomad "does not hold the secret" and should not be commodified purely as a trope (*Thousand* 466). In this way, nomadology emerges as continuous with aspects of its past and future.

The concept of nomadology (or "nomad thought") is linked to that of the rhizome, which describes the connections that occur between the most disparate and the most similar of objects, places and people:

any network of things brought into contact with one another, functioning as an assemblage machine for new affects, concepts, bodies, thought (Colman 231–232). The rhizome maintains that ideas are dynamic events or "lines of flight" which take us into an endlessly bifurcating system, while the term itself suggests the nomadic movement of thought by the intensities of a self in process, contrary to the hierarchical (arboreal) system of thought. Nomadic thought is spelled out most explicitly in *A Thousand Plateaus*, and as such is a construction of Deleuze and Guattari's "counter-philosophy," challenging authenticity and propriety. As mentioned, Deleuze speaks of traditional philosophy (and, by extension, traditional writing) as something that seeks to code the world and works within the codes of the world. "Nomad thought" is the philosophical process of thinking outside and across institutional boundaries, the decodification and recodification of thought, and therefore as a device it can be used as an alternative approach to understanding the history of civilization. Writers, filmmakers and artists can also be nomadic in this sense, in that they explore the potential of their respective media, and then break away from established paths.

Becoming-Woman, -Animal, -Minor

The ontology of becoming (also referred to as Process philosophy) identifies the interaction between metaphysical reality and change. Since Plato and Aristotle, traditional philosophy has posited reality as "timeless," based on permanent substances, while processes are denied or subordinated to timeless substances. For example, if a person is to suffer an illness, they remain the same (the substance of the person being the same), and the change (the illness) only glides over the substance: change is accidental, whereas the substance is essential. Therefore, classic ontology denies any full reality to change, which is conceived as only accidental and not essential. This classical ontology is commonly attributed to making possible a theory of knowledge, as it was thought that a science of something "becoming" was an impossible feat to achieve (Prigogine 53). Conversely, the ontology of becoming does not characterize change as illusory or as purely accidental to the substance, as in Aristotle's thought, but as the cornerstone of reality,

Introduction

or being. The endeavor to replace ancient Platonic theories of identity and being with concepts of difference are a vital constituent of modern philosophical thought. Despite significant contributions from the likes of Foucault and Jacques Derrida, it is Deleuze who has arguably furthered the field to the greatest degree, benefitting from having a philosophical position richly informed by biological thought. It is for this reason that Deleuzian theory is suited to the performance of a deterritorialization upon Wells's scientific romances, texts rich in issues concerning biology and concepts of human/animal/alien identity. Classic ontology conceives becoming merely as the comparison between a starting point and an end point, and as a consequence of this process the differences between the two are deduced. In Deleuzian terms, this is merely an abstract exercise that serves to distract from the richness of our experiences, as Deleuzian becoming is not the mere attribute or intermediary that occurs between events, but a characteristic of the very production of events themselves. Becoming is not a metaphor, not a matter of acting like something or imitating something; it is a deterritorialization, which involves more than simply undermining or doing away with hierarchy (Olkowski *Ruin* 34). With this state of constant transformation, we are removed from the rigid notion of being; the self as becoming is full of possibilities whereas the self as "being" is complete and has no further potential. Becoming is a process that never ends and, because of this, fixed categories are always at risk of being undermined.

As a result of this, Deleuzian theory assumes no essential divisions in the natural world, with no absolute differences between humans and animals. Instead, the material world is seen as a vast field of virtual forces and intensities that become actualized through interactions with the things and/or bodies with which we are familiar. These bodies are not stable entities, instead being assemblages of forces, undergoing constant change dependent upon the encounters they have with other entities with which they enter into relationships. In other words, bodies are not beings, but becomings. Hence, a body in question is not defined by its physical form, function, or resemblance to other bodies. Instead, a body is related materially to others, with its distinctiveness being the particular set of capacities and powers it actualizes through the medium of interactions. Human beings obviously have various distinctive characteristics, but so too have other forms, be they animal or mineral, yet none of these contain a fixed essence; they are all engaged in relations of becoming, which open up other modes of existence. In stating that all things and states are products of becoming, Deleuzian theory has significant ramifications for traditional philosophical concepts that emphasize being, originality and essence, such as the aforementioned Platonic ontology. For example, we can no longer conceive of a human being as a stable individual experiencing change but essentially remaining the same person (as with the example of illness presented previously). For Deleuze, the self must instead be envisaged as an assemblage of different forces in a state of constant flux.

In addition, the all-encompassing nature of the Deleuzian rhizome allows us to extend the analysis of such forms and their becomings into other realms, be they political, artistic, or in this case, a work of literary fiction. Wells's novels intrinsically contain their own distinctive characteristics and assemblages, not only between the reader and the work of literature itself, but also in the becomings and assemblage of forces present within the narrative. This leads to issues of becoming in literature specifically.

According to Deleuze, literature is the power of becoming beyond any already given "image of thought," or any rule of art; it has the power to mobilize desire, to create new pre-personal investments, and enables thought and affects beyond the human: "Writing is a question of becoming, always incomplete, always in the midst of being formed, and goes beyond the matter of any livable or lived experience. Writing is inseparable from becoming: in writing, one becomes-woman, becomes-animal or vegetable, becomes-molecule to the point of becoming-imperceptible" (Deleuze *Critical* 1). This "system of becomings" is intrinsically associated with the concept of literature and "becoming-minor." This is diametrically opposed to what Deleuze refers to as a "major" use of language, which serves to regularize and stabilize form and meaning, and thereby "reinforces categories and distinctions that compartmentalize existence, thereby fostering an isolation of the personal and the political … encourage[ing] both the reinforcement of the dominant views of the majority and the illusion of the autonomy of the single voice" (Khalfa 121). In contrast, becoming-minor refers to becomings that depart from dominant identities, inventing new forms of collective life, consciousness, and affectivity.[14] In the medium of literature, Deleuze and Guattari specifically locate Franz Kafka

Introduction

(1883–1924) and Herman Melville (1819–1891) as minor writers, whose works serve to "disturb dominant regularities and in the process connects the personal and the political in proliferating networks of becoming" (*Kafka* 121). In terms of these "dominant regularities," patriarchy could be used to provide a simple illustration of how the concept of "minority" is used: for example, even if there are more women than men in a numerical sense (either within a specific group, or in society as a whole), in Deleuze and Guattari's terms (which are sensitive to relations of power) men still constitute the majority whereas women form a minority. Thus the concept of "becoming-minor" converges with that of "becoming-woman," "becoming-animal," "becoming-molecular," "becoming-imperceptible," and, ultimately, "becoming-revolutionary." Each type of affective becoming marks a new phase of a larger process of Deleuzian deterritorialization. Suffice to say becoming-woman is not a transformation to a pre-given image of what a woman is or should be, and neither is becoming-animal a human being impersonating an animal. Becoming is a direct connection, where "the self contemplates nothing other than the singularities it perceives. To become-animal is thus to perceive the animal as if one were perceiving "its" world. To become-woman is to create what is other than man and fixity, or to become as such" (Colebrook *Understanding* 155).

As stated, Deleuze principally uses the literature of Kafka and Melville to demonstrate how literature expresses becoming-animal, but this is not to say that he emphasizes a particular type of literature; instead through these examples he expresses the power of literature, i.e., the power to perceive differently by the removal from the human. Instead of reading literature as a quest for meaning and interpretation, Deleuze and Guattari argue that literature is about affects and intensities; literature can be read for what it produces, for its transformations. Therefore the human fascination for the animal is a fascination for the world seen, not from an already organized position, but seen anew.

Wells's Oeuvre as Body Without Organs

Deleuze introduced the notion of the body without organs in *The Logic of Sense* (1969), but it was not until his collaborative work with

Wells, Deleuze and Science Fiction

Guattari (particularly *Anti-Oedipus* and *A Thousand Plateaus*) that the body without organs comes to prominence as one of his major ideas. The term itself is appropriated from a poem by Antonin Artaud.[15] It is not a literal term, being not an actual organless body, but instead a deterritorialized body, one without organization, an empty potential assemblage: "a body that breaks free from its socially articulated, disciplined, semioticised, and subjectified state (as an 'organism'), to become disarticulated, dismantled, and deterritorialized, and hence able to be reconstituted in new ways" (Best and Kellner 90–91). The body without organs is not a metaphor, Deleuze and Guattari insist, but actual matter, a sort of virtual space that the actual body presupposes as a zone of potentialities across which flows are directed thus not an empty body "stripped of organs," but a "body upon which that which serves as organs is distributed according to crowd phenomena ... in the form of molecular multiplicities" (*Thousand* 34). For example (as is subsequently discussed in a case study concerning *The Time Machine*), the Deleuzian nomad and the schizophrenic are fragmented, libidinal bodies, which seek to destroy the concept of identity based on representation. In *A Thousand Plateaus*, Deleuze and Guattari differentiate between three types of body without organs; in its "reconstitution," it has multiple potential destinations—"empty," "cancerous" or "full" (these specific terms are discussed more thoroughly in Chapter Two, in relation to *The War of the Worlds*). Deleuze and Guattari use the term body without organs in an extended sense, to refer to the virtual dimension of reality in general (which they more often call "plane of consistency" or "plane of immanence"). In this sense, they speak of a body without organs of the planet Earth: "The Earth ... is a body without organs. This body without organs is permeated by unformed, unstable matters, by flows in all directions, by free intensities or nomadic singularities, by mad or transitory particles" (45). This serves to challenge the assumption of the world being composed of relatively stable entities (such as bodies and beings); these bodies are actually composed of sets of flows moving at various speeds (rocks and mountains as very slow-moving flows, living things as flows of biological material, language as flows of information).

Extending this to Wells, we can argue that his oeuvre functions as a full body without organs: his concepts (alien invasions and time machines, for example) and source texts are subject to constant

Introduction

reinvention and adaptation (through the medium of literary criticism, countless references to his work in popular culture,[16] cinematic and literary adaptations and remakes, board and videogames,[17] the intersection of fan culture with the Wells canon, ad infinitum). In this manner the Wells universe is not "petrified by its original organization"; free to grow and expand, it is productive, always progressing in a multitude of rhizomatic directions, and hence is able to be reconstituted in new ways.

Literature and SF as Assemblage

Although the previous sections examine Deleuzian methodology in relation to sf, given that the specific case-studies are in novel form, it is also necessary to establish his relationship with literature as a genre. Deleuze repeatedly praises works of literature and art in almost rhapsodic terms; both are expressions of the virtual, of becoming, and of transformation. Philosophy, Deleuze states, is a question of what is going to happen and what has happened, "like a novel": "Except the characters are concepts, and the settings, the scenes are space-times. One's always writing to bring something to life, to free life from where it's trapped, to trace lines of flight" (Deleuze *Neg* 140–141). Hence, through the experience of literature, "we are not in the world, we become with the world; we become by contemplating it. Everything is vision, becoming. We become universes. Becoming-animal, plant, molecular, becoming-zero" (*Philosophy* 169).

One way of approaching a specific text is the assemblage, an intrinsic element of Deleuzian theory, defined by Deleuze as "a multiplicity which is made up of many heterogeneous terms and which establishes liaisons, relations between them" (Deleuze and Parnet *Dialogues II* 69). A Deleuzian assemblage is any number of "things" or pieces of "things" gathered into a single context. An assemblage can bring about any number of "effects": aesthetic, machinic, productive, destructive, consumptive, and so forth. Deleuze and Guattari's discussion of the nature of the book provides a number of insights into this loosely defined term: "In a book, as in all things, there are lines of articulation or segmentarity, strata and territories; but also lines of flight, movements of deterritorialization and destratification.... All this, lines and measurable speeds constitutes an assemblage." (*Thousand* 4–5). The assemblage can therefore serve as a sophisticated way of analyzing moments in fiction that are not simply a question of analyzing things and actions (what Deleuze refers to as "machinic assemblages") but also discourses, affects and other non-corporeal relations that link signifiers with effects. The recognition that these assemblages are continuously evolving and becoming can open up subtle readings of texts; interpretation becomes less about studying a fixed object and more about entering into a rhizomatic relationship with the text (Fancy 100).

A book, then, as described above, is an amalgamation of discrete parts or pieces that is capable of producing any number effects, rather than a tightly organized and coherent whole producing one dominant reading. The usefulness of the assemblage lies in the fact that, since it lacks its own inherent organization, it can draw into itself any number of disparate elements. A book itself can be an assemblage, but its status as an assemblage does not prevent it from containing other assemblages within itself, or entering into new assemblages with, for example, its readers, libraries, bookshops, bonfires, and so on. This concept of literature as an assemblage allows the viewing of a literary work in machinic terms. Through this, we can define the multitude of elements contained within the text, how these function individually, and as a consequence of this, how they are assembled to produce the overall work. Deleuze describes this process in relation to the works of Kafka in *Kafka: Towards a Minor Literature* (1986): "This functioning of an assemblage can be explained only if one takes it apart to examine both the elements that make it up and the nature of its linkages" (53). Initially, this approach would not appear to differ greatly from a standard textual deconstruction (an analysis or close reading), concerned with such themes as genre, plot, character, metaphors, analogies and so forth, the combination of which allows us to determine the meaning of the overall work. For example, in these terms, Wells's *The Time Machine* is an English Victorian science fiction novel concerning an unnamed protagonist who invents a time machine, journeys into the far future, and discovers a stratified society. Thematically the novel contains socialist warnings regarding the growth and abuse of capitalism, as well as issues of social Darwinism, evolution and the relativity of time. These elements are all identifiable individually, and also in terms of their function in relation to the novel as a whole.

Introduction

However, while this standard form of textual analysis serves its purpose, it is not what Deleuzian methodology is concerned with. A specific "active dismantling" of the work (i.e., the assemblage) involves the analysis of a multitude of its elements, investigating their more specific components, such as images, words, actions and spatial arrangements, and then demonstrating the differing relationships between these components. This not only provides a different interpretation of the work, but allows us to see what the work is capable of doing. For example, Deleuze maintains that differing assemblages of words and images can constitute "figures" that may not have inherent value of their own, but can result in determinate effects. These components are evaluated in terms of their relationship to forces that exist outside of the text itself, such as potentialities and desires. These allow the determination of how the work's many elements combine, and the consequences of these combinations. Ultimately, although the work as a whole is inherently a sum of its individual parts, the synthesis of these parts is not unifying and total, as the whole work itself is yet another individual aspect, another new facet that is added to the many other elements that form the work. In this way, a book then, can be viewed as "a little machine," and therefore "the only question is which other machine the literary machine can be plugged into in order to work" (*Thousand* 4–5). Of course, this study is discussing Wells's "literary machines" and their linkages to the broader sf genre; Fancy expresses the pertinence of conceptualizing sf as assemblage in regards to form, content, authorship and scholarship:

> those entering into a rhizomatic relationship with the assemblage of their thinking in the context of sf studies will, like the work of sf authors and filmmakers whose worlds they are entering, challenge themselves to engage in new lines of thinking in an open-ended exercise of concept creation and evolution. It is clear that sf, with its core concerns around future assemblages of technologies, humans, other planets and species, is a series of assemblages that can provide the lines of flight and Bodies without Organs Deleuze felt would be necessary to help undo the various stratifications he saw gathering [Fancy 105].

Hence, vital to Deleuze is the sheer fact of conceptual invention: the creation of new concepts (and hence the undoing of established stratifications) means that we can potentially see the world in a new way, one that was not available to us before: "a perception as it was before men (or after) ... released from human coordinates" (*Cinema* 122).

Wells, Deleuze and Science Fiction

In keeping with this notion of conceptual reinvention, via specific case studies the remainder of this study deterritorializes Wells, providing reinterpretations of existing readings, and unique perspectives upon a selection of his scientific romances. This process serves to recast Wells as a writer and thinker with remarkable resonance with Deleuze and Guattari's works and thus as an author who has much to say as to the world of contemporary philosophy, politics and society. This machinic splicing of the Wells and Deleuze machines demonstrates "productive use of the literary machine … that extracts from the text its revolutionary force" (*Anti* 116), allowing us to consider the elements of this revolutionary force personified in Wells. Ultimately, through his reading strategy, Deleuze strove to produce something recognizably new, distinctively "his." He infamously stated that he saw his philosophical approach as a form of immaculate conception: "I saw myself as taking an author from behind, and giving him a child that would be his own offspring, yet monstrous" (*Neg* 6). It is these monstrous "mutations" of Wells that are a major source of focus. In addition however, in the postscript to the essay "Dead Psychoanalysis: Analyze," Deleuze gives another remit for a literary reading:

> My ideal, when I write about an author, would be to write nothing that would cause him sadness, or if he is dead, that might make him weep in his grave. Think of the author you are writing about. Think of him hard so that he can no longer be an object, and equally so that you cannot identify with him. Avoid the double shame of the scholar and the familiar. Give back to the author a little bit of the joy, the energy, the love of life and politics that he knew how to give and invent. So many dead writers must have wept about what has been written about them [*Dialogues II* 119].

Therefore, it is the contrast and consistency of both "taking an author from behind," while positively and constructively engaging with a text, which determines the entire trajectory of any Deleuzian reading, and hence this study. Deleuze maintains that any work of art "points a way through life, finds a way through the cracks" (*Neg* 143), and how Wells's oeuvre engages with this process is demonstrated, taking into account the myriad of "mutations" to which it has been subject. Ultimately this serves to demonstrate the "untimely" power of Wells's literature.

One

The Island of Doctor Moreau
Transhumanism, Spaces and Becoming

> No matter how one takes you you are mad, ready for the straitjacket. By placing him again, for the last time, on the autopsy table to remake his anatomy. I say, to remake his anatomy. Man is sick because he is badly constructed. We must make up our minds to strip him bare in order to scrape off that animalcule that itches him mortally.
> —Artaud "To Have Done with the Judgment of God" 570

Wells, Deleuze and the Transhuman

This chapter principally demonstrates the concept of becoming, and how it can be used in a Deleuzian encounter with Wells's novel *The Island of Doctor Moreau*. Published in 1896, the novel concerns the surgical transformation of animals into human beings, inspired by the contemporaneous Victorian debate upon vivisection (and by extension eugenics) and hence is a commentary upon the potential horrors that Wells perceived reckless human experimentation with nature can produce (Harris 99). Wells's scientific romances refer repeatedly to both the attractive and potentially horrific possibilities of human evolution; for example, *The War of the Worlds* imagines an alternative posthuman history in which the assumed apotheosis that is Victorian civilization is superseded by more advanced and evolved aliens, while *The Time Machine* extrapolates such evolutionary issues into the far future. However, instead of focusing on these potential dangers, *The*

Wells Meets Deleuze

Island of Doctor Moreau is concerned with "the animal, chaotic, bloody origins and hidden nature of the human present," calling into question "the most basic tenet of the entire tradition of Western humanism: the belief in the specialty, the sublime individuality, the autonomy of the human species on this planet" (McConnell 89–90). The resulting depiction of the "dethronement of humankind from the centre of creation, with morality merely a conditioned reflex" (92) elicited an overwhelmingly hostile press reaction at the time of first publication, with reviewers nearly unanimous in their distaste for the novel's violence, cynicism and disturbing imagery: not least its portrayal of man as "little more than a half-trained, cannibalistic beast" (89). Arguably the novel still remains minoritised in terms of popularity and visibility in academia and popular culture (at least in comparison to *The Time Machine* and *The War of the Worlds*): of the scientific romances it is probably the least widely read or taught. Nevertheless, *The Island of Doctor Moreau* has still endured to produce a lasting legacy, with its influence evident in modern sf tales of scientific and medical experimentation,[1] and it has been subject to several cinematic adaptations (in 1933, 1977 and 1996 respectively).

Prior academic critique on the novel has been far reaching, with a multitude of studies examining its complex social, moral and religious allegories. More recent approaches include psychoanalytic readings of its representation of Victorian homosexuality, and arguments for the novel being positioned as a work of postmodern gothic literature).[2] However, while originally positioned as a commentary on evolution, divine creation, and the tension between human nature and culture, the novel is remarkably contemporaneous to today's issues of genetic engineering, gene splicing, and the augmentation of the human form through technology, as modern cinematic adaptations of the novel have been swift to embrace.

In the context of this study, the critical emphasis is upon the nature of Moreau's experiments themselves, which he describes as "the study of the plasticity of living forms" (*Moreau* 69). With its manifold of textual images of beast-people in a scientific context, Wells's novel provides unique opportunities to explore questions of human identity (Andriano 131), and through its representations of the surgical amalgamation and altering of animals and human beings, it can be argued that the novel provides an anticipation of what is now termed transhumanism.

One—*The Island of Doctor Moreau*

Transhumanism[3] as an ideology is based on the premise that the human species in its current form does not represent the end of our development but rather a comparatively early phase: the view that humans should (or should be permitted to) use technology to remake human nature (Campbell and Walker n. pag.). According to philosophers who have studied and written about the history of transhumanist thought,[4] human transcendentalist impulses in literature have been expressed at least as far back as the one of the oldest surviving works of narrative literature, the Mesopotamian poem *The Epic of Gilgamesh* (1300–1000 BC), which features a quest for eternal life. The pursuit of immortality, such as the search for fountains of youth or elixirs of life, and other efforts to stave off aging and death, are consistently recurring themes in human history and correspondently, in literature. Indeed, the transformation and/or end of the human is "a familiar topos in countless apocalyptic narratives from *Revelations* through H. G. Wells's *The Time Machine* to *The Matrix*" (Herbrechter and Callus n. pag.). It is however the use of technology (as opposed to mystical forces) to improve the human race that has sparked the imagination of sf writers, and it is Wells's novel (along with Mary Shelley's *Frankenstein*) that can be seen as an originator of these ideas. As Elaine Graham states: "human imagination, by giving birth to fantastic, monstrous and alien figures, has ... always eschewed the fiction of fixed species. Hybrids and monsters are the vehicles through which it is possible to understand the fabricated character of all things, by virtue of the boundaries they cross and the limits they unsettle" (Graham 37).

The Island of Doctor Moreau explores these conflicts between traditional conceptions of the unitary human and the onset of scientific theory and practice which renders the human body mutable. In the animal form, Moreau finds something that is completely inhuman and his goal is to reconfigure them as something more human: "I suppose there is something in the human form that appeals to the artistic turn of mind more powerfully than any animal shape can" (*Moreau* 71). Even though he has attempted non-human forms ("I've not confined myself to man-making" [71]), it is the transformation of animal to human that is his primary concern. He has "stuck to the ideal of humanity" (75), accordingly describing his procedures as "a humanizing process" (65).

Throughout fiction concerning transhumanism, science is often used in justification of the transgression of boundaries, as Wells originally stated in the novel's afterword: "strange as it may seem to the unscientific reader, there can be no denying that ... the manufacture of monsters—and perhaps even *quasi*-human monsters—is within the possibilities of vivisection" (Wells *Treasury* 157). It is notable that Wells's transformative visions are not restricted purely to the physical body: "the mental structure is even less determinate than the bodily," as Moreau states (70).

It is only now, well over a century after the publication of Wells's novel and its depiction of the malleability of the boundaries between the human and the animal, that ontologies are emerging through which to properly explore these ideas: postmodern and poststructuralist theories, posited by practitioners such as Jacques Derrida, Donna Haraway, and of course, Deleuze, place great emphasis upon such questions in regard to the categorization of the "animal" and the "human," and the many ramifications of their complex interrelationships.

Transhumanist issues are at the forefront of contemporary critical thought: Haraway's widely cited "Cyborg Manifesto," for example, revels in the cyborg's metaphorical power to destabilize binary oppositions.[5] However, Deleuze's own rhizomatic and the transhumanist direction are particularly suited to an investigation of this type; he often played with a motif of how we should learn to practice "a perception as it was before men (or after) ... released from their human coordinates" (*Cin1* 122). In furnishing us with a nuanced account of human and posthuman conditions, Deleuzian theory is as a consequence well suited for providing new interpretations of *The Island of Doctor Moreau*, with its animal to human transformations, and their subsequent reversals.

Deleuze and Guattari appear not particularly fond of animals, infamously declaring that anyone who likes cats or dogs is a "fool" (*Thousand* 265). Their issue here is that a pet cat or dog is not really an animal per se, but rather a creature "made" by humans in order to confirm an idealized image of the self, a construct which Deleuze and Guattari view as particularly regressive and restricting. Neither are they particularly interested in animality per se as a philosophical issue[6]; indeed, for Deleuze and Guattari, animals seem to operate more as a device of writing than as living beings whose conditions of life were of direct concern to the writers" (Baker "Becoming-Animal" 95). However, within *A Thousand Plateaus*, an intriguing hierarchy of animal representations is proffered, in which three kinds of animals are

One—*The Island of Doctor Moreau*

distinguished. Firstly are "individuated animals, family pets, sentimental, Oedipal animals each with its own petty history," followed by animals given characteristics or attributes, such as in "the great divine myths," from which structures, archetypes or models can be extracted. Finally, there are "more demonic animals pack or affect animals that form a multiplicity, a becoming, a population, a tale" (*Thousand* 265). One possible approach to a Deleuzian reading of *The Island of Doctor Moreau* would be to utilize these terms in order to classify the various specific forms of animals, humans and hybrids within the novel; for example, Montgomery's dog-based servant M'ling is very much an individuated pet, living in a kennel separate from the other beast-men. However, this would serve to ignore the manner in which it presents the dense network of affiliations and assemblages between the humans and animals, each experiencing their own becomings. As Cary Wolfe writes: "Deleuze and Guattari's distinctions aim to underscore that the figure of the animal, properly understood, is a privileged figure for the problematic of the subject in the most general sense because here we are forced to confront the reality that the subject is always already multiple" (Wolfe 170). In other words, the "individuated animals ... each with its own petty history" (*Thousand* 265) that are referred to, invite only regression, and it is therefore absurd to establish a hierarchy even of animal collectivities from the standpoint of a whimsical evolutionism according to which packs are lower on the scale and are superseded by nature (242). Instead of this, Deleuze and Guattari are instead concerned with what they call "becoming-animal," a theme they discuss at length in *Kafka: Towards a Minor Literature* and *A Thousand Plateaus*.[7] Becoming-animal does not mean imitation and should not be thought of as mere identification with an animal; it is not a psychoanalytic regression or an evolutionary progression, as all these ways of relating to the animal attribute to it a fixed identity that lies beyond becoming and change. On the contrary, for Deleuze and Guattari, animals serve to rupture notions of identity and sameness.

In *Francis Bacon: The Logic of Sensation* (1981), Deleuze speaks of a zone of "*indiscernibility* or *undecidability* between man and animal" (*Bacon* 16). For Deleuze this zone harbors something common to both man and animal, as both share an objective fate: to exist as flesh and as meat. Hence, the relationship between them is mutual, "affecting the animal no less than the human" (*Thousand* 261). That is not to say that the effect that one has upon the other is necessarily symmetrical nor reciprocal; Deleuze and Guattari cannot posit exactly what the animal will "become" as the result of the interaction between these two assemblages, except to say that it will "become other." They note, moreover, that the politics of becoming-animal remains, of course, extremely ambiguous (273). However, the animal/human hybrid creations that are the subject of *The Island of Doctor Moreau* allow us to pursue this line of enquiry: allowing the questioning as to what "other" that the animals become, the risks and consequences of their becoming, and ultimately, what their becomings teach us.

It is this concept of the malleability of the boundaries between animal and human that are explored within this chapter, using *The Island of Doctor Moreau* in conjunction with the conceit of "becoming-animal." Initially, a reading of the novel in terms of Deleuzian smooth and striated space is performed, before the various facets of the Deleuzian concept of becoming-animal are explored, preceding a close analysis from this perspective. As part of this process, it is demonstrated how *The Island of Doctor Moreau's* principal characters can be read in terms of their relationship to contemporary transhumanist texts (primarily the "body horror" genre) and philosophical issues of human transformation (both literal and ideological), and how such issues can be explored and unified through the concept of becoming-animal. Previous Deleuzian analysis of other texts involving becoming-animal shall be considered, as wells as issues concerning Wells, *The Island of Doctor Moreau* and Darwinian evolution. The chapter concludes with a Deleuzian explanation as to why the animal transformations that Moreau performs are ultimately not successful.

Moreau's Island: Smooth and Striated Spaces

Initially, Deleuzian theory is utilized to explore the significance of the physical setting and spaces of *The Island of Doctor Moreau*. As Ian Buchanan states by means of an introduction to *Deleuze and Space* (2005), Deleuze is:

> arguably the twentieth century's most spatial philosopher—not only did he contribute a plethora of new concepts to engage space, space was his very means of doing philosophy. He said everything takes place on a plane of

immanence, envisaging a vast desert-like space populated by concepts moving about like nomads. Deleuze made philosophy spatial and gave us the concepts of smooth and striated, nomadic and sedentary, deterritorialization and reterritorialization, the fold, as well as many others to enable us to think spatially [Buchanan and Lambert i].

The use of an island setting is hardly unique in fiction (sf or otherwise), being a common device throughout literary history; Plato's *Republic* (380 BC), Homer's *Odyssey* (800 BC), Daniel Defoe's *Robinson Crusoe* (1719), Arthur Conan Doyle's *The Lost World* (1912) and William Golding's *Lord of the Flies* (1954) being just a few notable examples. Wells himself uses the motif multiple times in various ways: both literally as in Moreau's eponymous archipelago[8] and *Mr. Blettsworthy on Rampole Island* (1928), and metaphorically in the depiction of communities isolated by other means, such as in *The Country of the Blind* (1904) (a valley estranged from the rest of the world by steep precipices), and also arguably in *The Time Machine* (an island not in space, but in time).[9]

The island metaphor lends itself particularly well to sf. Nicholas Ruddick, in his study of British sf, appropriately entitled *Ultimate Island* (1993), proposes that "the island is a metaphor for the (at once) positive separateness and negative alienation of the 'self' from 'other' as well as for the predicament of humanity itself on its island world encircled by the indifferent—or hostile—ocean of space" (Ruddick *Ultimate* 57). Paul Kincaid initiates his essay "Islomania? Insularity? The Myth of the Island in British Science Fiction" (2008) by listing a long selection of notable works in the history of British sf, stating that "everything I named would share one obvious characteristic: they are all island stories!" (Kincaid "Islomania" 141).[10] He sees the significance of the frequent use of islands in sf in the following terms:

> The island as dream state, the object of desire, the ideal; and insularity: the island as prison or fortress that holds us apart from the rest of the world.... Inevitably there are overlaps and linkages between these two responses. Utopia can only be the ideal state because it is set upon an artificially created island which cuts it off from the baleful influence of the rest of the world. It is, perhaps, the creative tension arising from this opposition in our response to the island that has kept it as such a vital aspect of British science fiction for some five hundred years [142].

Ryan Storment's *Other Spaces, Other Voices: Heterotopic Spaces in Island Narratives* (2008) encompasses a wide range of genres and time periods in its investigation of the island narrative; Plato's *Republic*, Shakespeare's *The Tempest* (1611), *The Island of Doctor Moreau*, the film *Star Wars*[11](1977) and the television series *Lost* (2004–2010) are given as examples of fiction set in these isolated spaces. He states: "as reshapable forms, islands become sites for conflict that often include competing spatial and socio-spatial regimes ... highlight[ing] conflicts between the premodern, modern, and postmodern organizations of space; contention is through smooth versus striated or the free flowing versus the controlled" (Storment vi). It is this concept of the "smooth versus striated" organization of space that this section explicates in relevance to *The Island of Doctor Moreau*. Deleuze's writings often feature allegorical uses of islands, but these are never simply geographical representations; rather they exist virtually, as an extended "plot point" or "plateau" for a special set of creatures and creatings. Plainly, this is especially pertinent with regard to Moreau's island and the transformations that occur upon it.

Deleuze and Guattari wrote much about the human desire to make various environments comprehensible by means of delineating, quantifying and measuring, while conversely also emphasizing the ways in which our world resists these attempts at over-coding and hierarchization. Islands often serve to represent that which is ideal and permanent, hence are intrinsically tied to the idea that systems of belief require a fixed basis. With their clearly definable borders, islands in literary fiction often function as a sanctuary for those who are lost, but this conversely often results in entrapment, and such islands also often harbor monsters, both real and imagined. Such themes are consistently present in island narratives. In his early essay "Desert Islands" (1953), Deleuze claims that the essence of the deserted island is "imaginary and not actual, mythological and not geographical.... At the same time its destiny is subject to those human conditions that make mythology possible" (*Desert* 11). For Deleuze, an island is always already inhabited by its own mythology; it represents a "golden age." In the act of coming to the island, humans "break the spell": "humans can live on an island only by forgetting what an island represents" (9). Hence, as the idea materializes, the dream dies. In this way, "islands are either from before or for after humankind.... Dreaming of islands—whether with joy or in fear—is dreaming of pulling away, of being already separate, far from any continent, of being lost and alone—or it is dreaming of starting from scratch, recreating, beginning anew" (9). It is this ideal of a new beginning and subsequent recreation (of society on his own terms) that Moreau personifies: "it is nearly eleven years since we came here, I and Montgomery and six Kanakas. I remember the green stillness of the island and the empty ocean about us, as though it was yesterday. The place seemed waiting for me" (*Moreau* 73).

Most significantly, islands are useful for their exemplification of Deleuzian readings of cultural space; these spaces can be physical, social, or psychological. In *A Thousand Plateaus*, Deleuze and Guattari distinguish between two kinds of cultural spaces: smooth space and striated space.[12] Cultural spaces are where culturally connected societies interact, societies that are made up of similar cultural constructs. In basic terms, smooth space is an area where individuals are free to do as they wish, contrasted with striated space, which is an area in which individuals are limited to predetermined roles. Highly striated cultures have very strict class structures, hierarchies, and rules that cannot be broken without penalty of law, an organizational manifestation of ideas and institutions whose significance and function are properly assigned. Smoother cultures may also have such hierarchies and class structures in place; however these are not enforced by law but instead are self-imposed by society. Smooth space is associated with a number of productive possibilities including nomadic bodies, minds and journeys (as is discussed in Chapter Three) through which occur the "dynamic process of unfolding subjectivity outside the classical frame of the humanistic subject" (Braidotti "Affirming" 21). Smooth and striated spaces are not in absolute opposition to each other *per se*, but are different manifestations of the self's alignment with space and are both simultaneous and anachronistic. To this end, both spaces continually interact with one another: "smooth space is constantly being translated, transversed into a striated space; striated space is constantly being reversed, returned to a smooth space" (*Thousand* 524). Deleuze asserts that all becoming (discussed subsequently) occurs in smooth space but progress is made by and in striated space. Smooth space is occupied by intensities and events; the sea and the desert are given as examples of smooth spaces that became striated. Striation seems to be, at least in part, the effects of technological mediation; for example, the town as force of striation upon countryside "invents agriculture" (531).

Wells Meets Deleuze

These spatial concepts are well suited to interpreting sf utopias and dystopias, which often use the medium of the physical landscape to negotiate and shape the concepts of self and identity. Such striation can be traced back to Plato's *Republic* (380 BC), and its stipulation of the placing of citizens into a rigid structure of socioeconomic classes. Thomas More's *Utopia* (1516) maintains the island theme: Tom Moylan explains that in More's time "the 'discovery' of non–European continents and islands provided visionaries of the fifteenth and sixteenth centuries with actual and imaginary space in which to create both practicing and literary experiments" (Moylan 3). Indeed, More's island is specifically created for this purpose, originally being a peninsula that is intentionally separated (both physically and ideologically) from the mainland.[13]

So, in being uninhabited and untouched, an island functions as a smooth space that encourages the process of striation. Moreau's island fits this remit; it is uncharted, an "unknown little island" (*Moreau* 17) that (according to Montgomery) "hasn't got a name" (10). Moreau relates to Prendick his initial processes of organizing the island space in physical terms: "The stores were landed and the house was built. The Kanakas founded some huts near the ravine. I went to work here upon what I had brought with me" (73). However, Moreau's true intentions lie not in the organization of the physical geography of the island itself, but in the organization of the animals that occupy it, in both physical and ideological terms. In the process of this striating procedure, the eleven years he spends on the island transforms it from "green stillness ... and empty ocean" (73) to a "landscape of total domination, total pain, and total, brutal irrationality masquerading as the total order of things, the true state of affairs.... Moreau's island is a totalitarian regime—perhaps the first really totalitarian regime imagined by Western man" (McConnell 92). The focus of the transformational process is Moreau's laboratory, the "house of pain," which functions as the central point of the striation: "Striating lines connect points, which are made to converge on a single central point, conjugating elements, enclosing space and then parceling it out" (Buchanan and Thoburn 210).

In this "parceling out" of space, Moreau's aim is to perform "a humanising process" (*Moreau* 65) upon the animals, reconfiguring them into human form. He describes the physical aspects of this restructuring process to Prendick: "You forget all that a skilled vivisector can do with living things.... Small efforts, of course, have been made,-amputation, tongue-cutting, excisions. Of course you know a squint may be induced or cured by surgery? Then in the case of excisions you have all kinds of secondary changes, pigmentary disturbances, modifications of the passions, alterations in the secretion of fatty tissue" (68–69). In this sense, Moreau's vivisection is in itself a form of extreme striation; he is taking smooth and natural animals, and is attempting to bring them into a striated human system. In the process, the body parts of the animals become categorized, removed, and then reconfigured to resemble human form (Storment 41). William Bogard notes how Deleuze emphasizes the effect of smooth and striated spaces on physical bodies themselves: "There is the smooth space of bodies, and the striated space of bodies. The latter is the space of 'body systems'—of the 'organism,' the 'human,' the "subject" and the "agent." These are the marked bodies, that bear the signs—contortions, wounds, scars—of their 'societalization'" (Bogard 285). This can clearly be equated to the beast-men, whose marked, contorted and wounded bodies bear physical witness to Moreau's attempt to socialize them; with their hybrid human/animal bodies which have "disproportion between the legs ... and the length of their bodies ... clumsy and inhuman curvature of the spine ... strangely-coloured or strangely-placed eyes" (*Moreau* 80), they quite literally bear the scars and signs of their socialization.

Giving the beast-men the capacity for language is the final act of striation, as Moreau closely associates the processes of speech and thought: "the great difference between man and monkey is in the larynx ... in the incapacity to frame delicately different sound-symbols by which thought could be sustained" (71). By virtue of this surgical modification the animals are literally given voice; ironically however, it is through this very voice that further subservience is forced upon them, through their verbal recitation of "the law." They must "say the words" in order to "learn the law" (56), regurgitating the text as an incantation. A yet further element of this stratification is the unification of the beast-men around the "Speaker of the Law" whose purpose is to reinforce their social structure; in this manner, the Speaker of the Law functions as another "central point of striation" other than the house of pain. In keeping with Deleuze's description of striated societies,

Moreau has hence created a highly striated culture with a strict hierarchy, and rules that cannot be broken without penalty of law.

Ultimately however, Moreau's attempts to striate the island society fail. The structure and hierarchy of the island deteriorates, and he is eventually killed, as is the Speaker of the Law, and the house of pain is incinerated and destroyed (109), thus removing the last physical vestiges of "humanizing" influence from the island. Once these purveyors of striation are removed, the beast-men gradually revert to their animal forms and behaviors; in other words, the striated society breaks down, and the physical spaces return from striated space to smooth space. With their central point of striation removed, firstly the language of the beast-men deteriorates, followed by their physical form. Prendick describes this process:

> I first distinctly perceived a growing difference in their speech and carriage, a growing coarseness of articulation, a growing disinclination to talk.... Can you imagine language, once clear-cut and exact, softening and guttering, losing shape and import, becoming mere lumps of sound again? ... they walked erect with an increasing difficulty ... held things more clumsily; drinking by suction, feeding by gnawing.... I realised more keenly than ever what Moreau had told me about the "stubborn beast-flesh." They were reverting, and reverting very rapidly [120–121].

Hence, over the process of the narrative, the initial smooth space of the island is striated, then this process eventually reverses to its smooth origins; ultimately the island and its occupants demonstrate a resistance to Moreau's ideals of perfect organization, in keeping with Deleuze's remit that smooth space always possesses a greater power of deterritorialization than the striated (*Thousand* 530). In order to explore this more thoroughly, the Deleuzian concept of becoming, specifically becoming-animal, permits a more specific reading as to the processes occurring within Moreau's experimentations, and the subsequent failings of the "stubborn beast-flesh" (*Moreau* 121).

Becoming-Animal

As stated in the introductory exploration of becoming, the human subject ought not to be thought of as a stable, rational individual, experiencing changes but remaining, principally the same person. Rather,

One—*The Island of Doctor Moreau*

for Deleuze, the "self" must be conceived as a constantly changing assemblage of forces, an "epiphenomenon arising from chance confluences of languages, organisms, societies, expectations and so on" (Stagoll "Becoming" 22). In the echelon of becomings, crucial to Deleuze is that of becoming-animal. If (for Aristotle, for example), the concept of "man" represents the paradigm of the human, then becoming other commences with "becoming-woman," as this is the first deviation from man. A further, and far more radical step, is becoming-animal. Deleuze uses many examples of becoming-animal through his writings; in terms of literature and art, he uses the works of Kafka, paintings of Francis Bacon, music of Mozart, and films such as *Taxi Driver* (1976), to name but a few.

As stated, Deleuze utilizes the term becoming-animal not only as a critique of basic philosophical values and assumptions, but also in the reappraisal of more specific disciplines such as literary theory and psychoanalysis. The key philosophical principle here involves the overcoming of dualisms in general, particularly the traditional opposition of man/nature, resulting in a radically non-anthropomorphic concept of nature. Throughout much of the history of philosophy (for example, from Aristotle to Aquinas, from Descartes to Kant, and from Hegel to Husserl) the essence of the human has been repeatedly determined in opposition to the animal, where the former is understood to be in possession of a certain capacity or trait. Deleuze and Guattari's concept of becoming in its pure form is analogous to what Derrida called "iteration," both involving a distinction between conditioned forms of becoming and an absolute or pure form (Patton and Protevi 22). Writing in *The Animal That Therefore I Am* (1997), Jacques Derrida performs a sustained meditation on the role of the animal in philosophy. He questions the logic, ethics, and the rhetorical and philosophical effects of establishing (or assuming) a boundary that seems to distinguish so clearly, so finally, and so permanently the human from the animal. Eschewing the notion of a rigid division between the human and the animal, Derrida instead imagines an altogether more mobile conception of interrelated being:

> There is no animal in the general singular, separated from man by a single indivisible limit. We have to envisage the existence of "living creatures" whose plurality cannot be assembled within the single figure of an animality that is simply opposed to humanity. This does not of course mean ignoring or effacing

everything that separates humankind from the other animals.... It is rather a matter of taking into account a multiplicity of heterogeneous structures and limits [Derrida *Animal* 369].

It is this argument that is further explored by the Deleuzian concept of becoming-animal. Deleuze is at pains to point out that becoming-animal does not have a privileged place in the continuum of becomings (becoming-woman, becoming-imperceptible and other becomings ad infinitum). The most exigent element of becoming-animal, and that most difficult to grasp, is Deleuze's claim that it is a real process and not one of resemblance, identification, imitation, nor is it an act of imagination, a dream or a fantasy. As has been noted previously in this chapter, the act of becoming-animal is not one of imitation, as it involves animal capacities and powers. If the human is to become animal, physical and emotional learning and behavior must be unlearned and new ones adopted, resulting in an enlargement of one's relationships and responses to the world. Becoming-animal does not however mean imitation and should not be thought of as identification with an animal; it is not a psychoanalytic regression, or an evolutionary progression, as these are all ways of relating the animal to a fixed identity that lies beyond becoming and change. On the contrary, for Deleuze and Guattari animals serve to rupture notions of identity and sameness. Like the revolutionary schizophrenic of *Capitalism and Schizophrenia* (discussed in Chapter Three in relation to *The Time Machine*), animality is "the line of flight" along which the human manages to escape Oedipal triangulation and identification. Becoming-animal is not just an issue within psychoanalysis, as it provides a new way of thinking about perceiving and becoming (as explored in *Anti-Oedipus*); life is desire, and desire is the expansion of life through constant metamorphosis, a positive and creative power.[14] The existence of these animal-becomings equates to the "traversing [of] human beings and [the] sweeping [of] them away, affecting the animal no less than the human" (261). Becoming-animal is therefore not merely the mimicry of animal behavior, as that would presuppose concepts of identity in terms of both the self and the animal, and as a consequence these would be deemed less "real" in accordance to Deleuze's critique as to the primary status of identity, representation and signification (Atterton and Calarco 101). Hence, it is asserted that what is real "is the becoming itself, the block of becoming, not the supposedly fixed terms through

One—*The Island of Doctor Moreau*

which that which becomes passes" (*Thousand* 262). This alliance (or "block") of becoming that is formed encompasses the zone of proximity that we enter into in our efforts to become the other, "sweeping up" the human being with the animal other into a relationship (Atterton and Calarco 103). However, this is not a linking together of two distinct points, instead resulting from the disappearance of these two discernible points, and as a consequence, the freeing from fixed forms.

As with any Deleuzian theory, the rhizomorphic concept of becoming and becoming-animal can be machinically linked to any number of subjects, be they (for example) politics, art, or literature. In terms of the latter, Deleuze states that the process of artistic creation itself involves becoming-animal: "writing is a becoming, writing is traversed by strange becomings that are not becomings-writer, but becomings-rat, becomings-insect, becomings-wolf etc." (*Thousand* 265). Through this we can see that the real radicalism of the becoming-animal concept does not lie in its reframing of the question of living subjects and their identities, but rather in its charting of the possibilities for experiencing an uncompromising sweeping-away of identities, whether they are human or animal (Rothfels 68). Hence, within literature, "there is no longer man or animal, since each deterritorializes the other" (Deleuze *Kafka* 22): becoming-animal is a means of undoing identity, and it is possible to step into the stream of animal-becomings through the act of writing, where there is no longer a "tripartite division" between a field of reality (the world), a field of representation (the book) and a field of subjectivity (the author) (*Thousand* 25).

Deleuze maintains that in terms of literature, Kafka's novels and short stories present good examples of this arrangement of radically heterogeneous elements, in that they not only depict the metamorphosing of the human into an animal, they also produce the chimerical becoming-animal of the author (Kafka) himself; indeed, "this is the essential object of the stories" (Atterton 99). These readings of Kafka shall be briefly examined, as various parallels can be drawn to *The Island of Doctor Moreau*. Indeed, both Kafka and Wells straddle the birth of both modern sf and technoculture, providing different takes on the reshaping of the body by said technoculture and technology (Dyens 55).

In his writings, Deleuze draws upon Kafka's *The Metamorphosis* (1912), which, with its allegory of man-turned-insect, is unsurprisingly a major subject of focus, but also examined are *A Report to an Academy* (1917), *Josephine the Singer, or the Mouse Folk* (1924), *Investigations of a Dog* (1922) and *The Burrow* (1923). Within these texts, Deleuze and Guattari characterize Kafka's becomings-animal in the following terms: "To become animal is to participate in movement, to stake out the path of escape in all its positivity, to cross a threshold, to reach a continuum of intensities that are valuable only in themselves, to find a world of pure intensities where all forms come undone, as do all significations, signifiers, and signifieds, to the benefit of an unformed matter of deterritorialized flux, of non-signifying signs" (*Kafka* 13). Later in the same chapter they comment directly upon Kafka's aphorism "Metaphors are one of the things that make me despair of literature" (Kafka *Diaries* 200), stating, "Kafka deliberately kills all metaphor, all symbolism, all signification, no less than all designation. Metamorphosis is the contrary of metaphor.... It is no longer a question of a resemblance between the comportment of an animal and that of a man" (*Kafka* 22). Hence, Kafka vividly presents how man transforms into insect, the process of becoming-animal, which enables us to imagine life from an inhuman perspective.

In terms of their human/animal transformations, Kafka's stories can be placed into two categories: either an animal becomes or behaves like a human, as in *A Report to an Academy*, *Investigations of a Dog*, or *The Burrow* (in these cases, an ape, a dog and an indeterminate burrowing animal respectively) or conversely where humans transform into animals, hence serving to display the unresolved animal potentiality in human beings, as in *The Metamorphosis*. It is vitally important to note however, that Deleuze argues that becoming is always double: stories of becoming-animal and stories of becoming-human are indissociable, like two sides of the same coin (Pedot 420). This point is emphasized in the fourth chapter ("Body, Meat, Spirit: Becoming-Animal") of *Francis Bacon: The Logic of Sensation*: "Meat is the common zone of man and the beast, their zone of indiscernibility ... animals are part of humanity ... the man who suffers is a beast, the beast that suffers is a man. This is the reality of becoming" (*Bacon* 17–18). Hence there is no contradiction in referring to the becoming-animal process in regards to Moreau's beast-men, who are in actually initially transforming into human beings prior to their reversal back to their animal forms.

Such becomings are of great significance in terms of reading of *The Island of Doctor Moreau*, in terms of both Moreau himself and his beast-men subjects. Frank McConnell notes that "the fatal paradox of Moreau's desire is that in his quest for rational perfection he creates a nightmarish world of monsters" (McConnell 92). In his attempts to "burn out the animal ... [and] make a rational creature of my own" (*Moreau* 76), he not only disfigures the animals into pathetic caricatures of humanity, but also "burns out," without even knowing it, the humanity that leavens his own overwhelming intelligence (McConnell 93). This constitutes an exemplification of Moreau himself becoming "no less than the one that becomes." The same can be said of Prendick; although not directly physically affected by Moreau's surgery, he nevertheless performs his own animal-becomings, in opposition to those of the beast-men: "I too must have undergone strange changes. My clothes hung about me as yellow rags, through which rents glowed the tanned skin. My hair grew long, and became matted together. I am told even now that my eyes have a strange brightness, a swift alertness of movement" (*Moreau* 122). Deleuze and Guattari note that in Kafka's *A Report to an Academy*, "man no less becomes an ape than the ape becomes a man" (*Kafka* 13). However, no linear process of transformation is to be expected; metamorphosis of human into animal or vice versa cannot lead to stable metaphor. This claim of stability (or rather, the lack of it) in terms of *The Island of Doctor Moreau's* human/animal hybrids is examined subsequently.

Moreau, Darwin and Deleuze

Just as the Deleuzian becoming-animal critiques the primary status of identity, representation and signification, the sf genre explores the social and philosophical implications of the ever-eroding boundary between animal and human, through (for example) the narration of genetic fusions, xenotransplantations,[15] and other technoscientific developments; as discussed, *The Island of Doctor Moreau* is arguably a forerunner of such an approach within fiction, and as a hybrid of sf and horror it is particularly suited to the exploration of such machinic assemblages. To this end, some of the overtly Darwinian elements in Wells's novel shall be briefly discussed, this process elaborating upon the relation to the Deleuzian philosophical methodology regarding evolution (as briefly discussed in the study introduction) in regards to the novel.

Despite containing themes that are a continuation of the social critique Wells initiated in *The Time Machine* (both novels featuring an aristocratic protagonist who finds himself woefully ill-equipped to deal with the alien circumstances into which he is thrown, and who is subsequently vulnerable to the tender mercy of manifestations of the "common man"), *The Island of Doctor Moreau* reverses the evolutionary process that results in the creation of the Eloi and Morlocks. The eminent biologist Thomas Huxley's 1893 book *Evolution and Ethics* was a great inspiration to Wells, and he constructed his novel as an extrapolation of Huxley's central conceit (as quoted below), which was in itself an exploration of the ethical questions raised by Darwin's evolutionary theories, namely whether biology has anything particular to say about moral philosophy: "And much may be done to change the nature of man himself. The intelligence which has converted the brother of the wolf into the faithful guardian of the flock ought to be able to do something towards curbing the instincts of savagery in civilised men" (Huxley 36–37). Subsequently, he states that "the thief and the murderer follow nature just as much as the philanthropist. Cosmic evolution may teach us how the good and the evil tendencies of man may have come about; but, in itself, it is incompetent to furnish any better reason why what we call good is preferable to what we call evil than we had before" (66).

For Darwin, evolution was driven by difference, variation and mutation, and hence evolution was the process by which species became other. He specifically noted the evolutionary difference of "monstrosities," which he remarked "cannot be separated by any clear line of distinction from mere variations" (Thompson 23). It is this theme of the monstrous that is present in Wells's own fictional engagement with evolutionary theory, as depicted in *The Island of Doctor Moreau*. Wells wrote retrospectively of his own novel (in the preface to a 1924 publication): "this story was but the response of an imaginative mind to the reminder that humanity is but animal, rough-hewn to a reasonable shape and in perpetual internal conflict between instinct and injunction…. It is written just to give the utmost possible vividness to that conception of men as hewn and confused and tormented beasts" (quoted in Showalter 178). Hence, the novel's beast-people are "grotesque parodies of humanity, whose carnivorous appetites equate with the Morlocks' cannibalism. These people-who-were-beasts live in a darkly comic travesty of human existence" (Dryden 163). The novel presents evolutionary theory from conflicting perspectives, with differing viewpoints voiced through the medium of specific characters. The narrator Prendick refers to the beast-men as "travesties" and "mockeries" of humanity, thus implying that no matter how Moreau assembled them, animals are by nature animals, not men, thereby implying that the qualities that define a human being transcend the physical body. Darwin's theory challenged this metaphysical barrier by suggesting that humans were merely exceptionally well evolved animals and hence, through Prendick, Wells appears to be trying to assert the case for human exceptionalism. Prendick frequently contemplates the issues of philosophical materialism (man is purely a physical form with no soul), despairing that "hunger and a lack of blood-corpuscles take all the manhood from a man" (*Moreau* 22). It is of particular note that what Prendick seems to find most human in the beast-men is their constant awareness of their inadequacy; that is, they are cognizant and desirous of an ideal (humanity) that they are unable to reach, and it is this shortcoming that results in their perpetual state of torment: "Before they had been beasts, their instincts fitly adapted to their surroundings, and happy as living things may be. Now they stumbled in the shackles of humanity, living in a fear that never died, fretted by a law they could not understand; their mock-human existence began in an agony, was one long internal struggle, one long dread of Moreau—and for what?" (93).

The character of Montgomery provides an alternative perspective, as he introduces a degree of relativity to the issue. Separated from civilization for a protracted period, he does not make as clear a distinction between himself and the beast-men as does Prendick. Further binary oppositions are blurred in that the beast-men are not uniform in their degrees of bestiality versus humanity (perhaps as a result of the variations in Moreau's experiments); this conforms with Darwinian theory in that some animals are by nature closer to men than others. Darwin's assertion that human evolutionary superiority is dependent entirely upon random selection is invoked in a brief exchange between Prendick and Montgomery early in the novel:

Wells Meets Deleuze

"If I may say it," said I after a time, "you have saved my life."
"Chance," he answered; "Just chance."
"I prefer to make my thanks to the accessible agent."
"Thank no one.... It's chance, I tell you," he interrupted, "as everything is in a man's life. Only the asses won't see it" [17].

Other examples of different perspectives upon the evolution debate include Montgomery invoking what could be interpreted as Malthusian principles: "'Increase and multiply, my friends,' said Montgomery. 'Replenish the island. Hitherto we've had a certain lack of meat here'" (28).[16] Darwin himself is explicitly referenced in chapter nine: "Each of these creatures, despite its human form, its rag of clothing, and the rough humanity of its bodily form, had woven into it—into its movements, into the expression of its countenance, into its whole presence—some now irresistible suggestion of a hog, a swinish taint, the unmistakable mark of the beast" (38). This specific passage could have been taken almost verbatim from Darwin's 1871 text *Descent of Man* (albeit without Wells's somewhat sensationalist embellishments): "Man still bears in his bodily frame the indelible stamp of his lowly origin" (Darwin *Descent* 492).

Intrinsic to the Deleuzian oeuvre are concerns of evolutionary theory, which make a rich contribution not only to the tradition of philosophical biology, but also to contemporary developments in neo-Darwinism and post–Darwinist paradigms. However, even the word "evolution" itself is called into question in Deleuze's work, as thinking "machinically" involves showing the artificial and arbitrary nature of the determination of boundaries and borders between living systems and material forms, and challenging linear schemas of becoming (Ansell Pearson *Difference Engineer* 17). Deleuze's perception of evolution stresses the striving for creativity and difference itself; it does not proceed in order to achieve the creation of species and beings, it is not governed by actual goals. Deleuze demonstrates that "evolution is itself a virtual power, a capacity or potential for change and becoming which passes through organisms.... The aim of evolution is change and creation itself, not the creation of an actual being" (Colebrook *Understanding* 2). Hence, "the species ... a notion that caused Darwin so much anxiety since an accurate definition proved so elusive, is a transcendental illusion in relation to the virtual-actual movement of life" (Ansell Pearson *Germinal* 93). In this way, the individual subject expands towards this infinite capacity through the movement out of the physical body and into the virtual body without organs. Such a body has no limitations and can allow itself to be occupied with plural subjectivities as forms of experience without attempting to center them in a finite subject (Pilsch n. pag.). Ultimately, it is apparent that just as Darwinism had shown that humans and animals were not finished, immutable products but were flexible subsets, we can argue that the Deleuzian concept of becoming-animal similarly critiques the primary status of identity, representation and signification. As Ansell Pearson asks, "can one speak of an end of evolution, granting it a final purpose, or is constant invention and re-invention the only end?" (*Germinal* 24).

The Island of Doctor Moreau serves to unite these concepts through the medium of Wells's visceral depictions of becoming and becoming-animal, which are subsequently investigated, initially through Deleuzian depictions of the hybridity of species within sf in general terms, before how these are manifested (and indeed, foreshadowed) in *The Island of Doctor Moreau* is demonstrated.

Wells and Beasts, Deleuze and Monsters

In thematic terms, more so than any of the other scientific romances, *The Island of Doctor Moreau* is a tale of horror. Of this, Wells himself spoke frankly: "*The Island of Doctor Moreau* is an exercise in youthful blasphemy. Now and then, though I rarely admit it, the universe projects itself towards me in a hideous grimace. It grimaced that time, and I did my best to express my vision of the aimless torture in creation" (*Moreau* xxxi). To this end, it has been frequently noted that the novel contains "barely disguised undertones of sadism, torture and even bestiality" (Worland 62), but the real horror appears to lie in the central theme, also evident in much recent literature and film in the sf and horror genres: how do we determine who or what is human? (Kirby 93). To this end, Powell states:

> Deleuze embrace[s] change as part of an evolutionary unfolding that cannot be predetermined, as the spontaneity of life is manifested by a continual creation of new forms seeking others ... structuralist templates are a fantasy of order which seeks to overlay our own already-happening change. The horror

genre and its monsters belong to both the old overlay and the ongoing flux, and are ripe for new becomings [*Horror* 104].

As has been previously explored, for Deleuze and Guattari, to become-animal is the epitome of their concept of becoming, being a strategy that challenges dualistic thinking by creating assemblages that involve the most historically prevalent "other" that exists outside of the human: i.e., the animal, or beast. To this end, Moreau's creations, being hybridic splicings of human and animal, can be placed in the realm of the sf assemblage of body-horror, a genre that has been subject to previous Deleuzian analysis. Simply put, body horror fiction is primarily based on the depiction of bodily alteration, mutilation and mutation, with the processes of transformation being usually slow, and often seemingly irreversible. Synonymous with physical alterations are major changes in personality: "when monstrosity erupts from within and graphically transforms the body of the character" (Cherry 22). Moreau's beast-men can be categorized in these terms, both in their initial physical form as man/animal hybrids, and their subsequently mental degeneration as they eventually revert back to animalistic behavior. As stated by Powell, this can be viewed in terms of "abjection of the flesh and disintegration of subjective wholeness by the violation and destruction of the body" (Powell "Face" 65). *The Island of Doctor Moreau* serves to present its physical subjects in such a manner that they can be viewed as an exemplar of Deleuzian philosophical concepts; the beast-men graphically "flesh out" the Deleuzian becoming-animal and body without-organs in an affective, literary dimension.

Such becomings of horror are expressed through hybridity, as in animals such as werewolves, shape shifting vampires, and often in the case of modern sf, genetic engineering (to which Wells's theme of vivisection in *The Island of Doctor Moreau* is an essential precursor). Hence, it can be maintained that Wells's beast-men play a pivotal role in the progression of the depiction of such becomings, arguably originating with H.P Lovecraft's[17] shape shifting "ancient-ones" and Mary Shelley's heterogeneous monster,[18] leading eventually (through a variety of forms) to the common trope in contemporary science fiction, the human/machine assemblage of the cyborg. Contemporary films such as *The Fly* (1986), *Alien Resurrection* (1997), and *District 9* (2009) also depict radical departures from the human body, fulfilling what Kelly Hurley describes as "the spectacle of the human body de-familiarized, rendered other" (Hurley "Alien" 203). *The Fly* in particular is a compellingly literal rendition of becoming-animal, and Powell directly equates Deleuzian becomings with the metamorphosis in the film: "becomings are incongruous, bizarre and repulsive, like the genetic hybrid of man and fly in David Cronenberg's *The Fly*, produced when a housefly is accidentally trapped inside a teleporter" (Powell *Horror* 10). The distinctive feature of David Cronenberg's film[19] is that neither human being nor fly retains any trace of its composition as an individual entity; as opposed to Kurt Neumann's 1958 version, in which two distinct human/fly hybrids result from the matter-transference, Cronenberg's film has only one subject remaining, a multiplicity of various fly and human parts and characteristics. These subjects of the body horror genre, be it *The Island of Doctor Moreau's* man/animal hybrids, or *The Fly's* man/fly splicing, are all in a process of actual becoming, being assemblages of different forces in a state of constant flux. The beast-men will never be completely human or animal, just as the cyborg can never be either human or machine, or the fly entirely insect or human. Becoming is ceaseless, as Deleuze and Guattari state, as "becoming produces nothing other than itself" (*Thousand* 262). All these examples are manifestations of "the body as the complex interplay of highly constructed social and symbolic forces" (Braidotti "Discontinued" 44). These forces are always in flux, always in the act of becoming. The individual manner of transformation is not important, only significant is the fact that it occurs: as Deleuze states "the becoming-animal of the human being is real, even if the animal the human being becomes is not" (*Thousand* 262).

Botched Becomings

Having discussed various aspects of *The Island of Doctor Moreau's* transhuman subjects from a Deleuzian perspective, critical focus now returns to the question posed at the outset of this chapter: what are the risks and consequences of the becomings of Moreau's beast-men? Moreau states that "to the study of the plasticity of living forms—my life has been devoted" (*Moreau* 69). When he performs surgery upon the animals, a rupture occurs of the representation that is supposedly animal. The resulting animals-becomings embodied through the medium of the beast-men, both human and animal, become something other than what they were, yet they never complete either transformation, remaining something between: "the human shape I can get now, almost with ease, so that it is lithe and graceful, or thick and strong; but often there is trouble with the hands and the claws, -painful things, that I dare not shape too freely" (75). These monstrous creatures produce in us identifications and sympathies, functioning to draw us into affective relationships with the non-human. In Deleuzian terms, these hybrids function as "advertisements for a new embodiment. They do not solicit our pity but summon ontological, ethical and aesthetic curiosity, provoking us to comport ourselves towards them as kin" (Thompson 24). Through the assemblages within the novel, we see a demonstration of the inter-species alliances that govern the natural world: the "blocks of becoming" that can be formed between human and animal through the exchange of genetic material, or (as is the case in *The Island of Doctor Moreau*) flesh itself.

Ultimately, it could be maintained that these conjoinings constitute a becoming that "operates in transgression not only of species boundaries but of boundaries between nature and artifice, science and art" (Thompson 24). The rhizomatic interaction between Wells, his Darwinian inspirations, his fiction (e.g., the beast-men and humans and their own interactions and becomings, as discussed), and Deleuze's concept of becoming-animal (along with a vast multitude of other assemblages) form just such a becoming. It is Moreau who, through his experimentations, instigates these becomings. Prior critical readings have read Moreau himself in a variety of ways. For example, in terms of literary tradition, he can be posited as "part of the neo-gothic horror tradition of the mad scientist"[20] who abuses his skills and interferes with the natural order out of scientific hubris (Powell *Horror* 148), with his death a consequence of "conventional gothic morality as he must be punished for dabbling in forbidden knowledge and unleashing monstrous forces" (35).[21] Wells himself described his novel as "theologically grotesque" (Bergonzi *Early* 99), and in this context many critics have developed interpretations based on perception of the novel as "a satiric parody of God and his creation" (Quade 293), and much has been made critically of Moreau's status as a God-like figure.[22] The monstrosities that he has created enable him to perceive himself as a God; that is, a human being who has transcended the terms of his own

One—*The Island of Doctor Moreau*

humanity by taking on the mantle of a creator, which is also how his creations regard him: "His is the House of Pain. His is the Hand that makes. His is the Hand that wounds. His is the Hand that heals" (*Moreau* 57).

Other readings play down this aspect, observing that Moreau never directly claims to be a deity, nor did he create the God-like image of himself among the beast-men; he does not hand down the commandment-style "Law" to them, rather that comes from the Kanakas, his human servants. Neither did he create the island, or bring forth the life upon it from scratch: he is a force of change, not creation, and this suggests that Moreau is instead a representation of evolution by natural selection. Prendick's observations would seem to concur with this: he sees "a blind fate, a vast pitiless mechanism seemed to cut and shape the fabric of existence" under which all "were torn and crushed, ruthlessly, inevitably, amid the infinite complexity of its incessant wheels" (93–94); the same delineation could easily be applied to Darwinian evolution as to Wells's "vision of the aimless torture in creation" (xxxi). In this way, *The Island of Doctor Moreau* serves as "Wells's critique of the institutions of religion that have attempted to control and civilize human beings by forcing them with fear of eternal damnation to adhere to a code of ethics contrary to the naturalistic laws of evolution" (Quade 293).

However, regardless of whether he is a God in the conventional understanding of the term, or a metaphor for Darwinian theory, in either sense Moreau functions as an agent of deterritorialization, in that his experiments create lines of flight from the dominant modes of life. Becomings are always multiple: just like becoming-animal, there is no longer man or animal, since "each deterritorializes the other, in a conjunction of flux, in a continuum of reversible intensities"; furthermore, "it is now a question of a becoming that includes the maximum of difference as a difference of intensity, the crossing of a barrier" (*Kafka* 22).

In spite of the multiple or pack nature of all beings, a human's becoming-animal must be initiated in an alliance with what Deleuze and Guattari describe in *A Thousand Plateaus* as an "anomalous individual." This is the animal in the pack that is situated at and helps define the borderline of the pack. The status of this individual is often unknown: they can be in the pack, on the border of it, or outside of it entirely. The role of the anomalous individual is to carry "the transformations of becoming or crossings of multiplicities always farther down the line of flight" (*Thousand* 275); it is this that Moreau is attempting through his experiments, specifically evident in his proclamation that "we find the promise of a possibility of superseding old inherent instincts by new suggestions, grafting upon or replacing the inherited fixed ideas" (*Moreau* 70–71).[23] In this sense, Moreau's vision for the potentials of the body adhere to a Deleuzian remit, as "we know nothing about a body until we know what it can do, what its affects are, how they can or cannot enter into composition with ... the affects of another body" (*Thousand* 284). In stating that "this extraordinary branch of knowledge has never been sought ... until I took it up! ... some such things have only been hit on as a last resort of surgery ... by accident" (*Moreau* 70), Moreau's medical techniques are inherently Deleuzian: to establish these relations is always precarious, as "becoming only operates by risk, danger, the throw of the dice, and contagion" (Sherman 8). He in fact perceives the subjects of his experimentations purely in terms of their rhizomatic potentialities: "You cannot imagine what this means to be an investigator, what an intellectual passion grows within him. You cannot imagine the strange colourless delight of these intellectual desires! The thing before you is no longer an animal, a fellow creature, but a problem!" (*Moreau* 72–73).

However, ultimately the experiments are unsuccessful. No matter the direction of these becomings (animal to man or vice versa), within the novel none of them succeed, and even at best they are perpetually unstable. As Moreau laments:

> These creatures of mine seemed strange and uncanny to you so soon as you began to observe them; but to me, just after I make them, they seem to be indisputably human beings. It's afterwards, as I observe them, that the persuasion fades. First one animal trait, then another, creeps to the surface and stares out at me ... and they revert. As soon as my hand is taken from them the beast begins to creep back, begins to assert itself again [76].

Hence it is clear that when Moreau performs vivisection upon his animal subjects, they do not become human, nor remain animal. As a converse example, the character of Montgomery, despite functioning as an intermediary between human and beast-man, loses his life in a misguided attempt to engage the beast-men in the "human" ritual of drinking alcohol (ironically shown throughout the novel to be the very source of the undermining of his human reasoning). Despite Moreau's best efforts of striation (both in terms of physical adaptation through surgery, and subsequent socialization through the medium of "the law") the beast-men slowly revert to their previous animalistic states, or do not survive at all, being killed in the process.

In this way, instead of a successful transformation, certain properties or potentials of both human and animal combine in new and monstrous amalgamations. Moreau's House of Pain itself therefore produces a new body or territory; but as previously explored, such becomings never complete, so the only choice is for the becoming to perpetuate until the process either makes a breakthrough or exhausts its potential, and the animal/human hybrid dies. As Deleuze stated, to become animal is to "participate in movement, to stake out the path of escape in all its positivity, to cross a threshold, to reach a continuum of intensities that are valuable only in themselves, and in the process to find a world of pure intensities where all forms come undone" (*Kafka* 13). The beast-men are unable to adhere to this remit, their becomings fail, and they return to their original forms. Essentially, for all the audacity of Moreau's attempted animal-becomings, and in spite of the act of imagination that produces the beast-men (both on the part of Moreau within the narrative, and Wells in creating the fiction itself) there is something within the narrative that blocks the success of the becomings.

Deleuze and Guattari note that becoming-animal is a risky experiment, and that its outcome cannot be guaranteed. A body may be alive and teeming with intensities and potentialities, but caution is advised, as there are risks inherent to becoming-animal, and the possibility that the process may be "botched" (*Thousand* 266). One needs to retain "a minimum of strata, a minimum of forms and functions, a minimal subject from which to extract materials, affects and assemblages in order to hold the becoming in the middle" (*Thousand* 298), otherwise becoming collapses in on itself, with no assemblages on either side to fuel it. It can actually be preferable, they say, to remain stuck on a stratum than to evacuate the model too fast, at the wrong time: "If you free it with too violent an action, if you blow apart the strata without taking precautions, then instead of drawing the plane [of consistency] you will be killed, plunged into a black hole, or even dragged toward catastrophe" (*Thousand* 178). Deleuze was very aware of such failed becomings, whose ultimate consequences are often worse than the conventional forms of subjugation they seek to escape. He questioned why this could occur: "Why such a parade of sucked dry, catatonicised, vitrified, sewn-up bodies, when the body without organs is also full of gaiety, ecstasy and dance.... What happened?" (*Thousand* 167). Indeed, a "parade of sucked dry, catatonicised, vitrified, sewn-up bodies" serves as an apt description of the beast-men, and in ascertaining "what happened," various perspectives pertaining to these "botchings" will now be discussed. This primarily consists of territorialized images and specific formations within the text, along with the ethical considerations of Moreau's experiments. Naturally these are not mutually exclusive, all forming their own machinic assemblage.

Firstly, parallels can again be drawn to Deleuzian readings of Kafka, which place their emphasis upon what is described as "territorialized images." The animal-becomings in Kafka's stories often end in failure on account of the persistence of these territorialized images; for example, towards the end of *The Metamorphosis*, the insectoid Gregor Samsa clings to his final possession, a photograph of a "lady dressed in copious fur" (Kafka *Metamorphosis* 50), and it is this action that interrupts "the lines of escape of the orphaned becoming-animal" (*Kafka* 14). Through this action, rather than letting desire deterritorialize and roam freely, Gregor's sexual attraction is territorialized, and his metamorphosis turns out to be "the story of a re-oedipalization that leads him into death, that turns his becoming-animal into a becoming-dead" (Baker *Postmodern* 119). Hence, according to Deleuze, Kafka's animals are "too formed, too significative, too territorialized" to be successful in their animal becomings (*Kafka* 15). A similar process appears to be occurring in relation to the beast-men. In their analysis of Kafka, Deleuze and Guattari propose that to become animal is "to find a world of pure intensities where all forms come undone" (*Kafka* 13), as do all meanings. This accounts for their fascination with "pack modes" and other forms of animal multiplicity, the hierarchy of animal representations discussed earlier: these are the "pack or affect animals that form a multiplicity, a becoming, a population, a tale" (*Thousand* 265). In accordance to this, in their forms as individual, recognizable animals, the beast-men are "still too formed, too significative, too territorialized" (*Kafka* 15). Moreau, through physical modification and insistence on their adherence to "the law," has removed the pack element from the animals; they still dwell together, but in a crude semblance of human society rather than an animal pack. This is illustrated through Prendick, who despite specifically referencing the beast-men in terms of their animal origins, such as the "Leopard-Man" and the "Hyena-Swine," is able to distinguish between individuals to the point of anthropomorphization. This is one of the "varied forces" that Deleuze states can undermine an animal pack, and instead (in line with his hierarchy of animal representation , as previously discussed) will establish in them "interior centers of the conjugal, family or state type," hence "replacing pack effects with family feelings, or state intelligibilities" (*Thousand* 271). Hence the beast-men are initially too territorialized, and despite Moreau's efforts, remain individuated subjects that cannot fulfill their becomings.

In specific terms of territorialized images, it is their conditioned adherence to Moreau's "law" that initially prevents the beast-men returning to their animal origins. The problem here is that the same system of laws that are meant to reinforce their physical humanization ironically actually work to fetishize objects and actions that are coded specifically to the animal: "Not to suck up Drink; that is the Law. Are we not Men? Not to eat Fish or Flesh; that is the Law. Are we not Men? Not to claw the Bark of Trees; that is the Law. Are we not Men?" (*Moreau* 57). The animals, through the process of Moreau's surgical attempts at humanizing them, have become hyper-perceptible and very subjectified; they are human-animals, susceptible to human laws and codes, as demonstrated by their initial adherence to "the law." For an animal to kill another is perceived as the order of nature, but for an animal forced into a becoming that would have otherwise been avoided if it were not for Moreau's direct intervention, to kill a human is murder, for which they must be punished. If becoming-animal demands a co-mixing of energies, an exchange of forces, in this case the animals have taken on some of what it means to be an ontological being in a human-centered world. However, the territorialized images of animalistic desire present in Moreau's laws prove impossible to resist, and once they have had "the taste of blood" (85) (of which the killing of a rabbit by the leopard man is the first occurrence), the law is broken, and the beast-men turn upon Moreau and Montgomery. The death of Moreau removes him and his "house of pain" from the human/animal mutual assemblage. This results in animal desire being reterritorialized; the assemblage is unsustainable, and its collapse ultimately results in the failure of the becomings, and the beast-men revert to their previous animalistic forms.

Moreau's medical procedures are usually interpreted in terms of his role as the archetypal mad scientist, and hence are reduced to merely being a manifestation of his perceived insanity. Indeed, Prendick dismisses him in these terms: "Had Moreau had any intelligible object, I could have sympathised at least a little with him. I am not so squeamish about pain as that. I could have forgiven him a little even, had his motive been only hate. But he was so irresponsible, so utterly careless! His curiosity, his mad, aimless investigations, drove him on" (93). But (disregarding the pain that he inflicts upon his subjects, which is discussed subsequently) from the Deleuzian perspective of desiring, his bizarre acts are in fact schizophrenic behaviors that actually reflect the positivity of desire; for life is desire and desire is the expansion of life through creation and transformation. It could be argued that Moreau is practicing lines of flight as a reaction against the oppressive and dehumanizing powers of imperialism; those that have stood in the way of his scientific experimentations. Prendick comments upon Moreau's back-story, stating:

> The doctor was simply howled out of the country. It may be that he deserved to be; but I still think that the tepid support of his fellow-investigators and his desertion by the great body of scientific workers was a shameful thing.... He might perhaps have purchased his social peace by abandoning his investigations; but he apparently preferred the latter, as most men would who have once fallen under the overmastering spell of research [32].

In his geographical position on the eponymous island, Moreau is conducting his experiments far from civilization's censure, and in this way, he is making himself a body without organs against the organization of the psyche imposed by imperialism/capitalism. This is a kind of freedom gained by no longer "seeing ourselves as a point of view detached from life. We become free from the human, open to the event of becoming" (Colebrook *Gilles Deleuze 129*). However, this line of flight is deemed by "civilized" society (voiced through the medium of Prendick) as a negative act; a degradation of soul, viewing him as "careless ... mad ... aimless" (*Moreau* 93).

In accordance to this, neither can Moreau himself or his actions be thought of as simply "evil": in Deleuzian terms, a body or action

One—*The Island of Doctor Moreau*

cannot be thought of as being "bad" in itself, but as only becoming bad (or good) in relation to the specific assemblage it forms with other bodies and the specific affects it enables. As Deleuze notes in one of his earlier texts on Baruch Spinoza: "there is no evil (in itself), but there is that which is bad (for me)" (*Spinoza* 33). In this way, transcendent categories of good and evil are abandoned, and instead, a "good" individual seeks to make connections that increase their power to act, while at the same time not diminishing similar powers in others. The "bad" individual does not organize their encounters in this way and either "falls back into guilt and resentment, or relies on guile and violence" (Marks, John "Ethics" 86). Moreau would appear to be applicable in either category; he believes that he is increasing the potentiality of his animal subjects (albeit for his own purposes of scientific curiosity), but is reliant on violence (in the form of his gruesome surgical operations) in order to achieve this.

However, intrinsically tied to this is another aspect of the failed becomings: the moral and ethical implications of Moreau's experiments themselves. Deleuze and Guattari observe that some acts of becoming-animal are violent, unnatural, and unanticipated, and this can be equated with the complete absence of ethical consideration that Moreau extends towards his creations. As Claire Colebrook notes, life for Deleuze and Guattari is an "open, creative whole of proliferating connections" (Colebrook *Gilles Deleuze* 5). The human subject is only the "effect of one particular series of experiential connections," one assemblage in the world among many (81). Human values in this case simply express the perspective of one form of becoming. Consequently, as Colebrook writes, it becomes necessary to expand our understanding of values as "effects of the flow of life. This means moving beyond morality to ethics, where we create and select those powers that expand life as a whole, beyond our limited perspectives" (96).

In this expanded view, ethical consideration is not tied to the organs or form which an entity owns or inhabits. Whether the body is animal or human is really not the point. Instead, ethics are tied to the limits and capacities of that body. Deleuze and Guattari emphasize that we must "come to know what a body can do, its potential for interacting with other bodies, whether or not that interaction will bring harm to either body and whether there is the potential for exchange or a joining together to form a still stronger body" (Brown 268). But Moreau is so concerned with overcoming what he perceives to be physical limits of the bodies on which he experiments, that he does not comprehend their virtual element, the ethical limitations tied to the same bodies: "to this day I have never troubled about the ethics of the matter ... the study of Nature makes a man at last as remorseless as Nature. I have gone on, not heeding anything but the question I was pursuing" (*Moreau* 73).[24]

Drawing on the work of Spinoza, Deleuze distinguishes between good and bad effects upon the body according to whether a particular assemblage enhances or harms each body's "life force"; in other words, whether it increases or reduces each body's power to act and its potential to go on forming new relations (Malins 97). This distinction is very complex, especially given that a body can form multiple relations with other bodies; some good, some bad: "we have many constituent relations, so that one and the same object can agree with us in one respect and disagree with us in another" (*Spinoza* 33). In essence, an ethical event for Deleuze and Guattari is one in which bodies emerge with a strengthened potentiality, or at least a potentiality which is undiminished. In these terms, the surgery that Moreau performs upon his animal subjects may not be intrinsically "bad" in itself; what is important is that bodies are able to go on connecting with other bodies, creating new flows of desire and undertaking new becomings. An embodied ethics of this sort aims to reduce unethical assemblages (which reduce bodily potentials) and increase ethical, life-enhancing assemblages; that is, assemblages that increase a body's power to form creative, productive relations and which increase its capacity for life (Malins 98). However, rather than enabling new becomings (as would appear to actually be his ambition), Moreau's actions are actually reducing bodily potentials.

The vital issue here is that ideally assemblages should be consensual, and in this case they have been enforced, with the existential rights of the "singularities" concerned being denied, causing terrible suffering (Powell *Horror* 74). Assemblages should be compositions of desire, and correspondingly Deleuze and Guattari's notion of becoming is itself a "theory of desire: the only possible way to undertake this process is to actually be attracted to change, to want it in the flesh" (Braidotti "Meta(L)Morphoses" 70). However, the animal subjects have had their becomings forced upon them regardless of their own desires, hence

One—*The Island of Doctor Moreau*

Moreau's efforts to come to know "what a body can do" (*Spinoza* 60) are nullified by the very act of his enforcing the assemblages of the self same bodies.

    In conclusion, this chapter has illustrated, through the medium of spaces, transhumanism, and becoming-animal, how a Deleuzian encounter can serve to reinterpret *The Island of Doctor Moreau*. The concepts of smooth and striated spaces allow a reading in regards to Moreau's intentions, and through animal-becomings we can bear witness to the various processes of his experimentations, and ultimately, why they fail. As part of this process, we also bear witness to the rhizomorphic connections between the novel and the multitude of texts, films and tropes it has inspired. The next chapter continues with the transhumanist theme in relation to *The War of the Worlds*, and through the medium of arguably Wells's most prominent and influential work, we are witness to an even more extreme vision as to the potential terminus of mankind: the future lies not in the transhuman, but in the extra-terrestrial.

Two

The War of the Worlds
Martians, Cyborgs and Bodies Without Organs

> I have seen machines fighting a lot but only infinitely far behind them have I seen the men who directed them.
> —Artaud "To Have Done with the Judgment of God" 557

Evolution, Religion and Technology

Having explored concepts of transhumanism, body-horror, and becoming in relation to *The Island of Doctor Moreau,* this chapter is concerned with *The War of the Worlds* and another of the seminal sf archetypes of which Wells was a major instigator: the alien invader. Initially, a brief introduction to the novel serves to establish the various religious, technological and evolutionary themes that are subsequently elaborated upon via theory. Subsequently, the novel is placed in an historiographic context in terms of the debt the alien trope owes to Wells, before the various interpellations of an "alien Deleuze" are considered; the focus being upon themes of becoming, signs, spaces, and the spiritual automaton. This leads into an argument concerning the novel's relationship with technology, the main crux involving the machinic alliances between Wells's Martians as cybernetic organisms (cyborgs) and the Deleuzian concept of the body without organs. In keeping with the rhizomatic nature of Deleuzian theory, and the study as a whole, there is a necessary crossover with previously established machinic concepts and themes.

Two—*The War of the Worlds*

The War of the Worlds (published in novel form in 1898, though initially serialized in *Pearson's Magazine* in 1897) arguably occupies the position of being the most popular and best known of Wells's scientific romances; influential sf publisher Hugo Gernsback goes as far as proclaiming it to be "Wells's best and more enduring story" (Flynn 5). Correspondingly, the novel was well received at the time of publication, in marked contrast to the reaction provoked by *The Island of Doctor Moreau*.[1] In keeping with the trend of "invasion literature" that had captured the public's imagination in the late nineteenth century (George Tomkyns Chesney's *Battle of Dorking* [1871] and Bram Stoker's *Dracula* [1897] being other notable examples), the novel successfully tapped into the zeitgeist of popular anxieties; to this end, it has been variously interpreted as a commentary on evolutionary theory and British imperialism, as well as a reflection of the general fears and prejudices of Victorian society. Apparent in the novel is Wells's scorn towards his culture, and the inequities he observed within it; this is forcefully depicted in the manner in which the novel depicts the destruction of the edifices and symbols of authority. Clearly enthused at the prospect, Wells wrote to his friend Elizabeth Healey: "I'm doing the dearest little serial for Pearson's new magazine, in which I completely wreck and destroy Woking—killing my neighbours in painful and eccentric ways—then proceed via Kingston and Richmond to London, which I sack, selecting South Kensington for feats of peculiar atrocity" (quoted in Smith, David *Correspondences* 261). The novel is specifically notable for being the earliest example of a narrative that details a conflict between mankind and an alien (that is to say, extraterrestrial) race. Being a vocal proponent of Darwinism, Wells depicted the Martian subjugation of the human race as a natural outcome in the battle for survival of the fittest; the Martians' longer period of evolution (the scientific theories of the period believing Mars to be a far older planet than Earth) having led to their development of superior intelligence, manifested in their ability to create weapons far in advance of human technology. They have no interest in negotiation or truce, fighting a total war and viewing the human race literally as cattle to be herded, bred and consumed.

Perhaps the most intriguing aspect of the novel, subsequently explored and emphasized in terms of the Deleuzian reading, is that there is little philosophical differentiation made between the Martian antagonists and their human victims; despite the former being far more advanced in evolutionary terms, they both subscribe to the same imperialist ideology. Wells does not invite his readers to take sides, and the Martians are portrayed without any real rancor; the narrative does not implore us to hate them, or even encourage humanity but rather to observe events dispassionately, just as Wells had his Martians scrutinize us like "the transient creatures that swarm and multiply in a drop of water" (*War* 3). In these terms, and in keeping with the novel's outlook of scientific rationalism, concepts of good and evil appear to be entirely relative and as a consequence the eventual defeat of the Martians does not involve any kind of divine power, being the result of an entirely material cause, the action of microscopic bacteria. The novel's engagement of religious themes corroborates this; a clergyman may be a key character, but his attempts to relate the invasion to biblical Armageddon serve only to reinforce his mental derangement (Draper 51–52). Unable to manage a theodicy in the face of the invasion, the curate begins to interpret the attack in terms of his faith: this is the end of days, and the Martians are actually God's messengers of destruction. His death, a direct consequence of his evangelical outbursts which attract the attention of the Martians, appears to be an indictment of his outdated religious attitudes making him a candidate for culling by natural selection at the hands of the superior evolved adversaries. Religious faith and the alien invasion (which the clergyman equates with forces of nature) cannot be reconciled: "Why are these things permitted? What sins have we done? ... Fire, earthquake, death! As if it were Sodom and Gomorrah! All are work undone, all the work—What are these Martians?" (*War* 53).

The novel also dramatizes the ideas of race that are present in social Darwinism. Being evolutionarily more advanced, the Martians exercise their "rights" over human beings in their position as the superior race. Adam Roberts observes that at the time of the novel's publication the British Empire was in its most aggressive phase of expansion, and while invasion literature had provided an imaginative foundation for the idea of the heart of the British Empire being conquered by foreign forces, it was not until *The War of the Worlds* that the reading public of the time were presented with an adversary so completely superior to themselves and the Empire they were part of (Roberts, Adam 148). A significant motivating force behind the success of the British Empire was its development and use of sophisticated technology; analogously, the Martians, also attempting to establish an empire on Earth, have technology superior to their British adversaries (Fitting 137). The novel places an imperial power in the position of the victim of imperial aggression, thus encouraging the reader to consider the nature of imperialism itself. This is implicitly stated early in the novel: "And before we judge them [the Martians] too harshly, we must remember what ruthless and utter destruction our own species has wrought, not only upon animals, such as the vanished Bison and the Dodo, but upon its own inferior races" (*War* 4). The Martians, with their "vast, and cool, and unsympathetic" intellects (3), are thus established as Darwinian competitors with mankind. *The novel* was all the more potent for its implication that the highly advanced British Empire was finally experiencing from the other side the "diplomacy" that it had meted out to others and as a consequence, this also challenged the Victorian notion of there being a natural order, in which the British Empire had a right to rule through their own superiority over subject races. In this manner, one of the novel's central conceits is to emphasize that the relentless Martians may be bent on "the rout of civilization, of the massacre of mankind" (81), but are doing so as an element of a ruthless industrial process: for example, the Martian tripods carry a contrivance "like a gigantic fisherman's basket" (*War* 35) for harvesting their human "catch." Consequently, they have more than a few things in common with their human "victims"; this central conceit plays an important role in the subsequent Deleuzian reading.

These Darwinist themes, both biological and social, can be equated with prior exploration of the relationship between Darwin and Deleuze (as exemplified previously in relation to *The Island of Doctor Moreau*). Deleuze demonstrates that "evolution is itself a virtual power, a capacity and potential for change and becoming which passes through organisms. The aim of evolution is change and creation itself, not the creation of an actual being" (Colebrook *Understanding* 2). This chapter investigates the form that this evolution takes, mediated through the representations of humans, Martians and technology. As stated in the introduction, in terms of these evolutionary becomings, Deleuze and Guattari maintain that becoming is an "antimemory" (*Thousand* 324); in this way, sf stories of becoming are also "anti-histories," challenging what we think we know about species dominion. Deleuze maintains that the individual subject expands towards this infinite evolutionary capacity through the movement out of the physical body and into the virtual body without organs, and it is the status of the Martians as bodies without organs that is the main focus of this chapter. Ultimately, the key theme of the novel, that both Martian and human races appear to subscribe to identical ideologies, provides the crux of the Deleuzian reading.

Deterritorializing the Alien: Becoming, Striation and Signs

This section is concerned with the concept of the extra-terrestrial itself, and how a Deleuzian encounter can position it in terms of a conceptual entity. The concept of the extraterrestrial being (regardless of the specific terminology involved: "Martians," "space invaders," "aliens" and so forth) is engrained into twenty-first century Western cultural consciousness, both in terms of their frequent depictions in sf or speculation as to their "real-life" existence. In literary terms, as early as the second century BC, the Greek satirist Lucian of Samosata described voyages to the sun and moon, and in the seventeenth century Cyrano de Bergerac describes the first space rocket and an encounter with "moon-men" in *Le Autre Monde: ou les États et Empires de la Lune* (1657), while John Milton's *Paradise Lost* (1667) briefly considers the possibility of life on the Moon. However, none of these fictions involved any actual encounters with life emphatically alien to human beings. Writers in the seventeenth and eighteenth centuries produced tales of travel to and from other inhabited worlds, but again they did not depict beings that were alien per se; Voltaire's *Micromégas* (1752) features "Saturnians" that are essentially human, albeit of giant proportions.[2] In the latter part of the nineteenth century the growing influence of Darwinian theory (*On the Origin of Species* having been published in 1859), and as a consequence a fuller understanding of natural history, enabled writers to imagine that life on other worlds might develop differently from that on Earth. In 1864 the astronomer and science popularizer Camille Flammarion published *Les Mondes Imaginaires et les Mondes Réels* (*Imaginary Worlds and Real Worlds*), depicting otherworldly forms of life that could evolve within alien biological environments.

Two—*The War of the Worlds*

This conceptual breakthrough was first exploited in fiction by J.H. Rosny Aîné, whose short story *"Les Xipéhuz"* (1887) describes an evolutionary war of extermination between prehistoric humans and a menacing crystalline life-form.

Despite these precursors, *The War of the Worlds* remains arguably the most famous and influential work in the formation of the sf genre, and along with his subsequent novel *The First Men in the Moon*[3] in 1901 (with its bug-eyed, insectoid lunar creatures) has served to cement Wells's position as the originator not only of modern sf, but of the trope of the alien in sf, and as a consequence, the malevolent alien invader (Roberts, Adam 48). Indeed, for more than a century since the novel's release, "readers, radio-listeners and movie goers have been tantalized by the prospect of an invasion from Mars" (Flynn 5). Wells's tale of invasion from another planet bestowed a significant legacy upon the subsequent sf genre, with a visionary foray into literary "special effects" (Martian heat rays, poisonous black smoke, bio-mechanical tripods, flying machines) that establish many of the key tropes, conventions and plot devices evinced in "alien invasion horror" fiction and/or cinema of the subsequent century and new millennium (Sheldon n. pag.). Aliens as invaders from a dying planet, as violent parasites, as brains without bodies, using high-tech weaponry on their human victims; all these originated in Wells's seminal work; the deeper levels of social criticism found in the novel also making their way into such texts and films. Stableford claims that "these images that became fundamental to sf's deployment of aliens were introduced by H. G. Wells: invaders of earth bent on genocidal conquest in *The War of the Worlds*" (*Historical* 3), while William Johnson notes that Wells effectively "encoded the DNA sequence, as it were, of all extraterrestrial invasion narratives, with its [the novel's] basic dialectic of war, anarchy, reconstruction, new society" (Johnson 5). Keith Williams concurs: "*War of the Worlds* mustered many of the cinematic techniques, motifs, themes and techniques that Wells tried out in other stories, into a full scale narrative of interplanetary invasion. In effect, he created a 'blockbuster' genre which developed in both filmic and textual forms in the coming century" (Williams 139).

Having served to establish the alien trope, the influence of Wells's Martians in present day sf is consequently vast, and we are witness to an extensive array of alien depictions in both literature and film. Ziauddin

Sardar claims that the alien presence is now such a basic element of sf that to properly understand the mechanics of how sf employs aliens one must "not travel forwards but backwards in time ... the very first alien encounter, H. G. Wells's *The War of the Worlds*, returns to the very beginning of western storytelling" (Sardar and Cubitt 6). Following Wells, the alien life form has become such a basic metaphor, so primal an allegory that it can be reworked to serve in many ways. For example, alien invasions in 1950s popular culture represented a fear of the cold war, while the less threatening aliens of the 1970s served to ease technological fears and provide spiritual guidance (Ellis 145).

The resonant opening paragraph of *The War of the Worlds* ("No one would have believed, in the last years of the nineteenth century, that human affairs were being watched keenly and closely by intelligences greater than man's and yet as mortal as his own" [*War* 1]), giving the matter-of-fact sense of humanity being caught in the gaze of another race, constitutes a founding moment in the history of the sf invasion fantasy, just as the novel itself has proven to be a model for alien invasion narratives (Hutchings 337). In terms of their debt to Wells's novel, particularly worthy of note are the "monster movies" of the 1950s (such as *The Day The Earth Stood Still* [1951 Dir. Robert Wise], and *The Blob* [1958 Dir. Irvin Yeaworth]), direct literary homages such as John Christopher's series of novels *The Tripods Trilogy* (1967–68), modern extraterrestrial cinematic classics such as *Alien* (1977 Dir. Ridley Scott), and *The Thing* (1982 Dir. John Carpenter), and the long running television series *Dr Who* (featuring the cyborg Daleks, discussed in detail later in this chapter). There have, of course, been radio broadcasts (obviously notable is the now notorious Orson Welles radio adaptation in 1938) and cinematic adaptations of *The War of the Worlds* (the latter in 1953 and 2005 respectively), as well as many films that are essentially deliberate facsimiles, such as *Independence Day* (1996 Dir. Roland Emmerich)[4] and its sequel *Independence Day: Resurgence* (2016).

So, as demonstrated, since their introduction and subsequent infiltration into cultural consciousness, aliens have become the image of marginality par excellence in both television and cinema. In doing so, they function to represent the antistudy of the human through their perceived physical and intellectual superiority, and in a simultaneous defamiliarization and even horrification of their flesh and substance.

Two—*The War of the Worlds*

Consequently, the extraterrestrial in fiction has been subjected to analysis from a wide variety of critical perspectives; Constance Penley states that "sf as a genre is concerned with the question of difference, typically posed as that of the difference between human and non-human" (Penley vii). In this way, the alien is often read as a personification of the "other" from political, gender, psychoanalytic or postcolonial positions.[5] However, from a poststructuralist, Deleuzian perspective we move beyond such binary oppositions: to this end Penley concedes that "other challenges to being able to "tell the difference" come from poststructuralist criticism, with its highly constructed and unstable subjects" (vii). To this end, Deleuzian readings of the alien are now discussed.

While Deleuze and Guattari do not specifically mention aliens within their works, many theorists have forged this alliance; to this end, MacCormack cites Rosi Braidotti, Eric White, Camilla Griggers and Steven Shaviro, who "all apply becoming with relative ease to the idea of the alien as an evolution of the human[6] ... [which] exists as radical departures from the human body, fulfilling the spectacle of the human body de-familiarized, rendered other" (MacCormack 5). As conceptual figures, aliens defamiliarize the human most commonly in two ways: their located defamiliarization (they originate from another world) and their temporal defamiliarization (where they have come from in time rather than in space); this allows subject to be rendered alien by virtue of making strange the place the subject exists at, both in space and in time. It is this "space of marginality" that is precisely the minoritarian space where Deleuze and Guattari demand we begin our processes of becoming.

Deleuzian theory also presents a conceptual figure referred to as the "Spiritual Automaton," a mode of thinking "alien and outside to normal thinking" (Frampton 65). The spiritual automaton relates to Deleuze's cinematic theory, being a "quasi-human figure" which appears again and again throughout the history of cinema. It is described by Roland Bogue in these terms:

"Though outside itself," the "unthought or unthinkable inside thought," the "alien thinker within the thinker"–all attest to an apersonal, de-realized "other" thought, the thought of the spiritual automaton. Various figures might represent the spiritual automaton—the robot, the computer brain, the zombie, the alien (Bogue *Cinema* 177).

Wells Meets Deleuze

As Deleuze puts it: "the spiritual automaton, mechanical man, experimental dummy, Cartesian diver in us, unknown body which we have at the back of our heads whose age is neither ours nor that of our childhood, but a little time in the pure state" (*Cin2* 164). Deleuze himself utilized the films of director Carl Theodor Dreyer, such as *Vampyr* (1932) to explore these motifs (principally in *Cinema 1: The Movement Image*). Bogue notes that when Dreyer's characters "intone their trance-like sentences" (Bogue *Cinema* 177) they are in fact the enunciators of a kind of "free indirect discourse ... as if their words issued from some place beyond any external world or some site further inside than any internal world" (178). He claims that "figures of the ... spiritual automaton ... are the stock in trade of classic sci-fi and horror" (177), going on to maintain that what is significant is the activation of these spiritual automatons as a "mode of thought" (179). Wells's Martians can arguably be placed within this construct: the "deafening howl that drowned the thunder" (*War* 35) emitted by the tripod machines, or the "peculiar hooting" of the Martians (102) are not merely Wells's alien beings being "alien" or obscure merely for the sake of defamiliarization or horrification, but in Deleuzian terms, are arguably performing this form of "free indirect discourse," enabling them to assume the role of the spiritual automaton. Viewing the alien as an act of becoming, or as the spiritual automaton are both viable approaches in general; however, in terms of a specific reading *of The War of the Worlds*, and as this chapter subsequently explores, the Martians do not necessarily represent a process of becoming-alien of the human: they are to all intents and purposes, already human beings themselves.

The Martian invasion itself can be read in terms of the previously discussed concepts of smooth and striated spaces. As noted, Deleuze's island is never simply a geographical representation; rather it exists virtually, as an extended plot point or plateau for a special set of creatures and creatings. In these terms, the planet Earth itself constitutes an island space, albeit one that (through the course of human evolution and civilization), has already been striated; the effect of technological mediation has altered the landscape both physically (industrialization and the resulting physical infrastructure) and virtually (in terms of the adoption of capitalism). It is this space that the Martians attempt to striate through the process of their invasion, though of course, it first must be rendered smooth, as both spaces interact with one another:

Two—*The War of the Worlds*

"smooth space is constantly being translated, transversed into a striated space; striated space is constantly being reversed, returned to a smooth space" (*Thousand* 524). This explains why the objective of the Martian attack is not random devastation, but the destruction of the very infrastructure of Western capitalism itself: "They do not seem to have aimed at extermination so much as at complete demoralisation and the destruction of any opposition. They exploded any stores of powder they came upon, cut every telegraph, and wrecked the railways here and there. They were hamstringing mankind" (*War* 81). This process is also particularly well manifested in the text via the medium of the "red weed": the seeds which the Martians bring with them which "gave rise in all cases to red-coloured growths" (101–102). The weed quickly overpowers terrestrial flora and fauna, functioning as a metaphor for imperialism and territorial expansion.[7] Echoing the progress of the Martian invasion, the growth of the weed (at least initially) is of "gigantic and of unparalleled fecundity" (115), transforming the formally green English landscape into a uniform "red swamp" (115). This xenoterraforming is representative of the smoothing process prior to subsequent re-striating; the latter we never get to see, as the Martians die before it can be achieved. Ironically, we learn that the genesis of the invasion is that Mars has itself been smoothed by external forces (that of entropy, echoing the dying future Earth as depicted in *The Time Machine*) to the point where it is no longer habitable: "the secular cooling that must someday overtake our planet has already gone far indeed with our neighbour" (4).

Leading from this, the planet Mars itself (as the essential genesis of *The War of the Worlds* narrative in that it is the source of the extraterrestrial invaders) can be read in Deleuzian terms. Mars has long been a specific focus for human knowledge and folklore,[8] but the popular idea that the planet was populated by intelligent beings only became prevalent in the late nineteenth century: "Mars came into focus at the end of the nineteenth century as fin de siècle anxieties propelled people to look toward the red planet for clues about the past and future of life on Earth. Percival Lowell saw canals on Mars, which he read as signs of a once great but now dying civilization" (Helmreich 67).[9] Lowell published his observations of strange lights emanating from Mars in the scientific journal *Nature* on 2 August 1894, from which Wells subsequently drew inspiration; in fact the opening of *The War of the Worlds*

Wells Meets Deleuze

implicitly references the article, with the narrator imagining the lights Lowell reported to be the launching of the Martian cylinders towards Earth: "During the opposition of 1894 a great light was seen on the illuminated part of the disk, first at the Lick Observatory, then by Perrotin of Nice, and then by other observers. English readers heard of it first in the issue of *Nature* dated August 2. I am inclined to think that this blaze may have been the casting of the huge gun, in the vast pit sunk into their planet, from which their shots were fired at us" (*War* 5). However, though modern advancements in space exploration have largely put to rest the hypotheses of life on Mars (or at least disproving the notion that that planet might harbor a civilization of canal builders),[10] the planet remains a potent source of inspiration in the realms of fiction: Mars and mythology remain inextricably linked in the human imagination.[11] To this end, in *Martian Metamorphoses: The Planet Mars in Ancient Myth and Religion* (1997), Ev Cochrane reflects that long prior to modern sf speculation upon the existence of Martian civilizations and consequent threats of invasion: "the red planet was regarded as a malevolent agent of war, pestilence, and apocalyptic disaster. In an attempt to appease the capricious planet-god, various ancient cultures offered it human sacrifices. What is there about this distant speck of light that could inspire such bizarre conceptions culminating in ritual murder?" (Cochrane 2). Attempting to answer this question, Cochrane examines in detail various mythological themes that reflect both ancient and modern man's obsession with the red planet, demonstrating its significance in human consciousness across the ages in a historiographic context. However, the significance of Mars as a source of myth (as well as the source of Wells's alien invasion) can also be examined in terms of Deleuzian signs and signifiers, specifically in terms of politics of identity.

In a plateau of *A Thousand Plateaus* titled "Year Zero: Faciality," Deleuze and Guattari discuss the manner in which a "face" (human or otherwise) "makes sense" of the rest of the body: "Although the head, even the human head, is not necessarily a face, the face is produced in humanity. But it is produced by a necessity that does not apply to human beings in general; there is even something absolutely inhuman about the face" (*Thousand* 189). It is maintained that the sign of the human face (being a collection of features we take for granted as the exterior guarantee of interior life) exists only insofar as it is a "wall that

Two—*The War of the Worlds*

the signifier needs in order to bounce off of" (186). This can be equated to both the planet Mars and its fictional inhabitants. Every face, Deleuze and Guattari say, contains a landscape, and every landscape contains a face: "all faces envelop an unknown, unexplored landscape; all landscapes are populated by a ... dreamed-of face" (191). Massumi (referring to a region of Mars named Cydonia, which has attracted much attention in astronomy and popular culture because its geological features resemble a human face) maintains that "[the] becoming-alien of Man is bounced back off the surface of Mars in the perceived face appearing in NASA photographs" (Massumi "Expression" xiii). Massumi maintains that the famous face on Mars is exemplary here, especially because Deleuze and Guattari write that "the face has a correlate of great importance: the landscape, which is not just a milieu but a deterritorialized world" (*Thousand* 191). This can be equated with *The War of the Worlds* description of the observation of the planet itself:

> Men like Schiaparelli watched the red planet—it is odd, by-the-bye, that for countless centuries Mars has been the star of war—but failed to interpret the fluctuating appearances of the markings they mapped so well.... Looking through the telescope, one saw a circle of deep blue and the little round planet swimming in the field. It seemed such a little thing, so bright and small and still, faintly marked with transverse stripes, and slightly flattened from the perfect round [*War* 5–6].

This passage reflects the manner in which Mars is both a source of fascination and the incarnation of myth (acknowledged by the narrator as the "star of war"), and myth is irresistible: "a kind of mythic arena onto which we have projected our Earthly hopes and fears" (Sagan 107). It is thus functioning as the previously referenced "wall that the signifier needs in order to bounce off of" (*Thousand* 186). Interestingly, the novel also presents us with something akin to this sign in reverse, from the perspective of the Martians looking across the gulf of space to the Earth:

> And looking across space with instruments, and intelligences such as we have scarcely dreamed of, they see, at its nearest distance only 35,000,000 of miles sunward of them, a morning star of hope, our own warmer planet, green with vegetation and grey with water, with a cloudy atmosphere eloquent of fertility, with glimpses through its drifting cloud wisps of broad stretches of populous country and narrow, navy-crowded seas [*War* 1].

Wells Meets Deleuze

As Deleuze states that every face contains a landscape and every landscape contains a face, the face of the landscape can also be equated with the physical, human face. However, the face-landscape here is not human, but (at least physically) an alien life-form, serving to challenge the very conception of human life. Deleuze and Guattari call this process "faciality": "The inhuman in human beings: that is what the face is from the start. It is by nature a close-up, with its inanimate white surfaces, its shining black holes, its emptiness" (*Thousand* 171). Wells's visceral depiction of the Martians can be equated to these surfaces and holes: "Two large dark-coloured eyes were regarding me steadfastly. The mass that framed them, the head of the thing, was rounded, and had, one might say, a face ... above all, the extraordinary intensity of the immense eyes—were at once vital, intense, inhuman, crippled and monstrous" (*War* 15). As a consequence, this face is "a horror. It is naturally a lunar landscape ... there is no need for a close-up to make it inhuman; it is naturally a close-up, and naturally inhuman, a monstrous hood" (*Thousand* 211). The significance here is that Deleuze and Guattari emphasize the image of black holes on a white surface because this dominating face is by definition white: "the face is not a universal. It is not even that of the white man; it is the white man himself" (196). In other words, they find a primordial horror in the white face that is historically defined by power, authority, and privilege. This is fitting; after all (as is subsequently further explored), the Martians are to all intents and purposes a depiction of evolved human beings, with an imperialist agenda identical to their human "ancestors": "The Tasmanians, in spite of their human likeness, were entirely swept out of existence in a war of extermination waged by European immigrants, in the space of fifty years. Are we such apostles of mercy as to complain if the Martians warred in the same spirit?" (*War* 3). Hence, Deleuzian faciality can be united not only with the representation of Mars as the source of the invasion, but also in terms of the Martian invaders themselves. This equates to Jameson's description of the novel as being "patently a guilt fantasy on the part of a Victorian man who wonders whether the brutality with which he has used the colonial peoples ... may not be visited on him by some more advanced race intent, in its turn, on his destruction" (Jameson *Archaeologies* 265).

As valid as these interpretations are, this chapter posits that another Deleuzian concept serves to provide a reading of the Wellsian

Martian in greater depth; that of the body without organs. As shown above, interpreting the alien in terms of becoming primarily revolves around the concept of difference, whereas the emphasis of this reading lies in the significance of the similarity of concerns between human and alien. The manner in which the Martians are depicted as an evolutionary possibility of the human being is also key to this exploration.

The Martian as the Future Human

The previous chapter was in part concerned with demonstrating the rhizomatic paths of association from *The Island of Doctor Moreau* and contemporary body horror. In a similar vein, it shall be posited that the Martians that Wells depicts so viscerally in *The War of the Worlds* are literary forerunners of the concept of the cyborg; the symbiosis between organic tissue and machine that has also become a familiar trope in contemporary sf.

A "traditional" reading of *The War of the Worlds* provides somewhat contradictory perspectives on concepts of technological and mechanical improvements and augmentations. On the one hand, the advanced technology wielded by the Martians is what defines them as superior to the human race; the characters in the novel fear the technological power of their enemies, and there is nothing that can be done in the face of such advanced intelligence. From this perspective the novel posits technological advance as the very thing that allows and facilitates the invasion and destruction of one culture by another. Conversely however, this also implies the necessity of science for the maintenance and propagation of a culture; Wells implies that technology should not be the main focus of a society, but also suggests that unless a country keeps up with the technology of the world, that country will eventually be destroyed by that same technology.[12]

Intrinsic to the Martians adoption of technology is their advanced evolutionary status. To this end, the genesis of the Martians is discussed, leading to an argument concerning their status as cybernetic organisms. *The War of the Worlds* conveys that the evolutionary development of the Martians has taken them to a point where they are merely a brain, some sense organs and a cluster of tentacular "fingers." Wells had previously explored this Darwinian concept in his 1893 essay

Wells Meets Deleuze

"The Man of the Year Million": "Ruskin has said somewhere, a propos of Darwin, it is not what man has been, but what he will be, that should interest us" (reprinted in Wells *Certain* 109). This text introduces us to the potent sf image of a far-future man as an overdeveloped head and brain, perched on top of a shrunken, atrophied body. "Great hands they have, enormous brains, soft, liquid, soulful eyes. Their whole muscular system, their legs, their abdomens, are shriveled to nothing, a dangling degraded pendant to their minds" (167). The future man, Wells believed, would strike us today as a grotesque alien, a theme which *The War of the Worlds* expands upon. Amusingly, the narrator of the novel refers implicitly to Wells's own article, stating that "a certain speculative writer of quasi-scientific repute ... writing in a foolish facetious tone" had prior to the invasion "forecast for man a final structure not unlike the actual Martian condition" (*War* 101). The Martian is in fact a direct analogue of the Man depicted in "Man of the Year Million," with the narrator's subsequent description of the Martians repeating Wells's previous scientific article almost verbatim: "huge round bodies—or, rather, heads—about four feet in diameter, each body having in front of it a face ... a pair of very large dark-coloured eyes.... They were heads, merely heads" (99–100). After further ruminations upon the Martian form, it is concluded: "To me it is quite credible that the Martians may be descended from beings not unlike ourselves, by a gradual development of brain ... at the expense of the rest of the body" (101).

So, though initially, the war between Earth and Mars appears to be about two competing species with differing levels of technology, it ironically becomes apparent that the two are bound by the same cosmic law, that of evolution: "we men, with our bicycles and road-skates, our Lilienthal soaring-machines, our guns and sticks and so forth, are just in the beginning of the evolution that the Martians have worked out" (102–103). Hence the struggle between the human and Martian forces is in effect humanity fighting against a speculative future version of itself. Thus, in much the same way as *The Time Machine*, *The War of the Worlds* functions as a prophetic warning as to the future of humanity: evolution becomes the "machine" of history through which we are destined to become the Martians. And, by extension, we are destined to be enslaved to the very technology on which they are dependent.

However, the novel's relationship between human and Martian

Two—*The War of the Worlds*

can in fact be even further extrapolated; we are not destined by evolution to become like the Martians; we are in fact already Martians. "The chances against anything manlike on Mars are a million to one" (7), states Ogilvy near the beginning of the novel, the implication being that, despite these long odds, something man-like does in fact exist on Mars. Later in the novel, the curate enquires of the narrator, "what are these Martians?," to which he retorts, "what are we?" (53), as if the questions were in all actuality one and the same. The Martians are a mechanistic, collectivist force indistinguishable from the machines they operate (as is discussed in detail later in the chapter), and this is analogous to the novel's depiction of nineteenth-century British man, who is also characterized by soulless conformity. The character of the Artilleryman, despite being portrayed as a drunken fantasist, has telling points to make about "respectable" society:

> They haven't any spirit in them—no proud dreams and no proud lusts.... I've seen hundreds of 'em, bit of breakfast in hand, running wild and shining to catch their little season-ticket train, for fear they'd get dismissed if they didn't; working at businesses they were afraid to take the trouble to understand; skedaddling back ... keeping indoors after dinner for fear of the back streets; and sleeping with the wives they married, not because they wanted them, but because they had a bit of money that would make for safety in their one little miserable skedaddle through the world [123].

Also, it should be noted that alien invasion in the novel takes place in the past: "The storm burst upon us six years ago now" (5). This chronological shift suggests that we are already in the future, with the narrator's speculations concerning the fate of humanity anticipating a projected future that is already taking place in the present; when the alien arrives, it turn out to be just like us, only living in a future that is already unfolding (Pinsky 70).

In these terms, both human and Martian are "two avatars of evolutionary law ... the real winner of the war is the true alien, an entity that exists outside the linear progression of evolution and obeys another law—the law of chance ... the Martians were merely unlucky" (Pinsky 71). However, from a Deleuzian perspective, simple bad luck does not figure in the failed invasion. Via a reading of the Martians as cybernetic organisms, and as an extrapolation of this argument, the Deleuzian body without organs, the true nature of the failure of the alien invasion can be ascertained. This commences with a reading of the cyborg in literature in general terms, before the concept is related to Wells and Deleuze respectively.

Evolving the Cyborg

Due to its position as a seminal work, Wells's scientific romances are frequently used as an archetype in sf to illustrate the shifting attitudes and concerns towards technology over time. Jameson states in his essay "Progress Versus Utopia; or, Can We Imagine the Future?" (1982) that contemporary sf does not envision a utopian future "like that described in earlier nineteenth-century sf of H. G. Wells" (151). It is apparent that Jameson believes Wells's sf to be simply the reflection of an older ideology, mirroring the expansion of rational humanism in which the dominance of the human mind over technology was unquestioned. In *Terminal Identity: The Virtual Subject in Postmodern Science Fiction* (1993), Scott Bukatman claims that contemporary sf introduces the imminent realization of the conquest of man's consciousness by technology, as opposed to "earlier" sf which depicts "the conquest of the inter-galactic in which man's consciousness was the dominant power over technology … an essentially anthropocentric and utopian vision of the future" (16–17). In regards to Wells, both of these readings reinforce the standardized perspective of how the scientific romances approach issues of the relationship between humanity and technology. However, though this may be inferred in terms of "early" sf in general terms, as previously stated, a Deleuzian reading will demonstrate that, far from a celebration of human rationalism and superiority in the face of burgeoning technology, *The War of the Worlds* actually demonstrates the possible dire consequences of "the conquest of man's minds" through technology to a startling degree.

The previous chapter concerned issues of transhumanism in *The Island of Doctor Moreau*. To briefly return to this theme, one only has to look to the Martians from *War of the Worlds* to find an example of a culture which has radically embraced transhumanism. Over a century after its initial publication, the novel remains a shocking image of the worst kind of technological society where the inhabitants so rely upon their artificial improvements that they are utterly unable to cope with a more primal threat: a simple virus. The figure of the cyborg, frequently recurring in contemporary sf, is a coupling of machine and organism, often appearing as something monstrous; this is unsurprising, since the intermeshing of human and machine defies a number of traditional binary oppositions (human/machine, spirit/matter, life/death, among others) and hence it is seen as incarnating something evil or at the very least, potentially evil (Melehy 14). The most obvious (and common) argument concerning the cyborg is that many of these narratives tell us something about our ambivalent relationship with technology: "fragile human flesh versus cold machines" (Parker 74). However, as this chapter demonstrates, in the destabilization of the organic structure of the human being, in Deleuzian terms the cyborg provides a site for different sorts of becoming.

In *Colonialism and the Emergence of Science Fiction* (2008), John Rieder considers themes such as hybrids, hypertrophied brains and cyborgs in early sf literature, concentrating on "the figure of the advanced alien race or the man from the future with an enormous brain and atrophied body" (19). He cites the very three novels that are the subject of this study as intrinsic to the origin of the cyborg in sf, claiming: "A survey of the hybrid-cyborg pair [in fiction] has to begin with the three great early novels of H. G. Wells.... *The Time Machine*, *The Island of Doctor Moreau*, and *The War of the Worlds*." More specifically, he states that "Wells's Martians are the prototypical cyborgs of early sf. Their combination of prosthetic supplementation and organic atrophy is one of the most influential, widely imitated inventions in the field" (111).[13] Rieder does not however overly elaborate upon this statement, but further investigation is indeed warranted in light of the proposed Deleuzian argument. It is important to note at this juncture that whereas the majority of cyborg theory concentrates upon the interface between human and machine, Wells's Martians are alien beings. However, as has been demonstrated, they are in essence highly evolved human beings, and therefore there is no inherent contradiction in positioning them as cyborgs in the "traditional" understanding of the term.

So how do Wells's Martians earn their place in the cyborg pantheon? As is befitting of such a complex metaphor, the narrator struggles throughout the novel to provide a satisfactory rationalization as to the specific physical nature of the creatures he encounters. Upon their landing and emergence from their metal cylinder, the Martians are initially regarded as repulsive but unthreatening due to their physical limitations: "They are the most sluggish things I ever saw crawl.... But the horror of them!" (*War* 23). However the narrator subsequently admits to having "overlooked the fact that such mechanical intelligence as the Martians possessed was quite able to dispense with muscular exertion at a pinch" (43), eventually conceding that in evolutionary terms "the perfection of mechanical devices must ultimately supersede limbs" (140). The narrator is perplexed in his attempts to ascertain a clear distinction between the organic and the machine, the tripods being the first source of confusion: "Seen nearer, the thing was incredibly strange, for it was no mere insensate machine driving on its way" (35). He questions whether they are "intelligent mechanisms? Such a thing I felt was impossible. Or did a Martian sit within each, ruling, directing, using, much as a man's brain sits and rules in his body?" (38). Subsequently, the tripods are referred to as "minds swaying vast mechanical bodies" (59). Ultimately, it is concluded that the Martians are "mere brains, wearing different bodies according to their needs" (140). In the narrator's description of the Martian "Handling Machine," the blurring of the organic and the mechanical is complete, with the Martians functioning as purely a brain augmented by mechanical means: "the handling-machine did not impress me as a machine, but as a crablike creature with a glittering integument, the controlling Martian whose delicate tentacles actuated its movements seeming to be simply the equivalent of the crab's cerebral portion" (99). Additionally, as opposed to the biological process of the ingestion of food, the Martians actually instead effectively take on fuel, much like machines: "entrails they had none. They did not eat, much less digest. Instead they took the fresh, living blood of other creatures, and injected it into their own veins" (100). A further affirmation concerning the Martians cyborg nature is via their method of reproduction. Wells's narrator informs us that "a young Martian, there can now be no dispute, was really born upon earth during the war, and it was found attached to its parent, partially *budded* off, just as young lilybulbs bud off, or like the young animals in the fresh-water polyp" (139). This can be related to the hybrid biology of the cyborg, which being a combination of tissue and technology, is considered outside of the scope of standard human classifications such as gender, health, race, age, and method of reproduction; the cyborg does not reproduce, it replicates (Haraway "Manifesto" 150). It is through these depictions of the hybridic splicing of

Two—*The War of the Worlds*

the organic body with technology that it can be argued that Wells anticipates the concept of the cyborg: "nightmare creatures to be fitted out with attachments fashioned by his [Wells's] heated imagination" (Kemp 25). The subsequent significance of the cyborg as both a dominant staple in the sf genre, and as an important concept in contemporary philosophy and cultural studies, cannot be overstated.

To ascertain the significance of Wells's Martians in the further development of the cyborg metaphor, *The War of the Worlds* can be placed in context of both its peers and successors. In terms of the development of the concept of a hybrid of natural and artificial systems in literature, the monster in Mary Shelley's *Frankenstein* (1818) is often cited as the first cyborg, being a creature assembled, not naturally born. Arguably the only other work containing similar themes preceding *The War of the Worlds* was Edgar Allan Poe's short story "The Man That Was Used Up" (1843), featuring a protagonist augmented with extensive external prostheses. Subsequent to *The War of the Worlds*, in 1908 the novel *L'Homme Qui Peut Vivre Dans L'eau* (*The Man Who Can Live in Water*) by Jean de la Hire introduced the character Léo Saint-Clair (otherwise known as "The Nyctalope"), a crime fighter with artificially augmented vision and a prosthetic heart; this character is arguably regarded as the first literal representation of a cyborg, in that he possesses intrinsic implanted machinic parts.[14] Edmond Hamilton presented space explorers with a mixture of organic and machine parts in his short story "The Comet Doom" in 1928, which features the conscious brain of a scientist transplanted into a box. In the short story "No Woman Born" (1944), C. L. Moore wrote of an actress whose body is immolated and whose brain is placed in a robotic body, raising issues as to whether her sense of humanity and femininity can be maintained in the absence of her human body.

Following these seminal examples, since the 1960s the cyborg has become an ever evolving form in the realms of sf television and film. Indeed, cyborgs such as Darth Vader in *Star Wars* (1977), the Replicants in *Blade Runner* (1982), the title character of *The Terminator* (1984) and *Robocop* (1987), and *Dr Who's* Daleks (1963–present), have become omnipresent figures not only in sf, but also in popular culture. The latter, being comprised of organic brains inside metal carapaces, are the most obvious modern successors to Wells's Martian war machines, and their significance in these terms is discussed later in this chapter. The cyborg trope continues to expand and diversify via the medium of contemporary sf television, with characters such as Seven of Nine in *Star Trek: Voyager* (1995–2001), the Cylon race in *Battlestar Galactica* (2003–2009) and *Caprica* (2009–2010) and Adam in season four of *Buffy The Vampire Slayer* (1997–2003). The latter is an interesting case, being a hybrid of human, machine and supernatural demon[15]: "a twentieth-century revision of Frankenstein's monster, and as such is part of an ongoing dispute concerning the legitimate experiments of science" (Pateman 118). In discussing the lineage of this specific cyborg, Matthew Pateman uses the term "involution" to describe its intertextual associations, which are "potentially endless both in terms of its intra- and paratextual elements, but especially [in terms] of its intertextual relations" (119). Described in this manner, the complex genealogy of the cyborg can be related to the previously discussed Deleuzian conception of evolution, which is construed as a process of repetition that is inherently creative. Deleuze also makes use of a system of involution, describing it as a "form of creative transformation where transversal movements engage forces and effects" (Parr 58). As stated in *A Thousand Plateaus*, "becoming is involutionary, involution is creative" (*Thousand* 263); hence through an example of the modern cyborg, such as *Buffy The Vampire Slayer's* Adam, rhizomorphic paths of association can to be drawn through literature and culture to all prior forms. In this manner, the evolution of the cyborg can be explored in both cultural terms and as a virtual entity in its own right, with Adam, Frankenstein's monster and Wells's Martians all forming elements of the cyborg rhizome. Inherent to these creative evolutions and associations is not only the physical form of the cyborg (that is, a hybrid of man and machine) but also their function as cultural object and ideas; indeed, as previously established, "ideas do not die ... ideas are always reusable, because they have been usable before" (*Thousand* 259). Indeed, via these multiple rhizomorphic manifestations, the cyborg figure has become an ever more powerful figure in sf, popular culture, and critical theory; a "condensed image of both imagination and material reality" (Haraway "Manifesto" 150).

In these terms, in discussing the cyborg concept not only are we referring to the physical symbiosis between human and machine, but also to the metaphor of the cyborg; the term has shifted from mere sf territory into the vast field of theoretical criticism. The splicing

Two—*The War of the Worlds*

together of biological organism and machine has become a very important signifier in postmodern and poststructural fields, particularly in regards to feminist studies, spearheaded by Donna Haraway's influential essay "A Cyborg Manifesto: Science, Technology, and Socialist-Feminism in the Late Twentieth Century" (1980). In Haraway's terms, a cyborg body is a representation of an imagined cyberspacial existence, not only a utopian and/or dystopian prophesy, but also a reflection of a contemporary site of possible being. Images of the cyborg body hence go some way to exemplify the fears and desires of contemporary culture in its practice of transformation. To this end, Haraway states: "A cyborg exists when two kinds of boundaries are simultaneously problematic: (1) that between animals (or other organisms) and humans, and (2) that between self-controlled, self-governing machines (automatons) and organisms, especially humans (models of autonomy). The Cyborg is the figure born of the interface of automaton and autonomy" (*Primate* 139).

So, for Haraway, the figure of the cyborg emerges at the breakdown of boundaries between human and animal, organism and machine, physical and non-physical, and nature and culture (150–153). In terms of their power as an intellectual device, she maintains that "cyborg writing is about the power to survive not on the basis of original innocence, but on the basis of seizing the tools to mark the world that marked them as other" (Haraway "Manifesto" 175). This concept of other is emphasized by Jeffrey Cohen, who states that the cyborg body quite literally "incorporates fear, desire, anxiety, and fantasy.... A construct and a projection, the monster exists only to be read" (Cohen 4). Because the cyborg is a symbiotic relationship between human and machine and is equally faithful to its organic components and its machine attributes, its manifestations vary according to which aspect is attributed dominance or materiality; hence the cyborg is fundamentally contradictory, its character consisting of "a condensed image of both imagination and material reality" (Haraway "Manifesto" 150). This combination of flesh and machine results in a union that, while containing significant elements of both, results in a symbiotic creature that is neither. Ultimately, it is this lack of boundaries between the biological and the machinic (just as Wells's narrator cannot distinguish between the Martians and their machines) that is the power of the cyborg as a concept: "The difference between machine and organism is thoroughly blurred; mind, body and tool are on very intimate terms" (165). The culmination of such a union is in effect a direct form of dialectical synthesis; partaking in both forms, yet the resulting combination subscribes to none; hence the cyborg is a being which stands alone, philosophically and ideologically.

The Martian Cancerous Cyborg

In her exploration of the figure of the cyborg, Haraway offers an intriguing, not to mention highly influential conceptualization of the relations between the body and technology in symbiosis. However, it can be maintained that prior to Haraway, Deleuze and Guattari developed a concept of the cyborg body of their own, through their notion of the body without organs.[16] In positioning the Martian cyborgs in terms of the body without organs, we produce rhizomatic connections to other elements of the Deleuzian tool-box that assist in understanding their motivations, and indeed their eventual failings. Tied directly to their conceptualizations of machine, desire and becoming, Deleuze and Guattari's significance to the cyberculture debate resides in *Anti-Oedipus's* concept of the "desiring machine" and *Difference and Repetition's* repeated engagements with the concept of the virtual (Lister et al. 384). Buchannan also emphasizes the potential in their approach to this theoretical field, stating: "It is indeed the material complexity of Deleuze and Guattari's plane of imminence that is missing from much cybertheory" (quoted in Stivale *Key* 196). Amusingly, Daniel Conway posits Deleuze himself as "a cyborg priest," who is "necessarily implicated in the junkheap of thanatos engines, zombie-machines, and grotesque prostheses" (Ansell Pearson *Engineer* 15).

As stated previously, sf narratives constructed around the cyborg customarily invoke human fears of these technological creations that are, in certain ways, superior to humans. Some of these narratives validate these fears, for example, *The Terminator*. Some assuage those fears by creating friendly cyborgs (for example, *Star Trek Voyager's* Seven of Nine); still others ask us to question the ethics of maintaining the boundary between man and machine. While these narratives can generally be said to speculate about the development of machinic intelligence in the future (while incorporating commentary upon the present), Deleuze and Guattari map the machine as an integral, historical element of human consciousness. As a result, where the conventional sf narrative might speculate upon the similarities between human and machine, the two remain very different forms of consciousness; however, the Deleuzian approach marks human consciousness as being already machinic. Rather than recognizing a schism between the human mind and machinic intelligence, human consciousness shares the same material space as the machine, mutating along with machinic developments (what Guattari terms "heterogenesis") (Reid n. pag.).

While Haraway's conceptualization of the cyborg as a human-machine hybrid implies that technology and humanity exist independently of each other, the body without organs breaks these polarities between man and machine. While both Deleuze and Haraway valorize the cyborgian coupling, networking, and fusion of organic and nonorganic parts, Deleuze however calls into question the idea of their fully integrated assembly; the notion of a single cybernetic organism is rejected in favor of the body without organs, an "imageless, organless body [which is] perpetually reinserted into the process of production" (*Anti* 9). Thus, the body without organs can be read as a cyborg construct, a "desiring machine," collapsing the distinctions between man/machine, man/nature, self/other, male/female and so forth. If the machinic assemblage is a multiplicity of forces in motion, not fixed components, then a physical organism is in itself a machinic meld of body, mind and brain. As Slavoj Žižek observes: "the true problem is not 'how, if at all, could machines imitate the human mind?' but 'how does the very identity of human mind rely on external mechanical supplements? How does it incorporate machines?'" (*Organs* 16). Lister and Dover summarize the Deleuzian position thus: "these are complex ideas, and perhaps the best way to sum up Deleuze and Guattari's work on the question of biology and machine relations is the following: Life is nothing but machines" (Lister et al. 387). Deleuze and Guattari therefore envision the body without organs as an assemblage of biological components that are capable of interfacing with other non-biological organisms, as every body without organs is itself a plateau in communication with other plateaus on the plane of consistency (*Thousand* 175). This state bears implications not only for individuals, but also for the society and culture to which they are machinically attached. In this way, the body without organs can be related to capitalism and capital; indeed, *Anti-Oedipus* defines the body without organs mainly in these terms. This is highly significant to the specific position that this study takes in positioning Wells's Martians as bodies without organs, in terms of their invasion taking the form of an industrializing process. Capitalism and technology have a mutual relationship; indeed, Deleuze along with the multitude of assemblages that influenced the emergence of capitalism ("a motley painting of everything that has ever been believed" [*Anti* 37]), technology can be seen as its symbiotic partner, with the interaction between the two serving to accelerate said symbiosis.

Intrinsic also to the invocation of the Martians as bodies without organs is the fact that the process is inherently dangerous and fraught with problems; Deleuze and Guattari warn that it can sustain "relations of violence and rivalry as well as alliance and complicity," and hence can ultimately be present as the "cancerous body without organs of a fascist inside us" (*Thousand* 180–181). As is now explored, despite the Martian/machine cyborg coupling, and resulting transformation theoretically opening up new potentialities, not all couplings are successful. Though it may be a site for potentialities, there is also inherent peril in the body without organs, and hence in the cyborg assemblage. To this end, Stivale notes that "due to the liberation of flows of desire, the cyborg is a machinic assemblage to be regarded with caution" (Stivale *Two-Fold* 125).

In the previous chapter the failure of Deleuzian animal-becomings in *The Island of Doctor Moreau* was discussed. In a similar manner, it can be ascertained why the Martian interactions between machine and flesh in *The War of the Worlds* are ultimately unsuccessful. This relates to what manner of body without organs (via the cyborg assemblage) that the Martians have become[17]; the distinctions that Deleuze makes between different types are integral in a reading of Wells's cyborg Martians. In *A Thousand Plateaus* Deleuze and Guattari differentiate between three potential destinations for the body without organs: full, empty and cancerous. To summarize briefly, the full body is healthy and productive, not petrified in its organization. The empty body without organs is described as "catatonic" because it is completely deorganized; all flows pass through it freely, with no stopping, and no directing. Even though any form of desire can be produced on it, the

Two—*The War of the Worlds*

empty body without organs is non-productive. The cancerous body without organs is caught in a pattern of endless reproduction of the self-same pattern. In terms of his political theory, Deleuze gives the example of capitalism as a cancerous body without organs; it can't die, it is but an endlessly reproducing, never-changing cycle. Bogue expounds upon this: "Deleuze and Guattari recognize ... that there are great risk and perils in the pursuit of a body without organs and thus in *A Thousand Plateaus* they speak of both a suicidal and a cancerous body without organs, each with their own specific dangers" (Bogue "Violence" 111). As previously referenced in terms of Dr Moreau's "botched becomings," such failings of the empty or cancerous body without organs are expressed in *A Thousand Plateaus* thus: "if you free [the body without organs] with too violent an action, if you blow apart the strata without taking precautions, then instead of drawing the plane [of consistency] you will be killed, plunged into a black hole, or even dragged towards catastrophe" (*Thousand* 178).

Obviously, the Martians cannot attain a full body without organs; not only are they unsuccessful in their "massacre of mankind" (*War* 81), but are doing so as an element of a ruthless industrial process; these actions could not be described as "healthy and productive," as the liberatory potential of the body without organs is unused. This can also be further justified by the manner in which the full body without organs rejects "any attempt to impose on it any sort of triangulation implying that it was produced by parents" (*Anti* 16). As has been discussed, the Martians are in effect our distant evolutionary ancestors, and by virtue of this they are to all intents and purposes our "children."

Neither are the Martians empty bodies without organs, in that they are not non-productive; they produce both destruction and capitalism. It is however these things that they produce that make them a cancerous body without organs. In evolutionary terms, they are literally a "mutation of capitalism" (*Neg* 180), who "war in the same spirit" (*War* 3) as we, their ancestors. Their adherence to the same capitalistic system makes them a "body of war and money" (*Thousand* 181), a cancerous body without organs to an extreme degree. Additionally, it is implied that through their telepathic communication, the Martians have a form of hive mind[18]: "I have seen four, five, and (once) six of them sluggishly performing the most elaborately complicated operations together without either sound or gesture ... in this matter I am convinced-as firmly as I am convinced of anything-that the Martians interchanged thoughts without any physical intermediation" (*War* 103). Compounding this, they are indistinguishable from one another, being wholly uniform in appearance: "they wore no clothing" and have "no conceptions of ornament and decorum" (102). Due to these uniformities, a single Martian appears to have no sense of individual personhood, and hence cannot be thought of apart from any other Martian, or indeed the machines which they inhabit. They literally embody their ideology in that their virtual bodies are part of the assemblage of human/alien/machine potentialities, but this assemblage is tied to the industrialized, capitalistic nature of this system, hence these parts are prevented from being "free flows" of Deleuzian potentiality. One cannot become a full body without organs if one is wired to a collective network, hence those trapped within this network are caught in a pattern of endless reproduction of the self-same pattern.

The body without organs also allows us to posit rhizomatic associations between the Martians and the bacteria that ultimately defeats them. As discussed, the body without organs is a site of decoded flows. It opens a zone of indeterminacy, for imagination as a new circuit between the actual and the virtual. In this way, Deleuze regards it as a molecular process.[19] The molecular sensibility is found in Deleuze's appreciation of microscopic things, in the tiny perceptions or inclination that destabilize perceptions as a whole (Conley 173). He speaks of how such sensibilities function "to pulverize the world" (*The Fold* 87). In this way, "there is no such thing as man or nature now, only a process that produces the one within the other and couples the machines together" (*Anti* 2). Bacteria are mentioned in the very first paragraph of *The War of the Worlds*: "With infinite complacency men went to and fro over this globe about their little affairs, serene in their assurance of their empire over matter. It is possible that the infusoria under the microscope do the same" (*War* 1). This subtly foreshadows the subsequent vital role they have to play subsequently in the narrative:

> These germs of disease have taken toll of humanity since the beginning of things—taken toll of our prehuman ancestors since life began here. But by virtue of this natural selection of our kind we have developed resisting power; to no germs do we succumb without a struggle, and to many—those that

cause putrefaction in dead matter, for instance -our living frames are altogether immune. But there are no bacteria in Mars, and directly these invaders arrived, directly they drank and fed, our microscopic allies began to work their overthrow. Already when I watched them they were irrevocably doomed, dying and rotting even as they went to and fro. It was inevitable [133–134].

A Thousand Plateaus states that insects, germs, bacteria and particles do not just denote biological categories of knowledge, but simultaneously can be seen as carriers of intensities and potentials: "Contagion, epidemic, involves terms that are entirely heterogeneous; for example, a human being, an animal, and a bacterium, a virus, a molecule, a microorganism.... These combinations are neither genetic nor structural; they are interkingdoms, unnatural participations. That is the only way Nature operates—against itself" (*Thousand* 267). Here, nature is conceptualized as no mere passive process. Instead, it is an image of mutation and violent force, turned against itself and everything that dwells within it. And, as explored previously, the cancerous body without organs is caught in a pattern of endless reproduction of the self-same pattern, and unlike the full body without organs, it is not open to other flows and potentials. Hence, the Martians are unable to explore or exploit the bacteria as carriers of potentialities, and it is this that assists in their demise.

So, as cancerous bodies without organs, the Martians fail in their campaign to conquer planet Earth, as they are a depiction of future man, or even man themselves who are subscribing to the same ideology as those they are assumed to be superior to. By their attempted invasion of humanity, they are the same as those that they attack, working within the same imperialist capitalistic system: an example of the "modern Prometheus punished by his own creation" (Parker 76). Vital here is the relationship between capitalism and technology. As stated, along with the multitude of assemblages that influenced the emergence of capitalism, technology can be seen as its symbiotic partner, with the interaction between the two serving to accelerate said symbiosis. Hence, in Deleuzian terms, they are still an element of the state apparatus, and hence cancerous, destined to repeat a non-productive system to no avail. Ultimately, the Martians, occupying the position of the cancerous body without organs, cannot break free from the imperialistic capitalist machine: instead of reterritorializing a culture, it collapses into cancerous inertness. Deleuze and Guattari maintain: "The revolution needs a war machine, and not a State apparatus, is only too obvious. It also needs an analytical instance, an ongoing analysis of collective desires, but not one brought about by an exterior apparatus of synthesis [by specialist bodies]" (*Desert* 267).

The cultural impact and influence of Wells's Martians was explored previously in this chapter, and it is worthy of note that the Martian cyborg body without organs can also be seen in context of their cultural legacy: one apposite example would be *Dr Who's* Daleks, which have previously been positioned as direct successors to the Martians in *The War of the Worlds*. Sutton states: "[*Dr Who's*] stories illustrate the varying organisation of the body without organs that Deleuze and Guattari outline … they [Daleks] create a cancerous body that relies on the rote repetition of form. This is the body that becomes a despotic, totaling body, well represented in the Daleks … the product of a fascist style government bent on the eradication of the impure" (Sutton and Martin-Jones 114). Indeed, *Cinema 2: The Time Image* depicts cybernetic machines as emblems of control societies, likening Hitlerian Germany to a "cybernetic race" (254–255). Obviously there is a clear differentiation between the capitalistic system of the Martians and the fascism adopted by the Daleks; however, Deleuze states that it is only in fascism the real cruel face of capital is revealed; capitalism is essentially "profoundly illiterate" and conservative and it turns to fascism it shows its real face (*Anti* 260). So, despite their fictional genesis being separated by some 65 years (Daleks having been first introduced in the *Dr Who* series in 1963), Wells's Martians and the Daleks clearly follow rhizomorphic paths of association.[20] The Martians are forefathers of the Daleks in both spiritual and ideological terms, and as a consequence have instilled in them identical failings: both function as cancerous body without organs. Hence, we can see that the Martian cyborgs are a direct source of inspiration for modern sf and cyborg narratives, in terms of both their physical composition, and (at least in the case of *Dr Who's* Daleks) inherent ideology. Ultimately, a Deleuzian reading, through its depiction of a cancerous cycle that we are destined to repeat upon ourselves, allows us to view Wells's novel, and its damning incitements of colonialism and capitalism, in a uniquely visceral way. However, in regards to the novel's somewhat ambiguous conclusion, it is necessary to debate as to whether there are potential "lines of flight" of escape from this predicament.

Two—*The War of the Worlds*

Positive Catastrophe, the Divine and the Expanded Universe

Despite its apocalyptic vision, an intriguing element of *The War of the Worlds* is that once the Martian invasion has been defeated (albeit inadvertently), the epilogue contains a marked change in tone, at least on a philosophical level, with emphasis placed both positively and negatively upon the impact that the thwarted alien invasion has had upon humanity. In regards to this, other theoretical elements can be brought into play; that of Deleuzian catastrophe and the expanded universe. The narrator speaks of how the world-altering events of the invasion have resulted in mankind's reappraisal of his position in the universe: "Our views of the human future must be greatly modified by these events.... The broadening of men's views that has resulted can scarcely be exaggerated. Before the cylinder fell there was a general persuasion that through all the deep of space no life existed beyond the petty surface of our minute sphere. Now we see further" (*War* 142). In regards to this, Parrinder states: "In *the War of the Worlds* we are told at the outset that the humanist conception of the universe has been shattered by the Martian invasion" (*Shadows* 120), and as Bukatman observes, this facilitates "an opportunity to reconsider human purpose" (Bukatman 17). We can view these reactions to the near annihilation of the human race from a Deleuzian perspective. This ties once again into the geographical and geological metaphors that are consistent in Deleuze's work, such as smooth and striated spaces, and the Earth as an illustration of the full body without organs. From *A Thousand Plateaus* to *What Is Philosophy?*, the concept of geological catastrophism is expressed through the ever-present processes of deterritorialization and reterritorialization; no well-defined territory is safe or static; it is constantly undone and remade (Ansell Pearson *Engineer* 234). Though species become "settled and attached to a particular form, they are the results of a series of dramatic changes, and they are destined to be engulfed by further ones; identity must be understood in terms of a potentiality that can come to destroy it" (235).

So in Deleuzian terms, catastrophe is only a stage that allows us to express the differential changes that underlie identity, in a world that is committed to identity and representation. Once these changes are expressed and understood our commitment to identity disappears and with it the need to relate to change purely in terms of the extreme violence of catastrophe. In its place, Deleuze puts forward the doctrine of "counteractualization," that is, the practice of expressing the catastrophic changes that come to constitute and destroy any actuality. In other words, disaster and destruction must be present in all things and must be put into motion in all great creations; there can be no construction without destruction. Gary Genosko provides a summary of this mode of thought: "For Deleuze disaster and destruction must be present in all things and must be put into motion in all great creations ... his reasons are not simply millenarian or tragic in the sense of the final disaster or undoing ... his catastrophe is any event 'subverting a system of things.' The subversion of systematicity and identity is the attraction of catastrophe rather that the harsh lessons of its violence" (Genosko 163).

Deleuze uses the examples of the disappearance of familiar landscapes and the creation of unfamiliar terrain, using examples of volcanic eruption, tidal waves or earthquakes. These life-shattering events, according to Deleuze, provide a turning point, allowing "the emergence of another world into the work" (*Bacon* 49); the near extermination of human life and collapse of civilization in the novel is just such an event, resulting in "the emergence of another world," or in the words of Wells's narrator, "it may be that in the larger design of the universe this invasion from Mars is not without its ultimate benefit for men; it has robbed us of the serene confidence in the future that is the most fruitful source of decadence, the gifts to human science that it has brought have been enormous, and it has done much to promote the conception of the commonwealth of mankind" (*War* 141).

The Martians' invasion leads to a planetary unification (a notion of humankind joined in opposition to the extraterrestrial threat) and, in doing so, existing social distinctions become obsolete or provisional in the struggle for survival.[21] Interestingly, here the emphasis is strictly on rational discourse; science has benefited, but the religion personified by the curate remains irrelevant. Possibly the most often quoted, and also arguably the most misunderstood paragraph from *The War of the Worlds* concerns the final death of the antagonists themselves: "laid in a row, were the Martians—dead!–slain by the putrefactive and disease bacteria against which their systems were unprepared; slain as the red

Two—*The War of the Worlds*

weed was being slain; slain, after all man's devices had failed, by the humblest things that God, in his wisdom, has put upon this earth" (133). Far from ending the novel with a last-minute affirmation as to humanity's triumphal destiny (Bukatman 17) as is often interpreted (as in Pal's 1953 film version, for example, in which humanity being saved by bacteria smacks both of a divine affirmation of humanity and retribution cast upon their desecrators), this is in fact "a profound humiliation for man [who] had not conquered" (Clarke, *Ignatius* 85). Or, in narrative terms, "hubris followed by nemesis ... logic so neatly rounded that it speaks of poetic even more than of scientific or cognitive justice" (Parrinder *Shadows* 11). Wells's sentiments in fact anticipate Deleuze's views regarding the role of the divine in catastrophic events, in that Deleuze is adamantly against any rationalization of catastrophe and destruction through divine processes of the transcendent: "disaster cannot be redeemed by reference to a will outside this world" (Ansell Pearson *Engineer* 236). Ansell Pearson equates Deleuze's views to those of Spinoza, as both philosophers despise those who do believe in such illusions: "among so many conveniences in nature they had to find so many inconveniences; storms, earthquakes, diseases, and the like. These they maintain happen because the Gods are angry on account of wrongs done to them by men" (Spinoza "Ethics" 111). The attitudes of the narrator and the curate reflect this; for Wells the curate undoubtedly represented the bankruptcy of established religion in the face of new scientific paradigms, whether they brought benefits or disasters. The Martians themselves are without pity, but also without rancor, and the narrator scorns any idea of divine retribution, instead equates the invasion to a natural disaster: "Think of what earthquakes and floods, wars and volcanoes, have done before to men! Did you think God had exempted Weybridge? He is not an insurance agent!" (*War* 54).

Despite this unification through disaster, questions are still raised as to the ultimate future of the human race, specifically in regards to the morality of expanding the reach of their empire beyond the limits of the Earth, even if it be through necessity: "When the slow cooling of the sun makes this earth uninhabitable, as at last it must do, it may be that the thread of life that has begun here will have streamed out and caught our sister planet within its coils. Should we conquer?" (194). Despite the "broadening of men's views" (142), relative normality (and hence imperialism and capitalism)[22] appear to have been restored.

Wells Meets Deleuze

Finishing on an ambivalent note, the novel questions whether mankind will suffer the same fate as the Martians; whether we are destined to repeat the path, both evolutionary and ideologically, that will result in humanity ultimately being indistinguishable from their Martian foes. Read in Deleuzian terms, the issue here is whether humanity can avoid the fate of the cancerous body without organs, and not be trapped in a perpetual loop of endless reproduction of the self-same pattern; if a culture cannot be reterritorialized, it collapses into cancerous inertness, and it is ultimately with this dilemma that the novel concludes.[23] In *Anti-Oedipus*, Deleuze and Guattari state that the creativity of evolution should be understood in terms of the production of machines: "Everywhere it is machines—real ones, not figurative ones: machines driving other machines, machines being driven by other machines, with all the necessary couplings and connections" (*Anti* 1). So, all organisms, in this sense, are cybernetic from the outset. As previously explored, the humans are already Martians; hence, by extension, the humans have always been cyborgs. In many ways, the irony of *The War of the Worlds* is obvious: because the Martians have rejected and become dissociated from the organic, they are at its mercy, whether in their unwieldy bodies, their pain in Earth air or gravitation, or their deaths through infection. The surest machines, Wells seems to be saying are not those that divorce mind from matter or separate technology from nature, but those that are organically and viscerally integrated, as man, through long ages of vicissitude, has become resistant to many germs of disease (Manlove 237): "By the toll of a billion deaths, man has bought his birthright of the earth, and it is him against all comers; it would still be his were the Martians ten times as mighty as they are. For neither do men live nor die in vain" (*War* 283). It would appear that in Deleuzian terms, this statement remains true, albeit in an ironic fashion; even if the Martians were "ten times as mighty" and succeeded in their invasion, then mankind would still own his "birthright of the earth" (134), for man and Martian are one and the same.

So in Deleuzian terms, ultimately the crux of the novel is the question as to whether mankind can achieve the journey towards becoming a full body without organs, without suffering the same fate as the Martians and collapsing into cancerous inertness. Wagar concludes *H.G Wells: Traversing Time* with much the same question in relation to the "real-life" possibility of Wells's proposed "World State": "He pointed

Two—*The War of the Worlds*

us in the right direction, but is anyone really following? Is there a shape of things to come.... The easy answer is no. The hard answer is no. Wells's last answer was no. This may be the right answer. It may be the wrong answer.... As Wells might have said, the world state lies in the womb of time, but whether it will be born live and grow to maturity is not assured, or even likely" (277). Just as Wagar uses "womb" as a metaphor for the potential gestation of Wells's ideas over time, Deleuze on occasion refers to the body without organs as an "egg" which in its incubation is conceptually full of potential traits and desires: "The egg is the body without organs.... The body without organs is desire; it is that which one desires and by which one desires.... Even when it falls into the void of too-sudden destratification, or into the proliferation of a cancerous stratum, it is still desire. Desire stretches that far: desiring one's own annihilation, or desiring the power to annihilate" (*Thousand* 182–183). Hence, through the medium of the body without organs, humanity as depicted in the novel and Wells's audience in the "real world" become indistinguishable from one another. Analogously, the finale of *The War of the Worlds* can be equated with the novel itself as a machinic cultural object. Just as the near-destruction of the Earth brings about reflection and ideological reappraisal (albeit with ambiguous results), Wells's novel has had a momentous cultural impact and (although not resulting in the societal revolution that he desired) his prophetic warnings to humanity are still being rhizomorphically extrapolated in many diverse forms; literature, cinema, sf, politics, ad infinitum. It is therefore fitting that Deleuze described the writer or artist as a potential "cosmic artisan: a homemade atomic bomb" (*Thousand* 380), an axiom than can readily be applied to Wells, whose vision remains "imperative" in our contemporary day and age (Wagar *Traversing* 277). Continuing from this, the next chapter, via the medium of *The Time Machine*, argues that Wells's vision provides a unique perspective not just on humanity, but also in terms of the very essence of time itself.

Three

The Time Machine
Time Travel, Crystals and Nomads

> What makes it serious is that we know that after the order of this world there is another. What is it like?
>
> —Artaud "To Have Done with the Judgment of God" 562

Time Travel Narratives

A text of great cultural significance, *The Time Machine* has been the subject of a vast ream of critical analysis since its publication, exploring variously its position as social commentary, its function as an exposition of Darwinian theory, and in terms of more recent criticism, its stance in the light of the development of psychoanalytic, postmodern and poststructuralist theories. Obviously a Deleuzian encounter will provide something different from these interpretations. This chapter utilizes two specific elements of Deleuzian theory in its reading of *The Time Machine*; the first section expands upon prior poststructural interpretations forwarded by Hollinger and Hardy, and demonstrates how the novel can be read in terms of the Deleuzian understanding of time and memory. Secondly, the novel is positioned in the context of Deleuze's political philosophy, using the character of Wells's time traveler as an exemplification of the concept of "nomadic thought." Again, these various processes shall naturally be rhizomorphic, demonstrating multiple connections between various elements of the text and theory.

The Time Machine, along with *The War of the Worlds*, is arguably

Three—*The Time Machine*

the best known and most influential work of Wells's entire oeuvre, and is responsible for inspiring the entire sf time travel genre: "Science fiction is, in essence, a time travel genre. Events either open in the altered past, the transformed present, or the possible future, transporting the reader or viewer to another age, place, dimension or world.... When science fiction time travels one truly knows that one is in science fiction ... time travel provides the futuristic narrative dynamic needed for the genre" (Redmond 114). Although *The Time Machine* was by no means the first piece of fiction to explore the concept of travelling through time, its significance lies in its pseudoscientific explanation of how time travel could possibly occur, and is thus credited with the universal popularization of the concept of time travel using a vehicle that allows an operator to travel purposefully and selectively. In its extrapolation from Wells's text, time travel in sf, with its paradoxes, ruptures, alterations and juxtapositions of past, present and future has "not passed with any modernist vogue, nor succumbed to postmodernist temptations for closure" but rather is "perhaps the hardiest form of sf" (Slusser "Spacetime" 181). Time travel narratives prompt us to ask intriguing questions about causality, identity, cognition and even ethics. Due to *The Time Machine's* eminent position as the work of fiction that popularized the concept of vehicular-controlled time travel, a multitude of other time travel narratives, in literature, cinema and other media, have consequently used the same archetype.[1] Although these subsequent narratives may feature a more complex structure, include time-loops and paradoxes not featured in Wells's novel (although the often assumed simplicity of Wells's time model is subsequently debated), they could be argued to still be existing (i.e., utilizing time) within the context of a Wellsian universe.[2] All such issues as depicted in fiction have their origin in the paradoxical idea of time travel, all derived (despite the novel not containing all of the features above) from Wells's time traveler who "flung [him]self into futurity" (*Time* 17–18).

Time travel stories through the medium of dreams and altered mental states are to be found throughout literary history, the "Sleeping Beauty" fairytale being an obvious example.[3] Madeline Stern relates that "about 600 AD Gregory of Tours told the story of the Seven Sleepers of Ephesus who slept for three hundred and seventy two years.... Let us not forget too that Mohammed had 90,000 conversations with God whilst he washed his hands. So the mind vanquishes time" (Stern

Wells Meets Deleuze

338–340). Wells also used this device in the novel *The Sleeper Awakes* (1910) in which the protagonist sleeps for over two centuries, awaking to a dystopian future. However, it is not until the mid-nineteenth century we are witness to the popular emergence of the literary time travel narrative that uses techniques other than over-sleeping to produce temporal displacement.[4]

The time travel technique is a useful vehicle for social criticism via the depiction of dystopian futures, though sometimes it is just a fantasy device for its own sake. *The Time Machine* is often positioned as an example for the former, depicting a world where humanity has degenerated into two distinct forms, one of which lives underground, controls machinery and practices cannibalism, while the other lives an emotionally immature, apathetic life above ground, not unlike that of grazing cattle. Obviously, in accordance to this interpretation, in order to extrapolate these evolutionary conceits to their furthest conclusion, a protracted period of time has to pass, so Wells required a special literary technique to plausibly present his version of a possible future. He solved this, ingeniously and very originally, by the invention of the time machine: an instrument that carries his hero to any temporal location he chooses. So tremendous is Wells's impact on the concept of time travel in fiction that he has ultimately become its synonym: when film, television or literature wish to work with the concept, Wells himself is often inserted as a character.[5]

The novella initially appeared in serialized form as "The Chronic Argonauts" in *The Science School Journal* in April 1888; it was then revised and published as *The Time Machine* in *The National Observer* in 1894 and *The New Review* in January 1895. Wells revised the story again for the Atlantic Edition, published in 1924, and since its initial appearance in book form, *The Time Machine* has never been out of print. Its influence can be seen in the manner in which its ideas have shaped modern sf, as well as its continued adaptation into various formats, including films (in 1960 and 2002 respectively, the latter directed by Wells's great grandson, Simon Wells), comics, and various sanctioned and unofficial sequels (Stephen Baxter's 1995 novel *The Time Ships* being an example of the former, and David Haden's 2010 *The Time Machine: A Sequel* of the latter). Gary Westfahl attempts to summarize the novel's appeal, claiming that it "encapsulates almost everything that characterizes the [sf] genre, from its nerdish opening

Three—*The Time Machine*

discussion of scientific ideas to its exotic adventures in a simultaneously futuristic and reprimitivized environment, all preceding a chilling final vista of cosmic futility and extinction" (Westfahl "Tainted" n. pag.). Hollinger concurs, emphasizing the transdisciplinary appeal of the novel:

> The idea of time travel has for many years exercised the ingenuity not only of sf writers, but of scientists and philosophers as well; neither the equations of quantum physics nor the rules of logic have managed definitively to prove or to disprove the possibility that this most paradoxical of sf concepts may someday be realized.... H. G. Wells's *The Time Machine*, the novella which first applied technology to time travel ... remains the most influential time-travel story ever written [Hollinger 201].

Subsequent to *The Time Machine*, time travel has become an intrinsic ingredient in popular culture, with a seemingly endless succession of novels, short stories, films and television programs featuring, in one of its many forms, time travel as a dramatic device. Correspondingly there is also a vast amount of literature documenting reactions to time travel narratives; whether such ideas are coherent, whether they are consistent with the understandings of modern physics, and what it would mean to be in the position of a time traveler. One only has to look at the large number of websites dedicated to unraveling the paradoxes found in popular time-travel films, such as *The Terminator* series and the *Back to the Future* trilogy, to see the prominent position that the concept occupies in the popular imagination.[6] The more conjectural implications originated by *The Time Machine* have long since crossed over to the scientific disciplines, with branches of speculative metaphysics occupied with discussions as to the validity of Wells's time travel vehicle; one such example is the essay "H. G. Wells: Why His Time Machine Won't Work" in Paul J. Nahin's *Time Travel in Physics, Metaphysics and Science Fiction* (1999). Nahin's objections are based on the fact that "as it travels through time, the machine must always be located in the same place ... a Wellsian-type time machine would have to occupy every instant of the intervening century and more. For observers outside the machine, [it] would appear to be sitting in the same place for all those years."[7] Nahin does conclude however that "Wells himself was well aware of the loss of story-telling credibility that such immobility entails, and he tried to explain the problem away" (25) citing the time travelers account of the time travelling process: "so long as I travelled through time.... I was, so to speak, attenuated—was slipping like a vapour through the interstices of intervening substances!" (*Time* 18).

Significantly, the questioning of the credibility of Wells's narrative device, and the possibility of an incredulous response from the novel's audience, is reflected in the narrative itself. Though he returns to the time and place where his journey began, the time traveler himself does not have a happy homecoming; his audience (a representative ensemble of professionals from the author's time) to whom he recounts his adventures in the far future do not believe his story. Only one member of the gathering, the unnamed primary narrator, makes an effort to suspend his disbelief, and even he remains strictly a man of his time, hoping that if the traveler were to go to the future again would choose "one of the nearer ages, where men are still men" (82), while his epilogue contains trite platitudes about the human race enduring in "gratitude and mutual tenderness" (82). Indeed, against all the evidence that the time traveler has presented to him in his account of his future experiences, he maintains that "it remains for us to live as if it were not so" (82). The reaction of the fictional audience corresponds with the initial skeptical critical response to the novel, Wells's Victorian peers believing time travel, even as a literary device, to be an outrageous conceit, with magazine reviews in the *Spectator* and *Daily Chronicle* referring to the novel as "hocus-pocus ... a fanciful and lively dream" and "bizarre" respectively, with such a reaction perpetuating for decades (Nahin 22). In the intervening century, *The Time Machine* has been critically reclaimed from these early dismissals, and is now lauded as a vital work. However, in discussing the shifting audience response over time, Slusser makes a very interesting statement:

> He [Wells] was writing, it seems, for a virtual audience, for the audience that would exist in the twentieth century and beyond, an audience that would grapple with such "wonders" as the fourth dimension, temporary displacement, time machines. All disciplines, scientific or literary, that were represented among the traveller's audience of professionals remained closed to the message of the future. For Wells's virtual audience, however—the readers we have become—these same disciplines have become dialogue partners, wrestling with the multiple complexities of the author's visionary work [Slusser *Perennial* 2001 xii].

Obviously Slusser does not intend his use of the term "virtual" to equate with the Deleuzian understanding of the term, but his claim does indeed resonate with a statement from *What Is Philosophy?*: "The creation of concepts in itself calls for a future form, for a new earth and people that do not yet exist" (*Philosophy* 108). Hence it is indeed through the concept of the Deleuzian virtual that we can imbue the text with a more radical reading, in this case, in its approaches to time, and the significance of the time traveler himself as a manifestation of concepts.

It is not the purpose of this analysis to claim that the novel subscribes exactly to the various aspects of Deleuzian time-theory (which is extremely complex and multifaceted), but it is posited that this method allows us to see a sense of anticipation of various poststructural approaches to temporality within *The Time Machine*. There has been much prior criticism (literary, scientific and philosophically based) as to the use and purpose of time within the novel, and a Deleuzian reading provides an alternative to these approaches. Issues of time are also inherently related to scientific discourse; however it is not the purpose of this investigation to debate Einsteinian or Newtonian physics. Hollinger makes an insightful observation on this point:

> Scientific discourse admits its own status as metaphor. Time has no reality outside our interpretations and it invites a potentially vast variety of possible "readings." In poststructuralist epistemology, of which Relativity Theory is one expression, this opposition has been subverted. Science, no longer privileged, has become subsumed under fiction as a particular system of discourse, and this has greatly expanded the possibilities for sf's explorations of the nature and structure of time [Hollinger 208].

Ultimately, if the text is to be understood in a Deleuzian context, we need to go beyond its actual elements; not just what it says, but beyond its manifest context, to the virtual problem from which the text is actualized (Colebrook "Actuality" 10). In Deleuzian terms, *The Time Machine* is the "virtual consciousness" (Moulard-Leonard 41) of these formations.

Rhizomes of Time and Memory

Through the medium of its fictional narrative, Wells's novel gives us his audience the capacity to step outside chronological time, and as a result facilitates our questioning as to its workings, and our place within it. Time is a vital element of Deleuze's philosophical encounter with literature, and he claims that the capacity to rethink time is one of the driving forces of art and philosophy. In this way, methods of thinking embodied in art and philosophy are not just idle cognitions, they are the very medium through which we become. This is more than just conjectural philosophy; it is only if we can rethink time, Deleuze argues, that we will be able to transform ourselves and our future (Colebrook *Gilles Deleuze* 37), and through the medium of literature (and cinema) we can free our perceptions of the world from a fixed and conventional viewpoint, thus bringing about transformation.

In thinking about the events that make up "the passage of time," narrative practice is not just informed by the idea of a linear sequenced sense of time, but also by notions of what time is, particularly in its relationship to memory. Deleuze draws on Henri Bergson's notion that time is a "thickness" of which the present is just a part, and in which the virtual past and the actual present co-exist. As previously discussed, this distinction between the virtual and actual is not a distinction between "not real" and "real." Deleuze demonstrates this by giving the example of a memory, which can interrupt the actual present because it sits virtually alongside the present (May 49). This implies that although memory is the conscious recollection of past events, these events are not recalled as discrete segments that can be separated into the past, the present and the future. Rather they are remembered in both the time in which the event took place and in the entire multiplicity of our lived past, which acts as a context for the memory: "the past does not follow the present that is no longer, it coexists with the present it was. The present is the actual image, and its contemporaneous past is the virtual image, the image in a mirror" (Deleuze *Cin2* 79). Correspondingly, in literature, Deleuze maintains that a character's linear chronological experiences can be disrupted by an event from the "past," which can take the form of memory. *The Time Machine* provides examples of these disruptions. In the opening of the novel, the time traveler's gathered audience are highly skeptical towards his invention. When the time traveler refutes his companion's claims that time travel is not possible, he uses memory as an example: "you are wrong to say that we cannot move about in time. For instance, if I am recalling an incident very vividly I go back to the instant of its occurrence: I jump back for a moment" (*Time* 6). From the Deleuzian perspective, this is not a jump into the past per se, but a jump into the virtual. This serves

Three—*The Time Machine*

as an illustration of Deleuze's claim that all history is timeless, in that it is contemporaneous with us, and we can "leap" to different parts or "sheets" of history, or past moments, and from past moments to other past moments, in no chronological order (*Cin2* 98–100). This takes the form of a two-step process: firstly, memory is accessed by means of a "leap into the past," enabling the most relevant plane to be located. Secondly, memory is brought into presence and given a new "life" or context in terms of the current circumstances (Stagoll "Memory" 160). This results in a special kind of synthesis that Deleuze considers to be essential to the flow of lived time. In this way, memory gives rise to the impression of a consistent and unifying self.

Correspondingly, the novel demonstrates the time traveler experiencing just such a lack of consistency of self, due to failures of memory. The significance of memory is an intrinsic theme in *The Time Machine*, and there are multiple references to memory, and the problems related with its inadequacy. To cite a few examples; confronted with the future dystopia, the time traveler laments that "the mere memory of Man as I knew him, had been swept out of existence" (*Time* 55). Subsequently, upon his return from the future, he is on the brink of self denial as to the authenticity of his story: "I'm damned if it isn't all going. This room and you and the atmosphere of every day is too much for my memory.... Did I ever make a time machine.... Or is it all only a dream?" (79). Michael Tague discusses memory in regards to physical edifices found in the future world, positing The White Sphinx and The Palace of Green Porcelain as "monuments only to the failure of memory" (Tague 9). The former provides a significant moment of memory's confusion when the time traveler realizes somebody or something has stolen his time machine: "I looked at the lawn again. A queer doubt chilled my complacency. 'No,' said I stoutly to myself, 'that was not the lawn.' But it *was* the lawn. For the white leprous face of the sphinx was towards it. Can you imagine what I felt as this conviction came home to me? But you cannot. The Time Machine was gone!" (*Time* 31). If we are to elaborate upon this argument in Deleuzian terms; the machine itself, the device by which the time traveler experiences time, is intrinsically tied to his memory, and hence sense of self. With the loss of his machine, the traveler can no longer return home; his literal ability to "leap into the past" and to locate a "relevant plane" is denied to him, resulting in the loss of memory and self.

Wells Meets Deleuze

Despite being a museum, and hence constructed solely for purposes of recollection, The Palace of Green Porcelain prevents the time traveler from remembering a single day, let alone the epochs of time it was intended to preserve; in recounting his explorations, the time traveler admits that he "cannot tell you all the story of that long afternoon" (61). Besides this failure of memory, the time traveler also learns nothing about the past, present or future in the museum. This unsound sort of remembrance, along with the incredible lack of basic retention that the Eloi display throughout the novel, is ultimately compounded by the lack of credibility we must place in the narrator who propounds it, in that at the novel's conclusion he seems to ignore the time traveler's entire tale (Tague 10). These failures can be related to Deleuze's writings in *Cinema 2*, in which he disputes the ability to ever find the truth of a historical event. The very sense of history itself is "lost in its discursive representation, in the layers of words and things that build up over it. Yet it is only by being inscribed in this way that it can be said to occur at all" (Marks, Laura "Politics" 245). The time traveler's "historical event" is ironically his future, which is subsequently lost through his attempts to "represent" it to others. Not only does he himself have doubts as to its occurrence, those to whom he relates his tale do not believe him, and neither does the narrator of the story itself, hence history is ultimately lost.

Deleuze puts forward the idea that in relation to time, rather than processing all of the differences that make up the flow of time, we edit and "fold" perceptions around our own sets of established concepts and stories. This forms the basis from which we act in the world: we use time to chart the changes around us, and the past exists as a series of images that we recall in order to live the present and future (Colebrook *Gilles Deleuze* 32). Hence the human perception of time is specifically located, with our past consisting of images that are recalled in order to position, and consequently make sense of, our present and future. In other words, we use our fixed point of observation to chart the changes that we perceive around us. In accordance, for Deleuze the power of literature (and cinema) lies in the manner in which they are able to give us both direct and indirect images of time itself that are not derived purely from movement; these take the form of the "movement image" and "time-image," which are discussed subsequently. Using the various Deleuzian approaches to time, we are able to examine the many processes occurring within the course of the narrative of *The Time Machine*. As with all fictions depicting the process of time travel, the novel raises various questions regarding philosophy and time; principally, the nature of how we "inhabit" time itself, and what it means for us to "endure" within the movement of time.

For Deleuze then, time is a rhizomatic multiplicity of singularities or "events," all of which are in motion, and exist simultaneously across many times. As an extrapolation of this, the concept of time travel itself in sf equates to rhizomatic as opposed to arboreal movement. Through the process of travelling through time, the very nature of linear chronological progression is disrupted: each random point in history becomes linked and accessible to other random points. Time is no longer a linear process; there are no logical consecutive events, but rather a system of connections without beginning and end, hence time itself becomes the ultimate rhizome. *The Time Machine* demonstrates this in a number of ways, which are now elaborated on.

Temporality and the Time Travel Narrative

If we are to view time as rhizomorphic, as opposed to arboreal, linear and sequential, how does this affect a reading of *The Time Machine*, both as a cultural object and as a narrative? At the simplest level the concept of temporality in a book or film is intrinsic to their very nature; both unfold in time, requiring duration to watch or read. More complex temporalities are transmitted through the various narrative layers, and most obviously time can be the book or film's subject or theme, either overtly or covertly; time can be a way of establishing a narrative,[8] or be an implicit premise, as present in *The Time Machine* and all the subsequent time travel stories that it has inspired. The organization of time is obviously vital to the time-travel narrative itself. However, when literature fractures the chronological order of time, it allows moments to be related to one another in multiple and non-linear ways. In such narratives, the beginning and end of a text take on a different role, not ceasing to exist, but marking the limits between which (for example) the time traveler is able to move, as an infinite number of journeys can be made within these limits. Deleuze maintains that this is the greatest thing that literature can do; we are released from finite and linear time: "Within the finitude of life (bounded by birth and death) there lies an infinity, since moments are not traversed only once and in only one direction, but an infinite number of times, from innumerable directions. Life, then, or what is 'in the middle' is raised to an infinite power for the reader of literature who undergoes its effect of de-chronologisation" (Baugh 51–52). Of course, in *The Time Machine*, this de-chronologisation occurs not only as the active process of reading, but also within the construct of the narrative itself.

Despite (or, perhaps, because of) his rhizomatic vision of time, Deleuze (writing in *Proust and Signs*) expresses that he is keen to hold onto a reading of a novelist as a purveyor of time. For example, if we do not grant an important role to time in the construction of the novel we lose all sense of the apprenticeship undergone by the narrator or the hero; in simple but vital terms, such things "take time." Deleuze writes that what is important is "that the hero does not know certain things at the start, gradually learns them, and finally receives an ultimate revelation" (*Proust* 26). This is certainly true of the time traveler, who is on a gradual journey of discovery, and it is only after many trials and false assumptions that he reaches the correct conclusion as to the true nature of the relationship between the Eloi and Morlocks. Hence, despite the chronological re-ordering inherent to the time travel process, a sense of order is clearly retained; this concept of disordered time ironically resulting in continuity will be further discussed subsequently.

In Cinema 1: The Movement Image (1983) and *Cinema 2: The Time-Image* (1989) Deleuze combines philosophy with film criticism, using the art form to formulate various conceits; theorizing time, movement and life as a whole (Colebrook *Gilles Deleuze* 29). Deleuze states in the preface of *Cinema 1* that "this study is not a history of cinema. It is a taxonomy, an attempt at the classifications of images and signs" (*Cin1* xiv), and later in *Negotiations* he claims that "there's a … period when I worked on painting and cinema: images on the face of it. But I was writing philosophy" (*Neg* 137). Though the concept of the time-image is provoked by cinema, it also enables us to rethink the very nature of concepts themselves. The more specific concepts contained within Deleuze's cinema theory will not be utilized, the emphasis here being *The Time Machine* as a work of literature, but the significance of time in the novel, combined with its close associations with

Three—*The Time Machine*

cinematic techniques, allows the use of the more general aspects of the theory, and through this it is argued that *The Time Machine* functions to create an image of time that is outside of the lived time of human experience.

In previous criticism, much has been made of *The Time Machine's* cinematic associations, which is unsurprising considering its chronological synchronicity with the development of this particular artistic medium; the novel was published in 1895, the same year that the Lumière brothers invented their "Cinèmatographe." Indeed, the emergence of time travel as a literary theme at the end of the nineteenth century may well be a phenomenon linked to the simultaneous emergence of cinema, with its capacity to manipulate the illusion of time (Coates 307). In *H. G. Wells: Modernity and the Movies* (2007) Williams explores many facets of the association between Wells and film, advocating him as a thinker who understood the social significance of this new technology, and as a writer whose prose itself invented cinematic devices. Williams concludes by positioning Wells as a prophet who foresaw the political and economic possibilities, as well as the dangers, of the moving image. Indeed, the manner in which Wells engages with the medium of film is "the most complete and complex among [late Victorian and Edwardian] writers, and in many ways his writing career ran parallel to the evolution of cinema" (Marcus "Literature" 337). This can be illustrated through the invocation of cinematic technique within *The Time Machine's* narrative; for example, as the time traveler first begins his journey into the future, he describes how the sun blurs across the sky, and the description of the alternation of light and darkness makes allusions to the flickering of early cinematic projectors: "The night came like the turning out of a lamp.... The laboratory grew faint and hazy.... To-morrow night came black, then day again, night again, day again, faster and faster still ... the twinkling succession of darkness and light was excessively painful to the eye" (*Time* 16). Compounding this analogy, the time traveler is invisible to the ages through which he passes as he observes events unfold outside his machine, just like the passive audience of a film. Williams states that, in narrative terms, the scientific romances as a whole display a cinematic self-reflexiveness; viewpoint and perspective are always foregrounded, while characters and narrators are constantly seeing or being seen through mediating frames (Williams, Keith *Modernism* 7). He elaborates: "Experimental intertextuality with cinema [was] arguably laid down by him [Wells]. For example: representations of relativistic 'space-time'; anatomisation of moment and movement; 'eidetic' or virtual visualisation; radical re-envisionings of subjectivity; 'optical' self-reflexivity; 'the cinematised city'; besides anticipatory critiques of film's manifold cultural, political and social impacts" (5).

Wells's definition of time travel as a visual experience, then, also suggests a commentary on technology's metaphysical effects. The time traveler's meddling with the chronological order of time is aligned with the newly prevalent treatment of time and movement by the cinema (Bruckner 66). Wells's depictions of alternate histories (within *The Time Machine* and *War of the Worlds*, for example) were in part informed by his anticipation of Einsteinian physics; this also suggests that he can be acknowledged for anticipating the new sense of temporality in modern thought and the temporal innovations present in much of pre-war modernist fiction and cinema. To this end, Hammond states that each of his novels is "a time machine, an argosy which permits the reader to escape from the tyranny of quotidian time into a world rich in possibilities of transcendence and wonder. By compelling the reader to define and redefine reality, Wells opens a door onto wider possibilities of perception" (Hammond *Modern* 70). In other words, the novel itself becomes a time machine, able to transport us to any era we desire.

As previously emphasized, in terms of influence, Wells's scientific romances (*The Time Machine* most obviously) also play with concepts of causality, space and time in ways that subsequently have become distinctive of film and other related media. Hence, to conceive of the fictional technology of the time machine is to imagine a vehicle, but also a kind of fantastic cinematic device allowing us to travel in time. Hollinger maintains that "it is first necessary to "read" time before writing a time-travel story," (201), stating that the time travel trope is "a sign without a referent, a linguistic construction originating in the metaphorical spatialization of temporality" (221). If time has classically been readable as a category of space, it becomes technologically writable with the emergence of the cluster of technologies that must have informed the original literary text: "clocks and watches, trains and their timetables, photographic motion studies, chronophotography, the kinetoscope" (Bruckner 66). The irony of this technical claim is not lost on Wells: in terms of a Deleuzian reading, his inaugural time

Three—*The Time Machine*

machine narrative is in fact a sharp critique of the "fourth dimension" concept itself, as shall now be discussed.

The Crystal Time Machine

In her primer *Understanding Deleuze*, by means of an introduction to the concept of the time-image, Colebrook refers to *The Time Machine* directly, positing it as an archetype of a narrative form that operates by directly thematizing the flow of time:

> [In] time-travel narratives ... more often than not the traveler moves along a line of unified time ... [in] H. G. Wells's *The Time-Machine*, for example, the central character ... moves back and forwards through history, as though the events of time were so many actual and already-given objects, with time being the chain upon which they are linked ... as if time were a single plane, with past and future in a linear causal sequence. Time is presented as nothing more than an actual series of events, with the future being the playing out of the possibilities in the past. The future can only be changed through an alteration in the actual events of the past [Colebrook *Understanding* 158].

Colebrook is hereby exemplifying *The Time Machine* as the antithesis of the Deleuzian model of time. For Deleuze, such a chronolinear concept of time (where time is a line and the past is behind us, the future before us, and the present is moving along this line into the future) simply does not make sense; as stated, for Deleuze the past exists only as memory and is entirely virtual. Only the present is actual, and it is impossible to measure, calculate, or separate it from the virtual past. Both past and present exist in every present instant, each doubling or reflecting the other; they are distinct, but indiscernible from one another (*Cin1* 50–52). Colebrook initially appears justified in defining the novel's depiction of time as a causal sequence; the narrator does indeed state that time is a fourth dimension through which his machine is capable of accelerating, both forward and in reverse. In claiming he can "stop or accelerate his drift along the Time-Dimension, or even turn about and travel the other way" (*Time* 6), he appears to be offering a model of movement through a chronologically linear sequence of events. However, it shall be argued that *The Time Machine* can in fact be understood in terms of providing an anticipation of the Deleuzian concept of time; that is, time as a rhizomatic multiplicity of singularities.

Wells Meets Deleuze

Hollinger argues that "the subversion of 19th-century scientific values which [the novel] undertakes on the level of narrative event is complemented on the level of textual discourse by its deconstruction of the metaphysics of presence" (221). This reading argues that through this process *The Time Machine* deconstructs the notion of absolute, chronologically progressive time, as it frees the perception of time from a standard fixed and ordered viewpoint. Although (as Colebrook maintains) the novel appears to present us with a clear sense of the past, present and future as the time traveler journeys from his present day to the future and back, this is complicated by several factors, such as the narrator's temporal positioning, as well as our position as contemporary readers. The time traveler's initial "present" (the Victorian era) becomes his "past" (when he is in the future dystopia of the Eloi and Morlocks), and his Victorian point of origin is in actuality our (as twenty-first century readers) past. His discoveries in the Palace of Green Porcelain are a good example of this temporal anachronism: upon entering he has the gradual revelation that the building is a museum, filled with relics and artifacts from a past age (in the fields of natural history, paleontology, and geology: books, skeletons and machines are specifically referenced) that is in fact his own future. The time traveler cannot however make sense of the majority of the objects or machines, making "only the vaguest guesses at what they were for" (*Time* 59). In Deleuzian terms, these objects have been subject to deterritorialization; as culturally and time specific subjects and objects, they have been removed from their own locations in space and time, and hence these elements are indiscernible from one another. Some sense of the past does exist through the medium of these objects in that they have duration; they are aged and subject to decay. However, this past has become indistinguishable from the present, which is also subject to the entropy that the traveler associates with "humanity upon the wane" (27), and indeed from the future, that is to say, the future of the time traveler. Hence, in keeping with a Deleuzian conception, time is "no longer reduced to the thread of chronology where present, past, and future are aligned on a continuum" (Rodowick 4). Hardy places this argument not only in terms of the novel's narrative, but also its discourse, stating that "an analysis of the narrative structure shows that neither the story (sequence of events) nor the discourse (text) *of The Time Machine* is linear" (Hardy "Victorian" 88). In narrative terms the

Three—*The Time Machine*

time traveler returns, after only a few hours, to the very place he started from, while in terms of discourse, the whole of the text is an anachrony: "an external prolepsis because the events occur at a time in the future beyond the time limits of the framing story." Hence, "the effect of time's arrow in the narrative structure ... is in fact a sleight-of-hand" (89).[9]

In the essay "The Legacy of H.G Wells's The Time Machine: Destabilization and Observation," Joshua Stein takes this abandonment of linear time to its logical extreme, stating that the novel in fact fractures all concepts of chronological causality: "His [the time traveler's] tour of the Palace of Green Porcelain gives an overview of the meaningful inventions of humanity, yet his own machine is not included amongst these objects. Causality has started to fracture because of his presence in the future ... the traveler is visiting and consequently drawing conclusions from his own time based upon a future that is not his or his society's" (Stein 154). Stein places specific emphasis upon the flowers that the time traveler takes from the future to the past. It can be argued that this also demonstrates the effect that the deterritorialized Deleuzian object has upon the sense of chronological time itself: "Adding to the fragmentation is the presence of the flowers he brings back from the future ... this future anachronism suggests one reason he never returns [to the future]. Taken to logical extremes, the traveler could even now be ... creating more fragmentation by his actions; creating and recreating a möbius strip of possibilities that never repeats—a labyrinth of time that never ends nor reverses itself" (154).[10] Hollinger affirms this assessment: "there is no vantage point outside the boundaries of the observable, no privileged observer, no completely innocent reading of "reality"" (Hollinger 203). Hence, although *The Time Machine* would initially appear to have an internal chronological logic, in fact we find ourselves as readers "fractured in the labyrinth of time" (Marks, John "Vitalism" 150). In this manner, it is fitting to argue that this enables the positioning of Wells as a forerunner of poststructuralist attacks on formal unities and ideologies: "Subjectivity is never ours, it is time, that is, the soul, the spirit, the virtual," as Deleuze states in *Cinema 2: The Time Image* (82).

Interestingly, however, when we take away this organization of time, we are not left with a chaotic structure, but instead one that actually allows a remarkably smooth transition from past to present to future, and vice versa. The time traveler's journey opens up "unimaginable and almost meaningless expanses of time, yet paradoxically *The Time Machine* renders a thirty million year future thinkable.... That is the 'virtual reality' effect of the story's ... hold over the reader" (Parrinder *Shadows* 40). In this way, all aspects of time (past, present and future) are revealed as one: a "non-linear, non-subjective entity,"[11] and the time traveler has become one with time itself. In the words of Deleuze then, in actuality the text "unites all the dimensions of time, past, present and future, and causes them to be played out in the pure form" (*Difference* 140). This allows us to think of time in the novel in context of the Deleuzian crystal image, which can be defined thus:

> when we see actions linked up into an ordered sequence, then time is tamed, ordered and spatialized; but when an image of the past disrupts the present sequence of images, we see time not as an ordered sequence but as a virtual whole. The past, other narratives, other viewpoints, and other lines of time all co-exist but are ordered by our day- to-day perceptions ... the time-image allows for past perceptions to cut into the present, displaying the very potential of time: time as disruption of what is (the actual) by difference [Colebrook *Understanding* 159].

Deleuze states that the transcendental form of time is not ordinarily visible to us, which is why he comes up with an image of time to make it thinkable, which he calls the crystal-image:

> What constitutes the crystal-image is the most fundamental operation of time: since the past is constituted not after the present that it was but at the same time, time has to split itself in two at each moment as present and past, which differ from each other in nature, or, what amounts to the same thing, it has to split the present in two heterogeneous directions, one of which is launched towards the future while the other falls into the past [Deleuze *Cin2* 81].

The crystal-image, which forms the cornerstone of Deleuze's time-image, fuses the pastness of the recorded event with the presentness of its viewing. The virtual image is subjective, in the past, and recollected. The virtual image as "pure recollection" exists outside of consciousness, in time; it is always somewhere in the temporal past, but still alive and ready to be "recalled" by an actual image. The actual image is objective, in the present, and perceived. Crystal-images, formed by the collision of the actual and virtual, allow us to see time. We could look at the concept of virtual and actual image in general terms of the process of reading the novel; the virtual image refers to the time of the actual writing of the text, a time which is securely in

Three—*The Time Machine*

the past, existing outside of consciousness and time. However, the virtual images can be "recalled" by the actual image. The actual image then, in this case refers to the act of reading Wells's text. When the reader reads the book, they therefore experience the "pastness" of the "captured" moment along with the "presentness" of the act of viewing it (Totaro 1–2). The idea of the crystal-image is particularly interesting when applied to *The Time Machine* since the present/pastness of the concept is reflected in both the structure and the subject matter of the novel.[12] Through the crystal image, the novelist himself becomes the primary agent in the construction of truth, a falsifying character through his editing, writing and overall construction of the text. The writer serves as the creator of reality who determines the action and dictates the progression of time in the work, "provoking undecideable alternatives and inexplicable differences between the true and the false" (*Cin2* 132).

The time traveler's experiences upon the "terminal beach" of the far future provides us with a good exemplification of the crystal image; as he advances deep into the future, he "perceives the gravel and dust of memory on the empty fringes of consciousness ... he sees ice along the sea margin,[13] a double perspective of past and future that follows a projection that vanishes into a nonexistent present" (Smithson 332). As Deleuze states: "What is specific to the image ... is to make perceptible, to make visible, relationships of time which cannot be seen in the represented object and do not allow themselves to be reduced to the present" (*Cin2* 246).

That these examples of the crystal image can be located within *The Time Machine* is fitting, given its position as the instigator of fictional time travel; in fact one could go as far as stating that Wells's text has encouraged us (in terms of the inspiration that his sf time travel device has provided, both to writers of fiction, scientists, and cultural consciousness as a whole) to explore time in the same manner that Deleuze advocates through his use of his crystal image.[14] It is therefore suggested that *The Time Machine* provides just such examples of "visible relationships of time." As Hollinger states: "the time travel story provides literary metaphors of our ideas about the nature of time; it is a means of working out the logical (and not-so-logical) implications of our interpretations of this most nebulous aspect of human experience" (Hollinger 201).

Wells Meets Deleuze

As stated, for Deleuze history is timeless, all of history is contemporaneous with us, and we can "leap" to different parts or "sheets" of history, or past moments, and from past moments to other past moments, in no chronological order (*Cin2* 98–100). We do not bring these moments forward into the present, they are contemporary with us in every present moment; history is now. The present moment contains everything, all of the past, all of the present, and opens to all of the future. Ultimately, Deleuzian time-images offer the possibility of sensing "a realm of virtuality and potential, where the imaginary conjured is just as much as real as our everyday "reality" (Ashton 19), and therein lies the legacy of *The Time Machine*.

The second section of this chapter focuses upon a reading of the time traveler character specifically, utilizing Deleuze's political philosophy; issues pertaining to the virtual will be returned to at the chapter's conclusion, in order to unite these two approaches.

The Image of Thought and the Nomad

As established, in *The Time Machine* we are witness to a journey through time via the testimony (albeit secondhand) of Wells's nameless time traveler. Specific emphasis upon the character himself is important to this reading; indeed, Deleuze stated that literary characters struck him with the same force as philosophical concepts, as both possess their own autonomy and style. Compounding this, there are also stylistic concerns that are comparable in both philosophy and literature. Deleuze suggests that great literary characters are also great thinkers: just as a philosopher creates concepts, within literature a concept adopts the form of a character, and as a result the character takes on the various dimensions of the concept that was their genesis (Deleuze *Dialogues II* 113–115). Hence, from the Deleuzian perspective, a literary character is not a self-contained and unified subject within itself or within the novel in which it appears, but instead is an amalgamation of different relations and forces, these forces extending beyond the novel containing the character and into the social sphere. Therefore, Wells's time traveler is not something unified and self-contained, but becomes "a functioning of a polyvalent assemblage of which the solitary individual is only a part" (*Anti* 42). In accordance, through the time

Three—*The Time Machine*

traveler we can witness these individual forces and their function, both inside and outside the text.

Over the course of the novel's narrative, we witness the time traveler journeying from Victorian London to 802,701 AD, through till the ends of the earth, and then back again to his point of origin. As previously explored, as a result of this process, *The Time Machine* necessarily deconstructs the notion of absolute, chronologically progressive time, as it frees the perception of time from a standard fixed and ordered viewpoint. This we can interpret as performing an act of transgression of linear time, in so far as the time traveler is not restricted in linear chronometric progression as we (as readers without time machines) are. To elaborate upon this argument, the result is a transgression of what Deleuze describes as the "image of thought."

In *Difference and Repetition*, Deleuze sets his own philosophy against a history of philosophy that has begun from an image of thought. Deleuze argues that the traditional image of thought to be found in the philosophies of (for example) Aristotle and René Descartes, misconceives thinking as a relatively unproblematic, common sense affair. Within this tradition, notions of "truth" may be hard to discover; it may require a life of pure theorizing, rigorous computation or systematic doubt, but in principle this processes allow us to correctly grasp facts, ideas, and concepts. It may be practically impossible to attain a God's-eye, neutral point of view (of the universe or reality), but this is the ideal for which to aim: a disinterested pursuit that results in a determinate, fixed truth, an orderly extension of common sense. Deleuze however rejects this view, instead claiming that genuine thinking is a violent confrontation with reality, an involuntary rupture of established categories (*Neg* 136). Truth changes what we think (and vice versa) and it alters what we think is possible. By setting aside the assumption that thinking has a natural ability to recognize the truth, Deleuze says we attain a "thought without image," a thought always determined by problems themselves rather than by the solving of them. In relation to *The Time Machine*, Wells's time traveler refutes the traditional image of thought in his very first line of dialogue: "You must follow me carefully. I shall have to controvert one or two ideas that are almost universally accepted" (*Time* 3). Conversely, his peers demonstrate their subscription to the traditional image of thought through their incredulous reactions to his theories:

Wells Meets Deleuze

> The fact is, the Time Traveller was one of those men who are too clever to be believed ... [he] had more than a touch of whim among his elements, and we distrusted him.... So I don't think any of us said very much about time travelling ... though its odd potentialities ran, no doubt, in most of our minds: its plausibility, that is, its practical incredibleness, the curious possibilities of anachronism and of utter confusion it suggested [11].[15]

The time traveler remains unaffected by the skepticism of his peers towards new modes of thought: "my dear sir, that is just where you are wrong. This is just where the whole world has gone wrong" (5), and in beginning his journey through time, he literally becomes a manifestation of his desire to "controvert universal ideas."

Deleuze argues for the process of thought itself as just such an encounter: "Something in the world forces us to think" (*Difference* 176). Subsequent to his initial proclamations, the time traveler experiences such an encounter, obtaining the thought without image by directly experiencing Deleuze's "violent confrontation with reality," in the act of travelling through time. In keeping with the transgressive nature of the thought without image, this act is manifested in the text as being both violent and unpleasant: "I am afraid I cannot convey the peculiar sensations of time travelling. They are excessively unpleasant. There is a feeling exactly like that one has upon a switchback—of a helpless headlong motion! I felt the same horrible anticipation, too, of an imminent smash" (*Time* 17). In Deleuzian terms, this "imminent smash" becomes an "*immanent* smash," and can be equated to the casting off of the traditional image of thought, and the adoption of a thought without image. In the process of the classical image of thought being rejected (and in acknowledging Deleuze's belief that literary characters can function in the same manner as philosophical concepts),[16] it can be argued that the time traveler has opened up the possibility of attaining nomadic thought.

The concept of nomadology is expounded upon principally in *A Thousand Plateaus*, and as a construction of Deleuze and Guattari's "counter-philosophy," it functions to challenge authenticity and propriety. As previously explored, Deleuze speaks of traditional philosophy (and, by extension, traditional writing) as something that seeks to code the world and that which works within the codes of the world. Deleuze defined the term nomad thought as the philosophical process of thinking outside and across institutional boundaries; the decodification and

Three—*The Time Machine*

recodification of thought, and therefore maintained that as a device it can be used as an alternative approach to understanding the history of civilization. The concept of nomadic thought is used in conjunction with his rhizomatic approach; a biological organism that grows horizontally, sprouting out nodes, roots in all directions, the rhizome represents an encompassing mode of philosophy opposed to dualistic and binary systems that work through inter-connectedness. Writers (along with filmmakers and artists) can be nomadic in this sense, in that they explore the potential of their respective media, and then break away from established paths, using thinking that operates outside the conceptual structures endorsed by and supportive of the established order. Specific cultural texts can therefore be models of nomadic and rhizomatic writing. Such writing "weds a war machine and lines of flight, abandoning the strata, segmentarities, sedentary, the State apparatus" (*Thousand* 26). The following analysis is concerned with positing the character of the time traveler as a nomadic thinker, and as a consequence, a war machine.

Writing in *A Short History of the World* (1920), Wells himself discusses the nomad in an ideological and geographical sense: "A different way of living, the nomadic life, a life in constant movement ... but the reader must not suppose that theirs was necessarily a less highly developed way of living on that account. In many ways this free life was a fuller life than that of the tillers of the soil. The individual was more self-reliant; less of a unit in a crowd" (16). Deleuze takes these very ideas of movement and freedom and uses the nomad as a concept in distinction from the "sedentary point of view" (*Thousand* 25) that he believes characterizes much western philosophy, history and science, instead advocating a nomadic subjectivity that allows thought to move across conventional categories and hence against "settled" concepts and theories. In *A Thousand Plateaus*, Deleuze and Guattari consistently refer to this concept of a philosophical nomadism, by which they mean the creation of new enquires and approaches (or "lines of flight") that require an ability to think outside of the dominant structure, hence the making of new connections and affirmations. In a characteristic departure from the traditional sense of the term, for Deleuze, a nomad does not have to move: a nomad can practice nomadology while being in one place,[17] as nomadic journeys need not have relative movement, but they must have intensity (Thousand 420). It is hence the nomadology of thought that is the journey to new territories, through the processes of deterritorialization and reterritorialization: "the nomad moves, but while seated, and he is only seated while moving ... the nomad knows how to wait, he has infinite patience. Immobility and speed, catatonia and rush, a stationary process.... He is a vector of deterritorialization" (*Thousand* 420). By examining this quotation in detail we can see that specific Deleuzian-delineated traits and representations of the nomad are evident in the novel. The processes of time travelling with its "immobility and speed, catatonia and rush"; all of these sensations apply to the imagery of travelling through time, as the traveler accelerates and slows, slipping in and out of consciousness: "for an indefinite time I clung to the machine as it swayed and vibrated, quite unheeding how I went.... So I travelled, stopping ever and again, in great strides of a thousand years or more" (*Time* 74). The time traveler himself also adheres to this remit; as he sits stationary upon the saddle of his machine, he is not a nomad of place, but one of time.

This emphasis upon the journey (be it through time or space) can be compounded by Paul Patten's description of the Deleuzian nomad: "for the migrant or transhumant, a journey is simply a trajectory between two points, whereas for the nomad, it is the journey that matters, points along the way being no more than relay stations between successive stages.... Nomadic life is essentially en route" (Patten "Conceptual" 71–72). Although the novel may concentrate upon three distinct chronological points (the Victorian "present," dystopian "future," and the far future of the "terminal beach") it is (at least initially) the journey that matters for the time traveler, not the destination, and he has the whole of time at his disposal: "Upon that machine," he states, "I intend to explore time. Is that plain?" (*Time* 10).

Also implicit in nomadism is the belief in imagination and myth-making, as Rosi Braidotti suggests: "The choice of an iconoclastic, mythic figure such as the nomadic subject is consequently a move against the settled and conventional nature of theoretical and especially philosophical thinking" (Braidotti "Difference and Diversity" 4). Although traditional readings of Wells's time traveler vary considerably (placing him variously as the quintessential Victorian hero, the classic mad-scientist figure of sf, a fictional avatar of Thomas Edison or Wells himself, or merely a latter-nineteenth-century everyman), there is no doubt that he contains many traits of the "mythic figure" that Braidotti

Three—*The Time Machine*

identifies with the nomadic subject: "The time traveler stands for much that Wells would consistently praise: he is resourceful, intrepid, and intensely curious about the world he occupies; he is then linked to a long line of literary heroes, to Ulysses and Aeneas, bravely facing a series of hard tests and gaining wisdom as he goes" (Murray 89). In addition to this, Robert Begiebing's essay "The Mythic Hero in H. G. Wells's *The Time Machine*" maintains that the time traveler "exhibits at least three characteristics of the primordial heroic figure" (202), while Bergonzi's essay "*The Time Machine*: An Ironic Myth" (1960) makes a case for the attribution of mythic content not only to the one character, but to the novel as a whole. Bergonzi cities the intensity with which the time traveler's momentary sensations are registered (his sudden moods, sense of alienation, irrational fears), and combined this with the manner in which his tale is sequentially disrupted, resulting in a change of "localized meaningfulness," giving the story attributes of a dream, and the character mythical status (Bergonzi "Ironic" 39–55). If we are to take into account the examples above, we can state that the time traveler does indeed posses nomadic traits in both literal and ideological terms, and hence can be viewed as nomadic in the light of Deleuze and Guattari's concept; he is the mythic iconoclast, empowered by his abandonment of chronological time, with an impulse to take a "line of flight" from normalization. The nomad, in a state of flux, thus becomes a natural conduit for many of Deleuze and Guattari's theories. Establishing that the time traveler is in possession of nomadic traits allows us to pursue a rhizomorphic path through various other aspects of theory in order to determine what the time traveler is, in Deleuzian terms.

Having achieved nomadic thought, the time traveler is put in the position of being, potentially at least, a body without organs. As previously discussed, Deleuze and Guattari's body without organs is a deterritorialized body, one without organization, an empty potential assemblage: as previously explored, this constitutes "a body that breaks free from its socially articulated, disciplined, semioticized, and subjectified state (as an 'organism'), to become disarticulated, dismantled, and deterritorialized, and hence able to be reconstituted in a new way" (Best and Kellner 90–91). Suffice to say; Deleuze and Guattari group the body without organs and the nomad together, both being "desiring machines," and the nomadic body can therefore constitute a body without organs.

Wells Meets Deleuze

However, in terms of *The Time Machine*, despite possessing nomadic traits, the time traveler does not contain the theoretical potential to achieve the status of a body without organs; his inability to draw out these virtual potentials is related to the body without organs being an element of Deleuzian schizoanalysis (or schizophrenic process). Schizoanalysis is a critique of psychoanalysis that Deleuze performs primarily in *Anti-Oedipus*; in these terms, schizophrenia is not an illness, but a "potentially liberatory psychic condition produced within capitalistic social conditions, a product of absolute decoding" (90). The Deleuzian schizophrenic is not mentally ill, but have simply allowed themselves to be defined as a clinical entity within an Freudian Oedipal framework. Instead, schizophrenics who assume other identities and have multiple personalities have actually discovered a truth about the unconscious itself: that contrary to the orthodoxy of psychoanalysis, it is cosmically unconcerned with attachments to our mother and father and the unconscious. The idea here is that the schizophrenic can perform an exploration of their own identity as a collective persona, and hence experience growth and development that employs a multiplicity of character traits, which make use of the unconscious, of repressed memories and desires, in the way that the non-schizophrenic cannot. However, the time traveler is unable to actualize as a body without organs due to his inability to reject the Oedipalisation process.

Much has been made critically of the connections between *The Time Machine* and the Oedipal myth on which Freud based his psychological model. Just as with Oedipus, the time traveler exiles himself from his own "kingdom," by virtue of his travel into time. Upon his return from the future, he is described by the narrator as "walk[ing] with just such a limp as I have seen in footsore tramps" (*Time* 12), the name Oedipus of course deriving from the Greek meaning "swollen-footed." On his travels he encounters the White Sphinx,[18] and must retrieve his machine which is trapped inside. David Ketterer notes that "the presence of the Sphinx suggests that, like Oedipus, the Time Traveler must solve a riddle" (Ketterer "Oedipus" 340), while Frank Scafella also makes the implicit connection between the White Sphinx and the Sphinx of the Oedipus myth: "*The Time Machine* must be a variation of Oedipus's encounter with the Sphinx on the road to Thebes" (Scafella 255). The figure of the sphinx is also subject to examination in

Three—*The Time Machine*

Deleuze's *Difference and Repetition*, in which he posits the hybrid monster, long persisting in arts and culture, as a mythical mask of the questioning and problematic nature of the unconscious. The Deleuzian critique of capitalism posits the Sphinx as the "condition of impossibility" for Oedipal subjectivity; Oedipus is simultaneously the denial and the expression of a capitalism that, on the one hand, unpicks all identities, and on the other, is defined by its continual thwarting of final collapse into schizophrenia (*Difference* 131).

Deleuze claims the schizophrenic to be an "enemy of capitalism," someone "free to roam outside of predictable paths" who refuses to be sublimated: "The schizophrenic deliberately seeks out the very limit of capitalism: he is ... its proletariat, and its exterminating angel" (*Anti* 38). It would appear that the time traveler partially fulfills these roles; he is the product of the Victorian capitalistic society that has created the future world of the Morlocks and Eloi, and though initially subjugated by it (he is attacked by the Morlocks, and they steal his machine), he eventually confronts the monstrous mutations of capitalistic excess that the Morlocks literally embody. This does not however result in its extermination, as it is apparent that the time traveler is unable or unwilling to refute the Oedipalization that the schizophrenic denies. His paternal relationship with the Eloi Weena allows him to maintain a sense of normalcy in the otherwise anomalous future, by virtue of an adherence to Oedipal (in a psychoanalytic sense) family roles: "The creature's friendliness affected me exactly as a child's might have done.... She was exactly like a child ... she was somehow a very great comfort ... by merely seeming fond of me, and showing in her weak futile way that she cared for me, the little doll of a creature presently gave my return to the neighbourhood of the White Sphinx almost the feeling of coming home" (*Time* 38–39). Deleuze maintains that the Oedipal family structure is "one of the primary modes of restricting desire in capitalist societies" (Bogue *Deleuze and Guattari* 88), and in accordance to this, it is his attachment to Weena that prevents the actualization of the Deleuzian schizophrenic process, thereby not actualizing as a body without organs. However, the very possibility that this has at least the potential to occur does raise many interesting issues as to what exactly the time traveler is in terms of Deleuzian assemblages, leading to other potentialities. Hence, it may be problematic positing the time traveler as a body without organs or a schizophrenic, but a strong case can be made for him fulfilling the role of the Deleuzian nomadic war machine, in that he emblematizes resistant force against the all pervasive power of the state, which is manifested in the form of the Morlocks.

The Time Traveler as Nomadic War Machine

In further engaging in the political aspects of Deleuzian nomadology, correlations can be drawn between Deleuzian political theory, and the three specific "aspects" (Morlock, Eloi and the time traveler) that occupy *The Time Machine's* future dystopia. Wells's novel is traditionally read as a warning against capitalism continuing unregulated and unchecked, but Deleuze's ruminations upon capitalism and the relationship between state and nomad allow us to view the relationship between Morlock and Eloi in terms other than basic capitalism run amok, while emphasizing the role occupied by the time traveler.

In the novel, the relationship between the Morlocks and Eloi is essentially symbiotic, although ultimately somewhat one sided; the Eloi are clothed and fed by the Morlocks, and in return, the Morlocks literally consume the Eloi. This relationship can be equated with Deleuze's arguments concerning the nature of the relation between war and the state. In their position as the controlling power in the future society, the Morlocks can be equated with the state. Deleuze sees the state as more than simply a specific institution existing in a particular historical stage; it is an abstract principle of power and authority that has always existed in different forms, yet is somehow "more than" these particular actualizations. The relationship between the Eloi and the Morlocks can be expressed through Deleuze's two-pronged function of the state, as depicted in *A Thousand Plateaus:* "Undoubtedly, these two poles stand in opposition term by term, as the obscure and the clear, the violent and the calm, the quick and the weighty, the terrifying and the regulated.... But their opposition is only relative, they function as a pair" (*Thousand* 388). In literal terms, the Morlocks are indeed obscure, in that they are secreted in their subterranean lair. They commit acts of violence, and are terrifying: "[they] made me shudder.... I felt a peculiar shrinking from those pallid

Three—*The Time Machine*

bodies.... You can scarce imagine how nauseatingly inhuman they looked" (*Time* 50). Conversely the Eloi are calm and regulated "fragile thing[s] out of futurity" (21), who are bred and controlled: "very pleasant was their day, as pleasant as the day of the cattle in the field. Like the cattle, they knew of no enemies and provided against no needs. And their end was the same" (69). This opposition is "only relative," however, as they function in union as a pair, in a symbiotic (if parasitic) relationship.

However, in conjunction with this system there exists a counter-force to the state, and this introduces another element, that of the war machine, which can be equated with the time traveler and his emergence into the future world. The war machine is an abstract machine, existing in the virtual realm, as the time traveler does literally, being outside "real" time. A political element of the nomadology concept, the war machine is in opposition to the apparatus of the state, and can take a variety of forms; for examples, ideological, scientific, or artistic movements can be potential war machines (*Thousand* 466). If the Morlocks can be equated with the state, then it can be maintained that the time traveler acts as a nomadic war machine when he encounters them. War is not necessarily the prime activity of the war machine (given that the initial object of the machine war is defined as producing a variety of social relations other than war, something that escapes the state), but war is the "supplement" of the war machine, even if such a machine does not see destruction as its main object.

If this analogy is to be pursued further, it can be argued that if the Morlocks fulfill the role of manifestations of the state, then the Eloi can read as an example of supplementarity. This term refers to the ways in which a system of significations or structural arrangements cannot satisfactorily complete or enclose itself; supplementarity in this sense is less an accident or a failure of a system than it is its very possibility. The Eloi are more than the Morlocks need, and this has led to an imbalancing of their social system. The time traveler inadvertently refers to the danger of societal imbalance when he makes his initial (and, as he subsequently discovers, incorrect) observation that the future world is based on communist (and hence in his eyes, balanced) principles: "the institution of the family, and the differentiation of occupations are mere militant necessities of an age of physical force; [here, the] population is balanced and abundant, much childbearing becomes an evil rather than a blessing to the State" (*Time* 26). In *A Thousand Plateaus* Deleuze describes how, as an invention of the nomad, the war machine "does not necessarily have war as its object," but if war is the result, it is because of a collision with the state; when this occurs, the war machine then has the state as its enemy and "adopts as its objective their [the state's] annihilation" (*Thousand* 460).

Hence, the war machine is a tool of the nomad, engaging in a resistance to control, war being only a consequence, not the intended objective. The time traveler is repulsed by the Morlocks upon their initial encounter, and as a consequence of their various interactions and their attempts to suppress him (via the stealing of the time machine), he becomes increasingly hostile, and eventually conflict between the two erupts on a grand scale. It is precisely after the war machine has been appropriated by the state that it tends to take war as its direct and primary object. This can be read in terms of a literal appropriation: for example, when the Morlocks steal the time traveler's machine, or their abduction and (presumed) killing of Weena, which is ultimately what triggers the savage conflict between the time traveler and Morlocks, i.e., the nomad and the state. It is in the Morlocks' interest to subdue the war machine, vanquish nomadism and hence "to striate the space over which it [the state] reigns" (425); the motivation for their attacks upon the time traveler, and the theft of his machine can therefore be exemplified in Deleuze's statement: "each time there is an operation against the State—subordination, rioting, guerrilla warfare or revolution as act—it can be said that a war machine has revived, that a new nomadic potential has appeared" (426). It is for such reasons that Deleuze and Guattari place value in the nomadic warrior precisely because of its otherness to the subjugated subject of the state: "war kills, and hideously mutilates ... the State apparatus makes the mutilation, and even death, come first. It needs ... [its] people to be born that way, crippled and zombie-like. The myth of the zombie, of the living dead, is a work myth and not a war myth.... The State apparatus needs ... pre-disabled people, pre-existing amputees, the still-born, the congenitally infirm" (470). The Eloi, in their state of "intellectual degradation" (*Time* 56), certainly qualify as literal manifestations of the zombified, living dead required by the state in order that it might function correctly. George Pal's 1960 film adaptation of *The Time Machine* emphasizes this further: as in Wells's text, Pal's Eloi appear to live in

Three—*The Time Machine*

pastoral utopia from which want and danger have been eliminated, but they are in reality parasitic drones, summoned en masse to their fate at the hands of the Morlocks by a conditioned Pavlovian response to an air-raid siren. It is through examples such as these that the "lines of flight" between Wells's imaginary dystopia and Deleuzian theory can be demonstrated.

    Ultimately, it is through Deleuze's concept of the virtual that these various rhizomatic elements can be assembled. Where these can be unified is in Wells's visceral depiction of the struggle for natural selection. This occurs in chapter nine of the novel, when the time traveler is slaughtering the Morlocks in the forest at night: "I struggled up, shaking the human rats from me, and, holding the bar short, I thrust where I judged their faces might be. I could feel the succulent giving of flesh and bone under my blows, and for a moment I was free. The strange exultation that so often seems to accompany hard fighting came upon me. I knew that both I and Weena were lost, but I determined to make the Morlocks pay for their meat" (66). It is through this depiction of the struggle for survival that we can see that Wellsian Darwinism and Deleuzian nomadology can meet in geological time; obviously they are allowed to do this because this is fiction, through the medium of Wells's imagination. It can be argued however, that what we can take from this is that the fiction suggests that they could meet in virtual time. For Deleuze, the virtual is that which allows all forms of life to connect in a way that does not depend upon prior divisions:

> The artist and philosopher do not conjure things out of thin air, even if their conceptions and productions appear as utterly fantastical. Their compositions are only possible because they are able to connect, to tap into the virtual and immanent processes of machinic becoming (there are no points on the map, only lines), even if such a connection and tapping into are the most difficult things to lay hold of and demonstrate.... One can seek to show the power, the affectivity, the alienated character of thought. One is drawn to the land of the always near future, reading the signs, and decoding the secrets of intelligent alien life within and without us [Ansell Pearson *Difference Engineer* 4].

Hence the aforementioned "tapping into the virtual" opens up a possibility for it to become-actual. As the "presentation of the unconscious, not the representation of consciousness" (Deleuze *Difference* 241), this leads to laying out a plane of immanence, in order to "bring into being that which does not yet exist" (185). Hence, a philosopher (or, in this case, an author) becomes capable of traversing a "fundamental distinction between sub representative, unconscious and aconceptual ideas and the conscious conceptual representation of common sense" (Bogue *Deleuze and Guattari* 58–59).

This returns us to the model of the crystal image, as explored in the first half of this chapter. Deleuze's crystalline conception of time is such that the past is constituted at the same time as the present, with memory existing virtually alongside this present. Singular moments in the past may continue into the present, growing and accumulating new layers of possibility and meaning. This crystal is, then, in essence itself a time machine enjoining the coalescence of actual time (the production of ordered sequences) with virtual openings into the past and future. As a result, "instead of a linear development, we get a circuit in which the two images are constantly chasing one another around a point where real and imaginary become indistinguishable. The actual and its virtual image crystallize, so to speak" (*Neg* 52). Hence, in certain images (time-images or crystal images) the actual and the virtual become indistinguishable: "actual images come along with a multitude of virtual other images and it is these other possibilities that the time-image knows how to make visible" (Posman 51–52). In this specific case, *The Time Machine* fulfills this Deleuzian remit: human timescales, bodies, forms of thinking and perception; each of these must be circumvented if one is ever able to grasp, as Deleuze puts it, "the thing itself" (*Difference* 80). The novel demonstrates this synthesis of the past in the future and a recreation of the future in the past simultaneously. In this manner, *The Time Machine* ties the future and the past together as one. Through the medium of Deleuze, Wells functions as "the visionary, the seer ... the one who sees in the crystal, and what he sees is the gushing of time as dividing in two, as splitting" (*Cin2* 81). This is but one example of the actual/virtual concepts, the full implications of which regarding Wells are now discussed in the study conclusion.

Four

H. G. Wells
Conceptual Personae, Minor Writing and Eternal Return

Deleuzian Experimentation

Previous chapters have demonstrated a variety of ways in which the Deleuzian "toolbox" and Wellsian texts function when machinically plugged into one another, thus providing a number of interpretations as to how and why they function in the manner that they do. In doing so, we are fulfilling the Deleuzian remit; to reiterate the quote cited at the beginning of this study: "make a rhizome. But you don't know what you can make a rhizome with, you don't know which subterranean stem is effectively going to make a rhizome, or enter a becoming, people your desert. So experiment" (*Thousand* 277). Through these experimental encounters, these readings throw new light upon the scientific romances, and in the process demonstrate how the themes that they inspired in sf and culture have been perpetuated and subjected to extrapolation up to the present day. However, the question remains whether the reading can be advanced further, not in regards to the scientific romances specifically, but in terms of Wells himself. Deleuze states that literature is always in a state of becoming, a flight that is justified by its own trajectory; to "lose one's face, to jump over or pierce through the wall" (*Dialogues* 34). However, this flight is not a retreat into the imaginary, or an escape from life. On the contrary, Deleuze argues that it is a flight into the real, that the flight is life itself: "to flee is to produce the real, to create life, to find a weapon" (*Dialogues* 36). Can Wells be positioned in terms of a "Deleuzian weapon"?

Wells Meets Deleuze

It is apparent that no single consensus has been reached in Wells studies thus far as to where his writings can be positioned in terms of critical theory. It has not been the aim of this study to engage in a protracted debate as to the relative merits of Wells's adherence to (or lack thereof) the relative teleology of modernist, postmodernist, or poststructuralist theory in general terms. This is also further compounded by the intrinsic nature of such theoretical approaches themselves, namely the lack of clear division between these various critical theories, and the manner in which they all rhizomorphically inform one another. However, even if Wells cannot be conveniently placed within any one specific theoretical movement, this paradoxically confirms him as an ideal candidate for Deleuzian analysis. The modernist Wells allows us to position him alongside authors such as Kafka and Conrad, who are the dominant sources of Deleuze's writings on literature. The postmodernist or poststructuralist Wells allows us to align him with various arguments and interpretations pertaining to Deleuze's own cultural positioning and methodology. All of these assist in placing Wells as a writer who exists "in-between" spaces, comparable with the concept of "minor literature" that informs Deleuzian literary theory; as a "productive use of the literary machine ... that extracts from the text its revolutionary force" (*Anti* 116).

The case studies have functioned as the Deleuze-sanctioned "experiment," though this study has only been able to cover a fragment of Wells's oeuvre. However, the final chapter approaches his work in more general terms. As discussed in the introduction, Hardy has previously posited Wells an anticipator of poststructuralist theory, primarily in terms of a discussion concerning Bakhtinian and Saussurean linguistics. As an extension of Hardy's arguments it is ascertained whether Wells can be explicitly posited as an "anticipator" of Deleuzian theory. To this end, Deleuzian theory shall be applied to Wells himself. Firstly, his legacy is examined in terms of the Deleuzian conceptual personae, before viewing his oeuvre in terms of the Deleuzian concept of minor literature (or minor writing). Issues concerning the latter have been touched upon briefly in the previous chapters (specifically in regards to Kafka and *The Island of Doctor Moreau*) but warrant further investigation. Finally, concepts of the virtual and eternal return are used to view Wells's literature in terms of a "transformative event."

Four—H. G. Wells

Wells's Legacy as Conceptual Persona

> The creation of concepts in itself calls for a future form, for a new earth and people that do not yet exist.
> —*Philosophy* 108

In a 1988 interview, Deleuze states (referring to his own writings, but this is obviously rhizomatically expandable to any other aspect of the critical process): "In the act of writing there's an attempt to make life something more than personal, to free life from what imprisons it.... There's a profound link between signs, events, life and vitalism: the power of nonorganic life that can be found in a line that's drawn, a line of writing, a line of music. It's organisms that die, not life. Any work of art points a way through life, finds a way through the cracks" (*Neg* 143). Or, as Bogue summarizes, "an organism has died but a life endures" (Bogue "Style" 251). Wells, of course, died in 1946, but his visionary, creative and analytical treatises on our "alien future" (Mayer 556) are still unfurling; or, as Deleuze puts it, they persist in their ability to "find a way through the cracks."

The introduction of this study briefly posited Wells's oeuvre as functioning as a full body without organs, in that his concepts and source texts are subject to constant reinvention and adaptation (through the medium of literary criticism, countless references to his work in popular culture, cinematic and literary adaptations and remakes, board and videogames, the intersection of fan culture with the Wells canon, ad infinitum). Analogously, the output of Wells's incessantly probing mind has also been reflected in modern technological innovations, such as the internet,[1] nuclear power, space travel, futuristic weaponry, genetic engineering, and mass transit (to name but a few), as well as through the medium of sf. In this manner the Wells universe is not petrified by its original organization; free to grow and expand, it is productive, always progressing in a multitude of rhizomatic directions, and hence is able to be reconstituted in new ways. An intrinsic element of this study has involved the enormous impact that Wells's writings and legacy have had upon sf and popular consciousness, and the manner in which his ideas are still now communicated; for example, Martians, alien invasions, time travel, invisibility, mad scientists, zombies[2] and transhuman transformations. However, there is another significant notion that his literature has spawned: the concept of H. G. Wells himself. As previously touched upon both in the introduction and at various stages through the investigation, so tremendous is Wells's impact on the sf genre that he has ultimately become its synonym: when film, television or literature wish to work with concepts of, say, time travel or alien invasion, Wells himself is often inserted as a character, functioning as a literal personification of these ideas. There are many such examples of Wells appearing in a variety of fictions including copious novels, films, and games.[3] Initially, the reasons for this would appear to be self-explanatory. The fact that his primary protagonists are frequently unnamed and often narrated from the first person has led to subsequent adaptations placing Wells himself in these roles (as the time traveler, for example),[4] serving as homage to the power of Wells's storytelling and imaginative foresight. Additionally, such characterization may function as a form of critique; "surmised lampooning," as Kenneth Bailey describes Wells's appearance in C. S. Lewis's novel *That Hideous Strength* (Bailey 226), while with the appearance of a "Dr Wells" in *Brave New World*, Huxley "openly avowed his aim to expose the horror of the Wellsian Utopia" (Firchow "Wells and Lawrence" 260). Huxley explicitly named Wells's *Men Like Gods* (1923) as the "inspiration for a parody which later got out of hand and turned into something quite different from what I [Huxley] intended" (quoted in Firchow "Brave" 261). It is also worthy of note that Wells consciously referenced himself within his fiction; for example (as previously mentioned in Chapter Two) the narrator of *The War of the Worlds* refers implicitly to Wells's own journal article "The Man of the Year Million," describing the author, possibly somewhat self-effacingly, as "a certain speculative writer of quasi-scientific repute" (*War* 101).[5] Clearly, Wells himself was not averse to contributing to his own fictionalization. Ultimately, via these processes, through the various media of history, biography, tributary fiction, academic analysis and so on, the "real" figure of Wells has become just as "constructed" as one of his characters.

However, Deleuze allows us to view these characterizations in different terms; the argument pursued is that in his appearance in these fictional roles, Wells becomes more than a mere archetypal tribute, character, or characterization. The many depictions of Wells in fiction take on a wide variety of forms; as the somewhat clichéd Victorian gentleman in the film *Time After Time* (Dir. Nicholas Mayer 1979), as the

Four—H. G. Wells

mentor of C. S. Lewis and J.R.R. Tolkien (under the pseudonym Bert) in James A. Owen's *The Chronicles of the Imaginarium Geographica* fantasy series (2006–2010), or as Helena Wells, a female mad-scientist cum evil genius, in the sf television series *Warehouse 13* (2009–2014), to cite but a few diverse examples. Hence, in a variety of unique ways, Wells himself is reconceptualized: these depictions are obviously not "true" representations of the man himself (even if such a thing could exist), being an assemblage of biographical details, attributes of his nameless fictional characters, and personifications (or indeed, celebrations) of his prophecies, politics, ideas and fictional inventions. A machinic hybrid of the "real" character of Wells (subject to numerous biographies) and his fictional creations (that many take to personify him; the nameless time traveler, for example), he has himself become a source of myth. Each Wells is different, each arising independently as a unique "solution" to a common disparity or problem, a concept that needs to be explored. In the context of this study, it is the occurrence of these "mutations" of Wells that is significant, as opposed to what each manifestation individually does, but to give just one example; the character of Helena Wells from *Warehouse 13* is a utilization of the Wells concept that serves to debate issues of gender equality; obviously this in itself can hardly be said to be unique in the realms of sf, a genre renowned for its feminist concerns.[6] However, via the concept of Wells himself, and the use of the time travel device with which he is intrinsically associated, varying attitudes towards gender in different historical eras (in this case, Victorian and present day) can be directly confronted, without the chronological transition between them that the actual progression of linear time insists upon. Admittedly, *Warehouse 13* may not do this in a particularly sophisticated way; Wells is depicted primarily as a misandrist due to her subjugation by patriarchal Victorian society (indeed, she specifically states that the Wells known to history was actually her brother, who took all the credit for her work).[7] However, in its unique way of extrapolating into a modern environment a variation of Wells's own (and for his time, fairly radical) stance towards gender equality, the virtual potential of the Wells concept is demonstrated. In broader terms, although the appearance of Wells as a character in fiction is not unique to the sf genre (he also appears in historical dramas, cartoons and even business training videos, for example), the flexible machinations of sf narratives with which he is inherently associated (specifically in this case, Wells's time travel device) allow him to "legitimately" make appearances, thus reinforcing the fact that sf is a genre of ideas to which Wells is still contributing.

Hence, what is significant in these various examples is that Wells's persona is not that of a character in the traditional sense. Rather, he is a figure that accompanies concepts, "a figure through whom thought moves" (*Philosophy* 63). In this manner, these manifestations of Wells can be examined via the concept of the Deleuzian conceptual persona.

Deleuze states that the role of conceptual persona is "to show thought's territories, its absolute deterritorializations and reterritorializations ... conceptual personae are thinkers ... and their personalized features are closely linked to ... the intensive features of concepts. A particular conceptual persona thinks in us" (*Philosophy* 69). In other words, the identity of a concept itself is conveyed through something referential, allowing the concept to be understood, reasoned with and questioned; this is the conceptual personae. Conceptual personae are "subjective presuppositions" (62), not identical to an author, philosopher, artist or self, but rather testifying to a third person: "we do not do something by saying it but produce movement by thinking it, through the intermediary of a conceptual person" (*Philosophy* 64). Hence, conceptual personae are figures of thought that give concepts their specific force, their raison d'être, and through them the concepts are given body. Deleuze and Guattari argue that conceptual personae, while often only implicit in philosophy, are decisive for understanding the significance of concepts. They are "becoming," the power of the concept itself.

The conceptual persona is one of Deleuze's more esoteric constructs, particularly in regard to how a "fictional" character can possess their own autonomy. However, it appears to makes sense to say that a novelist can "bring a character to life," even when such a character is purely fictional. Yet to insist that such characters are alive in the sense that they may free themselves from the manipulation of their creators, and hence can be thought of as more than mere representatives, is a substantially bolder claim. However, regardless of their status as free agents in themselves, Deleuze and Guattari suggest that conceptual personae play an important structural or intermediary role in philosophy. If philosophy demands the creation of concepts, and this creation

Four—H. G. Wells

takes place on a plane of immanence, then the conceptual personae is that which facilitates the creation of such concepts on the plane; the conceptual personae therefore link or draw together the creation of new concepts, and function as methodological tools for the philosopher. Through the process of this study, Wells has undeniably been functioning as a methodological tool and, in accordance with this, the conceptual persona can therefore demonstrate Wells as a Deleuzian "mutation" that gives him an eclectic variety of new identities.

However, it is important to note that the status of the conceptual persona cannot be applied to the "actual" Wells. Conceptual personae are not the authors of a concept, they are not the philosophers or theorists themselves who speak and create concepts; as Colebrook points out, the conceptual persona is "not the author but the figure presupposed by the concept" (*Gilles Deleuze* 74). These personae are not "signatures," that is, claimants whose ownership of a concept cannot be disputed; they are more like "friends ... internal to the conditions of philosophy" (*Philosophy* 4) who cultivate concepts rather than attach their signatures to them (Olkowski "Beside" 285). Instead, via the medium of various fictional extrapolations, Wells himself can be transformed into one of a myriad of "fluctuating figures who express the presuppositions or ethos of their philosophy and through their existence, no matter how inchoate or unstable, give life to concepts on a new plane of immanence" (Rodowick "Unthinkable" n. pag.). Importantly, these figures are not allegorical; they do not specifically "stand for" some idea, concept, or thought, but figure in the search for still unformed thoughts. Colebrook highlights romanticism as a specific example: "could we have 'Romanticism' without the figure of the Byronic individual (who is not the historical Byron but a broad-brushed character)?" (*Gilles Deleuze* 74). Deleuze himself provides examples in Socrates (who provided the conceptual persona for Platonism) and Homer (who provided the conceptual persona for the *Iliad* narratives). It is not necessary for these individuals to have actually existed *per se*, but it is necessary for them to have existed as vessels which contain a body of ideas. In *What Is Philosophy?*, Deleuze names several fictional characters he regards as conceptual personae; the multiple depictions of Don Juan, Herman Melville's Captain Ahab, Heinrich von Kleist's Penthesilea, and Nietzsche's Zarathustra, stating: "The conceptual persona is not the philosopher's representative, but, rather, the reverse:

the philosopher is only the envelope of his principal conceptual persona and of all the other personae who are the intercessors the real subjects of his philosophy. Conceptual personae are the philosopher's 'heteronyms,' and the philosopher's name is the simple pseudonym of his personae" (*Philosophy* 54).

The same status is possible for the various interpellations of Wells via numerous examples of his depiction in a fictional context. In these terms, a case can possibly be made for Well's characters themselves also being conceptual personae; the time traveler, for example. As demonstrated in the chapter focusing on *The Time Machine*, without doubt he is the figure through which concepts are given force; it is he who has shattered the image of thought as he flings himself into futurity (*Time* 17), achieving nomadic status as a result. He also remains conceptual in that he has no name; as previously discussed, he is an avatar, an amalgamation of various traits (mythic hero, scientist, everyman) and as such he can be said to function purely as a Deleuzian device for understanding the significance of concepts. He is not something unified and self-contained, but becomes "a functioning of a polyvalent assemblage of which the solitary individual is only a part" (*Anti* 42). However, as previously noted, when the character of the time traveler is used in fiction, it is often the figure of Wells himself who is being invoked. So in fact, a more convincing case can be made for delineations of Wells himself being conceptual persona via the medium of these "heteronyms." Wells is the figure through which various concepts (time travel, alien invasion, transhumanism and so on) are given force. He remains conceptual in that he has no consistent identity; his many depictions take on a variety of names, labels and even physicalities. To give but a few examples; in George Pal's 1960 film adaptation of *The Time Machine*, the time traveler is named as George, an obvious reference to his literary creator (and even more explicitly, "H. George Wells" can be seen inscribed on a plaque on the time machine itself). C. S. Lewis' novel *That Hideous Strength* (1945) features the character of Horace Jules, a pseudo-scientific journalist and caricature of Wells,[8] while in the context of the sf television series *Warehouse 13*, he is subject to gender reassignment. Rather than all being conceptual personae in their own right, the one constant in all of these "mutations" is, of course, that they invoke Wells in some form or other, regardless of the actual nature of the depiction. They are not however, functioning merely as Wells's representative; in conceptual terms they are the "fictional characters of philosophy" that Deleuze advocates; offering as examples the Socrates of Plato, the Zarathustra of Nietzsche, Pascal's gambler and Kierkegaard's "knight of the faith." These are not aesthetic figures, but "powers of concepts" (*Philosophy* 65). There are many different variations of Wells, which is in keeping with the manner in which the multitude of conceptual personae burgeon: "each persona has several features that may give rise to other personae, on the same or a different plane: conceptual personae proliferate" (76). And in these processes, the conceptual persona, in deterritorializing thought, assists in making concepts available that would otherwise remain stagnant on their plane; through these processes, the concepts of Wells endure, mutating into an abundance of new forms in the process.

Obviously, in their wide variety of manifestations, not all these "conceptual Wellses" are "accurate" depictions of his original ideologies, but are indeed Deleuze's "monstrous" mutations. So, more than a "reading" or "interpretation," we face a Deleuzian "production" of Wells, connected in a new philosophical space: a new and entirely Deleuzian plane of immanence (Khalfa 51). Deleuze would however argue that Wells would still recognize himself in the medium of his conceptual persona: "I am no longer myself but thought's aptitude for finding itself and spreading across a plane that passes through me at several places" (*Philosophy* 54). Indeed, it is the destiny of the "philosopher" to become his conceptual persona or personae, and "at the same time ... these personae themselves become something other than they are historically, mythologically, or commonly" (*Philosophy* 64). Such is Wells's legacy; ultimately, as a thinker, philosopher, prophet, and father of modern sf, through endless proliferations he has become something other; and as conceptual persona continues in the production of a legacy of "an infinite and plastic ambiguity" (Borges *Other* 87).

The Minor Wells

Instead of asking what a book or work of literature is (in terms of its placement into a specific structure), Deleuze and Guattari ask what it is a book does (in terms of how it utilizes language and actually subverts the formation of social structures). It is hence apparent that in these terms, the strength of literature lies in its rejection of the idea of the book as a representation of reality (and hence all of the adjacent problems with the dogmatic image of literature)[9] and presents the book as a machine (as something which does things, rather than merely signifying them): "What we find in great English and American novelists is a gift ... for intensities, flows, machine-books, tool-books, schizo-books" (*Neg* 23). Intrinsic to this is the concept of minor literature.

Initially it may appear incongruous that Wells could ever be located in a position that we could understand to be "minor," at least in the traditional sense of the term; after all, he was a white, middle class English male, writing at a time when the British Empire was at the peak of expansion, successful in his lifetime in terms of both critical and populist acclaim, and many of his works and principal themes (predominantly through the scientific romances, as discussed previously) have subsequently become hugely influential in terms of popular culture, literature, sf and the scientific community. None of these aspects would appear to position him as in any way a minority! However, the Deleuzian concept of minor presents the concept in an altogether different light; in these terms, "minor" is not simply defined as a literature written from the perspective of an oppressed group, nor is it secondary or neglected literature. It is in fact a form of political writing that undermines the high modernist distinction between elite and mass culture and its separation of life and art (Herron 177), and is hence work constructed by minorities within a major literature (*Kafka* 16). Minor literature takes the language of the dominant culture and warps it to new purposes, creating "lines of flight." Hence minor literature does not necessarily consist of literature written by ethnic, sexual, or any other kind of minorities. As Ronald Bogue clarifies:

> What constitutes minorities is not their statistical number, which may in actual fact be greater than that of the majority, but their position within asymmetrical power relationships that are reinforced by and implemented through linguistic codes and binary oppositions.... Minorities merely reinforce dominant power relations when they accept the categories that define them.... Only by blurring categories can new possibilities for social interaction be created [Bogue "Minoritarian" 168].

Bogue also notes that this creation involves a certain kind of becoming, becoming-imperceptible: "Becoming-imperceptible is a process of elimination whereby one divests oneself of all coded identity and engages in the abstract lines of a nonorganic life, the immanent, virtual lines of continuous variation that play through discursive regimes of signs and nondiscursive machinic assemblages alike" (*Wake* 73). In essence then, minor literature creates a type of living that is not merely a replication of dominant motifs but is modeled on the Deleuzian concept of the virtual. Arguments for Wells being regarded in these terms are now addressed, encompassing the case for him as a minor writer, and culminating with a debate upon the virtual.

It is in their 1975 study *Kafka: Towards a Minor Literature* that Deleuze and Guattari first map out the concept of a minor literature, positing Kafka as a primary exponent. They give a number of determining characteristics of a minor literature (or, in other words, the conditions in which a literature becomes revolutionary); with a minor literature everything is political, always collective (17), and should deterritorialize the major language (16):

> The three characteristics of minor literature are the deterritorialization of the language, the connection of the individual and the political, the collective arrangement of utterance. Which amounts to this: that "minor" no longer characterizes certain literatures, but describes the revolutionary conditions of any literature within what we call the great (or established).... To write as a dog who digs his hole, a rat who makes his burrow ... to find his own point of underdevelopment, his own jargon, a third world of his own, a desert of his own [*Kafka* 18].

So, to work in a minor way is not necessarily to be a "minority" in the way that the term is usually deployed, with negative connotations of economic, gender, racial and ethnic status. To be minor is to take a major voice and speak it in a way that expresses a preferred identity; in this way, minor art practices have the potential to destabilize the normal conventions of the major voices of society. This political aspect of the minor is crucial, for minor practices (art, literature, and language) have the potential to destabilize the conventions of the major voice of society. This serves not necessarily to directly oppose a dominant political system, but to inhabit it and change it from within (Sutton and Martin-Jones 52–53). Deleuze and Guattari's idea of the minor can be applied to any number of contexts; hence in this instance, to Wells.

What Deleuze defines as a major literature is a literature of masters: oppressive, hard and founded upon transcendental justifications. However, it need not necessarily remain petrified: "even when major, a language is open to an intensive utilization that makes it take flight along creative lines of escape which, no matter how slowly, no matter how cautiously, can now form an absolute deterritorialization" (*Kafka* 26). Nevertheless, although minor literature arises from the reactions of the minority within a major literature and culture, the project of "becoming-minor" is open to everyone. According to Deleuze and Guattari, "the political domain has contaminated every statement. But above all else, literature finds itself positively charged with the role and function of collective, and even revolutionary, enunciation" (*Kafka* 17). In doing so, "the literary machine becomes the relay for a revolutionary machine-to-come" (18). This machinic property of minor literature that Deleuze and Guattari propose corresponds to the performative aspect of the literary work, since minor literature performs (in major language) in a way that not only deterritorializes that major language but also creates new possibilities of speaking, thinking, writing in this major language. A minor literature is a project of deterritorialization: in the place of the exclusive rights of the privileged "majority," a minor literature gives free play to the disenfranchised, to minorities (for example, women or people from developing countries) even if they comprise the majority in literal, numerical terms. Although minor literature arises from the reactions of the minority within a major literature and culture, its literary and sociocultural project points toward a "becoming-minor" of the whole world, in which all structures of hegemony and privilege give way. While minor literature undermines the author as master and, in turn, the stable, despotic subject of which the author is but one manifestation, it also puts forward a new paradigm for literature and authority, open to multiplicity, difference and variation. As a result, a minor literature is political and revolutionary; it invokes another possible community, one without masters, literary and otherwise. Wells shall be examined in accordance with the three ways Deleuze specifies: in terms of the collective, language, and the political. Naturally there will be a degree of cross-contamination between these categories.

Firstly, a minor literature is always collective (*Kafka* 17). Hence, there is less emphasis on individual authors and talents (which are at any rate scarce within a minor literature) and more on the collective

Four—H. G. Wells

production of work (its collaborative status). It is in this sense that we can see the artistic production of statements as a kind of precursor of a community still in formation. This is the "utopian" function of the minor literary machine; it prepares the way (in fact in many senses, calls into being) the "revolutionary machine-to-come" (*Kafka* 18): "we might as well say that minor no longer designates specific literatures but the revolutionary conditions for every literature" (18). This is applicable to Wells in some ways but not others. Wells may not have been collective within his lifetime; indeed, this study has gone far to emphasize the fact that he stood very much alone in both literary and ideological terms, and that to present day he remains uncategorizable and unaligned with any specific literary movement. However, in terms of being a precursor of a community still in formation, his position as the not only the father of modern sf, but also of the discipline of futurism[10] allows him to be retroactively positioned in collective terms. With regards to constituting a "revolutionary machine-to-come," this study has argued for Wells's future orientation; for example, his bearing upon contemporary thought, and his infinitely malleable ideas, as shown in his position as conceptual personae. This can be equated to a "revolutionary machine": at the very least, Wells revolutionized the field of sf literature. Though it may have not led directly to the "world commonwealth" and political and sexual revolutions that he craved in his lifetime,[11] his influential ideas are still communicated today through his fictional works, arguably a revolution in another form. Indeed, to again quote Jorge Luis Borges's writings upon Wells: "Work that endures is always capable of an infinite and plastic ambiguity" (Borges *Inquisitions* 87). Indeed, Wells fulfills Deleuze's remit that our task is "not to draft the revolution or to proclaim that it has already happened. It is neither to appease the individual nor to create the classless society.... Our task is to ask and answer afresh, always once more because it is never concluded, the question of how one might live" (May 153).

The second act of a minor literature is that it should "deterritorialize the major language" (*Kafka* 19). Such a deterritorialization involves a neutralization of sense, or the signifying aspects of language, and a foregrounding of the latter's asignifying, intensive aspects (22). Again, this is not a language that is statistically minor (in terms of style and vocabulary, for example). A minor language is (potentially) a language of subversion, splintering and opposition, as opposed to major language's effects being that of control, uniformity and power. So it can be said that a "minor literature" is one which is in some way oppositional in relation to forms of language-use, and large-scale structures of power: "the literary machine alone is determined to fill the conditions of a collective enunciation that is lacking elsewhere in this milieu: literature is the people's concern" (*Kafka* 18). As previously discussed, Wells deliberately spurned experimental uses of language and style in his writings, to the point where he was rejected by critics from inside the modernist movement (such as Virginia Woolf), due to what they perceived as his reliance upon "traditional" forms of writing and narrative, conveniently disregarding his metaphorical and moral complexity.[12] While many argue that Wells's scientific romances do demonstrate continuity with the Victorian tradition of the novel in terms of narrative construction and style, the novels straddle different genres and eras, and consequently remain a complicated and consistently disputed body of work. To this end, Rolf Lessenich states that Wells's "epistemological normalization and perspectivism and his personal negation of natural norms and forms as well as providential purposes, found their expression in his grotesque or even pre-absurd inventions of plot and character" (Lessenich 299). Writing in "*The Time Machine*: An Ironic Myth," Bergonzi concurs: "I would claim that Wells's early fiction is closer ... to the fables of Kafka, than it is to the more strictly scientific speculations of Verne" (*Bergonzi* "Ironic" 39). So, although Wells's narratives "never departed from direct, accessible sentence structures and—ostensibly, at any rate—retained the illusion of reality conveyed by realist narrative conventions," these practices can be seen "as a direct consequence of his oft-expressed views on the power and purpose of literature" (Hardy "Poststructuralist" 114). In this way, if minor literature is oppositional in relation to large-scale structures of power and forms of language-use, by deliberately bucking the linguistic trends of the modernist movement (a major literary force at his time of writing), Wells was making a case for a minor literature. Of course, it must be borne in mind that this applies retrospectively, taking into account the subsequent canonization of many modernist authors.

In more specific terms of language use, Hardy's highly progressive essay "H. G. Wells the Poststructuralist" is of particular relevance. She cites Wells's staunch belief in the function of the novel as a conveyor of ideas and how this is the "fundamental principle underlying both

Four—H. G. Wells

his style and approach to fiction—his theory of language" (114). This serves to emphasize Wells's belief that "language does not represent pre-existing meanings, but mediates, and to that extent *creates*, meaning" (115). Significant here is the manner in which Hardy equates these statements, and various other aspects of Wells's writings, to the linguistic theories of Ferdinand de Saussure (1857–1913) and Mikhail Bakhtin (1895–1975), among others. A discussion of the genealogy of the relationship between Deleuze, Saussure and Bakhtin would constitute a study in itself and hence will not be tackled here, though suffice to say, Deleuze was heavily influenced by Saussurean linguistics.[13] However, while Hardy does not implicitly engage with Deleuze in her positioning of Wells in line with these theorists (and consequently as a poststructuralist), within the context of her argument a few examples of Wells's use of language can indeed be related to minor literature.

In minor writing, Deleuze and Guattari argue that "one has to lose one's identity" (*Dialogues* 45), hence literature should function to destroy the border between the perceiver and the perceived. This collapse of boundaries between the narrator and the reader results in the concept of Deleuzian becoming-minoritarian; the process of "no longer knowing who or what we are" results in "seeing with greater openness the differences, intensities and singularities that traverse us" (Colebrook *Gilles Deleuze* 130). Hardy makes references to literary techniques in a variety of Wells's novels that can be said to facilitate becoming-minoritian: "much of the power of the 1915 novel *The Research Magnificent* can be attributed to the fact that the story is recounted on three levels by three narrators, each of whom takes a different ideological stance to the events narrated, and each of whom has a different conception of what is required by literary form" (Hardy "Poststructuralist" 124). The reader's response to the novel's conclusion is problematic as a result of this interplay of voices and perspective. Similarly, *Mr Blettsworthy on Rampole Island* (1928) "sets up a complex dialectic between dreaming and waking, reality and illusion, the rational and the irrational through its narrative structure, and intertextual references" (125). In *Tono-Bungay* (1909), the narrator "insists on the inadequacy of words," giving "onomatopoeic rendering[s] of ... sound[s]," demonstrating that he is "unable to accept the imprecision and impermanence of ordinary language" (123). Hardy's investigation is primarily concerned with Wells's later works, and she states that as his career progressed, his theoretical approaches to language grew ever more sophisticated (115). However, "as early as 1891" (114) he was "fascinated by the nature and function of language," and hence it is unsurprising that similar examples are manifest in the narrative devices of the scientific romances. *The Time Machine* displays this in general terms, imagining the evolution of rival but interdependent posthuman species, resembling the Victorian bourgeoisie and proletariat, aesthetes and engineers. But, eventually the time traveler comes to realize that treating them as such would be a mistake, recognizing the danger of reading this future through his own limited perspective. He ascertains that an interpretation is not the truth, resulting in a radical destabilizing of traditional perspectives. In more specific terms, both *The Time Machine* and *The Island of Doctor Moreau* use the technique of "found manuscript" literature. In the former, the story is told through the medium of a guest at the time traveler's gathering, who for all but the first two chapters and the final chapter is taking dictation from the time traveler himself. In the introduction of *The Island of Doctor Moreau*, the main character's nephew introduces Prendick's manuscript which is "found amongst his papers ... unaccompanied by any definite request for publication" (*Moreau* 3) and it is up to the reader to ascertain its validity. Kimberly Jackson makes the point that "the story is being told from a point of view of a creature who is being slowly, tortuously and above all, consciously altered ... the narrator is undone, taken apart, and then patched together with bits and pieces from other sources" (Jackson 29). The result is that "once the reader senses that the narrator is himself vivisected, it becomes clear that every element of the text is susceptible to vivisection ... not only is the text torn open in various places ... the narrative is also a 'patchwork' of different discourses" (30). Hence, instead of presenting Prendick's and the time traveler's story and his inner world directly, Wells intentionally creates a multiple point of view in the narration of the stories. All these aspects contribute to a collapse of boundaries between the narrator and the reader, assisting in the process of Deleuzian becoming-minoritarian.[14]

Despite these examples, it may be too bold a claim to argue conclusively that these elements of Wells's oeuvre fulfill all the necessary criteria for minor literature. However, even if Wells's narratives do not seek to deterritorialize language itself, they do serve to deterritorialize the established stylistic conventions of the imperial fictions of the age.

Four—H. G. Wells

Indeed, while Wells's narrative may share similarities with his Victorian peers, he ventured where other writers did not in their attempt to reveal the truth behind imperial expansionism and to challenge the patriotic notion of Britain as a great "civilizing" nation. In this way, it is not merely the deterritorialization of its host-genre that qualifies Wells's narratives as minor literature but, in accordance with Deleuze and Guattari's criteria, the "political immediacy" (*Kafka* 18) of his works and the tendency to organize these principles in a "collective assemblage of enunciation" (*Kafka* 82). This can be tied into the third element of minor literature; the fact that it is inherently political. That is to say, political in the sense that the lives and individual concerns of the characters are always linked to the larger social milieu. To become-minor is to "jostle the reins of the majority identity in order to investigate new possibilities, new ways of becoming that are no longer bound to the dominant.... It is to investigate the virtual whose vision is often obscured by the molar lines of the majority. It is to break with identity, which is always the identity of the majority, in favor of difference as yet unactualized" (May 150).

Arguably, Wells's works fulfill this remit. As Deleuze states: "the truly great authors are the minor ones, the untimely ones. It is the minor artist that offers the true masterpiece: the minor artist does not interpret his times, mankind does not have a specific time, time depends upon mankind" (Deleuze and Bene 96). In this regard, it is undeniable that, despite being historically located in the Victorian/Edwardian era, and consequently a response to the events of these times, Well's scientific romances have truly transcended their specific point of historical origin in terms of their undeniable position of influence over the subsequent sf genre, and the manner in which they have been constantly and repeatedly reinvented for subsequent eras. Just as Wells's scientific romances have reached a mass audience, many of the minor authors exemplified by Deleuze (such as Lewis Carroll) have also had their works targeted for majority appreciation. But Deleuze points out that the contents ("excesses") of these works make them hard to normalize, domesticate and neutralize their productions; they persist in being difficult, ambiguous and hence qualify as minor. Indeed, Bogue notes that "Deleuze and Guattari extend Kafka's description of minor literature as defining it as literature that has an immediate social and political function" (Bogue *Deleuze and Guattari* 116). These functions are "not as they are imposed from without, but only as diabolical powers to come or revolutionary forces to be constructed" (117). It can be argued that in the still-present critical debates over many aspects of Wells's works (the problem of his cultural and critical positioning, for example), as well as in terms of their undeniable cultural influence, the productions have yet to be normalized, domesticated and neutralized.

It should be noted that the emphasis here has been upon Wells specifically as a proponent of minor literature, as opposed to the broader sf genre that owes him such a debt. A debate shall not be entered into regarding whether sf itself qualifies as a form of minor literature; indeed, given its previously discussed rhizomorphic and multidisciplinary nature, such a debate would constitute a study in itself. Suffice to say however, in terms of the criteria required for minor status, there is no denying sf's inherently political nature, or its collective power as a literature of ideas. Although this propensity towards becoming-minoritarian was arguably already present in the genre prior to Wells's vital contributions to the form (for example, its usefulness as a device for social critique, specifically the political elements that are intrinsic to utopian fictions), it can be argued that it is essential to acknowledge Wells's influence upon the sf genre, along with his practice (his use of extrapolation, epic scale, social issues, and scientific debate, for example), if engaging in a debate in order to establish the minor qualities of the genre.

In essence then, Deleuze and Guattari's concept of minor literature is defined in conjunction with their radical concept of life. If life is not just the actual world, but also all of its virtual potentials, then a minor literature will be great in its capacity to think of life not as it is, but what it might become (Colebrook *Perplexed* 29). That is to say, life from "new points of view" (*Kafka* 19), and it is ultimately herein that lies the value and power of Wells's literature. Roslynn Haynes comments: "Wells was a prophet, not merely in the popular sense of having predicted space travel, processed food and the common market, but in a wider sense of being able to think in a completely new way about the future. Such a way of thinking freed him ... it provided a new perspective" (Haynes x). And as Deleuze states, "the creative line of escape vacuums up in its movement all politics, all economy, all bureaucracy, all judiciary: it sucks them like a vampire in order to make them render still unknown sounds that come from the near future ... diabolical powers that are knocking at the door" (*Kafka* 41). Ultimately, in not only "freeing himself," but via the medium of his literature, also granting his readership possible insights into these future "diabolical powers," Wells has facilitated the viewing of life in terms of what it may become, from new points of view and it is this that is the purpose of minor literature. As Wagar expresses emotively in the "personal prologue" of *H. G. Wells: Traversing Time*: "Wide vistas. The passage of thousands and millions of years. The origin and destiny of Homo sapiens. I was a small, frail boy, a mote of human dust. But Wells expanded my universe until I felt almost godlike. This, uniquely, was his power" (4).

Eternal Return and the Virtual

Along with its collective, political and language aspects, Deleuze and Guattari also place significance upon the repetitive traits of minor literature. A minor literature "repeats," not in order to express what goes before, but "to express an untimely power, a power of language to disrupt identity and coherence" (Colebrook *Gilles Deleuze* 119). In doing this, a minor literature "repeats the past and present in order to create a future" (120). According to Deleuze, the only thing that is repeated or returns is difference, and the power of life itself lies in difference and repetition. In this manner, he interprets and uses Nietzsche's concept of "eternal return" as a constant repetition of difference.[15] His use of the Nietzschian concept must not be considered a simple rotation of a cycle, as this would only allow the return of something pre-existing. Instead, the eternal return is the repetition of that which differs-from-itself: "The subject of the eternal return is not the same but the different, not the similar but the dissimilar, not the one but the many" (*Difference* 126). Hence, the idea of the "new" is that it does not merely supersede the past; but that it is in itself "untimely." This untimely aspect of minor literature enables it to interdict history, and can be related to the Deleuzian "event": "Planes must be constructed and problems posed, just as concepts must be created.... If one concept is 'better' than an earlier one, it is because it makes us aware of new variations and unknown resonances, it carries out unforeseen cuttings out, it brings forth an 'Event' that surveys us" (*Philosophy* 27–28).

Wells Meets Deleuze

Deleuze's concept of eternal return is present in minor literature, as opposed to majoritarian literature which presents itself as a faithful description of a "law," "meaning" or "tradition," repeating what is already given with a minimum of difference (Colebrook *Gilles Deleuze* 121). As an example of the latter, Colebrook cites film adaptations of eighteenth-and nineteenth-century novels that use literary voice-overs, accurate period costumes and minimize any filmic or televisual aspects (121). By contrast, a minor literature does not repeat a voice or model but repeats the power of difference that produces the original. In this way, a filmic repetition of a literary work would have to transform the cinema in the same way that the literary work transformed literature. Hence, a minor literature may repeat a voice, but it does so not in order to maintain the tradition, but in order to transform it; not to copy a work, but to repeat the forces of difference that produced that work (122). It could however easily be stated that no film adaptation of Wells's work has transformed the medium in the same manner that the originals have transformed literature.[16] But the emphasis here is upon the virtual power and potential of Wells's originals, which is repeatedly displayed in the vast array of adaptations, tributes and references that permeate our contemporary culture; these are Deleuze's (sometimes) "monstrous mutations" that "find a way through the cracks" (*Neg* 143). Indeed, as Williams states, Wells's work remains "an inexhaustible rhizome for intelligent and visually self-aware sf on film and television" (Williams 130), and correspondingly Massumi posits that "imagination is the mode of thought most precisely suited to the vagueness of the virtual" (Massumi *Parables* 134).

If, as Deleuze posits, each event of life transforms the whole of life, and does so over and over again, then by extension all that is and will be (i.e., eternity) is always different from itself, always open to becoming, never at rest. Extending this concept, each event of literature transforms the whole of literature. In this way, if taken as minor literature, we can no longer read Wells's scientific romances merely as (for example) nineteenth-century novels, as all subsequent literary and cinematic transformations that Wells's oeuvre has been subject to function to make the originals different, for they disclose in the originals the power to "become." We do not read Wells in the same way after having read, say, Stephen Baxter's *The Time Ships*, or heard Orson Welles's radio broadcast of *The War of the Worlds* (1938), or having watched

Four—H. G. Wells

George Pal's adaptation of *The Time Machine* (1960), or Don Taylor's *The Island of Doctor Moreau* (1977). It is not so much that we have lost the original, but that the Wellsian texts already hold the virtual power of all these later repetitions. Wells himself also possesses this power of the virtual, and as conceptual persona, minor writer and "the Father of modern sf," is rhizomatically connected across space and time to all extrapolations of his work.

Conclusion

A century has passed since the publication of Wells's scientific romances, at least for those of us who are "passing along the Time-Dimension with a uniform velocity from the cradle to the grave" (*Time* 6), as described by Wells's time traveler; though of course both Wells and Deleuze's conceptions of time call this assumed linearity into question! However, despite (or indeed, because of) this passing of time, concepts and ontologies are still emerging through which Wells's ideas can be creatively explored. As demonstrated via the Deleuzian encounter with Wells that this study has provided, Wells's textual explorations of space, time, politics and biology (to specify but a few of the themes and concepts discussed) can be reinterpreted and reinvigorated, and in the resulting Deleuzian "production" of Wells, he can be positioned in a new philosophical space, or a new plane of immanence. Owing to both the sheer scope of Wells's prolific oeuvre, and the inherently dense nature of Deleuzian theory, this study has only been able to touch upon a small number of texts and corresponding philosophical conceptions. Nevertheless, via a demonstration of their mutual congruity, the aim has been to contribute not only to the canon of already existing Wellsian criticism and research, but also to be generative to the Deleuzian virtual potentiality of future approaches, which can obviously be taken in any number of rhizomorphic directions. Indeed, Deleuze and Guattari state that the task of art in all its forms is to "capture," "summon" and make visible these otherwise imperceptible potential forces (*Philosophy* 181–182). If "science fiction writes the future" (Pinsky 13), then both it and Wells are ideally placed to "produce or suggest worlds hitherto unseen but always produced from within the seen" (O'Sullivan 63). Wells's work fulfills this remit, proving itself to be an inexhaustible rhizome, to which an encounter with Deleuzian theory can only assist in the understanding.

Foucault once remarked that "perhaps, one day, this century [the twentieth] will be known as Deleuzian" (Foucault "Theatrum" 165). This status has yet to come, just as Wells is arguably denied his deserved status as one of the twentieth century's most influential authors and thinkers. Indeed, as one of the most significant minds at work in our times, and one of the few whose worldview remains fresh and imperative today, the answers he supplied to the most pressing issues of the human condition have lost none of their relevance (Wagar *Traversing* 277). However, beyond even this remit, Deleuze allows us to read Wells as more than just a great mind occupying a specific era of history: whatever rhizomorphic connections Wells and his works may form, they are ultimately truly "untimely," "acting counter to our time and thereby acting on our time, and let us hope, for the benefit of a time to come" (*Difference* xix). Wagar asks if, courtesy of Wells, there is "a shape of things to come," and suggests that "we can and must do our best to prepare the way [for it]" (277). In its encounter, deterritorialization and consequent reassessment of Wells, it is hoped that the variety of new perspectives provided by this study in some small way assist in this ambition: to "give back to the author a little bit of the joy, the energy, the love of life and politics that he knew how to give and invent" (*Dialogues* 119). It is through the medium of Deleuze that we are witness to the eternal and untimely power of Wells's literature, and as Wells himself stated in *The Discovery of the Future*: "It is possible to believe that all the past is but the beginning of a beginning, and that all that is and has been is but the twilight of the dawn" (60).

Appendix A
Fictional Portrayals of H. G. Wells

This appendix features notable examples of Wells's appearances as a character in novels, short stories, films and other media, presented in chronological order of appearance. Largely excluded are examples in which Wells is merely referred to or named or featured in historical documentary terms, or if it is only his machines or inventions (such as the time machine itself or chemical elements such as Cavorite and Carolinum) that are used. It is however worthy of note that the latter are legion in sf; for example, Cavorite (originating in *The First Men in the Moon* and *The War of the Worlds*), appears in *The League of Extraordinary Gentlemen*, Robert Buettner's *Orphan* series of novels (2004–2009), Vernor Vinge's *A Deepness in the Sky* (1999), and on television in *Warehouse 13* and in the *Star Trek* universe's fictional table of elements.

Novels and Short Stories

- Aldous Huxley's *Brave New World* (1932) features a scientist named Dr. Wells, openly alluding to the man himself.
- In C. S. Lewis's novel *That Hideous Strength* (1945), the character Jules is a caricature of Wells; much of Lewis's science fiction was inspired by (and in this case, a rebuttal to) Wells's oeuvre.
- Arthur Sammler, the main character of Saul Bellow's *Mr. Sammler's Planet* (1970), claims to know Wells, and is urged by other characters to write a biography of him.
- Wells makes an appearance *The Hollow Lands* (1975) by Michael Moorcock. The novel's protagonist travels back in time and recruits Wells to help him return to the future.

Appendix A

- In *The Space Machine* by Christopher Priest (1976), the main protagonist steals and damages Wells's time machine, and arrives on Mars just before the start of the invasion described in *The War of the Worlds*. Wells appears as a minor character.
- In Donald R. Bensen's sf novel *And Having Writ…* (1978) Wells is a major character, acting as an emissary between humans and invading aliens.
- Wells is a major character in John Kessel's award-winning short story "Buffalo," first printed in *The Magazine of Fantasy & Science Fiction*, February 1991. The narrative involves an imagined meeting between Wells and the author's father.
- In Ben Bova's short story "Inspiration" (1994), the narrator describes a fictional meeting between Wells and a young Albert Einstein.
- Stephen Baxter's novel *The Time Ships* (1995) features characters, situations and technobabble from several of Wells's stories, as well as a representation of Wells. The time traveler encounters his younger self, whom he nicknames "Moses." This is a reference to Wells's "The Chronic Argonauts," the story which grew into *The Time Machine*, in which the inventor of the Time Machine is named Dr. Moses Nebogipfel.
- Ronald Wright's 1997 novel *A Scientific Romance* tells of Wells's time machine arriving in the present day, carrying with it a letter from Wells himself.
- Issue 147 (2005) of the satirical UK comic *Viz* features a cartoon strip "H. G. Wells the Builder," which depicts Wells as a "speculative novelist-cum-building-contractor," assisted in his work by Martian tripod builders and invisible workmen.
- A time travelling Wells is a major character in James A. Owen's fantasy series *The Chronicles of the Imaginarium Geographica* (2006–2010).
- Kevin J. Anderson's *The Martian War: A Thrilling Eyewitness Account of the Recent Invasion As Reported by Mr. H. G. Wells* (2006) retells *The War of the Worlds* with Wells as the main protagonist, witnessing the Martian attack alongside Thomas Huxley and Percival Lowell. Anderson also edited *The War of the Worlds: Global Dispatches* (1996), featuring many other retellings of the novel, many of which featuring a variety of Wellsian characters from numerous works, as well as various depictions of Wells himself.
- Wells makes an appearance in the 2007 Stargate SG-1 novelization *Roswell* (Sonny Whitelaw), as a version of himself prior to the writing of *The War of the Worlds*. There are also multiple references to Lovecraft and his Cthulhu mythos.

Fictional Portrayals of H. G. Wells

- A teenage Wells is one of the heroes (along with a similarly youthful G. K. Chesterton) in *The Tripods Attack!: The Young Chesterton Chronicles* (2007), a sf/alternative history adventure series, written by John McNichol.
- Wells makes a brief appearance (as a staunch advocate of socialism) in Libba Bray's historical-fantasy novel *The Sweet Far Thing* (2007).
- David Lodge's *A Man of Parts* (2011) is a biopic predominantly focused upon Wells's personal relationships. Its fictionalized elements (principally in regards to descriptions of Wells's sexual liaisons) merit its inclusion here.
- Wells is featured as a character in Paul Levinson's 2013 time travel novelette, "Ian, George, and George" (2013), the other George of the title being Orson Welles.

Film, Television and Other Media

- Wells has made numerous appearances in comic book series, including "Real Fact Comics" (1946 DC Comics), "Marvel Classics Comics" (1976) "The Searchers" (1996 Caliber Comics) and "The Rook" (1979 Warren).
- In George Pal's film adaptation of *The Time Machine* (1960), the protagonist is named George Wells, placing the author in the character of his time traveler.
- Wells appears on the famous album cover of The Beatles' 1967 album "Sgt Pepper's Lonely Hearts Club Band" (positioned next to Karl Marx).
- Wells appears as the protagonist in the 1979 film *Time After Time*, which uses the conceit that Wells's works were based upon his actual escapades. Transported to modern day San Francisco, he pursues a time travelling Jack the Ripper, and meets and falls in love with a woman named Amy Robbins (the name of his real-life second wife), taking her back to the Victorian era with him at the culmination of the film.
- In the *Doctor Who* episode "Timelash" (1985), the time-travelling Doctor encounters a young man named Herbert in the Scottish Highlands, taking him on an adventure that is revealed to have been inspirational when it is revealed this is the pre-published Wells. He is also implicitly referenced in the 1975 episode "Pyramids of Mars," as well as various spin-off comics.
- *All Change* (1988) is a corporate business training video, in which

Appendix A

Wells is played by John Cleese; here, the time travel conceit is used to via demonstrate the potential future impact of various business strategies.
- *Testimony* (1988) is a film based on the memoirs of Shostakovich, in which Wells (played by Brook Williams) is a minor character.
- The Czechoslovakian film *Clovek proti zkáze* (*Man against Destruction*) (1989) features Wells as a character.
- The "Circlevision" film *From Time to Time* (also known as *The Timekeeper*) (1992), made as a Disney theme park attraction, features a ad feedprotagonist who invents the world's first functional time machine, kidnaps Jules Verne, and meets fellow time machine inventor Wells (played by Jeremy Irons).
- In the *Animaniacs* cartoon series episode "When Mice Ruled the Earth" (1993), cartoon mice are being kept in H. G. Wells's laboratory, and plan to steal his time machine.
- *The Time Machine: The Journey Back* (1993) is a sequel to Pal's 1960 film adaptation; as with the original, it features a time travelling George Wells.
- In an episode of the television series *Lois & Clark: The New Adventures of Superman*, titled "*Tempus Fugitive*" (1995), Wells seeks out Superman's help to stop a criminal from the future whom Wells had accidentally unleashed on the present. Notably, in its concept of Wells's time machine being stolen and used for evil, plot-wise this episode closely resembles *Time After Time*.
- "A Rip in Time," a 1997 episode of the Television series *Timecop* features an "Inspector Wells," who is pursuing Jack the Ripper through time. This is a clear homage to *Time After Time*, except the setting is the Victorian era, as opposed to modern day.
- The TV series *The Infinite Worlds of H. G. Wells* (2001) presents a fictionalized biopic account of Wells's youth, and incorporates many of his short stories into the narrative.
- In the 2002 film adaptation of *The Time Machine*, directed by Simon Wells, Wells's great-grandson), Wells's photo appears on the stairway wall of time traveler Alex Hartdegen's home.
- The predominant setting of The Disney Channel's time-travel comedy *Phil of the Future* (2004–2006) is H. G. Wells Junior/Senior High School.
- "George Herbert," an obvious allusion to Wells himself, is the main protagonist in the low-budget films *H. G. Wells's War of the Worlds* (2005) and *War of the Worlds 2: The Next Wave* (2008), both by Asylum Films.
- The television film *Grover's Mill* (2006) features Orson Welles and Wells besieged by aliens in a rural radio station. The New Jersey

Fictional Portrayals of H. G. Wells

town of the title was the location of the beachhead of the Martian invasion in Orson Welles's 1938 radio broadcast of *The War of the Worlds*; a monument to commemorate the "Martian Landing Site" was erected in 1988.
- *H. G. Wells: War with the World* (2006) presents a stylized documentary-style account of Wells's life, in which he is played by Michael Sheen.
- *Cataclysmo and the Battle for Earth* (2008), a webseries of short films, features a time travelling Wells.
- An elderly Wells appears as a character in the online serial *Solar Pons's War of the Worlds* (2008), in which he aids in repelling a Martian invasion in 1938.
- The 2009 video game *Prototype* pays homage to Wells by featuring him and naming many of its missions after his works, including *The Wheels of Chance*, *Open Conspiracy*, *Under the Knife*, *The Stolen Body*, *The Door in the Wall*, *First and Last Things*, *Men Like Gods*, *A Dream of Armageddon*, *The World Set Free*, and *Things to Come*.
- A gender-swapped "Helena Wells" appears as an anti-hero in several seasons of the sf television series *Warehouse 13* (2009–2014). She claims to be Wells's sister, and that the achievements that history has attributed to him are actually her own. Several Wellsian technologies are also featured throughout, including Cavorite (derived from *The First Men in the Moon*). A steampunk themed, Victorian-era spin-off series focusing purely upon the Wells character has been strongly rumored since the end of the series in 2014.
- Wells makes an appearance in the historical detective series *Murdoch Mysteries*; in the episode "Future Imperfect" (2010), he is the guest speaker at debate concerning eugenics, and a sub-plot features him having a romantic dalliance with one of the main characters.
- The satirical sf cartoon series *Futurama* features Wells's head in a jar in the 31st Century "Head Museum," a showcase of history's most important people. Wellsian references are unsurprisingly legion throughout the series; for example, the episode "Lrrreconcilable Ndndifferences" (2010) spoofs Orson Welles's infamous radio adaptation of *The War of the Worlds*, while "The Late Philip J. Fry" (2010) features a "forward time machine" based on Wells's descriptions in *The Time Machine.* Along with a multitude of tropes drawn from time travel sf, the episode also features a depiction of a future humanity split into two species, a clear allusion to Wells's novel, along with a reference to three books that could restore

Appendix A

human civilization, thereby citing the conclusion of George Pal's 1960 film adaptation.
- *Legends of Tomorrow*, a TV series based on superhero characters from DC comics, features Wells as a young boy in the episode "The Magnificent Eight" (2016).

Appendix B
Wells and Deleuze: Chronology of Publications Cited

Chronology of Publications Cited: H. G. Wells

Year	Publication
1891	"Zoological Retrogression"
1895	*The Time Machine*
	The Wonderful Visit
	The Stolen Bacillus, and Other Incidents
	"The Limits of Individual Plasticity"
1896	*The Island of Doctor Moreau*
1897	*The Invisible Man*
	Certain Personal Matters
	"The Crystal Egg"
1898	*The War of the Worlds*
1899	*When the Sleeper Wakes*
1901	*The First Men in the Moon*
	Anticipations
1902	*The Discovery of the Future*
1903	"The Land Ironclads"
1904	*The Food of the Gods*
1905	*A Modern Utopia*
1906	*In the Days of the Comet*
1908	*New Worlds for Old*
	The War in the Air
1909	*Tono-Bungay*
1910	*The Sleeper Awakes* (revision of *When the Sleeper Wakes*)
1911	*The Country of the Blind, and Other Stories*
	Floor Games
1913	*Little Wars*

Appendix B

Year	Publication
1914	*The World Set Free*
1915	*Boon*
	The Research Magnificent
1922	*A Short History of the World*
Year	Publication
1923	*Men Like Gods*
1928	*The Way the World Is Going*
	Mr. Blettsworthy on Rampole Island
	The Book of Catherine Wells
1930	*The Science of Life* (co-written with Julian S. Huxley and G.P. Wells)
1931	*The Work, Wealth and Happiness of Mankind*
1933	*The Shape of Things to Come*
1934	*Experiment in Autobiography*
1935	*Things to Come: A Film Story*
1937	"World Brain: The Idea of a Permanent World Encyclopaedia"
1939	*The Fate of Homo Sapiens* (U.S. title: *The Fate of Man*)
	The New World Order
1945	*Mind at the End of Its Tether*

Chronology of Publications Cited: Gilles Deleuze

Year	Text	English Translation
1962	*Nietzsche et la philosophie.*	*Nietzsche and Philosophy* (1983).
1964	*Proust et les signes.*	*Proust and Signs* (1973, 2d ed. 2000).
1967	*Présentation de Sacher-Masoch.*	*Masochism: Coldness and Cruelty* (1989).
1968	*Différence et répétition.*	*Difference and Repetition* (1994).
1968	*Spinoza et le problème de l'expression.*	*Expressionism in Philosophy: Spinoza* (1990).
1969	*Logique du sens.*	*The Logic of Sense* (1990).
1970	*Spinoza—Philosophie pratique.*	*Spinoza: Practical Philosophy* (1988).
1972	*Capitalisme et Schizophrénie: L'Anti-Œdipe* (with Félix Guattari).	*Anti-Oedipus* (1977).
1975	*Kafka: Pour une Littérature Mineure* (with Félix Guattari).	*Kafka: Toward a Minor Literature* (1986).
1977	*Dialogues* (with Claire Parnet).	*Dialogues* (1987, 2nd ed. 2002).

Chronology of Publications Cited

Year	Text	English Translation
1979	*Superpositions.*	
1980	*Capitalisme et Schizophrénie: Mille Plateaux* (with Félix Guattari).	*A Thousand Plateaus* (1987).
1981	*Francis Bacon—and Logique de la sensation*	*Francis Bacon: The Logic of Sensation* (2003).
1983	*Cinéma I: L'image-mouvement.*	*Cinema 1: The Movement-Image* (1986).
1985	*Cinéma II: L'image-temps.*	*Cinema 2: The Time-Image* (1989).
1986	*Foucault.*	*Foucault* (1988).
1986	*Nomadology: The War Machine* (with Félix Guattari).	Revised in *A Thousand Plateaus* (1987).
1988	*Le pli—Leibniz et le baroque.*	*The Fold: Leibniz and the Baroque* (1993).
1990	*Pourparlers.*	*Negotiations* (1995).
1992	*Qu'est-ce que la philosophie?* (with Félix Guattari).	*What Is Philosophy?* (1994).
1993	*Critique et clinique.*	*Essays Critical and Clinical* (1997).
2001	*Pure Immanence* (2001).	*Pure Immanence* (2001).
2002	*L'île déserte et autres textes 1953–1974.*	*Desert Islands and Other Texts 1953–1974* (2003).

Chapter Notes

Introduction

1. Though many of the texts and theories utilized in this study were authored by Deleuze and Guattari in conjunction, the term Deleuzian shall be used as opposed to Deleuzoguattarian. In keeping with the nature of a Deleuzian "encounter," when Deleuze collaborated with Guattari, he was in effect already in collaboration with Friedrich Nietzsche, Henri Bergson and others, and hence Deleuze is given primacy. A full chronology of publications used is provided in Appendix B.

2. One such example is the highly influential study *Nietzsche and Philosophy* (1962), which systematically explicates and reappraises Nietzsche's work, resulting in a convincing defence against allegations of fascism that were tarnishing his reputation post–World War II.

3. Obviously Deleuze's works have been translated into English from the original French; this study uses the standardized translated spellings of specific titles, words and concepts. A chronology of the original French publications, and the dates of their respective translations is presented in Appendix B.

4. In terms of these "early Wellsian narratives," Crossley lists *The Time Machine* (1895), *The Wonderful Visit* (1895), *The Island of Doctor Moreau* (1896), *The Invisible Man* (1897), *The War of the Worlds* (1898), *When the Sleeper Awakes* (1899), and *The First Men in the Moon* (1901).

5. Contents of Gollancz's *The Scientific Romances of H. G. Wells* and sources of original publication: *The First Men in the Moon* (*Cosmopolitan*, November 1900), *The Food of the Gods* (*Pearson's Magazine*, December 1903), *In the Days of the Comet* (*The Daily Chronicle*, 1905), *The Invisible Man* (*Pearson's Weekly*, June 1897), *The Island of Doctor Moreau* (*Saturday Review of Literature*, January 1895), *The Time Machine* (*The New Review*, January 1895), *The War of the Worlds* (*Pearson's Magazine*, April 1897), *Men Like Gods* (*Hearst's International*, November 1922).

6. Self-proclaimed literary sequels to Wells's works are numerous. A few notable examples include: Garrett Putman Serviss's *Edison's Conquest of Mars* (1898), Egon Friedell's *The Return of the Time Machine* (1972), Michael Moorcock's *The Dancers at the End of Time* (1981), George Pal and Joe Morhaim's *Time Machine II* (1981) and Ronald Wright's *A Scientific Romance* (1997).

7. Hardy notes that despite Saussure (1857–1913) being his contemporary, Wells would have been unaware of his linguistic theories. Despite having had an impact in the linguistic schools of Eastern Europe early in the twentieth century, Saussure had no direct influence in the West until the Structuralist movement of the 1960s (114).

8. A term first coined by William Gibson in the short story "Burning Chrome" (1982) and popularized via the novel *Neuromancer* (1984).

9. Stivale cites Rudy Rucker's *Software* (1982) and *Wetware* (1988), John

Chapter Notes—One

Shirley's *A Song Called Youth* trilogy and William Gibson's *Sprawl* trilogy (*Neuromancer* (1984), *Count Zero* (1986) and *Mona Lisa Overdrive* (1988), as well as the film *The Matrix* (The Wachowskis 1999).

10. Movies referred to in this text include *Star Wars* (1977), *Batman: The Dark Knight* (2008), *Dr Who* (1963–present) *E.T. The Extra-Terrestrial* (1982), and the *Grand Theft Auto* series of videogames (1997–2008)

11. These concepts are explored in detail within the case study concerning *The Island of Doctor Moreau* in Chapter Two.

12. Derived from the Greek; "Ou," meaning not, and "Topos" meaning place, therefore literally "Land of Nowhere."

13. The prefix "Dys" meaning "ill" or "bad" serving to subvert the original term.

14. Wells's relationship to the Deleuzian concept of minor literature is discussed in depth in the study conclusion.

15. The term is borrowed from Antonin Artaud's radio play "To Have Done with the Judgment of God" (1947): "When you will have made him a body without organs, then you will have delivered him from all his automatic reactions and restored him to his true freedom" (Artaud 571).

16. To briefly cite but one example; even just the title of *The Shape of Things to Come* has become a popular trope in contemporary sf; an episode (Season 9 Episode 4) of the television series *Lost* (2004–2010) is titled in direct reference, as is the coda of the final episode of *Caprica* (2009–2010). A 2014 episode of post-apocalyptic horror series *The Walking Dead* ("Self Help") explicitly features a character reading the novel itself; as Wells's text tells of a devastating world plague that destroys humanity (in the process anticipating Zombie Horror fiction) this is clearly an appropriate choice of book!

17. Wells's *Floor Games* (1911) and *Little Wars* (1913) are recognized as having established the conventions for all subsequent recreational war games and Wells is regarded by gamers and hobbyists as the "father of miniature war gaming" (Westfahl *Greenwood* 328).

Chapter One

1. There have been many unauthorized pastiches or sequels such as by Brian Aldiss's *Moreau's Other Island* (1980), Ann Halam's *Dr. Franklin's Island* (2001), and S. Andrew Swann's *Moreau Series* (1993–1999). Alan Moore and Kevin O'Neill's comic series *The League of Extraordinary Gentlemen* features Doctor Moreau prominently. In terms of cinematic example, the recent films *Splice* (2009) and *The Human Centipede: First Sequence* (2009) are both direct descendants of the novel's themes, and also make liberal use of its "mad scientist" trope.

2. See studies by: Ivan Canadas's "Going Wilde: Prendick, Montgomery and Late-Victorian Homosexuality in *The Island of Doctor Moreau*" (2010), Neville Hoad's "Cosmetic Surgeons of the Social: Darwin, Freud, and Wells and the Limits of Sympathy on *The Island of Dr. Moreau*" (2004), John R. Reed's "The Vanity of Law in *The Island of Doctor Moreau*" (1990) and Maria Beville's "Gothic Literary Transformations" (1999).

3. The term transhuman is used in this study as opposed to posthuman. The difference between the posthuman and other hypothetical non-humans is that a posthuman was once a human, either in its lifetime or in the lifetimes of some or all of its direct ancestors. As such, a prerequisite for a posthuman is a transhuman, the point at which the human being begins surpassing or transgressing from humanity, but is still recognizable as a human person or similar; hence the use of the term transhuman in the context of the study. Interestingly, the "World Transhumanist Association" (WTA) give an annual "H. G. Wells award" for "advances in the field of the ethical use of technology to extend human capabilities." See http://transhumanism.org/

Chapter Notes—One

4. See Nick Bostrom's article "A History of Transhumanist Thought" (2005).

5. Haraway's Cyborg is discussed in detail in relation to Deleuzian theory and *The War of the Worlds* in Chapter Three.

6. For an in-depth reading of the relationship between animals and philosophical thought, see Peter Atterton and Matthew Calarco, eds., *Animal Philosophy: Ethics and Identity* (2004).

7. The book on Kafka was written in 1975, between the two volumes of *Capitalism and Schizophrenia*, and contains many of the concepts also featured in these prior texts.

8. It is notable also that Moreau's island is described in the novel as being geographically located near the Galápagos islands, the study of the wildlife of which were key to the development of Darwin's theories.

9. There has been prior critical analysis of Wells's use of islands from colonial and postcolonial perspectives. See John Rieder's *Colonialism and the Emergence of Science Fiction* (2008).

10. Kincaid lists *Utopia* (Thomas More, 1516) *The Tempest* (William Shakespeare, 1611), *New Atlantis* (Francis Bacon, 1627), *Robinson Crusoe* (Daniel Defoe, 1719), *Gulliver's Travels* (Jonathan Swift, 1726), *The Island of Doctor Moreau* (1896), *Deluge* (Sidney Fowler Wright, 1928), *The Lord of the Flies* (William Golding, 1954), *Concrete Island* (J.G. Ballard, 1974), *A Dream of Wessex* (Christopher Priest, 1977), *Web* (John Wyndham, 1974), *The Wasp Factory* (Ian Banks, 1984) and *The Scar* (China Miévill, 2002).

11. Space-based sf (such as *Star Wars*) frequently have isolated planets and space stations which function in similar ways to terrestrial islands. For a detailed study of the island motif extrapolated into contemporary sf, see Westfahl's "Islands in the Sky: The Space Station Theme in Science Fiction Literature" (2009).

12. As Brian Massumi states in the introduction to *A Thousand Plateaus*, the work itself is an "effort to construct a smooth space of thought" (*Thousand* xiii). The plateau titled "The Smooth and The Striated" invites the reader to follow each section to the "plateau that rises from the smooth space of its own composition" (xv), and to move from one plateau to the next at pleasure.

13. Interestingly, Moylan also maintains that subsequent to More's *Utopia*, island narratives switched from utopian to dystopian forms as "after 1850 ... the works of Edward Bellamy (*Looking Backward*), H. G. Wells (*A Modern Utopia*), Charlotte Perkins Gilman (*Herland*), and Jack London (*The Iron Heel*) opposed what existed but could no longer look to an alternative located in the present time, [as] utopia on one island would not work ... consequently in the late nineteenth century utopias, subversive visions were relocated in a future time where the process of revolutionary, historical change brought about the utopian society" (Moylan 6). However, it appears that specifically isolated dystopias continue to use the device; though obviously *The Island of Doctor Moreau* only features a dystopian society based in the eponymous location; the rest of the world is in blissful ignorance as to the Doctor's exploits.

14. This is akin to Friedrich Nietzsche's "Will to power," what he believed to be the main driving force in human beings. Achievement, ambition, the striving to reach the highest possible position in life; these are all manifestations of the will to power.

15. The transplantation of living cells, tissues or organs from one species to another.

16. Malthusianism refers primarily to ideas derived from the political/economic thought of the Reverend Thomas Malthus (1766–1834), as laid out initially in "An Essay on the Principle of Population" (1798), in which he describes his theory of quantitative population development: human populations tend to increase at a faster rate than their means of subsistence. Unless checked by moral restraint or disaster, widespread poverty and degradation will inevitably result.

Chapter Notes—Two

17. Lovecraft was a contemporary of Wells, and it is generally accepted that Wells was an influence upon his work. Subsequent authors have attempted to make the connection explicit; for example, Don Webb's *To Mars and Providence* (1996) is a conflation of *The War of the Worlds* and Lovecraft's Cthulhu Mythos.

18. The connections between *The Island of Moreau* and *Frankenstein* are explored in *Making Humans* (2003), edited by Judy Wilt, which features both texts, along with a number of essays in context, including one by Charles Darwin.

19. Interestingly, Redfern claims that "the scientists [that] dominate [David] Cronenberg's films can be seen to be reformulations of Wells's Doctor Moreau" (Redfurn "Science" n. pag.).

20. See Ann Stiles's "Literature in Mind: H. G. Wells and the Evolution of the Mad Scientist" (2009).

21. The relationship between science and the Gothic response is an old one, existing as early as Mary Shelley's *Frankenstein* and continuing through nineteenth-century fiction with *The Island of Doctor Moreau*. The ingerent atmosphere generated by the Gothic form was thus seen very early as a means of symbolically expressing the cold objectivity of science and the sense of fearful power resident in the control of natural forces.

22. As an example, see Penelope Quade's "Taming the Beast in the Name of the Father: The Island of Doctor Moreau and Wells's Critique of Society's Religious Molding" (2007).

23. This statement echoes the sentiments within Wells's essay "The Limits of Individual Plasticity" (1895), published a year prior to *The Island of Doctor Moreau*: "We overlook only too often the fact that a living being may also be regarded as raw material, as something plastic, something that may be shaped and altered ... and the organism as a whole developed far beyond its apparent possibilities" ("The Limits of Individual Plasticity" 39).

24. Here we also observe in Moreau's attitude what Haraway refers to (and rejects as disembodied and distant) as the "God trick" of scientific discourse, where science is seen as some idealized practice based on "what escapes human agency and responsibility in a realm above the fray" (Haraway "Situated Knowledges" 196).

Chapter Two

1. Wells's critical reception is exhaustively studied by Ingvald Raknem in *H. G. Wells and his Critics* (1962). A typical magazine review of *The War of the Worlds* soon after its publication states that "among the young writers of the day, Mr Wells is the most distinctly original, and the least indebted to predecessors" (Raknem 401).

2. According to McConnell's *The Science Fiction of H. G. Wells* (1981), Voltaire's writings, specifically *Candide* (1759) and *Plato's Dream* (1756), were favorites of Wells, and hence are probable influences upon his work (90).

3. Brian Stableford argues that *The First Men in the Moon* is the first example of an alien dystopia in fiction. The lunar "Selenites" also launched a sf subgenre depicting intelligent social insects (Stableford "Dystopias" 360–362).

4. In which, akin to *The War of the Worlds*, the alien invaders are ultimately defeated by a virus, albeit of the computer variety.

5. See Ziauddin Sardar's *Aliens R Us: The Other in Science Fiction Cinema* (2002).

6. In reference to the following essays: Rosi Braidotti, "Meta(l)morphoses" (1997), Eric White, "Once They Were Men, Now They're Land Crabs: Monstrous Becomings in Evolutionist Cinema" (1995), Camilla Griggers, "Becoming-Woman: Theory Out of Bounds" Volume 8" (1997), Steven Shaviro, "The Cinematic Body: Theory Out of Bounds Volume 2" (1993).

7. Steven Spielberg's 2005 movie adaptation makes this metaphor even

more explicit; the Martians feed the red weed with human blood in order to assist with its growth.

8. In archeoastronomical terms, the Babylonian people were the first to record the existence of Mars in approximately 400 BC, but it was not until the seventeenth century that technological advances allowed serious scientific observations.

9. As early as 1698, Dutch astronomer Christiaan Huygens (1629–1695) speculated about the existence of life on Mars, but it was Percival Lowell (1855–1916) who did most to advance the cause, suggesting in his book Mars (1895) that features of the planet's surface observed through telescopes might be canals. He believing that these might be irrigation channels constructed by a sentient life form to support existence on an arid, dying world. Of course it was just a few years later in 1897 that *The War of the Worlds* was published, in which the Martians are losing the fight to irrigate their dying world (Baxter "Mythos" 186–187).

10. Although there has been much speculation, to date there is no proof as to the existence of life on Mars; pictures of a seemingly dead world taken by the Mariner space-probe in July 1965 seemingly put to rest previously-considered possibilities of life on the red planet (Momsen 1–2). However, cumulative evidence is now building that Mars once had a habitable climate, and that it may yet harbor as-yet undiscovered bacterial life.

11. Apart from *The War of the Worlds*, notable influential sf works concerning Mars included Ray Bradbury's *The Martian Chronicles* (1950), Edgar Rice Burroughs's *Barsoom* series (1912–1943), C. S. Lewis's novel *Out of the Silent Planet* (1938), Kim Stanley Robinson's *The Mars Trilogy* (1992–1996) and a number of Robert A. Heinlein stories, such as *Podkayne of Mars* (1963).

12. It is this reverent fear that perhaps explains Wells's other theoretical technological inventions which display enormous destructive capabilities; for example, the tanks in "The Land Ironclads" (1903), and the atomic bomb in *The World Set Free* (1914).

13. In the same publication, Rieder also considers *The Island of Doctor Moreau*: "Moreau is no cyborg—his only prostheses are the scalpel and the whip—but his alienation of intellect from emotion and his instrumentalization of bodies earns him a place in the cyborg's genealogy" (112).

14. Interestingly, the 1911 sequel *Le Mystère des XV* features a trip to Mars, and the adversaries in the subsequent battle are the Martians from The War of the Worlds themselves.

15. The demon element of this cyborg is an intriguing proposition, but not one that will be debated within the remit of this book. For an encounter between Deleuze, philosophy and demons, see Keith Ansell Pearson's "Spectropoiesis and Rhizomatics: Learning to Live with Death and Demons" (2000).

16. In terms of their relative popularity and academic impact, Noah Wardrip-Fruin maintains that Haraway's cyborg model of cultural and political engagement "is more accessible to many in the U.S. than that posited by Gilles Deleuze and Félix Guattari" as it "incorporates from the outset the cyborg world" resulting in being "an important element in the pop-culture phenomenon of the cyborg" (515).

17. Ironically, in purely literal terms, with their giant brains and shriveled appendages, the Martians are in fact "organs without bodies." Also the title of a 2003 book by Žižek, based upon Deleuze's early writings such as *Difference and Repetition* (1968) and *The Logic of Sense* (1969).

18. In sf a "hive mind" is a group mind with almost complete loss (or lack) of individual identity, a fictional version of real-life superorganisms such as ant or bee nests. Popularized as a trope in Olaf Stapledon's novel *Last and First Men* (1930), and hence arguably preceded by the Martians *of The War of the Worlds*. The Borg race of the *Star Trek* universe are a popular contemporary example of the hive mind.

19. In mechanics, molar properties are those of a mass of matter, as opposed to its parts, which are atoms or molecules. For Deleuze and Guattari, molarity is the site of coded wholes. The principle objective of their writing is to break down molar aggregates in favor of molecularity, and the "microphysics of desire."

20. Unsurprisingly, the long-running *Dr Who* series has contained many overt references to Wells's novels. The Doctor's first encounter with the Daleks (1963's "The Daleks") is a tale of a post-apocalyptic conflict between effete pacifists and the subterranean monsters who prey on them, hence very obviously modeled on *The Time Machine*. Wells himself features as a character in several episodes (most notably "Timelash" [1985]) as well as being referenced specifically by name ("Pyramids of Mars" [1975[). The spin-off comic *The Time Machination* (Tony Lee and Paul Grist 2009) depicts Wells's adventures with The Doctor being the inspiration behind the writing of *The War of the Worlds* and *The Time Machine*.

21. This theme is also explored in Wells's *The World Set Free* (1914). In the aftermath of "radiological" warfare, humanity is forced "to see the round globe as one problem; it was impossible any longer to deal with it piece by piece.... On this capacity to grasp and wield the whole round globe their existence depended" (190–191).

22. One such indicator is the resuming of the media; the narrator states that "I bought a copy [of the *Daily Mail*] for a blackened shilling I found in my pocket. Most of it was in blank, but the solitary compositor who did the thing had amused himself by making a grotesque scheme of advertisement stereo on the back page" (*War* 138). The coin (representing capitalism) may be damaged, but still functions as intended. The newspaper also contains advertisements, even in the absence of anything to sell.

23. In these terms, it can be see that this theme has inspired near identical narratives in contemporary sf, the most explicit example being the reimagined *Battlestar Galactica* series (2004–2009), in which mankind is destroyed by the return of his cybernetic creations. This is also reflected in the tag-line of the show: "what has happened before will happen again." This statement can be viewed as not only a description of the action of said cyborgs, but also serves as a reflection upon the alien invasion trope that *The War of the Worlds* has inspired.

Chapter Three

1. A few contemporary examples of iconic time travel devices that have been inspired by Wells's machine: The Tardis in *Dr Who* (1963–present) (though this travels in space as well as in time), the DeLorean car in the film *Back to The Future* (1985), and the time travelling phone booth in the film *Bill and Ted's Excellent Adventure* (1989).

2. It is worthy of note that Wells's concept of time as fourth dimension pre-empted Einstein's Theory of Relativity, which was not proposed until 1915; physically speaking, Paul J. Nahin claims that Wells's novel is set within the context of a "Newtonian universe, a three-dimensional Euclidean spatial manifold that changes along an inexorable arrow of time" (Nahin 25).

3. Though arguably now less evident in modern sf than "actual" time travel, this "sleeping into the future" or "suspended animation" narrative device still remains in popular usage. For example: Robert Heinlein's novel *The Door into Summer* (1957), the television shows *Buck Rogers in the 25th Century* (1979–81) and *Futurama* (1999–2013), and films such as *Forever Young* (1992), *Idiocracy* (2006) and Woody Allen's *Sleeper* (1973), the latter specifically based upon Wells's *When the Sleeper Awakes*.

4. Examples of such texts include: *The Forebears of Kalimeros* (Alexander Veltman, 1836), *The Clock that Went Backward* (Edward Page Mitchell, 1881), *A Crystal Age* (W. H. Hudson, 1887),

Chapter Notes—Three

Looking Backward (Edward Bellamy, 1888), *A Connecticut Yankee in King Arthur's Court* (Mark Twain, 1889), *Paris Before Man* (Pierre Boitard, 1861), *The Coming Race* (Edward Bulwer-Lytton, 1871), *Erewhon* (Samuel Butler, 1872), *After London* (Edward Richard Jefferies, 1885), *Sylvie and Bruno* (Lewis Carroll, 1889), *Pallinghurst Barrow* (Grant Allen, 1892) and *The British Barbarians* (1895), *The Lost World* (Arthur Conan Doyle, 1912), and, of course, Wells's *The Chronic Argonauts* (1888) and *The Time Machine* (1895).

5. For a list of examples see Appendix A. The full implication of these manifestations is discussed in the study conclusion.

6. For one example, see http://www.timetravelreviews.com, a website "devoted to exploring the themes of time travel and alternate history in books, movies, television, and pop culture in general."

7. One of the many literary "sequels," Christopher Priest's *The Space Machine* (1976) bases its plot around this perceived technical inaccuracy. Because of the movement of planets, stars and galaxies, for a time machine to stay in one spot on Earth as it travels through time, it must also follow the Earth's trajectory through space. In Priest's book, the hero damages the time machine, and arrives on Mars, just before the start of the invasion described in *The War of the Worlds*. Wells himself appears as a minor character.

8. A good example would be the traditional opening line of a fairy tale: "once upon a time...." In terms of an example from a modern sf variant, the films in the *Star Wars* franchise all famously commence with the legend "A long time ago, in a galaxy far, far away...."

9. Hardy proceeds to discuss *The Time Machine* in the context of mythic, cyclical time. Deleuze had much to say on this concept, chiefly in terms of his interpretation of Friedrich Nietzsche's concept of "eternal return." This is discussed in the conclusion of the study.

10. Stephen Baxter's authorized sequel *The Time Ships* (1995) uses this very conceit; by the very act of relating the tale of his original journey to his audience, the time traveler has altered the future, leading to an infinite branching of multiverses through which he must navigate in an attempt to reach his "original" future.

11. Time is described in this way in the 2007 *Dr Who* episode "Blink" ("People assume that time is a strict progression of cause to effect, but actually from a non-linear, non-subjective viewpoint, it's more like a big ball of wibbly-wobbly, timey wimey—stuff"). The character of The Doctor is of course heavily indebted to Wells's time traveler.

12. It is also interesting to note that crystal is also a vital physical element of the Wellsian time machine, which is described as possessing "Crystalline bars" (Time 10), or "some transparent crystalline substance" (7). Crystals also feature in Wells's other works, most notably "The Crystal Egg" (1897), in which a shop owner finds a strange crystal that serves as a visual portal to Mars.

13. "Ice along the sea margin" is an element of the time traveler's description of the future "terminal beach": "To the north-eastward, the glare of snow lay under the starlight of the sable sky and I could see an undulating crest of hillocks pinkish white. There were fringes of ice along the sea margin, with drifting masses further out; but the main expanse of that salt ocean, all bloody under the eternal sunset, was still unfrozen" (Time 74–75).

14. However, it should be noted that in stating that Wells anticipated (or his work contains elements of) Deleuzian concepts of time it does not of course automatically follow that all subsequent time travel narratives that he has inspired do the same.

15. Interestingly, with talk of "potentialities," this passage could readily apply to resistance to Deleuzian concepts themselves.

16. The conceit that literary characters can function in the same manner as philosophical concepts is examined in the conclusion.

Chapter Notes—Four

17. The movement of the nomad is intrinsically tied to issues of smooth and striated spaces. The nomad "distributes himself in a smooth space; he occupies, inhabits, holds that space" (*Thousand* 420). As an island in time, the future world of the Morlocks and Eloi is subject to these forces, but as it raises similar issues that were discussed in detail earlier pertaining to *The Island of Doctor Moreau*, issues of spaces will not be discussed in relation to *The Time Machine*.

18. The White Sphinx is a continuing source of fascination for critics. See Patrick Parrinder's *Shadows of the Future* (1996) and John Huntingdon's *The Logic of Fantasy* (1992) for discussions upon the significance of this monument.

Chapter Four

1. Wells's idea of a "World Brain," put forward in the essay "World Brain: The Idea of a Permanent World Encyclopedia" (1937) foresees the internet as a universal information system. Although Wells doesn't anticipate electronic computer networking as a specific form, he does raise the issue of the revolutionary potentials of such a global information resource (Williams 236). In an interesting parallel, the internet is often cited as an illustration of the Deleuzian rhizome. See Sutton: "Viral Structures of the Internet" (2008).

2. *The Shape of Things to Come* (1933) arguably anticipates later zombie fiction with its apocalyptic scenario and "wandering sickness," a highly contagious viral plague that causes the infected to wander slowly and insensibly, infecting others on contact. The 1936 film adaptation *Things to Come* demonstrates this even more explicitly. The implied association between Wellsian texts and the zombie is taken to its logical extreme in Michael Hickerson's *The War of the Worlds Plus Blood, Guts and Zombies* (2009), which splices a zombie subplot into the original text. Sarah Juliet Lauro and Karen Embry's essay "A Zombie Manifesto: The Nonhuman Condition in an Era of Advanced Capitalism"(2008) argues that it is actually the zombie, not the cyborg, that our current "historical and economic moment summons ... as our most apt metaphor" (92).

3. Refer to Appendix A for various examples of texts and other media in which Wells appears as a character.

4. In the case of *The Time Machine*, this could also be attributed to the lack of any clear consensus as to the origin of the character, be he a late Victorian scientist, scientific everyman, or a reflection either of Wells himself or of some mythic precedent. For a thorough debate on this issue, see Martin Willis's "Edison as Time Traveler: H. G. Wells's Inspiration for his First Scientific Character" (1999).

5. This could also be viewed as what would now be described as an act of postmodern self-reflexivity; indeed, the narrations of sf encourage explicit consideration of the nature of narrative worlds themselves (Rabkin 79). A similar technique is evident in *The Time Machine*: when challenged as to the truth of his story, the time traveler comments both upon his own story, and the act of creating the work of fiction itself in which it is contained: "I cannot expect you to believe it ... consider I have been speculating upon the destinies of our race until I have hatched this fiction. Treat my assertion of its truth as a mere stroke of art to enhance its interest. And taking it as a story, what do you think of it?" (*Time* 78).

6. Sf of course serves as an important vehicle for feminist thought, particularly as a bridge between theory and practice. Elyce Helford states that "no other genre so actively invites representations of the ultimate goals of feminism: worlds free of sexism, worlds in which women's contributions are recognized and valued, worlds in which the diversity of women's desire and sexuality, and worlds that move beyond gender" (Hetford 291).

7. The *Warehouse 13* episodes "Time Will Tell" and "Emily Lake" establish the

175

birth-year, birthplace, and later residence of Helena G. Wells to be the same as her real-world counterpart H.G. Wells (though it is unclear how much of the biographical information available on the historical H.G. Wells would apply to Helena due to her claim that her brother, Charles, is the person history remembers by her name). The Helena Wells character has proven to be popular with viewers; since the conclusion of *Warehouse 13* in 2014, a spin-off series has been rumored, focused purely upon this character, and is to be set in the Victorian era, albeit with a steam-punk aesthetic.

8. For a detailed analysis of Lewis's novel and his relationship to Wells, see Kenneth Bailey's essay: "H. G. Wells and C.S. Lewis: Two Sides of a Visionary Coin" in Parrinder's *H. G. Wells Under Revision* (1990).

9. This could be interpreted as a damning indictment of sf as a form, as the term itself could be said to be a defining label of a specific structure. However, though the term sf may be generic, this study has in part served to emphasize its multidisciplinary and rhizomorphic nature. Indeed, as discussed in the study introduction, Deleuze and Guattari recognize the potential of sf, stating that the genre "has gone through a whole evolution taking it from animal, vegetable and mineral becomings to becomings of bacteria, viruses, molecules, and things imperceptible" (*Thousand* 274).

10. See Wagar, "H. G. Wells and the Genesis of Future Studies" (1983).

11. See Wagar, *The Open Conspiracy: H. G. Wells on World Revolution* (2002).

12. Despite Woolf's exemplification of Wells as the standard against which she and other modernist novelists were rebelling, many characteristics of his fiction have actually been instrumental in defining what we now understand as being modernism; its genre-bending (from sf to socialist treatises, from Edwardian satire to sweeping historical accounts, from short stories to utopian novels), its incorporation of the discourses of science, and its prophetic voice. Wells of course was as much a critic of the Victorian era as any of the modernists.

13. For a detailed analysis of the relationship between Deleuze and Bakhtin, see Thomas Nail's "Deleuze, Bakhtin, and the Clamour of Voices" (2008). Nail maintains that not only does Deleuze refer to Bakhtin as a primary source for his emphasis on voice and indirect discourse, both thinkers also valorize heterogeneity and creativity. Indeed, Deleuze's notions of deterritorialization and reterritorialization parallel Bakhtin's idea of "heteroglossia" and "monoglossia."

In terms of Saussure, instead of the "sign," Deleuze and Guattari make their object of study the "regime" of signs. In studying these social regimes of signs (specifically linguistic ones, i.e., language), they propose not a linguistics like Saussure's but a "pragmatics" that would pay attention to the sociopoliticohistorical factors, as well as linguistic ones. Deleuze details this in the essay "How do we recognize Structuralism?" in *Desert Islands and other Texts*.

14. Additionally, in *The Shape of Things to Come*, Wells creates a framing device by claiming that the book is his edited version of notes written by an eminent diplomat. Many of Wells's short stories also utilize variants of this form: traveler's tales, seafarer's yarns, recounted anecdotes, and so forth (Priest "Wyndham & Wells," n. pag.). *The War of the Worlds* however does not strictly utilize such a device, although it is apparent from the introduction that the narrator is relating events that occurred previously; "the storm burst upon us six years ago now" (*War* 5).

15. Nietzsche's concept of "eternal return" (or "recurrence") is central to his writings, predominantly present in *The Gay Science* (1882) and *Thus Spoke Zarathustra* (1885). To wish for the eternal return of all events would mark the ultimate affirmation of life, and to comprehend eternal recurrence in thought, and to not merely come to peace with it

but to embrace it, requires "amor fati" or "love of fate" (Dudley 201).

16. Though, as briefly touched upon previously in relation *to The Time Machine*, Wells's early writings contain many kinds of imaginative speculations about the forms and potentials of the moving image and cinematic narrative. For a thorough investigation, see Keith Williams's *H. G. Wells, Modernism and the* Movies (2007).

Bibliography

Achenbach, Joel. "The World According to Wells." *Smithsonian 32*, April 2001, pp. 111–124.
Adorno, Theodor. *Minima Moralia*: *Reflections from a Damaged Life*. London: Verso, 2005.
Aldiss, Brian. *Moreau's Other Island*. Leeds: House of Stratus, 2001.
_____. *The Shape of Further Things: Speculations on Change*. London: Corgi, 1974.
_____, ed. *The Penguin Science Fiction Omnibus*: *An Anthology*. London: Penguin, 1973.
Alkon, Paul K. *Origins of Futuristic Fiction*. Athens: University of Georgia Press, 1988.
Allen, Grant. *The British Barbarians*: *A Hilltop Novel*. 1895. www.gutenberg.org/ebooks/4340. Accessed March 2015.
_____. "Pallinghurst Barrow." 1892. http://gaslight.mtroyal.ca/palling.htm. Accessed March 2014.
Anderson, Kevin J. *The Martian War: A Thrilling Eyewitness Account of the Recent Invasion as Reported by Mr. H. G. Wells*. London: Titan Books, 2012.
_____, ed. *The War of the Worlds: Global Dispatches*. London: Titan Books 1996.
Andriano, Joseph. *Immortal Monster: The Mythological Evolution of the Fantastic Beast in Modern Fiction and Film*. Westport, CT: Greenwood Press, 1999.
Ansell Pearson, Keith. *Deleuze and Philosophy: The Difference Engineer*. London: Routledge, 1997.
_____. *Germinal Life: The Difference and Repetition of Deleuze*. London: Routledge, 1999.
_____. "Spectropoiesis and Rhizomatics: Learning to Live with Death and Demons." *Evil Spirits: Nihilism and the Fate of Modernity*, edited by Gary Banham and Charlie Blake. Manchester: Manchester University Press, 2000, pp. 124–145.
_____. *Viroid Life: Perspectives on Nietzsche and the Transhuman Condition*. London: Routledge, 1997.
Artaud, Antonin. "To Have Done with the Judgment of God." *Antonin Artaud: Selected Writings*, edited by Susan Sontag. Berkeley: University of California Press, 1976.
Ashton, Dyrk. "Feeling Time: Deleuze's Time-Image and Aesthetic Effect." *Rhizomes* 16, Summer 2008, par. 19.
Asimov, Isaac. *Gold: The Final Science Fiction Collection*. New York: HarperPrism, 1995.
_____. *Isaac Asimov's Science Fiction Magazine* 69, September 1983.
Atterton, Peter, and Matthew Calarco, eds. *Animal Philosophy: Ethics and Identity*. London: Continuum, 2004.
Bacon, Francis. *New Atlantis*. 1626. www.gutenberg.org/files/2434/2434-h/2434-h.htm. Accessed July 2013.

Bibliography

Badiou, Alain. *Deleuze: The Clamor of Being (Theory Out of Bounds)*. Minneapolis: University of Minnesota Press, 1999.
Bailey, Kenneth Vye. "H. G. Wells and C.S. Lewis: Two Sides of a Visionary Coin." *H. G. Wells Under Revision*, edited by Patrick Parrinder. Selinsgrove, PA: Susquehanna University Press, 1990.
Baker, Steve. *The Postmodern Animal*. London: Reaktion Books, 2000.
_____. "What Does Becoming-Animal Look Like?" *Representing Animals*, edited by Nigel Rothfels. Bloomington: Indiana University Press 2000, pp. 67–98.
Bakhtin, Mikhail. *The Dialogic Imagination: Four Essays*, edited by Michael Holquist. Translated by Caryl Emerson and Michael Holquist. Austin: University of Texas Press, 1981.
Ballard, J. G. *Concrete Island*. London: HarperCollins, 2008.
Banham, Gary, and Charlie Blake, eds. *Evil Spirits: Nihilism and the Fate of Modernity*. Manchester: Manchester University Press, 2000.
Banks, Iain. *The Wasp Factory*. London: Abacus, 1984.
Batchelor, John. *H.G Wells*. Cambridge: Cambridge University Press, 1985.
Baugh, Bruce. "How Deleuze Can Help Us Make Literature Work." *Deleuze and Literature*, edited by Ian Buchanan and John Marks. Edinburgh: Edinburgh University Press, 2000, pp. 34–56.
Baxter, Stephen. "Further Visions: Sequels to *The Time Machine*." *Foundation* 65, Autumn 1995, pp. 41–50.
_____. "H. G. Wells's Enduring Mythos of Mars." *War of the Worlds: Fresh Perspectives on the H. G. Wells Classic*, edited by Glenn Yeffeth. Dallas: BenBella, 2005, pp. 181–188.
_____. *The Time Ships*. London: HarperCollins, 1995.
Beaumont, Matthew. "Red Sphinx: Mechanics of the Uncanny in *The Time Machine*." *Science Fiction Studies* 33, no. 2, July 2006, pp. 230–250.
Begiebing, Robert J. "The Mythic Hero in H. G. Wells's *The Time Machine*." *Essays in Literature* 11, Issue 2, 1984, pp. 201–210.
Bellamy, Edward. *Equality*. 1897. www.gutenberg.org/dirs/etext05/equal10h.htm. Accessed November 2014.
_____. "Looking Backward." 1888. www.gutenberg.org/files/25439/25439.txt. Accessed November 2014.
Beller, Jonathan L. "Cinema, Capital of the Twentieth Century." *Postmodern Culture* 4, no. 3. www.pmc.iath.virginia.edu/text-only/issue.594/beller.594. Accessed November 2014.
Bellow, Saul. *Mr. Sammler's Planet*. New York: Penguin, 1970.
Bennett, Arnold, ed. "The Invisible Man: Herbert George Wells and His Work." *Arnold Bennett and H. G. Wells: A Record of a Personal and Literary Friendship*, edited by Harris Wilson. Champaign: University of Illinois Press, 1960, pp. 260–276.
Bensen, Donald R. *And Having Writ...* Indianapolis: Bobbs-Merrill, 1978.
Bergonzi, Bernard. *The Early H. G. Wells: A Study of the Scientific Romances*. Manchester: Manchester University Press, 1961.
_____. "The Publication of *The Time Machine* 1894–1895." *SF: The Other Side of Realism*, edited by Thomas D. Clareson. Bowling Green: Bowling Green State University Popular Press, 1971, pp. 204–215.
_____. "*The Time Machine*: An Ironic Myth." *Critical Quarterly* 2, 1960, pp. 39–55.
_____, ed. *H. G. Wells: A Collection of Critical Essays*. Upper Saddle River: Prentice-Hall, 1976.
Best, Steven, and Douglas Kellner. *Postmodern Theory: Critical Interrogations*. Basingstoke: Macmillan, 1991.
Beville, Maria. "Gothic Literary Transformations: The Fin-de-Siecle and Modernism."

Bibliography

Gothic Postmodernism: Voicing the Terrors of Postmodernity, edited by Theo D'Haen and Hans Bertens. New York: Rodopi, 2009.
Bignell, Jonathan. "Another Time, Another Space: Modernity, Subjectivity and The Time Machine." *Alien Identities: Exploring Differences in Film and Fiction*, edited by Deborah Cartmell. London: Pluto Press, 1999, pp. 87–103.
Bishop, Michael. *No Enemy But Time*. New York: Pocket Books. 1982.
Bloom, Harold, ed. *H. G. Wells*. New York: Chelsea House, 2005.
Bogard, William. "Smoothing Machines and the Constitution of Society." *Cultural Studies* 14, no. 4, 2000, pp. 269–294.
Bogue, Ronald. *Deleuze and Guattari*. London: Routledge, 1993.
_____. *Deleuze on Cinema*. London: Routledge 2003.
_____. "Deleuze's Style." *Continental Philosophy Review* 29, no. 3, July 1996, pp. 251–268.
_____. *Deleuze's Wake*. New York: University of New York Press, 2004.
_____. "Minoritarian + Literature." *The Deleuze Dictionary*, edited by Adrian Parr. Edinburgh: Edinburgh University Press, 2005, pp. 167–169.
_____. "Violence in Three Shades of Metal." *Deleuze and Music*, edited by Ian Buchanan and Marcel Swiboda. Edinburgh: Edinburgh University Press, 2004, pp. 195–217.
Boitard, Pierre. *Paris avant les hommes* (*Paris Before Man.*) 1861. www.trussel.com/prehist/boitard1.htm. Accessed July 2013.
Borges, Jorge Luis. "A New Refutation of Time." *Other Inquisitions 1937–1952*. Translated by Ruth L. C. Simms. Austin: University of Texas Press, 2000.
_____. *Other Inquisitions 1937–1952*. Austin: University of Texas Press, 2000.
Bork, Alfred M. "The Fourth Dimension in Nineteenth-Century Physics." *Isis* 55, no. 3, September 1964, pp. 326–338.
Bostrom, Nick. "A History of Transhumanist Thought." *Journal of Evolution and Technology* 14, issue 1, April 2005. www.jetpress.org/volume14/bostrom.pdf. Accessed November 2015.
Boundas, Constantin and Dorothea Olkowski, editors. *Gilles Deleuze and the Theatre of Philosophy*. New York: Routledge, 1994.
Bova, Ben. "Inspiration." *Holt Anthology of Science Fiction*. Fort Worth: Harcourt College, pp. 175–187.
Bradbury, Ray. *The Martian Chronicles*. London: Harper Voyager, 2008.
Braidotti, Rosi. "Affirming the Affirmative on Nomadic Affectivity." *Rhizomes* 11, Spring 2006.
_____. "Difference, Diversity, and Nomadic Subjectivity." 1987. www.let.uu.nl/~rosi.braidotti/personal/rosilecture.html. Accessed July 2015.
_____. "Discontinued Becomings: Deleuze on the Becoming-Woman of Philosophy." *Journal of the British Society for Phenomonology* 24, no. 1, January 1993, pp. 44–55.
_____. "Embodiment, Sexual Difference, and the Nomadic Subject." *Hypatia* 8, no. 1, Winter 1993, pp. 1–13.
_____. "Meta(L)Morphoses." *Theory, Culture & Society* 14, no. 2, 1997, pp. 67–80.
_____. *Nomadic Subjects: Embodiment and Sexual Difference in Contemporary Feminist Theory*. New York: Columbia University Press, 1994.
Brake, Mark. "Aliens and Time in the Machine Age." *International Journal of Astrobiology* 5. Cambridge: Cambridge University Press, 2006, pp. 277–286.
Bray, Libba. *The Sweet Far Thing*. New York: Simon & Schuster, 2007.
Brecht, Bertolt. *Brecht on Theater: The Development of an Aesthetic*, edited and translated by John Willett. New York: Hill and Wang, 1964.
Broderick, Damien. *Reading by Starlight: Postmodern Science Fiction*. London: Routledge, 1995.

Bibliography

Brooks, Van Wyck. *The World of H. G. Wells*. London: Unwin, 1915.
Brown, Lori. "Becoming-Animal in the Flesh: Expanding the Ethical Reach of Deleuze and Guattari's Tenth Plateau." *PhaenEx: Journal of Existential and Phenomenological Theory and Culture* 2, no. 2, Winter 2007, pp. 260–278.
Bruckner, René Thoreau. "Travels in Flicker-Time." *Spectator* 28, no. 2, 2008, pp. 61–72.
Buchanan, Ian. *Deleuzism: A Metacommentary*. Edinburgh: Edinburgh University Press, 2000.
Buchanan, Ian, and Greg Lambert, eds. *Deleuze and Space*. Edinburgh: Edinburgh University Press, 2005.
Buchanan, Ian, and John Marks, eds. *Deleuze and Literature*. Edinburgh: Edinburgh University Press, 2000.
Buchanan, Ian, and Marcel Swiboda, eds. *Deleuze and Music*. Edinburgh: Edinburgh University Press, 2004.
Buchanan, Ian, and Nicholas Thoburn, eds. *Deleuze and Politics*. Edinburgh: Edinburgh University Press, 2008.
Buettner, Robert. *Orphanage*. New York: Warner Books, 2004.
Bukatman, Scott. *Terminal Identity: The Virtual Subject in Postmodern Science Fiction*. Durham: Duke University Press, 1993.
Bulwer-Lytton, Edward. *The Coming Race*. 1871. www.gutenberg.org/files/1951/1951-h/1951-h.htm. Accessed February 2015.
Burroughs, Edgar Rice. *Barsoom Series: A Princess of Mars*. 1917. www.gutenberg.org/files/62/62-h/62-h.htm. Accessed April 2014.
Busch, Justin E.A. *The Utopian Vision of H. G. Wells*. Jefferson: McFarland, 2009.
Butler, Samuel. *Erewhon*. Sydney: British Council, 1964.
____. *Luck or Cunning?* New York: AMS, 1968.
Campbell, Heidi, and Mark Walker. "Religion and Transhumanism: Introducing a Conversation." *Journal of Evolution and Technology* 14, no. 2, August 2005, pp. 1–10.
Canadas, Ivan. "Going Wilde: Prendick, Montgomery and Late-Victorian Homosexuality in *The Island of Doctor Moreau*." *JELL: Journal of the English Language and Literature Association of Korea* 56, no. 3, June 2010, pp. 461–485.
Cantor, Paul, and Peter Hufnagel. "The Empire of the Future: Imperialism and Modernism in H. G. Wells." *Studies in the Novel* 38, 2006, pp. 36–56.
Cantril, Hadley. *The Invasion from Mars: A Study in the Psychology of Panic*. London: Transaction Publishers, 2005.
Carroll, Lewis. *Sylvie and Bruno*. Middlesex: Echo Library, 2008.
Castrell, Deborah, ed. *Alien Identities*. London: Pluto Press, 1999.
Caudwell, Christopher. "H. G. Wells: A Study in Utopianism." *Studies in a Dying Culture*. London: Lane, 1938, pp. 73–95.
Caudwell, Larry W. "Time at the End of its Tether: H. G. Wells and the Subversion of Master Narrative." *H. G. Wells's Perennial Time Machine*, edited by George Slusser, Patrick Parrinder and Danièle Chatelain. Athens: University of Georgia Press, 2001, pp. 137–149.
Cherry, Brigid. *Horror*. New York: Routledge, 2009.
Chesney, George Tomkyns. *The Battle of Dorking*. 1871. www.gutenberg.net.au/ebooks06/0602091h.html. Accessed February 2014.
Christopher, John. *The Tripods Trilogy*. Middlesex: Puffin, 1984.
Cicero. *The Republic and The Laws*. Oxford: Oxford Paperbacks, 2008.
Clark, Andy. *Natural Born Cyborgs*. Oxford: Oxford University Press, 2003.
Clarke, Arthur C. *Childhood's End*. London: Pan Macmillan, 1990.
____. *Profiles of the Future: An Enquiry into the Limits of the Possible*. London: Indigo, 1999.

Bibliography

_____. *2001: A Space Odyssey.* London: Orbit, 2000.
Clarke, Ignatius Frederick. *Voices Prophesying War.* Oxford: Oxford University Press, 1992.
Clute, John. *Science Fiction: The Illustrated Encyclopedia.* New York: Dorling Kindersley, 1995.
Coates, Paul. "Chris Marker and the Cinema as Time Machine." *Science Fiction Studies* 43, no. 14, 1987, pp. 307–315.
Cochrane, Ev. *Martian Metamorphoses: The Planet Mars in Ancient Myth and Religion.* Ames: Aeon Press, 1997.
Cohen, Jeffery Jerome. *Monster Theory: Reading Culture.* Minneapolis: University of Minnesota Press, 1996.
Colebrook, Claire. "Actuality." *The Deleuze Dictionary*, edited by Adrian Parr. Edinburgh: Edinburgh University Press, 2005, pp. 9–11.
_____. *Deleuze: A Guide for the Perplexed.* New York: Continuum, 2006.
_____. *Gilles Deleuze.* Oxford: Routledge, 2002.
_____. *Understanding Deleuze.* Sydney: Allen & Unwin, 2002.
Colman, Felicity J. "Rhizome." *The Deleuze Dictionary*, edited by Adrian Parr. Edinburgh: Edinburgh University Press, 2005, pp. 231–233.
Conan Doyle, Arthur. *The Lost World.* 1912. www.gutenberg.org/files/139/139-h/139-h.htm. Accessed December 2014.
Conley, Tom. "Molecular." *The Deleuze Dictionary*, edited by Adrian Parr. Edinburgh: Edinburgh University Press, 2005, pp. 172–174.
Conrad, Joseph. *Heart of Darkness.* New York: St. Martin's Press, 1996.
Crossley, Robert "The Grandeur of H. G. Wells." *A Companion to Science Fiction*, edited by David Seed. Oxford: Blackwell, 2005, pp. 353–363.
Cubitt, Sean, and Ziauddin Sardar, eds. *Aliens R Us: The Other in Science Fiction Cinema.* London: Pluto Press, 2002.
Darwin, Charles. *The Descent of Man.* London: Adamant Media, 2005.
_____. *On the Origin of Species by Means of Natural selection.* New York: Signet Classics, 2003.
Davis, Eric. "The Witch's Flight: A Review of Deleuze & Guattari's What Is Philosophy?" *VLS*, Summer 1994. www.techgnosis.com/dg.html#top. Accessed September 2014.
De Bergerac, Cyrano. *Le Autre Monde: ou les États et Empires de la Lune.* 1657. www.bewilderingstories.com/issue27/cyrano1.html. Accessed May 2015.
De La Hire, Jean. *The Man Who Lived Underwater / The Nyctalope on Mars.* Tarzana: Black Coat Press, 2008.
Defoe, Daniel. *Robinson Crusoe.* 1719. www.gutenberg.org/ebooks/521. Accessed December 2014.
Delaney, Paul. *Decolonization and the Minor Writer.* www.kent.ac.uk/english/postcolonial/Deleuze%20and%20Guattari.pdf. Accessed 4 May 2015.
Deleuze, Gilles. *Cinema 1: The Movement-Image.* Minneapolis: University of Minnesota Press 1986.
_____. *Cinema 2: The Time Image.* London: Continuum Publishing Group, 2005.
_____. "Coldness and Cruelty." *Masochism.* New York: Zone Books, 1989.
_____. "Dead Psychoanalysis: Analyse." *Dialogues II.* Gilles Deleuze and Claire Parnet. New York: Columbia University Press, 2007, pp. 77–123.
_____. "Desert Islands." *Desert Islands and Other Texts 1953–1974.* London: Semiotext(e), 2004.
_____. *Desert Islands and Other Texts 1953–1974.* London: Semiotext(e), 2004.
_____. *Dialogues.* London: Althone Press, 1977.
_____. *Difference and Repetition.* London: Continuum, 2004.
_____. *Essays Critical and Clinical.* London: Continuum, 1998.

Bibliography

____. *Expressionism in Philosophy: Spinoza*. New York: Zone Books, 1990.
____. *The Fold: Leibniz and the Baroque*. Minneapolis: University of Minnesota Press, 1993.
____. *Foucault*. Minneapolis: University of Minnesota Press, 1988.
____. *Francis Bacon: The Logic of Sensation*. London: Continuum, 2003.
____. *Kant's Critical Philosophy*. London: Althone Press, 1963.
____. "Literature and Life." *Essays Critical And Clinical*. London: Continuum, 1998.
____. *The Logic of Sense*. New York: Columbia University Press, 1990.
____. *Negotiations: 1972–1990*. New York: Columbia University Press, 1995.
____. *Proust and Signs*. Minneapolis: University of Minnesota Press, 2000.
____. *Pure Imminence: Essays on Life*. Cambridge: MIT Press, 2001.
____. *Spinoza: Practical Philosophy*. San Francisco: City Light Books, 1988.
____. "What Is Structuralism?" *Desert Islands and Other Texts 1953–1974*. London: Semiotext(e), 2004, pp. 170–192.
Deleuze, Gilles, and Carmelo Bene. *Superpositions*. Paris: Minuit, 1979.
Deleuze, Gilles, and Félix Guattari. *Anti-Oedipus*. London: Continuum, 2004.
____. *Kafka: Towards a Minor Literature*. Minneapolis: University of Minnesota Press, 2003.
____. "On Capitalism and Desire." *Desert Islands and Other Texts*, edited by Sylvère Lotinger. London: Semiotext(e), 2004, pp. 262–273.
____. *A Thousand Plateaus: Capitalism and Schizophrenia*. London: Continuum, 2004.
____. *What Is Philosophy?* London: Verso, 1994.
Deleuze, Gilles, and Claire Parnet. *Dialogues II*. New York: Columbia University Press, 2007.
Derrida, Jacques. *The Animal That Therefore I Am*. New York: Fordham University Press, 2008.
____. "I'm Going to Have to Wander All Alone." *The Work of Mourning*, edited by Pascale-Anne Brault and Michael Nass. Chicago: University of Chicago Press, 2001, pp. 192–195.
Derry, Stephen. "The Time Traveller's Utopian Books and His Reading of the Future." *Foundation* 65, Autumn 1995, pp. 16–24.
Draper, Michael. *H. G. Wells*. New York: St. Martin's Press, 1988.
Dryden, Linda. *The Modern Gothic and Literary Doubles: Stevenson, Wilde and Wells*. Basingstoke: Pallgrave, 2003.
Dudley, Will. *Hegel, Nietzsche, and Philosophy: Thinking Freedom*. Cambridge: Cambridge University Press, 2002.
Dyens, Ollivier. *Metal and Flesh: The Evolution of Man: Technology Takes Over*. Cambridge: MIT Press, 2001.
Edwards, Malcolm, and Maxim Jakubowski, eds. *The SF Book of Lists*. New York: Berkeley Publishing Group, 1982.
Eliot, T.S. "Wells as Journalist." *H.G Wells: The Critical Heritage*, edited by Patrick Parrinder. London: Routledge and Kegan Paul, 1972, pp. 320–345.
Ellis, Carol Schwartz. "With Eyes Uplifted: Space Aliens as Sky Gods." *Liquid Metal: The Science Fiction Film Reader*, edited by Sean Redmond. London: Wallflower Press, 2004, pp. 145–153.
Elsenstein, Alex. "Very Early Wells: Origins of Some Major Physical Motifs in *The Time Machine* and *The War of the Worlds*." *Extrapolation* 13, 1972, pp. 119–126.
The Epic of Gilgamesh. Translated by Andrew George. London: Penguin, 1999.
Fancy, David. "Difference, Bodies, Desire: The Collaborative Thought of Gilles Deleuze and Félix Guattari." *Science Fiction Film and Television* 3, no. 1, 2010. Liverpool: Liverpool University Press, pp. 93–106.
Firchow, Peter. "H. G. Wells's Time Machine: In Search of Time Future and Time

Bibliography

Past." *Midwest Quarterly: A Journal of Contemporary Thought* 45, no. 2, 2004, pp. 123–136.
_____. "Wells and Lawrence in Huxley's *Brave New World.*" *The Journal of Modern Literature* 5, no. 2, April 1976, pp. 260–278.
Fitting, Peter. "Estranged Invaders: *The War of the Worlds.*" *Learning from Other Worlds: Estrangement, Cognition, and the Politics of Science Fiction and Utopia*, edited by Patrick Parrinder. Liverpool: Liverpool University Press, 2000, pp. 127–145.
Flammarion, Camille. *Les Mondes imaginaires et les mondes réels.* 1865.www.gallica.bnf.fr/ark:/12148/bpt6k834651. Accessed November 2015.
Fluet, Lisa. "Modernism and Disciplinary History: On H. G. Wells and T. S. Eliot." *Twentieth Century Literature* 50, no. 3, Autumn 2004, pp. 286–316.
Flynn, John L. *The War of the Worlds: From Wells to Spielberg.* Owings Mills: Galactic Books, 2005.
Foucault, Michel. "Theatrum Philosophicum." *Language, Counter-Memory, Practice: Selected Essays and Interviews*, edited by Donald F. Bouchard. Ithaca: Cornell University Press, 1977, pp. 165–196.
Friedell, Egon. *The Return of the Time Machine.* New York: Daw, 1972.
Fuglsang, Martin, and Bent Meier Sørensen, eds. *Deleuze and the Social.* Edinburgh: Edinburgh University Press, 2006.
Gedult, Harry M, ed. *The Definitive Time Machine: A Critical Edition of H. G. Wells's Scientific Romance.* Bloomington: Indiana University Press, 1987.
Genosko, Gary. *Deleuze and Guattari: Critical Assessments of Leading Philosophers.* London: Routledge, 2001.
Gernsback, Hugo. "Science Wonder Stories." *Science-Fiction: The Gernsback Years: A Complete Coverage of the Genre*, edited by Everett Franklin Bleiler and Richard Bleiler. Kent: Kent State University Press, 1988.
Gibson, William. "Burning Chrome." *Burning Chrome.* New York: HarperCollins, 2003.
_____. *Count Zero.* New York: Berkley Publishing Group, 1986.
_____. *Mona Lisa Overdrive.* New York: Bantam Books, 1988.
_____. *Neuromancer.* New York: Berkley Publishing group, 1984.
Gilman, Charlotte Perkins. *Herland.* 1915. www.gutenberg.org/files/32/32-h/32-h.htm. Accessed June 2014.
Godwin, Francis. *The Man in the Moone.* Peterborough: Broadview Press, 2009.
Golding, William. *Lord of the Flies.* London: Faber & Faber, 2005.
Goodwin, Barbara and Taylor, Keith. *The Politics of Utopia: A Study in Theory and Practise.* London: Hutchinson & Co., 1982.
Gollancz, Victor. *The Scientific Romances of H. G. Wells*, London: Gollancz, 1933.
Gomel, Elana. "Shapes of the Past and the Future: Darwin and the Narratology of Time Travel." *Narrative* 17, no. 3, October 2009, pp. 334–352.
Goodchild, Philip. *Deleuze and Guattari: An Introduction to the Politics of Desire.* London: Sage Publications, 1996.
Gott, Samuel. *Nova Solyma, the Ideal City: Or, Jerusalem Regained.* Charleston, SC: BiblioBazaar, 2010.
Graham, Elaine L. *Representations of the Post/Human: Monsters, Aliens and Others in Popular Culture.* Manchester: Manchester University Press, 2002.
Gray, Chris. *The Cyborg Handbook.* New York: Routledge, 1995.
Gregory of Tours. *Seven Sleepers of Ephesus.* www.breviary.net/martyrology/mart07/mart0727.htm. Accessed April 2015.
Griggers, Camilla. *Becoming-Woman: Theory Out of Bounds.* Minneapolis: University of Minnesota Press, 1997.
Grisham, Therese. "Linguistics as Indiscipline: Deleuze and Guattari's Pragmatics." *SubStance* 66, 1991, pp. 36–54.

Bibliography

Grosz, Elizabeth. "A Thousand Tiny Sexes: Feminism and Rhizomatics." *Topoi* 12, no. 2, 1993, pp.167–179.
_____. *Volatile Bodies: Towards a Corporeal Feminism.* Sydney: Allen and Unwin, 1994.
Guattari, Félix. *Chaosmosis: an Ethicoaesthetic Paradigm.* Bloomington: Indiana University Press, 1995.
Haden, David. *The Time Machine: A Sequel.* Stoke-on-Trent: Burslem Books, 2010.
Halam, Ann. *Dr. Franklin's Island.* New York: Laurel Leaf, 2001.
Halberstam, Judith, and Ian Livingstone, eds. *Posthuman Bodies.* Bloomington: Indiana University Press, 1995.
Hall, Joseph. *The Discovery of a New World, 1613.* Charleston, SC: BiblioLife, 2010.
Hamilton, Edmond. "Comet Doom." *The Collected Edmond Hamilton Volume 1: The Metal Giants and Others.* Royal Oak, MI: Haffner Press, 1999.
Hammond, John. R, ed. *H. G. Wells: Interviews and Recollections.* London: Macmillan, 1980.
_____. *H. G. Wells and the Modern Novel.* New York: St. Martin's Press, 1988.
_____. *H. G. Wells's The Time Machine: A Reference Guide.* Westport, CT: Praeger, 2004.
Haraway, Donna J. "A Cyborg Manifesto: Science, Technology, and Socialist-Feminism in the Late Twentieth Century." *Simians, Cyborgs and Women: The Reinvention of Nature.* London: Free Association Books, 1991, pp. 149–181.
_____. *Primate Vision: Gender, Race & Nature in the World of Modern Science.* New York: Routledge, 1989.
_____. "Situated Knowledges: The Science Question in Feminism and the Privilege of Partial Perspective." *Simians, Cyborgs and Women: The Reinvention of Nature.* New York: Routledge, 1991, pp. 184–202.
_____. "The Promises of Monsters: A Regenerative Politics for Inappropriate/d Others." *Cultural Studies*, edited by Lawrence Grossberg, Cary Nelson and Paula Treichler. London: Routledge, 1991, pp. 295–337.
_____. *When Species Meet.* Minneapolis: University of Minnesota Press, 2008.
Hardt, Michael. *Gilles Deleuze: An Apprenticeship in Philosophy.* Minneapolis: University of Minnesota Press, 1993.
Hardy, Sylvia. "H. G. Wells the Poststructuralist." *H. G. Wells's Fin-de-Siecle: v. 2: Twenty-First Century Reflections on the Early H. G. Wells*, edited by John S. Partington. Oxford: Peter Lang, 2007, pp. 113–125.
_____. "The Time Machine and Victorian Mythology." *H G. Wells's Perennial Time Machine*, edited by George Slusser, Patrick Parrinder and Danièle Chatelain. Athens: University of Georgia Press, 2001, pp. 76–96.
Harrington, James. *Oceana.* 1656. www.gutenberg.org/ebooks/2801. Accessed December 2015.
Harris, Mason. "Vivisection, the Culture of Science, and Intellectual Uncertainty in The Island of Doctor Moreau." *Gothic Studies* 4, no. 2, 2002, pp. 99–115.
Hayles, N. Katherine. *How We Became Posthuman: Virtual Bodies in Cybernetics, Literature, and Informatics.* Chicago: University of Chicago Press, 1999.
Haynes, Roslynn D. *H.G Wells: Discoverer of the Future: The Influence of Science on His Thought.* London: Macmillan, 1980.
Heinlein, Robert A. *The Door into Summer.* Toronto: Ballantine Books, 1986.
_____. *Podkayne of Mars.* New York: Baen Books, 1995.
Helford, Elyce Rae. "Feminism." *The Greenwood Encyclopedia of Science Fiction and Fantasy*, edited by Gary Westfahl. Westport, CT: Greenwood Press, 2005, pp. 289–290.
Helmreich, Stefan. "The Signature of Life: Designing the Astrobiological Imagination." *Grey Room 23*, Spring 2006, pp. 66–95.

Bibliography

Herbrechter, Stefan, and Ivan Callus. "What's Wrong With Posthumanism?" *Rhizomes* 7, Fall 2003. www.rhizomes.net/issue7/callus.htm. Accessed November 2014.

Herron, Jerry. *The Ends of Theory*. Detroit: Wayne State University Press, 1996.

Herzogenrath, Bernd. *An [Un]Likely Alliance: Thinking Environment[s] with Deleuze/Guattari*. Newcastle upon Tyne: Cambridge Scholars, 2008.

Hickerson, Michael. *The War of the Worlds Plus Blood, Guts and Zombies*. Winnipeg: Coscom Entertainment, 2009.

Higdon, David Robert. "A Revision and a Gloss: Michael Bishop's Postmodern Interrogation of H. G. Wells's *The Time Machine*." *H G. Wells's Perennial Time Machine*, edited by George Slusser, Patrick Parrinder and Danièle Chatelain. Athens: University of Georgia Press, 2001, pp. 176–187.

Hillegas, Mark. *The Future as Nightmare: H. G. Wells and the Anti-Utopians*. New York: Oxford University Press, 1967.

Hinton, Charles Robert. *The Scientific Romances: First and Second Series 1884/1885*. New York: Arno Press, 1976.

Hoad, Neville. "Cosmetic Surgeons of the Social: Darwin, Freud, and Wells and the Limits of Sympathy on *The Island of Doctor Moreau*." *Compassion: The Culture and Politics of an Emotion*, edited by Lauren Berlant. London: Routledge, 2004, pp. 187–217.

Holland, Eugene, Daniel W. Smith, and Charles J. Stivale, eds. *Gilles Deleuze: Image and Text*. London: Continuum, 2009.

Hollinger, Veronica. "Deconstructing *The Time Machine*." *Science Fiction Studies* 14, no. 42, July 1987, pp. 201–221.

Homer. *The Iliad* and *The Odyssey*. Translated by George Chapman. Ware: Wordsworth Classics, 2000.

Hudson, W. H. *A Crystal Age*. Charleston, SC: BiblioLife, 2004.

Hughes, David Y. "The Garden in Wells's Early Science Fiction." *H. G. Wells and Modern Science Fiction*, edited by Darko Suvin and Robert M. Philmus. Lewisburg: Bucknell University Press, 1977, pp. 48–69.

Hughes, David Y., and Robert M. Philmus. *H. G. Wells: Early Writings in Science and Science Fiction*. Berkeley: University of California Press, 1975.

Hume, Katherine. "Eat or be Eaten: H. G. Wells's Time Machine." *H. G. Wells*, edited by Harold Bloom. Philadelphia: Chelsea House, 2005.

Huntington, John. *The Logic of Fantasy: H.G Wells and Science Fiction*. New York: Columbia University Press, 1992.

_____. "*The Time Machine* and Wells's Social Trajectory." *Foundation* 65, Autumn 1995, pp. 6–15.

Hurley, Kelly. *The Gothic Body: Sexuality, Materialism, and Degeneration at the fin de siècle*. Cambridge: Cambridge University Press, 1996.

_____. "Reading Like and Alien: Posthuman identity in Ridley Scott's *Alien* and David Cronenberg's *Rabid*." *Posthuman Bodies*, edited by Judith. Halberstam, 1995, pp. 203–224.

Hutchings, Peter. "'We're the Martians Now': British Sf Invasion Fantasies." *Liquid Metal: The Science Fiction Film Reader*, edited by Sean Redmond. London: Wallflower Press, 2004, pp. 337–345.

Huxley, Aldous. *Brave New World*. London: Vintage Books, 2007.

Huxley, Thomas. *Evolution and Ethics*. 1893. www.gutenberg.org/cache/epub/2940/pg2940.html. Accessed July 2015.

Jackson, Kimberly. "Vivisected Language in H. G. Wells's The Island of Doctor Moreau." *H. G. Wells's Fin-de-Siecle: v. 2: Twenty-First Century Reflections on the Early H. G. Wells*, edited by John S. Partington. Oxford: Peter Lang, 2007, pp. 27–40.

Jameson, Fredric. *Archaeologies of the Future: The Desire Called Utopia and Other Science Fictions*. London: Verso, 2005.

Bibliography

———. "Progress versus Utopia; or, Can We Imagine the Future?" *Science Fiction Studies* 9, no. 1, March 1982, pp. 147–158.
———. *A Singular Modernity*. London: Verso, 2004.
Jamieson, Theresa. "Working for the Empire: Professions of Masculinity in H. G. Wells's *The Time Machine* and R. L. Stevenson's *The Strange Case of Dr Jekyll and Mr Hyde*." *Victorian Network Journal* 1, no. 1, Summer 2009, pp. 72–91.
Jefferies, Richard. *After London: Or, Wild England*. Charleston, SC: BiblioBazaar, 2007.
Jeter, K W. *Morlock Night*. London: Grafton, 1989.
Johnson, William, ed. *Focus on the Science Fiction Film*. Upper Saddle River: Prentice-Hall, 1972.
Kafka, Franz. *Collected Stories*. London: Everyman, 1993.
———. *Diaries 1914–1923*. New York: Schocken, 1965.
———. *The Metamorphosis*. Morrisville: Aventura Press, 2008.
Kaku, Michio. *Hyperspace: A Scientific Odyssey Through Parallel Universes, Time Warps, and the Tenth Dimension*. New York: Anchor Books, 1995.
Kemp, Peter. *H. G. Wells and the Culminating Ape: Biological Themes and Imaginative Obsession*. London: Macmillan, 1982.
Kern, Stephen. *The Culture of Time and Space 1880–1918*. Cambridge: Harvard University Press, 2001.
Kessel, John. "Buffalo." *The Magazine of Fantasy & Science Fiction* 80, no. 1, January 1991.
Ketterer, David. *New Worlds for Old: The Apocalyptic Imagination, Science Fiction and American Literature*. New York: Anchor Books, 1974.
———. "Oedipus as Time Traveller." *Science Fiction Studies* 9, 1982, pp. 340–341.
Khalfa, Jean. *Introduction to the Philosophy of Gilles Deleuze*. London: Continuum, 1999.
Kincaid, Paul. "Islomania? Insularity? The Myth of the Island in British Science Fiction." *What Do We Do When We Read Science Fiction?* Essex: Beccon Publications, 2008, pp. 141–148.
———. "Popularly Ignored." *Science Fiction Studies* 108, July 2009. www.depauw.edu/sfs/birs/bir108.htm. Accessed August 2014.
King, Geoff, and Tanya Krzywinska. *Science Fiction Cinema: from Outerspace to Cyberspace*. London: Wallflower, 2000.
Kirby, David A. "Are We Not Men?: The Horror of Eugenics in *The Island of Doctor Moreau*." *Paradoxa* 17, 2002, pp. 93–108.
Kirkup, Gill, ed. *The Gendered Cyborg: A Reader*. New York: Routledge, 2000.
Klass, Philip. "Welles or Wells: The First Invasion from Mars." *Synergy SF: New Science Fiction*, edited by George Zebrowski. Detroit: Gale Group, 2004.
Kleist, Heinrich Von. *Penthesilea*. 1808. www.gutenberg.org/cache/epub/6648/pg6648.html. Accessed April 2013.
Lambert, Gregg. "On the Uses and Abuses of Literature for Life." *Deleuze and Literature*, edited by Ian Buchanan and John Marks. Buchanan. Edinburgh: Edinburgh University Press, 2000, pp. 135–166.
———. *Who's Afraid of Deleuze and Guattari?* London: Continuum, 2006.
Land, Chris. "Becoming Cyborg: Changing the Subject of the Social." *Deleuze and the Social*, edited by Martin Fuglsang and Brent Meier Sorensen. Edinburgh: Edinburgh University Press, 2006, pp. 112–132.
Lauro, Sarah Juliet, and Karen Embry. "A Zombie Manifesto: The Nonhuman Condition in an Era of Advanced Capitalism." *Boundary 2* 35, no. 1, 2008, pp. 85–108.
Le Guin, Ursula. *The Dispossessed*. London: Orion Publishing, 2002.
———. *The Left Hand of Darkness*. London: Orion Publishing, 1988.

Bibliography

Lee, Tony, and Paul Grist. *Dr Who: The Time Machination.* San Diego: IDW Publishing, 2009.
Lessenich, Rolf. "The World of the Novels of H. G. Wells." *Zeitschrift für Englische Philologie* 115, issue 3, 1997, pp. 299–322.
Lewis, C. S. *That Hideous Strength.* New York: Scribner, 1996.
_____. *Out of the Silent Planet.* New York: Scribner, 2003.
Lister, Martin, Jon Dovey, and Seth Giddings. *New Media a Critical Introduction.* London: Routledge, 2002.
Lloyd, David. *A Man of Parts.* London: Harvill Secker, 2011.
_____. *Nationalism and Minor Literature.* Berkeley: University of California Press, 1987.
_____, ed. *20th Century Literary Criticism: A Reader.* London: Longman House, 1972.
London, Jack. *The Iron Heel.* 1907. www.gutenberg.org/ebooks/1164/. Accessed January 2014.
Lovecraft, H.P. *Tales of the Cthulhu Mythos.* New York: Ballantine, 1995.
Lucian of Samosata. *Lucian's Dialogues.* 1893. www.lucianofsamosata.info.html. Accessed December 2016.
Lyotard, Jean François. *The Postmodern Condition: A Report on Knowledge.* Minneapolis: University of Minnesota Press, 1984.
_____. *The Postmodern Explained to Children.* London: Turnaround, 1992.
MacCormack, Patricia. "Becoming Hu-Man: Deleuze and Guattari, Gender and *Third Rock from the Sun.*" *The Journal of Cult Media* 1, Autumn 2001.
Malins, Peta. "Machinic Assemblages: Deleuze, Guattari and Ethico-Aesthetics of Drug Use." *Janus Head* 7, no. 1 2004, pp. 84–104.
Malthus, Thomas. *An Essay on the Principle of Population.* 1798. www.econlib.org/library/Malthus/malPop.html. Accessed January 2013.
Manlove, Colin. "Charles Kingesly, H. G. Wells and the Machine in Victorian Fiction." *Nineteenth-Century Literature* 48, no. 2, September 1993, pp. 212–239.
Marcus, Laura. "Literature and Cinema." *The Cambridge History of Twentieth Century English Literature*, edited by Laura Marcus and Peter Nicholls. New York: Cambridge University Press, 2006, pp. 335–358.
Marcus, Laura, and Peter Nicholls, eds. *The Cambridge History of Twentieth Century English Literature.* New York: Cambridge University Press, 2006.
Marks, John. "Ethics." *The Deleuze Dictionary*, edited by Adrian Parr. Edinburgh: Edinburgh University Press, 2005, pp. 85–87.
_____. *Gilles Deleuze: Vitalism and Multiplicity.* London: Pluto Press, 1988.
Marks, Laura U. "A Deleuzian Politics of Hybrid Cinema." *Screen* 35, no. 3, 1994, pp. 244–264.
_____. *The Skin of the Film: Intercultural Cinema, Embodiment and the Senses.* Durham: Duke University Press, 2000.
Martin-Jones, David. *Deleuze, Cinema and National Identity.* Edinburgh: Edinburgh University Press, 2006.
Massumi, Brian. *A Users Guide to Capitalism and Schizophrenia: Deviations from Deleuze and Guattari.* Cambridge: MIT Press, 1999.
_____. "Deleuze, Guattari and the Philosophy of Expression." *Canadian Review of Comparative Literature* 24, no. 3, September 1997, pp. 754–782.
_____. *Parables for the Virtual.* Durham: Duke University Press, 2002.
May, Todd. *Gilles Deleuze: An Introduction.* Cambridge: Cambridge University Press, 2005.
Mayer, Ruth. "Africa as an Alien Future: The Middle Passage, Afrofuturism, and Postcolonial Waterworlds." *American Studies* 45, no. 4, 2000, pp. 555–566.
McLean, Steven. *The Early Fiction of H. G. Wells: Fantasies of Science.* Basingstoke: Palgrave Macmillan, 2009.

Bibliography

_____, ed. *H. G. Wells: Interdisciplinary Essays*. Newcastle upon Tyne: Cambridge Scholars, 2009.

McConnell, Frank. *The Science Fiction of H. G. Wells*. New York: Oxford University Press, 1981.

McNichol. *The Tripods Attack! The Young Chesterton Chronicles*. Manchester: Sophia Institute Press, 2008.

Melehy, Hassan. "Images Without: Deleuzian Becoming, Science Fiction Cinema." *Postmodern Culture* 5, no. 2, January 1995, n. pag.

Melville, Herman. *Moby Dick*. 1851. http://www.gutenberg.org/files/2701/2701-h/2701-h.htm/. Accessed January 2014.

Mercier, Louis-Sébastien. *L'An Deux Mille Quatre Cent Quarante*. 1773. http://gallica.bnf.fr/ark:/12148/bpt6k844569/f8.image. Accessed October 2014.

Merril, Judith. "What Do You Mean: Science? Fiction?" *Science Fiction, The Other Side of Realism: Essays on Modern Fantasy and Science Fiction*, edited by Thomas D. Clareson. Bowling Green: Bowling Green State University Popular Press, 1971.

Mieville, China. *The Scar*. London: Macmillan, 2002.

Milton, John. *Paradise Lost*. 1667. www.paradiselost.org/. Accessed December 2016.

Mitchell, Edward Page. *The Clock that Went Backward*. 1881. http://www.horrormasters.com/Text/a2221.pdf. Accessed November 2013.

Momsen, Bill. "Mariner IV—First Flyby of Mars: Some Personal Experiences." www.home.earthlink.net/~nbrass1/mariner/miv.htm. Accessed February 2013.

Moorcock, Michael. *Hollow Lands: The Dancers at the End of Time*. London: Orion, 1983.

Moore, Alan, and Kevin O'Neill. *Absolute League of Extraordinary Gentlemen: The Black Dossier*. London: Knockabout Comics, 2007.

Moore, C.L. "No Woman Born." *The Best of C.L. Moore*. New York: Del Ray, 1980.

More, Thomas. *Utopia*. Leeds: Scholar Press, 1966.

Morton, Arthur, ed. "Cellophane Utopia." *The English Utopia*. London: Lawrence & Wishart, 1952, pp. 183–194.

Moulard-Leonard, Valentine. *Bergson-Deleuze Encounters: Transcendental Experience and the Thought of the Virtual*. Albany: SUNY Press, 2008.

Moylan, Tom. *Demand the Impossible: Science Fiction and the Utopian Imagination*. London: Methuen, 1986.

Murray, Brian. *H. G. Wells*. New York: Ungar, 1990.

Nahin, Paul J. *Time Machines: Time Travel in Physics, Metaphysics and Science Fiction*. New York: Springer/Verlag, 1999.

Nail, Thomas. "Deleuze, Bakhtin, and the Clamour of Voices." *Deleuze Studies* 2, no. 2, December 2008, pp. 178–200.

Neil, David. "The Uses of Anachronism: Deleuze's History of the Subject." *Philosophy Today* 4, no. 42, Winter 1998, pp. 418–431.

Neimanis, Astrida. "Becoming-Grizzly: Bodily Molecularity and the Animal That Becomes." *PhaenEx: Journal of Existential and Phenomenological Theory and Culture* 2, no. 2, Winter 2007, pp. 279–308.

Neville, Henry. *The Isle of Pines*. 1668. www.gutenberg.org/ebooks/2801. Accessed December 2014.

Nichols, Ryan, and Fred Miller. *Philosophy through Science Fiction: A Course Book with Readings*. New York: Routledge, 2009.

Nicholls, Peter. *New Encyclopedia of Science Fiction*. London: Orbit, 1999.

Niederland, W.G. "The Birth of H. G. Wells's Time Machine." *American Imago* 35, 1978, pp. 106–112.

Nietzsche, Friedrich. *The Gay Science*. Cambridge: Cambridge University Press, 2003.

_____. *Thus Spoke Zarathustra*. Hertfordshire: Wordsworth Editions, 1997.

_____. *Untimely Meditations*. Cambridge: Cambridge University Press, 2003.

Bibliography

Olkowski, Dorothea. "Beside Us, in Memory." *Man and World* 29, 1996, pp. 283–292.
_____. *Gilles Deleuze and the Ruin of Representation*. Berkeley: University of California Press, 1999.
Orwell, Sonia, and Ian Angus, eds. *Vol. 2 of The Collected Essays, Journalism, and Letters of George Orwell*. London: Secker & Warburg, 1968.
O'Sullivan, Simon. *Art Encounters Deleuze and Guattari: Thought Beyond Representation*. New York: Palgrave Macmillan, 2006.
Owen, James A. *The Chronicles of the Imaginarium Geographica: Here, There Be Dragons*. New York: Simon & Schuster, 2006.
Pal, George, and Joe Morhaim. *The Time Machine II*. New York: Dell, 1981.
Palumbo, Donald E. "The Politics of Entropy: Revolution vs. Evolution in George Pal's 1960 Film Version of H. G. Wells's *The Time Machine*." *Modes of the Fantastic*, edited by Robert Latham and Robert A. Collins. Westport, CT: Greenwood Press, 1995.
Pamboukian, Sylvia A. "What the Traveller Saw: Evolution, Romance and Time Travel." *H. G. Wells: Interdisciplinary Essays*, edited by Steven McLean. Newcastle upon Tyne: Cambridge Scholars, 2009, pp. 8–24.
Parker, Martin. "Manufacturing Bodies: Flesh, Organization, Cyborgs." *Body and Organization*, edited by John Hassard and Ruth Holliday. London: Sage Publications, 2000, pp. 71–86.
Parr, Adrian, ed. *The Deleuze Dictionary*. Edinburgh: Edinburgh University Press, 2005.
Parrinder, Patrick. *H. G. Wells*. Edinburgh: Oliver and Boyd, 1970.
_____. *H. G. Wells: The Critical Heritage*. London: Routledge, 1972.
_____. *Science Fiction: A Critical Guide*. Harlow: Longman, 1979.
_____. *Science Fiction: Its Criticism and Teaching*. Suffolk: Methuen, 1980.
_____. *Shadows of the Future: H. G. Wells, Science Fiction and Prophecy*. Syracuse:Syracuse University Press, 1996.
_____, ed. *Learning from Other Worlds: Estrangement, Cognition, and the Politics of Science Fiction and Utopia*. Liverpool: Liverpool University Press, 2000.
Parrinder, Patrick, and John Partington, eds. *The Reception of H. G. Wells in Europe*. Continuum: London, 2005.
Parrinder, Patrick, and Robert M. Philmus, eds. *H. G. Wells's Literary Criticism*. Sussex: Harvester Press, 1980.
Parrinder, Patrick, and Christopher Rolfe, eds. *H. G. Wells under Revision: Proceedings of the International H. G. Wells Symposium*. London: Associated University Presses, 1990.
Parsons, Deborah. *Theorists of the Modernist Novel: James Joyce, Dorothy Richardson and Virginia Woolf*. New York: Routledge, 2007.
Pateman, Matthew. *The Aesthetics of Culture in Buffy The Vampire Slayer*. Jefferson: McFarland, 2006.
Partington, John S. "*The Time Machine* and *A Modern Utopia*: The Static and Kinetic Utopias of the Early H. G. Wells." *Utopian Studies Journal* 13, no. 1, 2002, pp. 57–68.
_____, ed. *H. G. Wells's Fin de siècle: Twenty-First Century Reflections*: *Selections from the Wellsian*. Frankfurt: Peter Lang, 2007.
_____. *Building Cosmopolis: The Political Thought of H. G. Wells*. Farnham: Ashgate Publishing, 2003.
Patton, Paul. "Conceptual Politics and the War-Machine in *Mille Plateaux*." *SubStance* 44/45, 1984, pp. 61–80.
_____. *Deleuze and the Political*. New York: Routledge, 2000.
_____. *Deleuzian Concepts: Philosophy, Colonization, Politics*. Palo Alto: Stanford University Press, 2010.

Bibliography

Patton, Paul, and John Protevi. *Between Deleuze and Derrida*. New York: Continuum, 2003.
Pedot, Richard. "Kafka's Ape." *Comparative Critical Studies* 2, no. 3, 2005, pp. 411–425.
Penley, Constance, ed. *Close Encounters: Film, Feminism, and Science Fiction*. Minneapolis: University of Minnesota Press, 1991.
Philimus, Robert M. *Into the Unknown: The Evolution of Science Fiction from Francis Godwin to H. G. Wells*. Berkley: University of California Press, 1970
_____. "The Time Machine: Or, The Fourth Dimension as Prophecy." *PMLA* 84, no. 3, May 1969, pp. 530–535.
_____. "Wells and Borges and the Labyrinths of Time." *Science Fiction Studies* 1, no. 4, Autumn 1974, pp. 237–248.
Philmus, Robert M., and David Y. Hughes, eds. *Early Writings in Science and Science Fiction by H. G. Wells*. Berkley: University of California Press, 1975.
Piercy, Marge. *He, She and It: A Novel*. New York: Ballantine, 1991.
Pilsch, Andrew. "'He Called It 'Utopia': The Transhumanism of Jameson & Aurobindo." www.sciy.org/?p=6884. Accessed December 2016.
Pinsky, Michael. *Future Present: Ethics and/as Science Fiction*. Madison: Fairleigh Dickinson University Press, 2003.
Pisters, Patricia. *The Matrix of Visual Culture: Working with Deleuze in Film Theory*. Palo Alto: Stanford University Press, 2003.
Plato. *The Republic*. Indianapolis: Hackett, 1992.
Plattes, Gabriel. *A Description of the Famous Kingdome of Macaria*. 1641. www..gutenberg.org/articles/eng/A_Description_of_the_Famous_Kingdom_of_Macaria. Accessed November 2016.
Poe, Edgar Allen. "The Man That Was Used Up." 1843. http://www.readbookonline.net/readOnLine/811. Accessed October 2015.
Posman, Sarah. "Where Has Gertrud(e) Gone? Cinematic Journey from Movement-Image to Time-Image." *Gilles Deleuze: Image and Text*, edited by Eugene Holland, Daniel W. Smith and Charles J. Stivale. London: Continuum, 2009, pp. 41–62.
Powell, Anna. *Deleuze: Altered States and Film*. Edinburgh: Edinburgh University Press, 2007.
_____. *Deleuze and Horror Film*. Edinburgh: Edinburgh University Press, 2006.
_____. "The Face Is a Horror Story: The Affective Face of Horror." *Diagrams of Sensation: Deleuze and Aesthetics. The Warwick Journal of Philosophy* 16, 2005, pp. 53–65.
_____. "Selling Space: King and Krzywinska's Science Fiction Cinema." *Film-Philosophy* 7, no. 19, August 2003. www.film-philosophy.com/vol7–2003/n19powell. Accessed May 2015.
Priest, Christopher. *Dream of Wessex*. London: Abacus Books, 1987.
_____. "John Wyndham & H. G. Wells." www.christopher-priest.co.uk/essays-reviews/contemporaries-portrayed/john-wyndham-h-g-wells/. Accessed April 2013.
_____. *The Space Machine: A Scientific Romance*. London: Faber & Faber, 1976.
Prigogine, Ilya. *From Being to Becoming*. San Francisco: W.H. Freeman, 1980.
Prince, John S. "The True Riddle of the Sphinx in The Time Machine." *Science Fiction Studies* 27, no. 3, November 2000, pp. 543–546.
Pritchett, Victor Sawden, ed. "The Scientific Romances." *The Living Novel*. London: Chatto & Windus, 1946, pp. 122–129.
Quade, Penelope. "Taming the Beast in the Name of the Father: The Island of Doctor Moreau and Wells's Critique of Society's Religious Molding." *Extrapolation* 48, no. 2, Summer 2007, pp. 292–301.
Rabkin, Eric S. "Metalinguistics and Science Fiction." *Critical Inquiry* 6, no. 1, Autumn 1979, pp. 79–86.

Bibliography

Rajchman, John. *The Deleuze Connections*. Cambridge: MIT Press, 2000.
Raknem, Ingvald. *H. G. Wells and his Critics*. Oslo: Scandinavian University Books, 1962.
Raunig, Gerald. *A Thousand Machines: A Concise Philosophy of the Machine as a Social Movement*. Translated by Aileen Derieg. Los Angeles: Semiotext(e), 2010.
Redfern, Nick. "Abjection and Evolution in *The Island of Doctor Moreau*." *The Wellsian: The Journal of the H. G. Wells Society* 27, 2004, pp. 37–47.
_____. "From Science to Chaos with David Cronenberg." http://nickredfern.wordpress.com/category/david-cronenberg. Accessed March 2016.
Redmond, Sean, ed. *Liquid Metal: the Science Fiction Film Reader*. London: Wallflower Press, 2004.
Reed, John R. *The Natural History of H. G. Wells*. Athens: Ohio University Press, 1982.
_____. "The Vanity of Law in *The Island of Doctor Moreau*." *H. G. Wells Under Revision: Proceedings of the International H. G. Wells Symposium: London, July 1986*, edited by Patrick Parrinder and Christopher Rolfe. London: Selinsgrove, 1990, pp.134–44.
Reid, Alexander. "Panoptic to Cyberoptics." *Posthuman Destinies*, December 2009. http://www.sciy.org/2009/12/16/panoptic-to-cyberoptics-by-alexander-ried-2/. Accessed January 2014.
Renzi, Thomas C. *H. G. Wells: Six Scientific Romances Adapted for Film*. Lanham: Scarecrow Press, 2004.
Rieder, John. *Colonialism and the Emergence of Science Fiction*. Middletown, CT: Wesleyan University Press, 2008.
Roberts, Adam. *The History of Science Fiction*. New York: Palgrave Macmillan, 2006.
Roberts, Charles. *The History of Science Fiction*, New York: Routledge, 2000.
Robinson, Kim Stanley. *The Mars Trilogy: Red Mars*. New York: Spectra, 1993.
Rodowick, David Norman. *Gilles Deleuze's Time Machine*. Durham: Duke University Press, 1997.
_____. "Unthinkable Sex: Conceptual Personae and the Time-Image." *Invisible Culture: An Electronic Journal for Visual Studies* 3, 2000. http://www.rochester.edu/.in_visible_culture/issue3/rodowick.htm. Accessed October 2014.
Rose, Mark. *Alien Encounters: Anatomy of Science Fiction*. Cambridge: Harvard University Press, 1991.
Rosny, J.H. *Les Xipéhuz*. 1887. www.archive.org/stream/lesxiphuz00rosnuoft#page/n7 /mode/2up. Accessed August 2015.
Rothfels, Nigel. *Representing Animals*. Bloomington: Indiana University Press 2002.
Rowlands, Mark. *The Philosopher at the End of the Universe*. London: Ebury Press, 2005.
Rucker, Rudy. *The Ware Tetralogy*. Rockville, MD: Prime Books, 2010.
Ruddick, Nicholas. *Ultimate Island: On the Nature of British Science Fiction*. Westport, CT: Greenwood Press, 1993.
Russell, W. M. S. "Time Before and After The Time Machine." *H G. Wells's Perennial Time Machine*, edited by George Slusser, Patrick Parrinder and Danièle Chatelain. Athens: University of Georgia Press, 2001, pp. 50–61.
Sagan, Carl. *Cosmos*. New York: Random House, 1980.
Sardar, Ziauddin, and Sean Cubitt. *Aliens R Us*. London: Pluto Press, 2002.
Sayeau, M. "H. G. Wells's *The Time Machine* and the Odd Consequence of Progress." *Contemporary Justice Review* 8, no. 4, 2005, pp. 431–446.
Scafella, Frank. "The White Sphinx and the Time Machine." *Science Fiction Studies* 8, no. 3, November 1981, pp. 255–265.
Seed, David, ed. *Anticipations: Essays on Early Science Fiction and its Precursors*. Syracuse: Syracuse University Press, 1995.

Bibliography

_____. *A Companion to Science Fiction*. Oxford: Blackwell Books, 2005.
Serviss, Garrett Putman. *Edison's Conquest of Mars*. 1898. www.gutenberg.org/files/19141/19141-h/19141-h.htm. Accessed August 2016.
Shakespeare, William. *The Tempest*. 1611. www.shakespeare.mit.edu/tempest/full.html. Accessed July 2014.
Shaviro, Steven. *The Cinematic Body: Theory Out of Bounds Volume 2*. Minneapolis: University of Minnesota Press, 1993.
Sheldon, Leslie. "The Great Disillusionment: H. G. Wells, Mankind, and Aliens in American Invasion Horror Films of the 1950s." *The Irish Journal of Gothic and Horror Studies* 4, June 2008, n. pag.
Shelley, Mary. *Frankenstein*. 1818. www.literature.org/authors/shelley-mary/frankenstein/. Accessed May 2016.
_____. *The Last Man*. 1826. www.gutenberg.org/files/18247/18247.txt. Accessed April 2016
Shelton, Robert. "Images of Health and Disease: Pathology and Ideology in Looking Backward and *The Time Machine*." *The Utopian Studies Journal*, 1991, pp. 17–21.
Sherborne, Michael, ed. *The Wellsian: Selected Essays on H. G. Wells*. London: University of Westminster, 2003.
Sherman, Jacob Holsinger. "No Werewolves in Theology? Transcendence, Immanence, and Becoming-Divine in Gilles Deleuze." *Modern Theology* 25, no. 1, January 2009, pp. 1–20.
Shildrick, Margrit. *Leaky Bodies And Boundaries: Feminism, Postmodernism and (Bio)ethics*. London: Routledge, 1977.
Shippey, Tom. *Tolkien: Author of the Century*. London: HarperCollins, 2000.
_____, ed. *Fictional Space: Essays on Contemporary Science Fiction*. Highlands, NJ: Humanities Press, 1991.
Shirley, John. *Eclipse: A Song Called Youth Trilogy*. Northridge, CA: Babbage Press, 1990.
Showalter, Elaine. *Sexual Anarchy: Gender and Culture at the Fin de Siècle*. London: Bloomsbury, 1991.
Sidney, Philip. *The Countess of Pembroke's Arcadia*. Charleston, SC: Nabu Press, 2010.
Slusser, George and Danielle Chatelain. "Conveying Unknown Worlds: Patterns of Communication in Science Fiction." *Science Fiction Studies* 29, no. 2, 2002, pp. 161–85.
_____. "Spacetime Geometries: Time Travel and the Modern Geometrical Narrative." *Science Fiction Studies* 22, no. 2, 1995, pp. 161–186.
Slusser, George, Patrick Parrinder and Danièle Chatelain, eds. *H. G. Wells's Perennial Time Machine*. Athens: University of Georgia Press, 2001.
Smith, Daniel W. "Deleuze and the Question of Desire: Toward an Immanent Theory of Ethics." *Parrhesia* 2, 2007, pp. 66–78.
_____. "A Life of Pure Immanence: Deleuze's 'Critique et Clinique' Project." *Philosophy Today* 41 SPEP Supplement, 1997, pp. 168–79.
_____. "The Place of Ethics in Deleuze's Philosophy: Three Questions of Immanence." *Deleuze and Guattari: New Mappings in Politics and Philosophy*, edited by Eleanor Kaufman and Kevin Heller. Minneapolis: University of Minnesota Press, 1998, pp. 251–269.
Smith, David C. *The Correspondences of H. G. Wells Volume 1: 1880–1903*. London: Pickering & Chatto, 1998.
_____. *H. G. Wells, Desperately Mortal: A Biography*. New Haven: Yale University Press, 1986.
Smithson, Robert. "The Shape of Future and Memory." *Robert Smithson: The Collected*

Bibliography

  Writings, edited by Jack Flam. London: University of California Press,1966, pp. 332–333.
Spinoza, Baruch. *Ethics*. Translated by Edwin Curley. Princeton: Princeton University Press, 1994.
Stableford, Brian. *Historical Dictionary of Science Fiction Literature*. Lanham, MD: Rowman & Littlefield, 2004.
_____. *The Scientific Romance in Britain: 1890–1950*. London: Forth Estate, 1985.
_____. "Dystopias." *The Encyclopedia of Science Fiction*, edited by Brian Stableford, John Clute and Peter Nicholls. London: Orbit, 1993, pp. 360–362.
Stableford, Brian, John Clute, and Peter Nicholls, eds. *The Encyclopedia of Science Fiction*. London: Orbit,1993.
Stagoll, Cliff. "Becoming." *The Deleuze Dictionary*, edited by Adrian Parr. Edinburgh: Edinburgh University Press, 2005, pp. 21–23.
_____. "Memory." *The Deleuze Dictionary*, edited by Adrian Parr. Edinburgh: Edinburgh University Press, 2005, pp. 159–161.
Stapledon, Olaf. *Last and First Men*. 1930. www.gutenberg.net.au/ebooks06/0601101h.html. Accessed April 2014.
Starr, Michael. "'I've Watched You Build Yourself From Scratch': The Assemblage of Echo." *Joss Whedon's Dollhouse: Confounding Purpose, Confusing Identity*, edited by Sherry Ginn, Alyson R. Buckman and Heather M. Porter. Lanham, MD: Rowman & Littlefield, 2014, pp. 3–20.
Stein, Joshua. "The Legacy of H.G Wells's The Time Machine: Destabilization and Observation." *H. G. Wells's Perennial Time Machine*, edited by George Slusser, Patrick Parrinder and Danièle Chatelain. Athens: University of Georgia Press, 2001, pp. 150–159.
Stern, Madeline B. "Counterclockwise: Flux of Time in Literature." *Sewanee Review* 44, July–September 1936, pp. 338–365.
Stiles, Ann. "Literature in Mind: H. G. Wells and the Evolution of the Mad Scientist." *Journal of the History of Ideas* 70, no. 2, April 2009, pp. 317–339.
Stivale, Charles J. *Gilles Deleuze: Key Concepts*. Durham: Acumen, 2009.
_____. "Mille/Punks/Cyber/Plateaus: Science Fiction and Deleuzo-Guattarian Becomings."
SubStance 20, no. 3, Issue 66: *Special Issue: Deleuze & Guattari*. Madison: University of Wisconsin Press, 1991, pp. 66–84.
_____. *The Two-Fold Thought of Deleuze and Guattari*. London: Routledge, 1998.
Stoker, Bram. *Dracula*. Berlin, NJ: Townsend Press, 2003.
Storment, Ryan Lee. *Other Spaces, Other Voices: Heterotopic Spaces in Island Narratives*. Königswinter: Tandem Verlag, 2008.
Stubbes, Philip. *The Anatomie of Abuses*. 1583. www.archive.org/stream/phillipstubbessa00stubuoft/phillipstubbessa00stubuoft_djvu.txt. Accessed November 2016.
Sullivan, Cat. "H. G. Wells the Builder." *Viz* Magazine 147, 2005, pp. 29.
Sutton, Damian. "Viral Structures of the Internet." *Deleuze Reframed*. London: I.B. Tauris, 2008, pp. 27–41.
Sutton, Damian, and Martin-Jones, David. *Deleuze Reframed*. London: I.B. Tauris, 2008.
Suvin, Darko. "Locus, Horizon, and Orientation: The Concept of Possible Worlds as a Key to Utopian Studies." *Not Yet: Reconsidering Ernst Bloch*, edited by Jamie Owen Daniel and Tom Moylan. London: Verso, 1997, pp. 122–137.
_____. *Metamorphoses of Science Fiction: On the Poetics and History of a Literary Genre*. New Haven: Yale University Press, 1979.
_____. *Positions and Presuppositions in Science Fiction*. London: Macmillan, 1988.
_____. "Theses on Dystopia 2001." *Dark Horizons: Science Fiction and the Utopian*

Bibliography

Imagination, edited by Raffaella Baccolini and Tom Moylan. New York: Routledge, 2003, pp. 187–201.
_____. "Wells as the Turning Point of the SF Tradition." *Critical Essays on H. G. Wells*, edited by John Huntington. Boston: G. K. Hall & Co., 1991, pp. 23–33.
Suvin, Darko, and Robert Philimus, eds. *H. G. Wells and Modern Science Fiction.* Lewisburg: Associated University Presses, 1977.
Swann, S. Andrew. *Moreau Omnibus.* New York: Daw Books, 2003.
Swift, Jonathan. *Gulliver's Travels.* 1726. www.gutenberg.org/files/829/829-h/829-h.htm. Accessed December 2014.
Tague, Michael. "H. G. Wells and the Failure of Memory." *Philomel: Past Conceptions of the Future* 35, 2009, pp. 8–13.
Telotte, J.P. *A Distant Technology: Science Fiction Film and the Machine Age.* Hanover, NH: Wesleyan University Press, 1999.
Thompson, Nato, ed. *Becoming Animal: Contemporary Art in the Animal Kingdom.* Cambridge: MIT Press, 2005.
Timberlake, John. "Forgotten Cameras and Unknown Audiences: Photography, *The Time Machine* and the Atom Bomb." *Photography and Literature in the Twentieth Century.* Saarbrücken: Scholars Press, 2005, pp. 11–24.
Totaro, Donato. *Gilles Deleuze's Bergsonian Film Project.* 1999. www.horschamp.qc.ca/9903/offscreen_essays/deleuze1.html. Accessed December 2014.
Trushell, John. "Mirages in the Desert: *The War of the Worlds* and fin du globe." *Extrapolation: A Journal of Science Fiction and Fantasy*, Winter 2002, pp. 439–455.
Turetzky, Philip. *Time: The Problems of Philosophy.* London: Routledge, 2000.
Twain, Mark. *A Connecticut Yankee in King Arthur's Court.* 1889. www.gutenberg.org/files/86/86-h/86-h.htm. Accessed December 2013.
Urpeth, James. "Animal Becomings." *Animal Philosophy: Ethics and Identity*, edited by Peter Atterton and Matthew Calarco. London: Continuum, 2004, pp. 119–110.
Vallorani, Nicoletta. "The Invisible Wells in European Cinema and Television." *The Reception of H. G. Wells in Europe*, edited by Patrick Parrinder and John Partington. London: Continuum, 2005, pp. 302–320.
Veltman, Alexander Fomich. "The Forebears of Kalimeros." *A.F. Veltman: Selected Stories*, edited by James J Gebhard. Evanston: Northwest University Press, 1998.
Verne, Jules. *From the Earth to the Moon.* 1865. www.gutenberg.org/ebooks/83. Accessed December 2013.
_____. *Journey to the Centre of the Earth.* 1864. www.gutenberg.org/ebooks/18857. Accessed December 2014.
_____. *Twenty Thousand Leagues Under the Sea.* www.gutenberg.org/ebooks/188571869. Accessed December 2014.
Vernier, J. P. "Evolution as a Literary Theme in H. G. Wells's Science Fiction." *H. G. Wells and Modern Science Fiction*, edited by Darko Suvin and Robert M. Philmus. Lewisburg, PA: Bucknell University Press, 1977.
Vinge, Vernor. *A Deepness in the Sky.* New York: Tor Books, 1999.
Voltaire. *The Works of Voltaire.* Charleston, SC: BiblioBazaar, 2009.
Wagar, W. Warren. "H. G. Wells and the Genesis of Future Studies." *World Future Society Bulletin*, January/February 1983, pp. 25–29.
_____. *H. G. Wells and the World State.* New Haven: Yale University Press, 1971.
_____. *H. G. Wells: Traversing Time.* Middletown, CT: Wesleyan University Press, 2004.
_____. *A Short History of the Future London.* Chicago: University of Chicago Press, 1992.
_____. *Terminal Visions: The Literature of Last Things.* Bloomington: Indiana University Press, 1982.

Bibliography

Wardrip-Fruin, Noah, and Nick Montfort, Nick. *The New Media Reader*. Cambridge: MIT Press, 2003.
Watt, Ian. *Conrad in the 19th Century*. Berkley: University of California Press, 1979.
Waugh, Patricia. *Practising Postmodernism, Reading Modernism*. New York: Routledge, 1993.
Webb, Don. "To Mars and Providence." *The War of the Worlds: Global Dispatches*, edited by Kevin J. Anderson. New York: Bantam Books, 1997.
Weeks, Robert P. "Disentanglement as a Theme in H. G. Wells's Fiction." *Papers of the Michigan Academy of Science, Arts, and Letters* 39, 1954, pp. 439–444.
Welles, Orson, dir. "The War of the Worlds." H. G. Wells, Adaptation by Howard Koch. *Mercury Theatre on the Air*. CBS Radio. New York: WCBS, 30 October 1938.
Wells, Amy Catherine. *The Book of Catherine Wells*. New York: Doubleday, 1928.
Wells, Herbert George. *Anticipations of the Reactions to Mechanical and Scientific Progress Upon Human Life and Thought*. New York: Dover Publications, 1999.
_____. *Certain Personal Matters*. Fairfield, IA: 1st World Library, 2006.
_____. "The Chronic Argonauts." 1888. www.colemanzone.com/Time_Machine_Project/chronic.htm. Accessed August 2014.
_____. *The Complete Science Fiction Treasury of H. G. Wells*. New York: Avenel, 1991.
_____. *The Complete Short Stories of H. G. Wells*. London: Dent, 1998.
_____. *The Country of the Blind*. London: Penguin, 2005.
_____. "The Crystal Egg." 1897. www.online-literature.com/wellshg/2878. Accessed May 2016.
_____. *The Discovery of the Future* with *The Common-sense of World Peace* and *The Human Adventure*. London: Polytechnic of North London Press, 1989.
_____. *An Experiment in Autobiography*. New York: Macmillan, 1934.
_____. *The First Men in the Moon*. Rockville, MD: Arc Manor Publishing, 2008.
_____. *Floor Games and Little Wars*. London: Hogshead Books, 1995.
_____. *The Island of Doctor Moreau*. London: Everyman 2003.
_____. "The Land Ironclads." 1903. www.gutenberg.net.au/ebooks06/0604041h.html. Accessed January 2014.
_____. "The Limits of Individual Plasticity." *H.G. Wells: Early Writings in Science and Science Fiction*, edited by Robert Philmus and David Y. Hughes. Berkley: University of California Press, 1975, pp. 36–39.
_____. "The Man of the Year Million: A Scientific Forecast" (Retitled "Of a Book Unwritten"). *Certain Personal Matters: A Collection of Material, Mainly Autobiographical*. London: Lawrence and Bullen, 1897, pp. 161–171.
_____. *Men like Gods*. Whitefish, MT: Kessinger Publishing Co., 2005.
_____. *A Modern Utopia*. London: Penguin Classics, 2005.
_____. *Mr Blettsworthy on Rampole Island*. La Vergne, TN: Lightning Source, 2011
_____. *New Worlds For Old*. 1908. www.archive.org/details/newworldsforold06wellgoog. Accessed November 2016.
_____. *The Research Magnificent*. 1915. www.gutenberg.org/ebooks/1138. Accessed January 2013.
_____. *Seven Famous Novels*. New York: Knopf, 1934.
_____. *The Shape of Things to Come*. London: Penguin Classics, 2005.
_____. *A Short History of the World*. London: Penguin, 2000.
_____. *The Sleeper Awakes*. London: Penguin Classics, 2005
_____. "The Stolen Bacillus." 1895. www.classicreader.com/book/1423/1.Accessed March 2014.
_____. *The Time Machine*. London: Everyman, 2001.
_____. *Tono-Bungay*. London: Penguin Classics, 2005.
_____. *The War in the Air*. London: Penguin Classics, 2005

Bibliography

____. *The War of the Worlds*. London: Heinmann, 1968.
____. *The Way the World Is Going*. New York: Doubleday, 1929.
____. "The Work, Wealth and Happiness of Mankind." *The Open Conspiracy: H. G. Wells on World Revolution*. Westport, CT: Praeger, 2002.
____. "World Brain: The Idea of a Permanent World Encyclopaedia." 1937. www.sherlock.ischool.berkeley.edu/wells/world_brain.html. Accessed May 2014.
____. *The World Set Free*. London: Collins, 1956.
____. "Zoological Retrogression." *The Gentlemen's Magazine* September 1891, www.en.wikisource.org/wiki /Zoological_ Retrogression. Accessed March 2014.
Wells, Herbert George, Julian Huxley, and Phillip George Wells. *The Science of Life*. London: Cassel, 1934.
West, Anthony. *H. G. Wells: Aspects of a Life*. London: Hutchinson, 1984.
Westfahl, Gary. *Islands in the Sky: The Space Station Theme in Science Fiction Literature*. Rockville, MD: Wildside Press, 2009.
____. *Science Fiction, Children's Literature, and Popular Culture: Coming of Age in Fantasyland*. Westport, CT: Greenwood Press, 2000.
____. "Tainted Wells: A Review of *The Time Machine*." www.locusmag.com/2002/Reviews/Westfahl_TimeMachine.html. Accessed November 2015.
____, ed. *The Greenwood Encyclopaedia of Science Fiction and Fantasy*. Westport, CT: Greenwood Press, 2005.
White, Eric. "Once They Were Men, Now They're Land Crabs.": Monstrous Becomings in Evolutionist Cinema." *PostHuman Bodies*, edited by Judith Halberstam and Ira Livingstone. Bloomington: Indiana University Press, 1995, pp. 244–266.
White, Hayden. *Metahistory: The Historical Imagination in Nineteenth Century Europe*. Baltimore: Johns Hopkins University Press, 1973.
Whitelaw, Sonny. *Stargate SG-1: Roswell*. Surbiton: Fandemonium Books, 2007.
Williams, Keith. *H. G. Wells: Modernism and the Movies*. Liverpool: Liverpool University Press, 2007.
Williamson, Jack. "The Evolution of the Martians." *War of The Worlds: Fresh Perspectives on the H. G. Wells Classic*, edited by Glenn Yeffeth. Dallas: BenBella, 2005, pp. 189–198.
____. *H. G. Wells: Critic of Progress*. Baltimore: Mirage Press, 1973.
Willis, Martin T. "Edison as Time Traveler: H. G. Wells's Inspiration for His First Scientific Character." *Science Fiction Studies* 26, 1999, pp. 284–300.
Wilson, Harris, ed. *Arnold Bennett and H. G. Wells: A Record of a Personal and a Literary Friendship*. Champaign: University of Illinois Press, 1960.
Wilt, Judith, ed. *Making Humans: Frankenstein and the Island of Doctor Moreau*. New York: Houghton Mifflin, 2003.
Wolfe, Cary. *Animal Rites: American Culture, the Discourse of Species, and Posthumanist Theory*. Chicago: University of Chicago Press, 2003.
Wolfe, Gary K. *Critical Terms for Science Fiction and Fantasy*. Westport, CT: Greenwood Press, 1986.
Woolf, Virginia. *Mr. Bennett and Mrs. Brown: Collected Essays Vol. 1*. London: Hogarth, 1966.
Worland, Rick. *The Horror Film: An Introduction*. Oxford: Blackwell, 2007.
Wright, Ronald. *A Scientific Romance*. Ealing: Black Swan, 1999.
Wright, Sydney Fowler. *Deluge*. 1928. www.sfw.org/www.deluge.shtml. Accessed August 2014.
Wyndham, John. *Web*. New York: Penguin, 1979.
Yang, Che-ming. "Representing The Unspeakable Trauma: A Deleuzian Reading of Conrad's Heart of Darkness." *Arts and Social Sciences Journal*, 2010, pp. 1–10.
Yeffeth, Glenn, ed. *The War of the Worlds: Fresh Perspectives on the H. G. Wells Classic*. Dallas: BenBella, 2005.

Bibliography

Žižek, Slavoj. *In Defence of Lost Causes.* New York: Verso Books, 2008.
_____. *Interrogating the Real.* London: Continuum, 2005.
_____. *Organs Without Bodies: Deleuze & Consequences.* New York: Routledge, 2003.
_____. *Plague of Fantasies.* New York: Verso Books, 1997.
_____. *The Sublime Object of Ideology.* New York: Verso Books, 1989.
_____. *Welcome to the Desert of the Real.* New York: Verso Books, 2002.
Žižek, Slavoj, and Gkyn Daly. *Conversations with Žižek.* Cambridge: Polity Press, 2004.

Filmography

Alien. Dir. Ridley Scott. 20th Century Fox, 1979.
Alien Resurrection. Dir. Jean-Pierre Jeunet. 20th Century Fox, 1997.
All Change. Dir. Peter Robinson. Video Arts Productions, 1988.
Animaniacs. Dir. Various. Amblin Entertainment, 1993–1996.
_____. "When Mice Ruled the Earth." Dir. Michael Gerard. Fox Kids, November 1993.
Back to the Future. Dir. Robert Zemeckis. Universal Pictures, 1985.
Batman: The Dark Knight. Dir. Christopher Nolan. Warner Bros, 2009.
Battlestar Galactica. Dir. Various. SyFy, 2003–2009.
Bill and Ted's Excellent Adventure. Dir. Stephen Herek. Orion Pictures, 1989.
Blade Runner. Dir. Ridley Scott. Warner Bros, 1982.
The Blob. Dir. Irvin Yeaworth. Paramount Pictures, 1958.
Buck Rogers in the 25th Century. Dir. Various. NBC. 1970–1981.
Buffy the Vampire Slayer. Dir. Various. WB/UPN, 1997–2003.
Caprica. Dir. Various. SyFy, 2009–2010.
The Day the Earth Stood Still. Dir. Robert Wise. 20th Century Fox, 1951.
District 9. Dir. Neill Blomkamp. Tristar Pictures, 2009.
Doctor Who. Dir. Various. BBC, 1963-Present.
_____. "Blink." Dir. Hettie MacDonald. BBC, June 2007.
_____. "Pyramids of Mars." Dir. Paddy Russell. BBC, October 1975.
_____. "Timelash." Dir. Pennant Roberts. BBC, March 1985.
E.T. The Extra-Terrestrial. Dir. Steven Spielberg. Universal Studios, 1982.
Eternal Sunshine of the Spotless Mind. Dir. Michael Gondry. Focus Features, 2004.
Event Horizon. Dir. Paul W.S. Anderson. Paramount Pictures, 1997.
The Fly. Dir. Kurt Neuman. 20th Century Fox, 1958.
The Fly. Dir. David Cronenberg. 20th Century Fox, 1986.
Forever Young. Dir. Steve Miner. Warner Bros, 1992.
From Time to Time. Dir. Jeff Blyth. Disney, 1992.
Futurama. Dir. Various. Fox Network/Comedy Central, 1999–2013.
_____. "The Late Philip J. Fry." Dir. Peter Avanzino. Comedy central, 2010.
_____. "Lrrreconcilable Ndndifferences." Dir. Crystal Thompson. Comedy Central, 2010.
Grand Theft Auto. (Videogame). Rockstar Games, 1997.
Grove's Mill. Dir. Paul St Amand. Vancouver Film School, 2006.
Hardware. Dir. Richard Stanley. Palace Pictures, 1990.
H. G. Wells: War with the World. Dir. Colette Flight. BBC2, 2006.
H. G. Wells's War of the Worlds. Dir. David Michael Latt. The Asylum, 2005.
The Human Centipede: First Sequence. Dir. Tom Six. Bounty Films, 2010.
Idiocracy. Dir. Mike Judge. 20th Century Fox, 2006.
Independence Day. Dir. Roland Emmerich. 20th Century Fox, 1996.

Filmography

Independence Day: Resurgence. Dir. Roland Emmerich. 20th Century Fox, 2016.
The Infinite Worlds of H. G. Wells. Dir. Various. Hallmark Channel, 2007.
The Island of Lost Souls. Dir. Erle C. Kenton. Paramount Pictures, 1933.
The Island of Doctor Moreau. Dir. Don Taylor. American International Pictures, 1977.
The Island of Doctor Moreau. Dir. John Frankenheimer. New Line Cinema, 1996.
Jurassic Park. Dir. Steven Spielberg. Universal Studios, 1993.
Legends of Tomorrow. Dir. Various. The CW Network, 2016-present.
_____. "The Magnificent Eight." Dir. Thor Freudenthal. The CW Network, April 2016.
Life on Mars. Dir. Various. BBC2. 2008–2009.
Lois & Clark: The New Adventures of Superman. Dir. Various. Warner Bros, 1993–1997.
_____. "Tempus Fugitive." Dir James R. Bagdonas. ABC, 1995.
Lost. Dir. Various. ABC, 2004–2010.
Man Against Destruction (Člověk proti zkáze). Dir. A. Matuska. Turkey, 1989.
Mars Attacks! Dir. Tim Burton. Warner Bros, 1996.
The Matrix. Dir. Wachowskis. Warner Bros, 1999.
Metropolis. Dir. Fritz Lang. UFA, 1929.
Murdoch Mysteries. Dir. Various. City TV, 2008-present.
Phil of the Future. Dir. Various. The Disney Channel, 2004–2006.
Prototype (Videogame). Activision, 2009.
Robocop. Dir. Paul Verhoeven. Orion Pictures, 1989.
Sleeper. Dir. Woody Allen. United Artists, 1973.
Solar Pon's War of the Worlds. Accessed April 2014. http://www.solarpons.com.
Solaris. Dir. Andrei Tarkovsky. Visual Programme Systems, 1972.
Splice. Dir. Vincenzo Natali. Dark Castle, 1999.
Star Trek. Dir. Various. Paramount Television, 1966–1969.
Star Trek: Voyager. Dir. Various. Paramount Television, 1995–2001.
Star Wars Episode IV: A New Hope. Dir. George Lucas. 20th Century Fox, 1977.
Taxi Driver. Dir. Martin Scorsese. Columbia Pictures, 1976.
The Terminator. Dir. James Cameron. Orion Pictures, 1984.
Terminator 2: Judgement Day. Dir. James Cameron. Tristar Pictures, 1991.
Terminator 3: Rise of the Machines. Dir. Jonathan Mostow. Warner Bros, 2003.
Testimony. Dir. Tony Palmer. Digital Classics DVD, 2007.
The Thing. Dir. John Carpenter. Universal Pictures, 1982.
Things to Come. Dir. William Cameron Menzies. United Artists, 1936.
Time After Time. Dir. Nicholas Mayer. Warner Bros, 1979.
The Time Machine. Dir. George Pal. Metro-Goldwyn-Mayer, 1960.
The Time Machine. Dir. Simon Wells. Dreamworks, 2002.
The Time Machine: The Journey Back. Dir. Clyde Lucas. PBS, 1993.
Timecop. Dir. Various. ABC, 1997–1998.
2001: A Space Odyssey. Dir. Stanley Kubrick. MGM, 1968.
The Vampyr. Dir. Carl Theodor Dreyer. Vereinigte Star-Film, 1932.
Videodrome. Dir. David Cronenberg. Universal Studios, 1982.
The Walking Dead. Dir. Various. AMC. 2014-Present.
_____. "Self Help." Dir. Ernest Dickerson. AMC. 2014
The War of the Worlds. Dir. Byron Haskin. Paramount Pictures, 1954.
The War of the Worlds. Dir. Steven Spielberg. Amblin Entertainment, 2005.
The War of the Worlds 2: The Next Wave. Dir. C. Thomas Howell. The Asylum, 2008.
Warehouse 13. Dir. Various. SyFy Channel, 2009–2014.
_____. "Emily Lake." Dir. Millicent Shelton. SyFy Channel, 2011.
_____. "Time Will Tell." Dir. Stephen Surjik. SyFy Channel, 2010.

Index

abjection 60; *see also* psychoanalysis
actual (Deleuzian concept) 20, 24, 30, 46, 58–61, 98, 111–112, 119–122, 135–136; *see also* virtual
After London (Jefferies) 174*n*4
Aldiss, Brian 13, 169*n*1
Alien (film series) 21, 60, 78
aliens: in contrast to humans 85–87; invasion narratives 19, 25, 73–78, 87, 173*n*23; *see also* Martians
All Change (Robinson) 161
And Having Writ... (Bensen) 160
animals: Deleuzian hierarchy of animal representations 42–43; ethics 42, 170*n*6; human and animal differences 30–31, 51–52; *see also* becoming animal
Animaniacs (television) 162
Anticipations (Wells) 24
antimemory (Deleuzian concept) 75; *see also* becoming; memory
Anti-Oedipus (Deleuze) 5, 7, 33, 52, 94, 96, 104, 130
arboreal (thought process) 5, 27–29, 115; *see also* rhizome
Aristotle 29, 51, 125
Artaud, Antonin 7, 33, 39, 72, 106, 169*n*15
Asimov, Isaac 23
assemblage (Deleuzian concept) 29, 30–33; cyborg 94–96; ethics 68–71; science fiction literature as 34–37
Le Autre Monde: ou les États et Empires de la Lune (Cyrano de Bergerac) 76

Back to the Future (Zemeckis) 109, 173*n*1
Bacon, Francis (artist) 43, 51, 54

Bacon, Francis (author) 23
Bakhtin, Mikhail 138, 151, 176*n*13
Ballard, J.G. 170*n*19
Banks, Ian 170*n*10
Barsoom Series (Burroughs) 172*n*11
Barthes, Roland 16–17
Batman: The Dark Knight (Nolan) 169*n*10
The Battle of Dorking (Chesney) 73
Battlestar Galactica (television) 92, 173*n*23
Baxter, Stephen 16, 108, 156, 160
beast-men (in *The Island of Dr. Moreau*) 43, 49–50, 54–68
becoming: animal 42–44, 51–52, 60–69, 71; botched 61–65, 97; in Deleuzian philosophy 7–8, 21, 27, 30–32, 34–35; imperceptible 27, 31–32, 52, 146; minor 31–32, 145–154; not being 30; woman 21, 29–31, 51
Bellamy, Edward 23, 170*n*4, 174*n*4
Bensen, Donald R. 160
Bergonzi, Bernard 11, 15, 62, 129, 150
Bergson, Henri 6, 112, 168*n*1
Beville, Maria 169*n*2
Bill and Ted's Excellent Adventure (Herek) 173*n*1
Bladerunner (Scott) 91
Blanchot, Maurice 9
The Blob (Yeaworth) 78
body horror 44, 60–61, 85
body without organs (Deleuzian concept) 60, 66, 94, 169*n*15; in relation to cyborgs 94–100, 104–105; in relation to evolution 58–59; in *The Island of Dr. Moreau* 66–68; in *The Time Machine* 129–131; in *The War of the Worlds* 94–100, 104–105; Wells's oeuvre as 32–33, 129, 139

201

Index

Bogue, Roland 97, 131, 136, 139, 146, 153
Boon (Wells) 166
Borges, Jorge Luis 16, 149
Bostrom, Nick 170*n*4
Bradbury, Ray 172*n*11
Braidotti, Rosi 47, 79, 128, 171*n*6
Bram Stoker 73
Brave New World (Huxley) 140, 159
The British Barbarians (Allen) 174*n*4
British Empire 74–75, 146; *see also* colonialism; postcolonialism
Buchanan, Ian 44–45, 48
Buck Rogers in the 25th Century (television) 173*n*3
Buettner, Robert 159
"Buffalo" (Kessel) 160
Buffy the Vampire Slayer (television) 92
Butler, Samuel 24–25, 174*n*4

Candide (Voltaire) 171*n*2
capitalism 35, 81; Deleuzian conceptualization of 96–97, 100; in *The Island of Dr. Moreau* 68; relationship with technology 75, 96, 99; in *The Time Machine* 35, 130–132; in *The War of the Worlds* 80–81, 96–97, 173*n*22
Capitalism and Schizophrenia (Deleuze) 5, 10, 24, 52, 170*n*7
Caprica (television) 169*n*16
Carpenter, John 78
Carroll, Lewis 7, 153, 174*n*4
Cataclysmo and the Battle for Earth (webseries) 163
catastrophism (Deleuzian concept) 65, 97, 101–103
Caudwell, Christopher 14, 16
cavorite (fictional mineral) 159
Christopher, John 88; *see also The Tripods*
The Chronic Argonauts (Wells) 108, 160, 174*n*4
The Chronicles of the Imaginarium Geographica (Owen) 141, 160
cinema 3, 5, 11, 14, 21, 34, 139, 177*n*16; Deleuze and 114, 116, 156; as time travel 117–118, 177*n*16; Wellsian cinematic adaptations 34, 40, 78, 171*n*19, 175*n*2
Cinema 1: The Movement-Image (Deleuze) 80, 116

Cinema 2: The Time-Image (Deleuze) 114, 116, 121
Clarke, Arthur C. 5
clergyman (*The War of the Worlds* character) 74; *see also* religion
The Clock That Went Backward (Mitchell) 173*n*4
Colebrook, Claire 58, 68–69, 111–112, 119–120, 143, 154–156
colonialism 84, 89, 100, 170*n*9; *see also* British Empire; postcolonialism
"The Comet Doom" (Hamilton) 91
The Coming Race (Bulwer-Lytton) 174*n*4
conceptual personae (Deleuzian concept) 11, 137–139, 142–144, 149
Concrete Island (Ballard) 170*n*10
Conan Doyle, Arthur 45, 174*n*4
A Connecticut Yankee in King Arthur's Court (Twain) 174*n*4
Conrad, Joseph 138
counteractualization (Deleuzian concept) 102; *see also* catastrophism
The Country of the Blind (Wells) 45
Cronenberg, David 61, 171*n*19
Crossley, Brian 11, 13–14, 168*n*4
A Crystal Age (Hudson) 173*n*4
The Crystal Egg (Wells) 174*n*12
crystals (in *The Time Machine*) 174*n*12; crystal image (Deleuze) 122–123, 136
cyberpunk (genre) 21–22
cyberspace 21
cyborg: "A Cyborg Manifesto" (Haraway) 42, 90–95, 172*n*12; in fiction 60, 78, 88–92, 172*n*13; in *The Island of Dr. Moreau* 172*n*13; in relation to the body without organs 94–100, 104–105, 172*n*16; in *The War of the Worlds* 89–100
Cyrano de Bergerac, Savinien de 76

Daleks 78, 91, 100, 173*n*20; *see also Dr. Who*
The Dancers at the End of Time (Moorcock) 168*n*6
Darwin, Charles 106, 170*n*8; Social Darwinism 34, 74; and Wells 86, 169*n*2, 170*n*8, 171*n*18; *see also* evolution, Darwinian theory of; *On the Origin of Species*
The Day the Earth Stood Still (Wise) 78
DC Comics 161, 164

Index

A Deepness in the Sky (Vinge) 159
defamiliarization 78–80
Defoe, Daniel 45, 170*n*10
Deluge (Wright) 170*n*10
Derrida, Jaques 16, 30, 42, 51–52
Descartes, René 6, 51, 125
Desert Islands and Other Texts (Deleuze) 46, 176*n*13
desire (Deleuzian concept) 7, 31, 36, 52, 66–68, 70, 94, 96, 100, 105, 130–131, 173*n*19
deterritorialization 2,7–8, 19, 24, 30–33, 45, 50, 63, 101, 120, 128, 142, 147–149, 153, 176*n*13; *see also* reterritorialization
Dialogues (Deleuze) 119, 124,137, 151, 158
Dialogues II (Deleuze) 6, 34, 37, 124, 137, 151
Difference and Repetition (Deleuze) 10, 20–21, 24, 94, 125–126, 131
difference and repetition (Deleuzian concept) 153, 155–156; *see also* eternal return
The Discovery of the Future (Wells) 24, 158
District 9 (Blomkamp) 60
Dr. Franklin's Island (Halam) 169*n*1
Dr. Moreau (*The Island of Dr. Moreau* character) 40–44, 47–50, 62–63; as cyborg 172*n*13; ethics of 63–64, 69–71; as mad scientist 13, 62, 68, 169*n*1, 171*n*20; in other media 169*n*1; as a religious figure 62–63, 171*n*24
Dr. Who (television) 78, 100, 169*n*10, 173*n*1, 174*n*11; Wells's appearances in 161; *see also* Daleks
The Door into Summer (Heinlein) 173*n*3
Dostoyevsky, Fyodor 7
Dracula (Stoker) 73
A Dream of Wessex (Priest) 170*n*10
Dreyer, Carl Theodor 80
dystopia 15, 23–24, 108, 170*n*13, 171*n*3; *see also* utopia

Earth (Planet) 25, 73; as body without organs 32
Edison, Thomas 128, 175*n*4
Edison's Conquest of Mars (Serviss) 168*n*6
Eloi (*The Time Machine*) 114–120, 131–134; *see also* Morlocks
entropy 81, 120

The Epic of Gilgamesh 41
Erewhon (Butler) 24–25, 174*n*4
E.T.: The Extra-Terrestrial (Spielberg) 169*n*10
eternal return (Nietzschean concept) 138, 155–156, 174*n*9, 176*n*15; *see also* eternal return
Eternal Sunshine of the Spotless Mind (Gondry) 21
ethics: Deleuzian conception of 51; in *The Island of Dr. Moreau* 3, 69–70; time travel 107
eugenics 39,163
Event Horizon (Anderson) 21
evil: Deleuze and 68–69; evolutionary 56; in *The War of the Worlds* 74
evolution: Darwinian theory 26–27, 56–9; Deleuzian conception 27–29; *see also* Darwin, Charles; *On the Origin of Species*
extraterrestrials *see* aliens

faciality (Deleuzian concept) 82–84
fascism: in relationship to capitalism 100
feminism 93, 175*n*6
The First Men in the Moon (Wells) 77, 159, 163, 168*n*4–5, 171*n*3
Flammarion, Camille 11
Floor Games (Wells) 169*n*17
The Fly (Cronenberg) 60–61
The Fold: Leibniz and the Baroque (Deleuze) 98
The Food of the Gods (Wells) 168*n*5
The Forebears of Kalimeros (Veltman) 173*n*4
Forever Young (Miner) 173*n*3
Foucault, Michel 6–7, 16, 30
Francis Bacon: The Logic of Sensation (Deleuze) 43, 54
Frankenstein 41, 91–92, 171*n*18; *see also* Shelley, Mary
Freud, Sigmund 130, 169*n*2; *see also* psychoanalysis
From Time to Time (Blyth) 162
Futurama (television) 163, 173*n*3
futurism 149, 176*n*10

Gibson, William 168*n*8–9
Golding, William 45, 170*n*10
Gothic (genre) 40, 62, 169*n*2, 171*n*21
Grand Theft Auto (Videogame) 169*n*10

203

Index

Griffin, George 11
Grover's Mill (St. Amand) 162
Guattari, Félix 95; as collaborator with Deleuze 168*n*1
Gulliver's Travels (Swift) 23, 170*n*10

Hamilton, Edmond 91
Haraway, Donna 42, 90–95, 171*n*24, 172*n*16; *see also* "A Cyborg Manifesto"
Hardware (Stanley) 21
Hardy, Sylvia 9, 18–19,106, 120, 138, 150–152, 168*n*7, 174*n*9
Hegel, Georg Wilhelm Friedrich 51
Heidegger, Martin 6
Heinlein, Robert A. 172*n*11, 173*n*3
Herland (Gilman) 170*n*13
H.G. Wells: War with the World (television) 163
H.G. Wells's War of the Worlds (Latt) 162
hive mind 97, 172*n*18
The Hollow Lands (Moorcock) 159
Homer 45, 143
L'Homme Qui Peut Vivre Dans L'eau (La Hire) 91
horror (film) 21–22, 55, 59–62; *see also* body horror
House of Pain (*The Island of Dr. Moreau*) 48–49, 65, 67
The Human Centipede: First Sequence (Six) 169*n*1
Hume, David 6
Huxley, Aldous 140, 159; *see also Brave New World*
Huxley, Thomas 26, 56, 160
hybridity 21, 41, 44, 49, 59–65, 89–95, 131, 141

"Ian, George, and George" (Levinson) 161
Idiocracy (Judge) 173*n*3
image of thought (Deleuze) 6, 20, 31, 124–126, 144
Imaginary Worlds and Real Worlds (Flammarion) 11
imminence (Deleuzian concept) 94
In the Days of the Comet (Wells) 168*n*5
Independence Day (Emmerich) 78
The Infinite Worlds of H.G. Wells (television) 162
"Inspiration" (Bova) 160

internet 139, 175*n*1 *see also* rhizome; World Brain (Wells)
invasion literature 73–74
The Invisible Man (Wells) 168*n*4, 168*n*5
The Iron Heel (London) 170*n*13
The Island of Dr. Moreau (Wells): animals in 42–44, beast-men in 43, 49–50, 54–68; becoming animal in 42–44, 51–52, 60–69, 71; capitalism in 68, cinematic adaptations of 30, 40; critical response 39–40; cultural legacy 40; ethics 56, 63, 69–71; eugenics 39, 163; evolution 56–59; as horror 59–61; island spaces 44–50; narrative techniques 150–153; religion 62–63; transhumanism 40–44; vivisection 49, 60, 64, 152; *see also* Dr. Moreau (character); scientific romance
The Island of Dr. Moreau (films: Taylor 1977, Frankenheimer 1996) 30, 40
islands: as conceptual spaces 44–50; in science fiction 44–45

James, Henry 17–18
Jameson, Fredric 22, 84, 88
Joyce, James 18

Kafka, Franz 7, 10, 31–32, 35, 51–55; as Deleuzian minor writer 147–148
Kafka: Toward a Minor Literature (Deleuze and Guattari) 147
Kant, Immanuel 6, 20, 51

La Hire, Jean de 91, 172*n*14
The Land Ironclads (Wells) 172*n*12
language: Deleuzian conceptions 31–33, 150–154, 176*n*13; in *The Island of Dr. Moreau* 49–50; Wells's use of 18
Last and First Men (Stapledon) 172*n*18
The League of Extraordinary Gentlemen (Moore) 159, 169*n*1
Legends of Tomorrow (television) 164
Le Guin, Ursula 13, 15
Lewis, C.S. 140–141, 144, 159, 172*n*11, 176*n*8
The Limits of Individual Plasticity (Wells) 171*n*23
line of flight (Deleuze) 52, 64, 69, 129, 155
literary theory 17–19, 51, 138

204

Index

literature: major and minor (Deleuze) 145–154
Little Wars (Wells) 169*n*17
The Logic of Sense (Deleuze) 7, 31
Lois & Clark: The New Adventures of Superman (television) 162
Looking Backward (Bellamy) 174*n*4
The Lord of the Flies (Golding) 45, 170*n*10
Lost (television) 46
The Lost World (Conan Doyle) 174*n*4
Lovecraft, H.P. 60, 160, 171*n*17
Lowell, Percival 81, 82, 160, 172*n*9

machine (Deleuzian concept) 6–7, 12; 29; *see also* assemblage; rhizome
mad scientist (fictional trope) 13, 62, 68, 128, 139, 141, 169*n*1, 171*n*20
major literature 31–32, 146–147, 154; *see also* minor literature
Malthus, Thomas Robert 58, 170*n*16
Man Against Destruction (Turkey) 162
A Man of Parts (Lodge) 161
The Man of the Year Million (Wells) 86–87, 140
"The Man That Was Used Up" (Poe) 91
Mars (planet): in fiction 25, 73; prospect of life on 81, 172*n*8; *see also* Martians
The Mars Trilogy (Robinson) 172*n*11
Martians: as cyborgs 94–100; and evolution 25, 73–75; Martian war machines 15; in *The War of the Worlds* 72–87, 89–91; *see also* alien invasion
The Martian Chronicles (Bradbury) 172*n*11
The Martian War (Anderson) 160
Marx, Karl 161; Marxism 14
Massumi, Brian 83, 156, 170*n*12
The Matrix (Wachowskis) 41, 169*n*9
Melville, Herman 7, 31, 143
memory (Deleuzian conception of) 111–114; *see also* antimemory
Men Like Gods (Wells) 24, 140, 163, 168*n*5
Metamorphosis (Kafka) 53–54
Micromégas (Voltaire) 76
Miévill, China 170*n*10
minor literature 138–145–154; minor language 149–152; minor writers 31–32; Wells as minor 147–154; *see also* major literature

Mr. Blettsworthy on Rampole Island (Wells) 45, 151
Mr. Sammler's Planet (Bellows)
A Modern Utopia (Wells) 23–24, 170*n*13
modernism: Wells as modernist 18, 176*n*12
Montgomery (*The Island of Dr. Moreau* character) 43, 47–48, 57–58, 64, 67, 169*n*2
Moorcock, Michael 159, 168*n*6
Moore, C.L. 91
More, Thomas 13, 22–23, 48, 170*n*10
The Moreau Quartet (Swann) 169*n*1
Moreau's Other Island (Aldiss) 169*n*1
Morlock Night (Jeter) 16
Morlocks *seen also* Eloi 56–57, 116, 120, 131–135, 175*n*17
movement image 80, 114, 116; *see also* cinema; time image
Murdoch Mysteries (television) 163
Le Mystère des XV (La Hire) 172*n*14
mythology 16, 43, 46, 175*n*4; Mars and 82–83; time traveler as mythic figure 128–130

narration: in *The Island of Dr. Moreau* 48–50, 55, 57, 63, 67–68, 70, 152, 169*n*2; in *The Time Machine* 24, 110, 114, 115–117, 119, 120, 130, 140, 152, 175*n*5; in *The War of the Worlds* 82–83, 86–87, 89–90, 93, 101–103, 140; Wellsian techniques 151–152; *see also* Prendick; the time traveler
Negotiations (Deleuze) 6, 116
Neuromancer (Gibson) 168*n*8, 169*n*9
New Atlantis (Bacon) 170*n*10
New Worlds for Old (Wells) 12
Nietzsche, Friedrich 6, 16, 143; and Deleuze 155, 168*n*1; *see also* eternal return; will to power
Nietzsche and Philosophy (Deleuze) 168*n*2
No Enemy But Time (Bishop) 16
nomadic thought (Deleuze) 28–29, 33, 106, 126–130; nomad as conceptual figure; nomadology 2, 9–10, 126; nomadic space 45–47, 175*n*17; nomadic war machine 132–135
No Woman Born (Moore) 91

Oedipus Complex 130–131; *see also* psychoanalysis; schizoanalysis

205

Index

On the Origin of Species (Darwin) 56–58, 76; *see also* evolution
Organs Without Bodies: Deleuze and Consequences (Žižek) 172*n*17
Orphanage (Buettner) 159
Out of the silent Planet (Lewis) 172*n*11

Pal, George 134, 144, 157, 161, 168*n*6 *see also* The Time Machine (1960 film)
The Palace of Green Porcelain (*The Time Machine*) 113–114, 120–121
Pallinghurst Barrow (Allen) 174*n*4
Paradise Lost (Milton) 76
Paris Before Man (Boitard) 174*n*4
Parrinder, Patrick 14–15, 101, 175*n*18, 176*n*8
Pearson, Keith Ansell 94, 101, 103, 135
Pearson's Magazine 73, 168*n*5
Phil of the Future (television) 162
philosophy: Deleuze's Counter Philosophy 5–8, 24–5, 29, 126; and science fiction 21, 34–37; Western traditions 6–8, 29–30, 51, 56
Plato 6, 20, 22, 29, 31, 46, 48, 143, 145
Plato's Dream (Voltaire) 171*n*2
Podkayne of Mars (Heinlein) 172*n*11
Poe, Edgar Allan 91
postcolonialism 79, 170*n*9
posthumanism 39, 42; 152, 169*n*3 *see also* transhumanism
postmodernism 5, 16–17, 19, 42, 46, 93, 106–107, 175*n*5; Wells as 9, 16–19, 40, 88, 138, 175*n*5
poststructuralism: in relation to Deleuze 5, 42, 79, 106, 111; Wells as 9, 18–19, 121, 138, 151
potentiality (Deleuzian concept) 1, 8, 54, 70, 98, 101, 157
Powell, Anna 21, 59, 60–61
Prendick (*The Island of Dr. Moreau* character) 48–50, 55, 57, 63, 67–68, 70, 152, 169*n*2
Prototype (videogame) 163
Proust, Marcel 7
Proust and Signs (Deleuze) 7, 116
pseudoscience 107, 144; *see also* technobabble; time machine (vehicle)
psychoanalysis 14, 40, 43, 51–52, 60, 130–131; Deleuzian critique 43, 51–52, 130–131; *see also* schizoanalysis

quantum physics 109

red weed (in *The War of the Worlds*) 81, 172*n*7
Redfern, Nick 171*n*19
religion 63, 74, 102–103, 125
A Report to an Academy (Kafka) 54–55
The Research Magnificent (Wells) 151
reterritorialization 45, 67, 99, 101, 128, 142, 176*n*13; *see also* deterritorialization
The Return of the Time Machine (Friedell) 168*n*6
rhizome (Deleuzian concept) 8, 25–29, 31, 92, 127, 137; internet as 175*n*1; Well's work as 139, 156–158; *see also* arboreal (thought process)
Rieder, John 89, 170*n*9, 172*n*13
Robinson Crusoe (Defoe) 170*n*10
Robocop (Verhoeven) 91

Sacher-Masoch, Leopold von 7
Sardar, Ziauddin 78, 171*n*5
Saussure, Ferdinand de 18–19, 138, 151, 168*n*7, 176*n*13
The Scar (Miévill) 170*n*10
schizoanalysis 52, 68, 130–132; *see also* psychoanalysis
science fiction: definitions 11–16, 22; as philosophy 19–22, 176*n*9; Wells as "father of modern science fiction" 5, 13–16, 28, 145, 149, 157; *see also* scientific romance
The Science of Life (Wells) 25
scientific romance 11–19, 25–29, 73, 88, 117, 150–153, 156–157; critical responses to 11–19, 110, 171*n*1
A Scientific Romance (Wright) 160, 168*n*6
"Sgt. Pepper's Lonely Hearts Club Band" (*Beatles* album) 161
The Shape of Things to Come (Wells) 158, 169*n*16, 175*n*2, 176*n*14
Shelley, Mary 13, 41, 60, 91, 171*n*21; *see also* Frankenstein
A Short History of the World (Wells) 127
Short Stories (Wells) 76
sign (semiotics) 24, 176*n*13; *see also* Saussure, Ferdinand de
singularity (Deleuzian concept) 25, 32–33, 70, 115, 119, 151
Sleeper (Allen) 173*n*3
Slusser, George 16, 107, 110

206

Index

smooth space 47–50, 81, 170n12, 175n17; *see also* striated space
social Darwinism 35, 74
Socrates 143, 145
Solar Pons's War of the Worlds (web-series) 163
Solaris (Tarkovsky) 21
A Song Called Youth Trilogy (Shirley) 169n9
space (physical) *see* smooth space; striated space
The Space Machine (Priest) 160, 174n7
speculative fiction 12, 23; *see also* science fiction; scientific romance
Spinoza, Baruch 69–71, 103
spiritual automaton (Deleuzian concept) 79–80
Splice (Natali) 169n1
Stapledon, Olaf 15, 172n18
state apparatus 99–100, 127, 134; *see also* war machine (Deleuze)
Star Trek: The Original Series (television) 159
Star Trek: Voyager (television) 92, 94, 172n18
Star Wars (film series) 46, 91, 169n10, 170n11, 174n8
Stargate SG-1 (television) 160
Stivale, Charles J. 21, 94, 96, 168n9
The Stolen Bacillus (Wells) 26, 163
striated space 44–50, 80–81, 101, 170n12, 175n17; *see also* smooth space
The Sweet Far Thing (Bray) 161
Swift, Johnathan 13, 23, 170n10
Sylvie and Bruno (Carroll) 174n4

Taxi Driver (Scorsese) 51
technobabble 163
technology: science fictional depictions 26, 40–41, 53, 72–76, 85–86, 88–99, 104–109, 118
The Tempest (Shakespeare) 170n10
terminal beach (in *The Time Machine*) 26, 123, 128, 174n13
The Terminator (film series) 21, 91, 94, 109
Testimony (Palmer) 162
That Hideous Strength (Lewis) 140, 144, 159
The Thing (Carpenter) 78
Things to Come (film) 175n2

A Thousand Plateaus (Deleuze and Guattari) 5, 10, 21, 27–29, 33, 42–43, 63, 82, 92, 96–99, 101, 126–127, 132–134, 170n12, 175n17
time 5, 17, 24, 26–28, 107, 125; causality 107, 118, 121; Deleuzian conception 111–117, 120–123; Einsteinian conception 17, 111, 111, 118, 173n2; geological 26, 135; linearity of 17, 28, 87, 112, 115–116, 119–120, 125, 136, 141, 157; *see also* time machine (vehicle); time travel
Time After Time (Mayer) 140, 161
time image (Deleuzian concept) 21, 100, 114, 116, 119–124, 136; *see also* movement image
The Time Machine (Wells): cinematic adaptations 108, 134; and the cinematic image 116–117, 176n16; class representation 27; Communism in 133–134; critical response 106–110, 136; as critique of capitalism 35, 131–132; cultural legacy 107–108; Deleuzian crystal image in 122–123; entropy in 81, 120; evolution in 26–27, 108, 152; mythic elements of 130–131; narrative techniques 108, 141, 150–153, 176n14; nomadology in 124–130; sequels to 16, 108, 168n6, 174n7; technology in 109, 117–118; terminal beach 26, 123, 128, 174n13; *see also* Eloi; Morlocks; time machine (vehicle); time travel; time traveler (character)
The Time Machine: The Journey Back (Lucas) 162
time machine (vehicle): in popular culture 16, 110, 173n1; in *The Time Machine* 107, 109–111
The Time Ships (Baxter) 16, 108, 156, 160, 174n10
time travel 10, 14, 16–17, 19, 26–27, 106–114, 118–128, 133; as cinematic experience 117–118, 176n16; as literary device 25–26, 107–113, 174n6; paradoxes 107, 120; in physics 109–111, 117–118, 174n7; via altered mental states 107–108; via sleep 108, 173n3; *see also* scientific romance; time; time machine (vehicle)
the time traveler (*The Time Machine* character) 26–27, 106–118, 120; as mad scientist 128; as mythic figure

207

129, 144; as nomad 126–128, 144; as Wellsian avatar 140–144, 175*n*4
Timecop (television) 162
The Timekeeper (Disney attraction) 162
To Mars and Providence (Webb) 171*n*17
Tono-Bungay (Wells) 151
transhumanism 39–44, 88–128, 139, 144, 169*n*3
tripod (Martian war machine) 75–80, 90; in popular culture 160, 161
The Tripods (Christopher) 78
The Tripods Attack!: The Young Chesterton Chronicles (McNichol) 161
2001: A Space Odyssey (Kubrick) 21

utopia 11–15, 22–25, 48, 88, 93, 154, 170*n*13; *see also* dystopia
Utopia (More) 13, 22–23, 48, 170*n*10

vampires 60, 92; capitalism as 154; Martians as 90
The Vampyr (Dreyer) 80
Verne, Jules 11, 13, 150, 162
Victorian (era) 8, 17, 35, 39, 73, 75, 84, 117, 131, 140, 150–153, 163, 169*n*2
videogames 34, 139, 169*n*10
Vinge, Vernor 159
virtual (Deleuzian concept) 19–24, 28–34, 46, 58–59, 70, 75–76, 94, 98, 110–112, 118–119, 121–124, 135–136, 154–157; see *also* actual
vivisection 39, 42, 49, 60, 64, 152
Viz (magazine) 160
Vonnegut, Kurt 13

Wagar, Warren 4–5, 16–17, 26–27, 104–105, 155, 176*n*10
The Walking Dead (television) 169*n*16
war machine (Deleuzian concept) 100, 127, 132–134
The War of the Worlds (Wells): cinematic adaptations of 78, 103, 171*n*7; as cinematic blockbuster 77; critical response to 73–74, 78, 171*n*1–2; as critique of capitalism 80–81, 96–100, 103, 173*n*22; as critique of colonialism 84, 89, 100, 103; cultural legacy of 77–78, 100; cyborgs in 88–100; evolution in 85–87, 90–92, 97, 104; 78; narrative techniques 82–83, 86–87, 89–90, 93, 101–103, 140; religion in 74, 102–103; sequels 78, 162; technology in 75, 78, 80, 85–86, 88, 90, 94–96; *see also* invasion literature; Mars; Martians; scientific romance
The War of the Worlds (films: Haskin 1953, Spielberg 2005) 78, 103, 171*n*7
The War of the Worlds: Global Dispatches (Anderson) 160
War of the Worlds 2: The Next Wave (Howell) 162
The Ware Tetralogy (Rucker) 168*n*9
Warehouse 13 141, 144, 159, 163, 175*n*7
The Wasp Factory (Banks) 170*n*10
Web (Wyndham) 170*n*10
Welles, Orson 156, 161–163
Wells, Simon 108, 162
Westfahl, Gary 108, 169*n*17
What Is Philosophy? (Deleuze and Guattari) 10, 24, 101
When the Sleeper Awakes (Wells) 108
The White Sphinx (*The Time Machine*) 113, 130–131, 175*n*18
will to power (Nietzschean concept) 170*n*14
Williams, Keith 77, 117, 156, 176*n*16
The Wonderful Visit (Wells) 168*n*4
Woolf, Virginia 150, 176*n*12
The Work, Wealth and Happiness of Mankind (Wells) 4
World Brain: The Idea of a Permanent World Encyclopedia (Wells) 175*n*1
The World Set Free (Wells) 163, 172*n*12, 173*n*21

Les Xipéhuz (Rosny) 77

Zarathustra (Nietzschean concept) 143, 145
Žižek, Slavoj 95, 172*n*17
zombies: as metaphor for capitalism 79, 134; in science fiction 79, 94, 139, 169*n*16, 175*n*2
Zoological Retrogression (Wells) 26

208